HAPPY WIFE

HAPPY WIFE

A NOVEL

MEREDITH LAVENDER

AND

KENDALL SHORES

BANTAM

NEW YORK

Bantam Books
An imprint of Random House
A division of Penguin Random House LLC
1745 Broadway, New York, NY 10019
randomhousebooks.com
penguinrandomhouse.com

Library of Congress Cataloging-in-Publication Data
Names: Lavender, Meredith author | Shores, Kendall author
Title: Happy wife: a novel / Meredith Lavender and Kendall Shores.
Description: First edition. | New York: Bantam Books, 2025.
Identifiers: LCCN 2025007271 (print) | LCCN 2025007272 (ebook) |
ISBN 9780593974377 hardcover acid-free paper |
ISBN 9780593974384 ebook
Subjects: LCGFT: Thrillers (Fiction) | Novels
Classification: LCC PS3612.A9442359 H37 2025 (print) |
LCC PS3612.A9442359 (ebook) | DDC 813/.6—dc23/eng/20250307
LC record available at https://lccn.loc.gov/2025007271
LC ebook record available at https://lccn.loc.gov/2025007272

Printed in the United States of America on acid-free paper

2 4 6 8 9 7 5 3 1

FIRST EDITION

Book design by Mary A. Wirth

The authorized representative in the EU for product safety and compliance
is Penguin Random House Ireland, Morrison Chambers, 32 Nassau Street,
Dublin D02 YH68, Ireland, https://eu-contact.penguin.ie.

To anyone looking for a sign to chase a wild dream,
let this book be that sign.

HAPPY WIFE

PROLOGUE

I watch through the window as a police car turns up my driveway. And then another one. A squad car would usually be out of place on this upscale street, but with everything going on, they've been frequenting this neighborhood.

I should have known better. I should have seen this coming.

When exactly the fait accompli was set into motion, though, is harder to put my finger on.

"Uh . . . Nora . . . ," Este says from somewhere behind me.

The tone of her voice drives home the certainty that something bad is about to happen.

I open the front door and step outside, the Florida heat hitting me about the same time the blood drains from my face. Three more cars follow behind the first two. An ominous processional.

"Nora, what is going on?" she calls from inside the house.

I try to answer, but my breath catches.

Detective Travis Ardell gets out of the lead car, followed by a cop from the shotgun seat. The other cars all have two, three, and four officers in them. They're taking out kits, brown evidence bags, gloves, and booties. They're preparing to descend on the property, and they've brought enough equipment to dismantle my life.

Ardell makes eye contact with me, a damning accusation behind his eyes, and I swear I can hear the thought inside his head. The one saying, *I've got you now, Nora.*

A memory of Will's face momentarily eclipses the scene unfolding in front me. His piercing blue eyes twinkle—he's almost in reach. I blink and he disappears. Again.

"Come inside," Este calls to me.

But there's no point. I stand there, waiting.

I know they are coming for me.

CHAPTER 1

THE NIGHT OF THE PARTY

*I*t's just a party, Nora. All you have to do is make it through the next couple of hours. Make it through a party. That's the whole job.

Our nine-thousand-square-foot house has never felt smaller, filled up with hundreds of Will's friends and colleagues. Various shades of pink streak the late afternoon sky, and I can hear the distant hum of conversation coming from the veranda. Guests have spilled out into our manicured backyard to sip cocktails and watch the sun slip beneath the horizon beyond the lake. There's plenty of room to socialize. The yard stretches from the house to the water, broken only by a huge pool and sweeping lawn that sprawls down to the boathouse and dock at the bottom.

And here I am, huddled in the corner. Hiding.

Este walks up to me and nudges my side. "Beau brought a weed pen," she whispers. "Want me to find him?" She scans the partygoers in my living room for her husband.

"Jesus. Do I look that nervous?" I try to sound offended, but Este nods without hesitation. "It's just a stupid party," I say, more to myself than to her.

The irony of dreading such a frivolous activity after all of the truly grueling jobs I've had in my life is not lost on me. For a brief second, the entry-level dues, mundane tasks, and menial labor of my past life spin through my mind like a shitty highlight reel. Baby-sitting unruly neighborhood kids, serving up ice cream in sticky Florida summers, lifeguarding on the weekends, and burning my fingers on hot plates as I waited tables.

You name it, I've probably done it.

But that was all before Will Somerset swept me off my blistered feet and retired me from minimum-wage jobs forever. Before everything changed. Now, I no longer mentally visualize my bank balance before swiping a card at the grocery store or dread the first day of the month and looming bill payments. And the blisters on my feet? Nonexistent thanks to regular spa days and pedicures.

I have no real problems. I know this.

Everything I've ever wanted is right here. A handsome, successful attorney husband. A sprawling lakefront estate. His influential circle of friends. The only thing I *don't* have is the respect of the crowd of people gathered here tonight.

As Will's twenty-eight-year-old second wife, I'm something between arm candy and dinner theater to most of his friends. A spectacle to be sure. At best, I am a strange interloper, someone new who doesn't know any of their inside jokes. At worst, all the wives jeer at me like I'm the Ghost of Christmas Future, a harbinger of younger second wives yet to come. Never mind that Will's divorce from his first wife, Constance, is well behind him—a divorce *she* initiated.

But this party, Will's forty-sixth birthday, is meant to change Winter Park's perception of me. After tonight, I won't feel like an outsider anymore. After tonight, they will see I'm not just the interloper. After tonight, I will be one of them.

But first, I need my hands to stop shaking.

Este nudges me again, reaches into her McQueen clutch, and produces a small white pill. "Xanax?"

I gently push her hand back into the bag. "Are you just keeping loose pills and weed in there?"

"Nooo," she says, drawing out the word. "I told you. *Beau* brought the weed. I brought pharmaceuticals, but only in case you needed them. And stop looking at me like I'm crazy. A whole pill bottle would never fit in this bag." She holds up the black leather pouch as if that should be obvious.

"I love you, but I'm not taking drugs six feet away from the mayor."

"The mayor's here? I should offer her something." Este looks past me to search the crowd. "I bet she fears the country club moms more than you do. They're always worked up over something inane like adding more quinoa to hot lunches."

"Please don't offer the mayor drugs."

"Prescription drugs aren't real drugs," she fires back.

Here's the thing about Este: If anyone else spoke to me the way she does, I might cry. But with her, somehow dismissive and aloof are part of a breezy, no-fucks-to-give charm.

Este assures me that the mayor attending isn't headline news. I should know that by now. We're talking about a town small enough to fit in your pocket. Spanning a mere ten square miles, Winter Park is known not for its footprint but rather for its sweeping mansions, brick-paved streets, meticulously curated lawns, and wealth per capita. Founded as a sunny escape for well-heeled New Englanders, Winter Park is now a haven for the affluent. And the estates established by snowbirds a century ago have been taken over by anyone willing to pay the steep housing prices in exchange for access to the tax shelters Florida has to offer—from professional athletes to hedge fund managers and old-guard sugar barons.

When I decided to host this celebration, my brilliant idea was that a party might help nurture stronger connections with some of Will's friends. I had visions of a small dinner party and good conversation. But when I asked Autumn Kensington—the "it" girl of all things event planning in this part of the world—to help, she made it clear that in Winter Park, gossip and party invitations are social currency. The party rapidly ballooned from an intimate gathering to something more closely resembling a state dinner.

"I don't fear the country club moms, by the way," I say under my breath. "I just see them for what they are: status-obsessed social snipers who hate me."

"You worry too much about what people think of you." Este swipes a flute of champagne off a passing silver tray and hands it to me like a jaded parent soothing a rowdy child with a toy. "Here. Calm down."

Again, dismissive and yet somehow not offensive. She silently raises her red wine, and we clink glasses before I take a measured sip so as not to appear unhinged. This crowd can smell fear.

In smaller groups, I can rely on Will to shield me from the unfriendly wives and unwelcome questions about his first marriage. He always changes the subject and then pulls me close to whisper a compliment in my ear. But as the party got started, the crowd swelled and engulfed him in a sea of backslapping and handshakes, leaving me standing alone. Thank God Este found me.

"So, you're just going to white-knuckle it through this soirée? No narcotics? What about hallucinogens?" She looks a little disappointed. As a California transplant with a relatively new, but massive, fortune, Este has not even attempted to fit in among the country club set. We became fast friends once we realized we were both outsiders. But for her, the on-the-fringes lifestyle was by choice.

"I'll stick to wine. I should keep my wits about me." I shake my head, thinking Will might actually kill me if I got high. What a gift *that* would be to all of his judgy friends.

"Well, the food is incredible. Have you tried Marcus's ceviche? That man is a fucking genius. He must have driven to the coast this morning for fish that fresh."

I smile. "At least they won't be able to complain about the food."

I still can't believe Marcus closed his restaurant to cater the party tonight. Even though he and I aren't exactly seeing eye to eye these days, I'm relieved he's here.

"Let's take a lap," Este says, grabbing my hand and guiding me toward the terrace.

The gossip is in high supply tonight, and I'm thankful this means shit-talking me is off the table. For now, Winter Park's morbid curiosity is focused on something other than my marriage. The topic du jour is a car accident that happened just up the street around two the previous morning. Someone ran off one of the brick roads that curl through Winter Park's most extravagant estates and crashed their Buick into Carol Parker's wrought-iron fence. The driver of the Buick was life-flighted to the nearest hospital, leaving a gnarled vehicle at the scene for almost a day before a tow truck could come and collect it. Carol has been beside herself about the damage to her lawn and her grandfather's prized wrought-iron fence—purchased at the World's Fair in 1893 and transported here to adorn the house. As hors d'oeuvres circulate through the party, so do second- and thirdhand accounts of the accident. Guests speculate over whether the driver was drunk, whether Carol came out in her house robe to render aid, and whether Will should be hired as the attorney to represent Carol in a civil suit against the driver.

Petty gossip, small-town intrigue, and fresh-caught ceviche. By all accounts, it's a perfectly normal night at a Winter Park party. I can't believe I pulled this off unscathed. Este notices the success of the event, too.

"I almost hate to say it, but this is a proper Winter Park fête." She raises her glass and beams. "Hear, hear."

But as her arm goes up, a misstep from a nearby guest causes her hand to jerk back, sending the entire glass of red wine hurtling toward me. The glass shatters on impact as it lands at my feet, and the room falls into a tense hush. The wives do a lackluster job of hiding their amusement as they take in the Jackson Pollock splash of wine trailing down the front of my white silk dress.

Disaster. Of course.

"Oh, *shit*," Este says.

I catch my reflection in the window, the red stain bleeding across the white silk. I look like I've survived a massacre.

CHAPTER 2

Autumn materializes out of thin air, waving a white napkin. "Go change. Leave the dress on your bed, and I'll stain-treat it before the end of the night. You might have a shot at wearing it again. *Might.* I'll have someone bring a broom for the glass."

This is why everyone in Winter Park trusts Autumn. Everyone but Este, who rolls her eyes.

"Go change," Autumn repeats.

I know better than to challenge the doyenne of parties in Winter Park. Heading toward my room, I slip through the scullery, where dishes and lipstick-stained wineglasses are being quietly rinsed and wiped clean by two cater-waiters. I try not to think about the wine that's dripping into my underwear and fake a smile as I pass them and enter the kitchen.

But the kitchen frenzy I expect to find—a crowded scuffle of dishes being plated—isn't here. The only person in the kitchen is Marcus, and in spite of myself, I exhale a sigh of relief.

Maybe he notices the softening in my posture at the sight of him, because his lips bloom into a boyish smile as he says, "What's up, boss? Dinner's running on time, and I've got a plate of sea bass if you want to give it a try." His cheer gives way to concern as he takes in my appearance. "What happened?"

"This is what I get for wearing white." I gesture at the crime scene on my dress, and he is already in motion, grabbing a clean towel, but I wave him off. "Marcus, it's an entire glass of red wine on white silk. The only thing that's going to fix this is lighter fluid."

"Have you considered the fact that arson is a dangerous stress behavior?" He raises an eyebrow.

"This isn't funny." My voice cracks, and I fan my eyes to keep the threatening tears from smearing my mascara.

Marcus puts his hands up in mock surrender as the air falls silent between us. An unspoken tension fills the kitchen. I know why it's there. I treated him terribly the last time I saw him.

"Marcus, about what I said . . ."

"Hey." Marcus's voice tightens a little. "Tonight isn't about that. We're good."

The tears I have been holding at bay spill over, blurring my vision. I wipe at my eyes as Marcus takes a step toward me. He puts his hands on my shoulders, and his gaze meets mine, concern etched in his features.

"Are you still worried about winning this crowd over?" I can tell he's trying to hide the thrum of frustration in his voice. "These people are not your friends, and what they think of you is none of your business. At best, they're a pack of drunken fakes, and that's the nicest thing I could say about them. Some of the people out there are truly vile human beings. Sociopaths. And that's just the stay-at-home moms from the country club. Don't even get me started on the career politicians." Then he adds with conviction, "Fuck them, Nora."

A genuine, albeit faint smile tugs at the corners of my lips.

"You're better than all of them. I'd bet my life on that. So, don't let them get to you. They don't deserve it. And besides, you're throwing the *biggest* party with the *best* chef in town, so all is right in the universe."

His brown eyes are so intensely kind that it almost breaks my heart. "I'm sorry, Marcus," I whisper. Because he deserves to hear me say it, and when he's looking at me like this, the regret is so heavy I can barely stand it. "I made such a mess of things."

He shifts on his feet. Something flashes in his eyes, but it's gone before I can place it. "You want to leave?" He smirks, lightening the mood and changing the subject, closing the door that keeps unlatching. "We'll let your husband take it from here, then Thelma and Louise our way across the country before they even realize we're gone."

"What a weird way to tell me you have a thing for Brad Pitt."

"Cute. But I'm just disappointed I've made it thirtysomething years and never properly carried out a crime spree." Marcus winks before he practically chucks me on the chin. "Go change your dress while I tamp down my itch to go out in a blaze of glory by driving a car over a cliff."

I let out a weak but grateful laugh. He gently releases his grip on my shoulders, giving me the space to collect myself. I choke down my self-pity and plaster a coy half smile on my face. My eyes are still watery as I say, "It's last year's dress anyway."

From the corner of my eye, I try to catch another glimpse of the damage to my dress in the bay window. That's when I see Will, standing outside, and—is he watching us?

No. You're just being paranoid.

I shake my head and go upstairs to change.

CHAPTER 3

Twenty minutes later, I reemerge, heading outside in a fresh dress—black this time. The neckline of the long-sleeved bandage dress gives away the sunburn on my shoulders from this morning's boat ride with Will and his daughter, Mia. In my head, my mother chides that tan lines are gauche. But at least the dress is clean.

Down at the dock, I spot Will engaged in what looks to be a relatively heated conversation with his law partner, Fritz. As in Frederick Hall III, a descendant of one of the founding families of Winter Park.

A hundred years ago, the Halls split their time between textiles in Chicago and lakeside retreats in Florida, patronizing Winter Park's artists and pulling strings in every kind of circle that matters—political, social, and the like. Sometime in the 1940s, they became full-time mainstays. In other words: The Halls are hard-core Winter Park royalty.

I watch as Will and Fritz's argument goes quiet, and they turn back toward the house to rejoin the party. Will picks up his pace toward me as Fritz sidesteps, half nodding in my direction, looking flushed. Probably from too much bourbon.

"Why'd you change?" Will murmurs in my ear, wrapping an arm around my waist. "I liked the white."

"Unfortunately, white silk and red wine are natural enemies," I quip, hoping to drop it.

Before Will can react, Fritz loudly starts to tell the story of a recent weekend he spent at his family's hunting camp on the St. Johns River, sucking up all the attention within a hundred-yard radius as he is known to do. Fritz is the quintessential example of Florida wealth, an avid hunter with a designer wardrobe. Golf and guns by day with a crisp Brioni tux always at the ready.

He's clutching a glass of bourbon that waves precariously over designer shoes, with every gesture threatening to douse nearby listeners. We've heard the story before, but we join the listening crowd, playing along. Will pulls me close to him, a warm surge of energy sparking between us.

"We were there to hunt turkeys, but after a few too many bourbons, catching alligators seemed like a more reasonable pursuit," Fritz booms, holding court. His faintly Southern accent is an old-money sleight of hand—angling toward gentility. In truth, there's nothing genteel about him. He's the kind of person you either love or find yourself needing an escape from.

People are wide-eyed as he describes "gator shining," the practice of stunning baby alligators by shining a floodlight in their eyes and lifting them up with a hand wrapped around their snouts so they can't bite you when they come to.

In contrast to Fritz's exuberance, Will embodies quiet confidence. Their partnership—forged in law school and tested through more than twenty years of building a successful firm—has weathered the highs and lows of their journey, including working out of their cars and cherry-picking which bills to pay as they struggled to get their momentum. Will is the careful anchor to Fritz's inflated ego, but without Fritz's hubris in the beginning, they might have folded. To put it frankly, Fritz had the name and the money, and Will had the brains.

Now, they stand at the pinnacle of their profession. Their firm is recognized as one of the most formidable in the state, and their partnership is the longest-running relationship in Will's life.

"So, at this point, we've got five or six baby gators in a bucket, and we were going to put them in your swimming pool, Nora." Fritz laughs. "But with Will pushing fifty, I thought that might give him a heart attack. We can't have him keeling over just yet."

"Who's pushing fifty? We're the same age," Will shoots back lightly, but the grip he has around my waist tightens a notch.

Fritz ignores Will, arriving at the part of the story where he's in possession of six baby alligators that need to be released back into the wild. "Now, I'm starting to wonder about alligators' memories and whether they can hold a grudge like crows do, because I can't say for certain if I'm putting these fuckers back in the right nests."

Fritz's wife, Gianna, rolls her eyes so dramatically that it's almost audible.

Gianna Hall is a stunning woman, with piercing eyes and sharp features—a few of them frozen in time by a delicate touch of Botox and the latest technology in peels. From what Autumn tells me, Fritz and Gianna met as freshmen at the University of Florida, when she took one look at his pedigree and locked him down for good. Having grown up perfectly upper middle class, Gianna was by no means born to the fuck-you money that Fritz's family had. And though she'll haughtily advise that speaking about money or wealth is tacky—while wearing a blinding stack of diamond rings—she makes very good use of the family plane and their bottomless bank accounts. And who can blame her? She bagged a winning lottery ticket—even if that ticket came in the form of Fritz and all his vainglorious personality.

Every few years, some gossip about Fritz bubbles up—a DUI or even a cocaine-fueled dalliance with a college-aged babysitter—but the rumors disappear as quickly as they surface. It's all at the hands of Gianna, or so the urban legend goes. How she squelches the gossip in a town like this, no one ever asks.

She and Will's ex-wife, Constance, have always been close, so naturally, Gianna hates me. Constance and I are the antithesis of each other. She is Scully & Scully to my Target home décor. I wouldn't put it past Gianna having been the one to crown me "Interloper," withholding the approval of her social connections just to ice me out.

As Fritz's oration continues, Will takes a step back from the crowd, pulling on my arm. We're just out of earshot of the guests when he says tightly, "Seriously. What happened to your dress?"

"I told you. Este spilled a glass of wine down the front of it. Autumn is going to stain-treat it. I'll get it to the cleaners." I sound more defensive than I intend to. I just want everything to be perfect. "It's not a big deal, really. It'll get sorted."

"Is Este drunk already?"

Este isn't Will's favorite person. She's too carefree for his taste. He's worked so hard to get where he is, and he expects everyone else to have his level of care. Still, the accusation stings.

"No. But accidents happen."

"Accidents happen a lot more when you're high as often as Este is."

"She likes to have fun. That's not a crime." Behind the group, I watch Marcus step out of the French doors and ring a tiny, tasteful dinner chime. Grateful for the interruption, I nudge Will and point in Marcus's direction. "I think it's time for dinner."

Will raises a hand for Fritz to pause his storytelling. It's a gesture that commands respect, carrying the weight of their long-standing friendship.

"If we wait for Fritz to finish his story, dinner will be cold. The punch line is that the gators got away, but Fritz was convinced one of them was stuck in the trunk of his car for a week."

The crowd lets out a polite laugh, shifting their attention to dinner even as Fritz glares at Will for cutting his story short. Then we follow the pebbled path down toward the lake. All morning, I watched as Autumn and her team raised a white tent on the lawn and transformed the space with green garlands and delicate fairy lights. Chandeliers dangle from above, casting a soft glow. In the center of the tent, a long white table serves as the focal point, adorned with elegant candelabra and vibrant bouquets of ranunculus and freesia, the sweet, earthy fragrance mingling with the evening breeze.

Beyond the tent's edges, the moonlight shimmers on the surface of the lake, creating a play of light and shadow, and the clean-cut hedges that separate our lawn from Este and Beau's add a touch of structure to the wild beauty that surrounds us.

As I go to take my seat at the table, I'm a little worried that Will won't be able to let the dress thing go, but he pulls out my chair and kisses me.

"This is something else," Will says. "Thank you."

I smile. "Between Marcus's food and Autumn's party planning, I'm afraid I can't take much credit."

Dinner is served with precision, a choreographed dance of waiters in white gloves presenting all the plates in perfect unison. Marcus stands on the edge of the tent, orchestrating the delivery like a conductor.

"Autumn is a real master of ceremonies," Fritz says. "She once threw a Monte Carlo–themed party for the firm, and if I didn't know any better, I would have thought I was in Monaco. I got so caught up in the moment that I lost about ten grand before Gigi cut me off."

Gianna's lips press into a chilly smile as she avoids my eye. "Will, how is Mia?"

She reaches for her wineglass, and the soft glow of light catches on the bejeweled ring on her pointer finger. I take note of the mosaic of gems, and Gianna's deft ability to showcase her new bauble. Half-blinded by the sparkle, I can make out seven or eight flawless stones fixed in an artistic shape. Just flashy enough to display power without appearing too gaudy.

"Land of conspicuous consumption" should be scrolled on the city's crest.

Will smiles at the mention of his only daughter. "She's good. Nora and I took her out on the boat this morning. She wanted to stay for the party, but I couldn't think of a more boring way for a fourteen-year-old to spend a Saturday night than at a party for her dad."

He's sugarcoating the fact that Constance refused to let Mia stay for the party.

But Gianna probably already knows that.

The divorce might be far behind him, but Constance has hated me since Will and I first started dating. While she was fine with Will spending the morning with Mia, hell would freeze over before she entertained the idea of her daughter attending a party I hosted—even if Mia and I have built a sort of friendship. And, unlike some people in Will's life, she doesn't seem to wish her parents were still together.

As dinner progresses—to my relief—the evening finally finds an easier rhythm. Maybe it's the champagne or just being next to Will, but when he leans in to ask if I'm having a good time, I find myself nodding quietly and smiling. And by the time cake is served with Fritz leading the crowd in a roaring rendition of "Happy Birthday," there's a lightness in the air that everyone seems to be enjoying.

For tonight, for now, everything seems to be just right.

CHAPTER 4

The French doors are still open, offering a seamless view from the living room to the pool and the lake beyond. A remaining few stragglers drank the last of their Dom Pérignon and left about a half an hour ago. Out on the pool deck, Will is sitting on a chaise, a scotch in hand, his gaze fixed on the night sky. I slip my Louboutin heels off by the couch and pad out barefoot.

"I have a good feeling about forty-six," he says, still looking up at the stars.

"Oh?" I sit down beside him and pull my knees into my chest.

"If tonight is any indication? It's going to be one for the books."

It's almost a compliment. Almost. And I can't resist fishing for more praise. "Good party, then?"

"Best forty-sixth birthday I've ever had."

He's going to leave me hanging. I roll my eyes. "Very funny."

He turns his gaze to me. "You looked beautiful tonight. In white *and* in black."

"Thank you." I smile. "So how does it feel to be forty-six?"

"You mean officially closer to fifty than forty? Will you still love me when I'm fifty-six?"

"Of course."

"If my hair goes gray?"

"Salt and pepper hair? Sexy."

"What if I start getting little white hairs in my ears?" he continues.

I feign disgust, pretending to gag. "Oh, ick. You really know how to flirt with a girl."

He turns toward me, amused. "I didn't know we were flirting."

"Well, we're certainly not now."

He plants his feet on the ground, preparing to stand, but the mischievous glint in his eye tells me he has something else in mind. I kick a leg up in the air, mounting a feeble defense.

"No, no!" I giggle. "Don't you bring your weird ear hair over here. Stay in your chair."

With a burst of energy, he launches toward me, catching my leg and wrapping it around his hip. He pulls me close, settling between my legs and grazing my collarbone with his teeth in a playful nibble. My laughter slows as the nips become tender kisses on my collarbone and then up my neck, his lips warm against my skin.

I love him like this—unhurried, a little tipsy, and playful. And I can't remember the last time he was in such a good mood. Wrapping my arms around his neck, I pull him closer and unbutton his shirt, untucking his shirttail so the open shirt drapes around us.

"Let's go upstairs," he urges, pushing the hem of my dress up.

And I want to say: Who's going to see us? The house is at the end of a small peninsula that juts out over the lake. We might as well be on an island. I want to tell him to live a little. But I know Will, and he isn't going to go for spontaneous sex on the lawn furniture when Italian cotton percale sheets are right upstairs. So I sit up carefully and straighten my dress, trying not to break the moment.

"Let's go upstairs," I repeat as I retrace my steps toward the living room.

He follows close behind, holding my hand so loosely that sometimes it's just my fingertips balancing in the palm of his hand. As we reach the top of the stairs, I turn to face him, fantasizing that he'll pull me into him and hike my legs around his waist, then carry me to bed like some scene in a movie.

Instead, his phone starts buzzing in his pocket. He looks at the caller ID and then to me. "Sorry," he mouths.

And the moment—the one I had been hoping not to break—shatters. I nod, letting out a heavy sigh.

"Hey," he says, putting the phone to his ear. "It's Mia. Just a minute," he whispers to me, and I believe him because he doesn't walk away like he would if it was a work call. Instead, he wraps an arm around my waist and pulls me close. I put my head on his bare chest.

"Where?" he says to her. "Okay. Just give me a second." Her side of the conversation is inaudible, but I can tell from his tone that she's upset about something.

He hangs up and loosens his grip on me as he puts his phone back in his pocket.

"Mia left her Taylor Swift hoodie in the boat."

I kiss his jaw. "Get it in the morning."

"She's all worked up. It's her prized possession, and she's worried it'll rain."

I wonder if this is when all of the composure I've been working so hard to maintain tonight might dissolve. My lower lip is threatening full pout, and Will must see it because he kisses my forehead and says, "Give me five minutes."

I don't agree, but I don't disagree either. So, I watch him descend the stairs, shirt still unbuttoned, then turn on my heel and head to our bedroom.

Standing in the bathroom, I debate if I should let him undress me in some sort of tantalizing foreplay, or if I should just cut to the chase and be stark naked and waiting when he gets back. Deciding on the latter—it *is* his birthday—I slip onto the bed and prop myself up, ready, waiting, my head a little heavy from the wine. But sometime after 1:00 A.M., the wine wins, and I fall asleep.

CHAPTER 5

THE DAY AFTER

Every morning at nine, a kayak tour pushes off from a public park called Dinky Dock, near downtown Winter Park. Boaters put in under the shade of mossy trees, and over the stretch of a couple of hours, they paddle through part of what is known to locals as the Chain of Lakes—the six lakes of Winter Park, connected to one another through a collection of canals spanning almost a thousand acres.

Save for the odd hurricane days, the boating conditions hold up almost year-round, offering a perennial playground for water sports. It takes time and effort to paddle past the waves kicked up by wakeboarders and Jet Skis. And of course the wildness of Florida is never far from view: Snakes and egrets linger near the sandy shorelines. No alligators, though. In a state that boasts a seven-digit alligator population, Winter Park residents will tell you they "got rid of" the alligators in their lakes in the seventies.

Money really can buy most anything.

Those who aren't scared off by the wake or the wildlife are rewarded with views of some of the city's most historic and beautiful architecture. On Lake Osceola, they can take in the Palms, a Colonial Revival–style home that gained prominence in the 1920s for its architectural beauty and then notoriety in the 1980s when it was occupied by a drug trafficker and seized by the federal government.

Paddling through the Venetian Canal, the last and longest of the connecting waterways on the tour, will bring you to Lake Maitland. Home to the Rollins College crew team's boathouse, the Winter Park Racquet Club, and an ultraprivate, less-than-a-quarter-mile-long peninsula called the Isle of Sicily.

It sounds kind of ridiculous when you say it out loud. It's a place in Florida with Venetian canals. But around here, you get what you pay for. And people pay a lot for it.

On a good day, I'm up before the tour reaches our lake. Este and I go for a run through the neighborhood and then grab a coffee on one of our pool decks. But the morning after Will's birthday party, the blackout shades in our bedroom stay drawn long past the time the tour ends. And it's not until the sound of a humming vacuum creeps into my dreams that I realize it's time to wake up. In fact, it's well past noon, and Autumn's cleaning crew is downstairs.

I roll over, stretching out a searching hand for Will. This is wishful thinking, of course. Will doesn't sleep until noon. Will doesn't sleep past seven unless he's at death's door. But I open my eyes when I feel that his side of the bed is still neatly made. I remember washing my face and brushing my teeth, and then getting into bed naked to wait for him. Did I fall asleep that quickly?

Poor Will. He came upstairs expecting birthday sex and found me out cold.

I grab my cellphone off the nightstand. There are three missed texts from Este waiting for me.

11:00 A.M.
Wanna come over for green juice before hot yoga?

Shit. I completely forgot about the hot yoga torture session I said we'd go to.

11:50 A.M.
Are you alive?

The most recent message was sent five minutes ago.

12:42 P.M.

I'm coming over.

Naturally.

Este lives next door, and we quickly adopted an open-door policy between our houses. It's not unusual for her to let herself in through the side kitchen door to borrow something, even if I'm not home. She knows the alarm code.

Looking again at my phone, I see there are no messages waiting from Will, so I fire off a text to him:

12:48 P.M.

Sorry I fell asleep last night. Where'd you go?

I hurry to the bathroom knowing Este won't stand on ceremony if I'm still naked when she walks in. As I hear the French doors by the kitchen creak open, I splash cold water on my face, and hastily pull on workout clothes.

"Morning!" Este trills as she strolls in, making herself comfortable on the edge of the tub while I attempt to revive my blowout from yesterday.

"Was Will downstairs?"

She shakes her head. "Just the cleaning crew."

"Right. He's probably at the office." I call him twice, but each time, it goes straight to voicemail. "Hey, Will, it's me. Where are you? Call me when you get this."

Este's tastefully Botoxed brow attempts a frown. "Working? The Sunday after his birthday?"

I give her a "be serious" look. "He's a trial attorney. He'd work twenty-four hours a day if he could. It was a miracle I got him to take his birthday off. I bet he's heads down, making up for lost time somewhere."

I don't expect Este to get it. Beau retired at the ripe old age of thirty-four after making a boatload of money out in California in a tech acquisition. Sometimes, I get the feeling the second he sold his company she forgot about the long hours that he undoubtedly had to pour into his job to get to the acquisition stage.

And good for her, by the way. Who among us wouldn't take

selective amnesia in exchange for endless amounts of cash? It's not time that heals the wounds. It's money.

I open the shared iCal that I had insisted Will make for big cases so that I would understand when he was completely absent even when he was sitting in the same room. He's never posted anything in it, so I'm not surprised to see it empty.

"Hey, you know who else I didn't see downstairs? That world-class kiss-ass Autumn."

"Last night was fun, right? She did a good job." I walk down the stairs with Este trailing behind. "And she went straight from our place to Jacksonville to set up for another job this weekend. I don't think she sleeps."

I can't help myself. Part of me will always root for a hardworking underdog.

"It was a good party." Este shrugs.

"Was it? I mean, I thought it was. Maybe the icy hearts of the country club shrews are thawing a bit?"

"Oh, please, there're, like, ten more parties before you can even expect to get an invite to 'Carol's Carols Extravaganza' this Christmas." The tone in her voice makes it clear being included in Carol Parker's holiday tradition would still be one of the lower rungs of the social ladder. "*You* threw a great party. Don't give that credit to Autumn. Ask yourself: What did she do besides arrange the flowers? It's your gorgeous house, Marcus's amazing food, and your fabulous friends."

Will's fabulous friends.

Even though I think it, I don't correct her. "Why do we hate Autumn? Do we have to hate her?"

Este's face pinches like she smells something sour. "Autumn has been mainlining the Kool-Aid of this place for too long."

She follows me into the kitchen, where I grab a protein bar before we head for the door. "Said the woman who moved here a few years ago," I say. "Do you not like living here?"

"I like tax breaks. I like boat rides and sunsets on the lake and summer all year. But people like Autumn act like this place is fucking Paris or something. It's Florida, not the goddamn center of the universe."

"You're spicy this morning. Who hurt you? Did someone at

the party try to tell you the Morse Museum is better than the MoMA again?" The small art museum is a long-lauded Winter Park landmark best known for housing the most comprehensive collection of Louis Comfort Tiffany's stained glass.

"It's just a bunch of glass!"

"It's *Tiffany* glass," I counter.

This earns me a deadpan glare. "Thankfully, no one tried to gaslight me with another 'I'll never leave Winter Park because everything I could ever need is right here' speech last night. But Beau did get hammered and hurled in your jasmine bushes on the walk home."

There it is. Este is salty because she likely spent part of the evening getting Beau to bed. I pull a face in her direction. "My jasmine? He puked on my jasmine? Damnit. I like those flowers."

"I know. They're going to smell like whiskey for like a month."

"Gross."

We go out through the garage, and I see Will's car parked neatly in its space. Maybe his car being here when he's gone would be suspicious for anyone else, but I know that Will hates to drive when he's deep in trial mode. He thinks it's a waste of time. He's always Ubering.

I double-check inside the sports car. I don't know what I think I am going to find. All I see is a coffee cup from last Friday that is probably growing mold. I'll tackle that petri dish later.

Just as soon as I figure out where the hell Will is.

CHAPTER **6**

As we pull out of the driveway in Este's electric Mercedes SUV, I open the Find My app and search for Will's location. After watching the "loading" wheel spin as we drive a few blocks, I look over at Este.

"Does your cellphone service suck? I'm trying to find Will, and it's taking forever to load."

"Want me to ask Beau to jailbreak your phone? If you want to start a bar fight in Silicon Valley, ask them about jailbreaking devices. But he swears it improves processing speed."

I stare down at my screen, watching the hash marks illuminate and dim as absolutely nothing loads. "No. It's fine."

"Last night, he was talking to Beau about some big trial coming up. Do you think he work-widowed you again?"

Work-widowed. This is what Este calls it anytime Will has a trial to prepare for and he basically falls off the grid. Holing up in a room at the Ritz-Carlton—somewhere out of the Winter Park bubble to avoid distractions—he works twenty-two-hour days and survives on room service while he storyboards opening statements and talks to his experts and witnesses.

"Despite his inability to document anything in our shared calendar, usually he has the decency to tell me before he fucking disappears."

We pull onto Park Avenue, a street at the heart of Winter Park.

The shopping hub—with its oak-shaded walks and brick-paved roads—spans less than a few blocks. It's about as old as the city itself, dating back to the late 1800s, when the train station that ran parallel to Park Avenue served as the arrival point for travelers. The influence of the New Englanders who settled here can be seen in the architectural style and street names in the Park Avenue district. There's even a miniature Central Park, an eleven-acre green space that's home to art and jazz festivals, which sits between Park Avenue and the train tracks.

The quaint provision shops from Winter Park's founding era have given way to Rolex dealers, but the shopping district has withstood the pressure of big-box stores, shopping malls, and super-centers. Small businesses line the shopping strip—independent restaurants, including Marcus's, and the charming local shops and boutiques that sell high-end clothes, books, and home goods. Like a lot of Winter Park's history, Park Avenue is fiercely protected by people who believe the community stands a cut above.

Este parallel-parks her car next to the fountain in the center of the park, and we walk to our favorite yoga studio, tucked down a narrow redbrick pathway. Hoping my phone will pick up a better signal on the studio's Wi-Fi, I outpace Este slightly to grab a mat and sit down. When I open my phone, the network connection seems stronger, but when I try again to search for Will's location by way of his phone, the processing wheel spins for what feels like an eternity. I know his work can be all-consuming, but I'll feel better if I know where exactly he's disappeared to.

"Just call the Ritz after we're done," Este offers, setting up her mat next to mine.

"Yeah." I lay out a towel over my yoga mat to keep from slipping when we start to sweat. "Good idea."

When Aliyah comes in, dims the lights, and starts the gonging spa music, Este doesn't seem to notice that I'm getting concerned about Will's whereabouts.

"I'm sorry, but we are not able to share any information about the guests staying on the property without a confirmation number for your stay," the front desk employee at the Ritz-Carlton advises when I call from Este's car on the drive home.

Este rolls her eyes at my phone, which is on speaker.

"Ma'am," she says to the phone. "We just want to know if my friend's husband is Beautiful-Minding his way through some legal prep in one of your suites. You don't even have to tell us the room number. Is there a guest that keeps ordering, like, an alarming amount of coffee? Someone you might describe as 'Howard-Hughes–level sequestered'?"

"I'm very sorry. But I'm not able to discuss guest activity."

"Don't you know someone there? Can you be transferred to the concierge or something?" Este says to me.

"All of our ladies and gentlemen follow the same protocol for the safety of our guests," the desk employee chimes in, her voice firmer than before. "Is there anything else I can help you with?"

"No," I say, biting at my thumbnail. "Thank you."

Este pulls into her driveway. "You want to drive up there? I'm pretty sure if one of us flashed the right bellman, we could have a master key in about fifteen minutes. The traffic to get there will take longer than the actual grift."

She's not kidding. If I asked, Este would beeline it to the hotel and lift her shirt in the name of getting more information about where Will is.

But I just sigh. "It's okay. We'd still be looking for a needle in a haystack. We can't exactly knock on every door." I press the Ritz number again. "Hang on a minute," I say. The same front desk employee answers, and in a fit of panic, I choose a weird hackneyed English accent to say, "Mr. William Somerset's room please." I sound so ridiculous that Este can't stifle her laugh. I hear the front desk employee clacking away on a keyboard.

"I'm sorry, there is no guest here by that name."

My "thank you, goodbye" comes out with a full-blown Southern twang, and Este almost does a spit take with her chai latte.

"You should talk like that all the time. What accent was that? Liverpool by way of the Floribama coast? Christ, you are clearly not destined to be an actor."

I crack up for a second before trying Find My again.

"Want to try any of the hotels downtown?" she asks.

"He wouldn't go anywhere but the Ritz. Everyone else's sheets are 'like sandpaper and make too much noise.' I didn't know sheets made noise."

"What about his assistant? She might know what's on the docket."

I shake my head. "It's Sunday. I'm not going to bother Lenore just because Will is forgetful."

Although it might be closer to the truth to say that I don't want to shoulder the humiliation of telling Lenore he regularly disappears into his job—this time, he up and vanished without a courtesy call to his wife, the town's favorite punch line. Lenore might tell Fritz, and Fritz could tell Gianna, and Gianna would be all too eager to let Constance know. The Winter Park gossip mill rules more in my life than I'd ever care to admit.

"You know Will." Este's voice softens, and we climb out of the car. "He's going to come walking through the door at any minute, telling you about some amazing settlement. And when he does, you'll make him buy you something shiny to repent for leaving you without an explanation."

This is entirely possible. Half of Will's work seems like a professional game of chicken. Will and the opposing counsel run full speed toward each other with all manner of threats, legal motions, and dismissed proposals for settlement. And then the night before a trial—even after weeks of prep—someone floats the right amount of money for a settlement, and a deal is done.

"You think that's how Gianna got that new ring she was flashing last night?" Este asks. "The way they packed so many precious stones onto that bony-ass finger of hers is a modern feat of science."

I pull a disgusted face. "Neither one of us wants to know what Gianna does for her jewelry."

Este laughs and then encircles me in a warm hug. "Go shower and then come over for dinner."

This is our usual routine when I'm work-widowed. I third-wheel it with Beau and Este at their house, marveling at the life they've made together.

"That sounds nice," I say, swallowing how lonely I suddenly feel.

We part ways in her driveway with me promising to head back over around five, and I take an hour-long bath, soaking until my fingers and toes wrinkle. Every now and then I text Will.

3:00 P.M.
Going to Este and Beau's for dinner. Should we set a place
for you?

4:30 P.M.
What time do you think you'll be home?

4:45 P.M.
Are you mad at me?

By dinnertime, I eagerly accept the glass of Chablis Este hands me, and I don't even bother putting my phone on the table as I sit down—my worry now boiling over into anger.

I understand Will is driven, but he can't find thirty seconds to be considerate? I tried to track him down. If Will wants to find me now, let him work for it.

CHAPTER 7

THIRTY-SIX HOURS AFTER

"Nora," Este pants behind me on our morning run. "If I had known we were training for the Boston Marathon, I wouldn't have had so much to drink last night."

"That's a lie." I pick up the pace a little bit, enjoying the fact that this is one of the few areas where I am legitimately better than Este. Plus, running is the only thing keeping me from spiraling about Will's absence at this point.

Most wives would've tossed all their spouses' monogrammed dress shirts on the front lawn and lit them on fire by now, but being a trial attorney's wife, I've come to understand the ghosting isn't personal.

It's more likely he's covered up with work, yet again. He spends weeks or even months poring over deposition transcripts and evidence, looking for the perfect arguments to help his clients. The level of focus required is a kind of meditative state, and when he falls completely off the grid, it's because he's had a breakthrough, like the defense destroyed evidence and he has them dead to rights, or his client said something stupid in a deposition and he can see the defense's path to victory in the error. Either way, it sends him down a rabbit hole and the rest of the world ceases to exist. The possibility of finding the perfect case, the ideal set of facts to win big for his client, is the white whale he'll never stop chasing.

As much as he loves the glory of his clients winning, Will has never been one for scenes. And I know he would be pissed if I drew attention to his disappearing act, so I've quietly called the Ritz a handful of times. I texted, GPS-tracked, even searched by the dock for signs of Mia's hoodie or his walk down there, and there's nothing. Every hour, I cycle through worried, lonely, pissed, and then processing the fact that this is the price I pay for marrying a trial attorney who is very committed to what he does.

And I guess I'm taking all the emotion out on the pavement.

It's good to keep moving. I have to keep moving.

"For fuck's sake, Nora, I'm going to die."

"Sorry." I slow my pace so she can catch up.

Este and I agreed that we'd run to the Racquet Club for breakfast and back after—a mile each way. But I'm a realist, and odds are we'll walk back after a couple of mimosas.

Once the morning reaches office hours, I'll call Lenore to check Will's calendar for the day. I haven't thought much about what happens after that, but showing up wherever he's supposed to be and reading him the riot act feels like a near certainty.

I glance over at Este, and her face is white, which stops me in my tracks. We haven't even made it out of our street yet. When I left her and Beau the night before, they were opening a third bottle of wine, and he was laughing, charmed by her as she slow-danced with herself in the moonlight, looking like some ethereal fairy queen.

"Can we just walk a minute?" She huffs, one hand grabbing at her right side.

"Yeah. Want me to call an Uber?"

"No." She's still a little breathless, but after a beat, she flashes a mischievous grin. "I want to see if Carol Parker's fence is still down."

"How is it that the mere mention of Carol Parker's wrecked fence immediately brings the color back to your face? I swear to God, your schadenfreude is pathological."

"What does it say about me that I fetishize the idea of perfect Carol's perfect yard being perfectly destroyed?"

"Ask your therapist," I say with a laugh. "Diagnoses are above my pay grade."

"Hey, is that Fritz?" She frowns as a black Porsche SUV pulls over the narrow bridge at the entrance to our street, just past the posted placard that reads ISLE OF SICILY: PRIVATE.

Isle of Sicily Road is a narrow cul-de-sac. Each of the few homes on the street is waterfront property, all so private Google Maps doesn't even offer street views. Fritz would have no reason to be here unless he's visiting someone.

We both watch as he drives by without noticing either one of us, and I instinctively start following his car. Este says something about breakfast behind me that I can't quite make out. I'm too busy searching the shadows in the back window of the SUV for signs that Will might be with him. My heart rate kicks up as Fritz pulls into our driveway, and I jog to get to him just a little bit faster.

Fritz steps out of the car with a questioning look on his face. "Hey, I'm looking for Will. We had a mediation this morning, but he didn't show. He's not answering calls." Fritz heads for the front door. "What'd y'all get up to after the party? Is he still sleeping it off? I need to talk to him."

Fritz's words catch me off guard. I feel like I'm falling backward.

How can Fritz not know where Will is?

I look down at my feet to confirm I'm still standing. The story I'd been counting on—the Will-is-tied-up-with-work song and dance—comes to a screeching halt, and I can almost hear the record scratch.

"Fritz," Este calls from behind me. "Will's not home. Nora hasn't seen him since the night of the party."

I spin around to look at her, somehow stung that she put it all out there like that—like she's given away a personal secret.

"Jesus." A million questions pass on Fritz's face as he turns to me with a blend of confusion and concern in his eyes. "Nora?" His voice is accusing.

An onslaught of dread lands so heavy on my chest I can barely breathe, never mind speak.

What the fuck is happening?

"Let's talk inside," Este says, leading the way and waving her hands like a crossing guard.

But we don't even make it past the threshold of the front door before Fritz is dialing someone.

"This is Frederick Hall," he says. "I need to speak to Detective Ardell."

Fritz walks down the hall toward Will's home office, and I look at Este. "Is this happening? We're calling the police now?"

Before Este can answer, Fritz comes back into the kitchen. "Detective Ardell is headed this way. Have you filed a report?"

"A report? No. I thought . . ." I'm struggling to catch up. "Why do we need that?"

I glance between Este and Fritz—my best friend and Will's—wondering if I've ever seen them speak to each other before. They're an odd pairing now. Fritz's expression is pulled tight while Este keeps rolling her eyes at him as if he's overdramatizing a whole lot of nothing. I'm still trying to get my mind around the fact that Will isn't with Fritz.

"He's been gone for thirty-six hours, and you haven't thought to call the police?" Fritz demands.

What could I possibly say to this? Where the hell is he?

"Considering how often Will ghosts Nora for work, he'll probably come waltzing through that door any second," Este pipes up. "Plus, everyone knows you have to wait a couple days to report someone missing."

"Where did you hear that?" Fritz snaps. "There's no waiting period to report a missing person in Florida. And I'm telling you he didn't ghost you for work. I *am* work, and he's not there." He's roaring now. "He missed a seven-figure mediation this morning. That doesn't happen."

My heart begins to pound. Este's head jerks back with a wince like she's physically rejecting this information.

Mediation is Fritz's love language—a chance to get paid on a case without having to work it up for trial. The irony is taking a settlement can leave money on the table. But it's often less work. And he could bully the mediator for sport. A perfect day by his standards.

"Is his car here?" Fritz asks.

"Yes, but he Ubers to the office all the time. He says commuting eats into work."

"Nora." Fritz grabs my arm and squeezes it. "You should have called me."

"I *would've*"—I shake my arm free from his grip—"if I thought there was a reason to. I figured you were with him. Which, considering the two weeks you two disappeared for that last legal conference, wouldn't be totally unrealistic, right?" I glare at him. The anger is misplaced, but I dig in anyway. I'm terrified, and I don't like what Fritz is implying.

"You really have never been able to let that go."

"Two weeks in Hawaii to 'learn about trucking law'? Why can't lawyers have their conferences in the Midwest like normal people?"

Fritz bristles at the insinuation that they were just fucking off in Hawaii. But he's a lawyer, so he doubles down and takes a step toward me, boxing me in between him and the refrigerator.

Este folds her arms. "Hey, Fritz, how about you give her a little space?"

Fritz doesn't move. I take a defiant step toward him until we're almost nose to nose, his breath hot on my face.

I won't be threatened in my own home.

He looks down at me and sneers. "So, what? Will works long hours so you don't have to give a shit where he is?"

"I knew where he was."

"Which is *where*?" he shouts.

It doesn't matter what I thought. Everything has changed in the last few minutes. I don't get a word out before the doorbell chimes.

"I'll get it." Este looks relieved to have a reason to get out of the room, but Fritz is quick on her heels.

"Ardell's a friend," he chides. "I'll talk to him."

I storm after them both, agitated as hell.

It's my fucking house.

CHAPTER 8

"Hey, Travis." Fritz extends a hand to the uniformed officer at the front door and invites him in with a gesture. Where only a second ago Fritz was wide-eyed and shouting, now he's perfectly composed. "Thanks for coming over so quickly. Listen, we've got an issue with Will."

"Sure." Ardell moseys into the house, checking it out as he does. "I know Will. Nice to see you again, Mrs. Somerset." He tips a polite nod in my direction.

His badge says ARDELL. And it dawns on me that Will introduced me to him at the Christmas party at the club earlier this year. Ardell had been a witness for Will in a hit-and-run lawsuit. When he introduced us at the club, Will commented that Ardell was on the fast track to a role in public service, and Ardell's boyish face had broken into a hopeful smile. Will and his friends are kingmakers in this city, and Ardell knows it. The most memorable thing about Ardell that night, though, came about ten minutes after I met him, when I saw him putting his hand up Tippy Schaeffer's skirt. I had wandered outside to get a breath of fresh air after too much of whatever cranberry punch they were slinging. Fortunately, I managed to sneak back inside without them noticing me.

As he closes in on me now, he smells a little like sweat and aftershave—thanks to the polyester police uniform that's hugging his HGH-fueled biceps. Ardell seemed like the kind of guy who would make Este's ears bleed waxing poetic about the wild peacocks that roam the city. He's a Winter Park lifer, like Fritz, although his station in the pecking order is not at Fritz's level.

"So, what seems to be the problem?" His brow creases with concern.

"Will's gone," Este blurts out.

Fritz and I both shoot her a glare, and Ardell's eyebrows go up.

"Gone?" he repeats, his face etched with fresh concern.

"No." I shake my head aggressively. "He's just not responding to calls is all."

"And Nora can't find him on Find My. And he's not physically here." Este waves her arms around the room.

Ardell's eyes bounce from me to Este and finally back to Fritz. "Are y'all wanting to make a missing person report, then?"

A chilly silence overtakes the room.

This is too real. It can't be real.

In the blink of an eye, Will went from being an absent-minded workaholic to . . . missing?

Fritz speaks first. "Play the optics out with me." He rubs his chin. "We file the report. The BOLO goes out over the radio. Some reporter hears over the police scanner that Will Somerset is missing. How long are we talking before this city is on its head with speculation and wild theories?"

"Are you fucking serious?" Este hisses. "This is your best friend, Fritz. Who gives a fuck about gossip and optics? Nora?"

Before I can say a word, Ardell chimes in.

"Is this a social call, Mr. Hall? Off the record?" He folds his arms across his chest, unruffled by Fritz or Este.

"We're just trying to understand the best way to proceed. Is there a way to track him down without calling too much attention to the situation? Our firm really doesn't need this kind of press."

I shoot a look at Este.

Is Fritz really talking about the press? And the firm?

"When was the last time you saw or heard from him?" Ardell asks me.

"We had his birthday party on Saturday. So, maybe around one A.M. on Saturday night. Well, Sunday morning, I guess. His daughter, Mia, called, begging him to go find her Taylor Swift sweatshirt, and he went down to the boat to see if it was there."

"And did he come back up?"

"I don't know. If he did, I didn't hear him. I fell asleep. It was late." Stomach churning with worry, I fold my arms across my chest. But then I remember a true crime podcast I heard once said folded arms look defensive and drop them. "Sometimes he sleeps in the guest room downstairs—if he's working late and doesn't want to wake me."

I don't mention that the guest bedroom was undisturbed when I checked it. A detail that suddenly feels so much more sinister.

"And then yesterday and today, no word from him?"

"That's right." I can see Fritz shaking his head with disapproval from the corner of my eye. "But it's just like Will to do something like this. He's always working late and he can be forgetful about his calendar. Fritz, you know that better than anyone, right?"

I look over at Este and Fritz, who are watching as if this were a weird one-act play.

"Since we don't have a report filed and I don't have a warrant, this isn't an official police matter. I want you to know that, okay? You don't have to be nervous."

"I just want him to come home." The words come out sounding like a prayer.

"Sure, of course you do." Ardell nods as if I've just said the most logical thing in the world. "So he was headed down to the boat dock last you saw him? Would it be all right with you if I walk down that way?"

"Of course. Can I get you some water or an iced tea?"

"I'm just fine. Thank you kindly." He heads for the pool door and then pauses. "I noticed a camera at the front door. Y'all have cameras anywhere else? Maybe there's something there that could help us."

That would be convenient, wouldn't it?

Half the people on this street forget to lock their doors. Between insurance policies and liquid wealth, my neighbors could replace the entire contents of their homes ten times over. With money like that, you don't worry about something as pedestrian as petty theft. I had asked Will about security cameras once, but he just laughed it off, insisting there could be no safer place to live in the world.

"Just the doorbell camera." I shake my head, wishing I could go back in time and change his mind. "I looked through the footage. He didn't leave through the front door, but he never does."

Ardell nods and heads for the back of the house. "I'll go take a look around the dock."

Este and I watch from the living room as Ardell and Fritz walk down to the dock.

"Maybe you should go out there." Este eyes the two of them talking, putting their hands on their hips as they walk the length of the dock. Then they survey the boatlift with hands shielding their eyes from the sun. "Fritz looked like he was ready to have you thrown in jail earlier. I don't trust him alone with a cop."

"It's fine," I say. "I don't have anything to hide."

Este nods, but her eyes linger on me for a few extra seconds.

Ardell takes out his iPhone and snaps a few photos of the dock and the boathouse, and I hold my breath a little.

Este squints, leaning closer to the window. "Do you think they found something?"

But then they're turning around and heading back to the house. Empty-handed.

"No," I assert. I had already searched the dock for what felt like hours early that morning, and there was no Taylor Swift hoodie, no sign of where Will went that night.

Ardell and Fritz make their way back inside and into the living room.

"Mr. Hall seems to think . . . ," Ardell starts, looking at Fritz like he's hoping for a signal of approval. "If it's all right with you, Mrs. Somerset, I'll go ahead and file that missing person report."

I look at Fritz, Este, and then Ardell. A chilling numbness pours over me. "Yeah, okay."

"We're going to see what we can dig up, but we might have some more questions for you once our digging is done." Ardell chuckles as Fritz claps him on the back. "Bastard better be somewhere working without his phone plugged in."

Ardell heads toward the door, and Este hangs back as Fritz and I walk him out to the driveway.

"Thanks for coming over so quickly, Travis." Fritz offers him a handshake.

"Hey, no problem. One of our own, you know."

And then it's just Fritz and me, watching the police car wind its way down the road.

"Someone has to give Constance a heads-up before she hears this through the grapevine," Fritz says.

"Okay," I say, but the word tastes bitter. Will's first wife left him in a fit of rage, and she still loathes the fact he had the gall to remarry.

Fritz turns back to me, and he must see the reluctance on my face because he adds, "I'll handle Constance, all right? And don't talk to anyone without me around. I'll call you if I hear anything from Travis."

"What? Why? And what makes you think they'd call you if they find something? I'm his wife."

"That's cute," he snipes. "But I'm his business partner of twenty years. I don't think you understand what's at stake here."

"I guess I don't," I say, voice hardening. "Are we talking about Will's safety or your law firm?"

Fritz's preoccupation with the firm makes me want to tell him to fuck off, but he glowers at me and heads to his car, robbing me of the opportunity. He gets in his Porsche and drives away.

I close my eyes and turn my head up to the sky, feeling the heat on my face, letting the sun and the helplessness bear down on me.

Jesus, Will, where are you?

"Hey," Este calls from the front door, snapping my attention back down to earth.

I turn to look at her.

"Come inside. You've earned a glass of wine."

I look at my watch. "It's eleven in the morning."

"So what?"

"Okay." But I stay in the driveway for just a second longer.

That's when I see it. A gray sedan creeping slowly up the road. The make and model seem out of place for the neighborhood, but

I dismiss the prickling feeling under my skin. DoorDash and Uber Eats always come through here at the beck and call of the wealthy and lazy. Still, I turn toward the house, shivering a little when the gray sedan completes the loop of the cul-de-sac and slowly drives by again. I quickly head inside, locking the door behind me.

CHAPTER 9

BEFORE

Before Will Somerset and boat rides around Winter Park's Chain of Lakes to cool off on a hot Saturday morning, and before Este and rosé by the pool on random Wednesday afternoons, I was hot. Not, like, check-out-those-curves hot, but rather, wondering-why-the-fuck-did-I-choose-to-live-on-the-surface-of-the-sun hot. I understand that Northerners will tell a Floridian to take a seat with weather complaints when they *willingly* live with minus-forty-degree winter days, but Florida's climate is a special kind of unforgiving. There's a heaviness that comes with the humidity that can feel impossible to shake. It's an ass-sweat-sticking-to-the-seat-of-your-car, perspiration-gathering-under-the-cups-of-your-bra kind of heat. Unless, of course, you have the luxury of spending your days poolside with a little umbrella drink, best not to be outside at all.

Back in those days, I spent most of my time working as a receptionist at the front desk of a children's museum in Loch Haven Park, a hub for museums and theaters just outside the boundaries of Winter Park. And my daily dose of sunshine came during my lunch break, when I would find a shady tree in the park where I could eat my brown bag lunch before the most oppressive heat of the day, and daydream about how I was going to reboot my life.

When I took the museum job just out of college, I had high hopes of parlaying the nonprofit role—with its fundraiser events and donor cocktail parties—into something with more upward mobility, like a job in marketing or public relations. At every event, I held my breath with the fantastic expectation that I would meet someone looking for a plucky young upstart. But three years into answering phones and doling out visitor stickers at the front desk, no one had taken me under their wing to help me find a bigger and better job. For all intents and purposes, my career was stalled, which was too bad, because living on a nonprofit receptionist's salary was, as the title implies, not exactly lucrative.

Meager funds and dwindling career prospects were why I snagged a second job as a swim instructor at the Winter Park Racquet Club. One of the three private clubs in town, the Racquet Club is nestled among the enormous estates and historical homes on one of the town's most coveted streets, Via Tuscany, and its lakeside location meant that members could arrive by boat and leave their vessels at the property's dock. Neighborhood moms would bring younger kids here because they could keep a close eye on their children between Chardonnays.

Teaching swimming was a nice way to escape the heat for a few hours on the weekends. And the second income stream from giving one-on-one lessons to children with deeper pockets than my own meant that, if I was thrifty, I could save up enough money to move out of my mom's place in a year or so.

"You want a Diet Coke?" Quinn, my 10:00 A.M. student, always offered as her lesson wound down. "I can charge it to my parents' account."

I'm not proud of the number of times I took her up on her offer, but the swimmer I saw after her was always my toughest student of the day. Fearful of water and not in command of his own limbs half the time, three-year-old Spencer tugged on my one-piece bathing suit like it was a life raft. More than once I had to pull his hands out of my neckline when, in plain sight of most of the club's guests, he grabbed wildly for anything that he could use to haul himself out of the water. And sometimes, a Diet Coke from Quinn felt like a well-earned treat.

One Saturday morning, I was trying to teach Spencer how to dive for small Paw Patrol figurines and keep his wandering hands from coming near me when I spotted two girls sneaking drinks from abandoned pool chairs. Frowning, I watched them giggle and hide behind the snack stand, and I looked around to see if anyone else had noticed.

It was another sunny day in Winter Park. The moms, perpetually in an arms race to see who could be the most agelessly beautiful while also jockeying to snag the latest designer bag or priciest Cartier bangle, sunned themselves on lounge chairs while a veritable army of babysitters and nannies sat fully dressed under umbrellas with strollers or wrangled kids and their snack stand hotdogs and instantly melting Popsicles. Everyone seemed too engrossed in their own afternoons to notice the girls.

But over the course of a thirty-minute swim lesson, I watched as they became more brazen in their thefts, swiping fresh drinks as busy bartenders left them on the bar tops for servers to carry off. Given the relatively small size of the club, it came as a surprise to me that the girls weren't being caught or even noticed.

"All done!" Spencer shrieked as he rescued a Dalmatian figurine in a red fireman hat from the second step of the pool for the umpteenth time.

"You ready to be done, buddy?" I checked the clock on the side of the snack stand. "Yeah. We can be done for the day. Did you have fun?"

"Nooo." He shook his head with a cheeky grin.

"Noo?" I parroted. "Should I bring some Spider-Man figurines next time?"

"Spider-Man!"

"If I bring Spider-Man, will you try jumping in the pool?"

He nodded.

"You've got a deal. Let's go find your mom."

After bundling Spencer up in a towel and handing him off to his mother, I headed into the locker room, braced for the stale scent of pool water. Pushing through the door, though, I heard a faint sound echo off the tiles, a blend of a mewling kind of cry and something else that got louder with every step.

It didn't take long for the second sound to come into sharp focus: retching.

I scanned the gaps beneath the bathroom stalls until I saw a small pair of white Keds on the beige square tiles.

"Hello?"

The white Keds drew closer to their owner at the sound of my voice. I could see cutoff denim shorts and knobby knees. It was one of the drink thieves from the pool. I looked around at the other stalls and realized she was alone.

"You okay?" I offered. "Where's your friend?"

This only provoked fresh tears and a whining sound from the girl.

Walking to the sink, I grabbed a handful of paper towels and ran them under cold water, then crouched down beside the stall door and showed the towels to her.

"I'm going to put my hand under the door, okay?" When the girl didn't object, I reached in, and she tentatively accepted the towels. "Clean up a little, and I'll go get you some water."

Approaching the bar outside, I caught the attention of Andres, the manager on duty for Saturday mornings. "Can I get a water for a guest?" He nodded, grabbing a plastic cup. Feeling a little protective of the girl curled up in the bathroom, I raised an eyebrow in his direction. "Hey, did you see those kids stealing drinks?"

He just made a noncommittal shake of his head. "I don't know."

"What do you mean?"

"I try not to get involved."

"So you *did* see them?" My voice was accusatory.

He handed me the water. "If we catch them, they just say we're lying and then their parents try to get us fired."

I started to say that the club could lose its liquor license, that someone could get hurt. But I could already imagine Andres's response. The district attorney for this county lived three houses over, and the member directory included judges and other higher-up city officials. The rules were whatever members wanted them to be. What did I expect Andres to do about it?

"Nice." Rolling my eyes, I reached across the bar to grab a handful of saltine packets, then made a beeline back to the bathroom.

When I reached the stall, the girl had opened the swinging door, but she was still sitting with her legs drawn to her chest. Her head was on her knees.

"Here." I sat down beside her and put the water and crackers between us.

She lifted her head for a second before groaning and putting it back down.

"What's your name?" I asked.

"Mia," she whimpered.

"I'm Nora. Is there someone I can call for you? Someone who can help you get home safely?"

Without lifting her head, she pulled a cellphone from her back pocket and handed it to me. "Just don't call my mom."

Her lock screen was a picture of her and her friends on the back of a boat flashing duck faces and peace signs. I tried to swipe it open, but her phone was password protected.

"Okay. Look up for a second, Mia."

She begrudgingly obliged, her face in a pathetic scowl, and I held the phone up to her face to unlock it. It seemed like a positive sign that she could respond to basic questions. Not alcohol poisoning. I hoped not, anyway.

I opened her contacts and scrolled through a list of unfamiliar names—Alwyn, Answell, Axley—and raised my eyebrows. "Your friends have . . . really interesting names. Who do you want me to call?"

"My mom is crazy. Don't call my mom. She'll kill me. She'll literally kill me."

I thought about all of the times in my life when my mother ditched me for a new boyfriend, including the one she was currently jet-setting around Europe with while I watched her place, but decided this wasn't the time to commence a one-upmanship game on whose mom sucked more.

"What about your dad?" I searched her contacts for Dad.

She reached for the water and nodded. "Pal."

"What?" I frowned, wondering if I had misheard her, but when I searched Pal, a contact showed up. I hit the phone icon.

After two rings, a warm male voice picked up. "Hey, Buggy."

Andres's warning echoed in my head for a fraction of a heartbeat before I said, "Hi, this is Nora at the Racquet Club."

"Is Mia okay?" His voice went taut with concern.

"She's okay. I'm sitting with her in the bathroom. She's not feeling well, I'm afraid."

There was a pause on the other end of the line. I couldn't think of a delicate way to say that Mia had been stealing alcohol and was now in the fetal position post-yacking without making him defensive. It turned out that one of the few things Andres and I had in common was that neither of us had any interest in losing our jobs to a dad who couldn't hear the truth about his kid.

"Jesus." The man on the phone sighed. "Did Mia and her friends use leftover drinks to make a hunch punch again?"

A sigh of relief slipped past my lips. "I can say with a fair degree of certainty that they did."

Should I be more surprised that this isn't the first time she's done this or that he isn't trying to cover for her?

"All right. I'll be right there." There was movement on his side of the conversation like he was heading for the door or grabbing car keys. "Listen, could you do me a favor and keep this quiet? If Mia's mom finds out, she'll crucify us both."

"Yeah," I said. "Why don't you text when you get here and I'll walk her through the service entrance?" There was a grassy pathway on the side of the club that guests used often to avoid dripping pool water on the dining room floor, but if I took Mia through the kitchen, I could walk her out the same way the servers took the garbage.

"I appreciate it." Instead of saying goodbye, he added, "I live close. I'll be right over."

I handed the phone back to Mia. "Your dad's on his way. Have some crackers. They'll soak up the alcohol."

She took a few bites, looking pallid. "My friend ditched me when I got sick," she grumbled. "My dad's a lawyer. Everyone thinks he'll sue them if something bad happens to me."

How fun for me.

I helped Mia off the floor as she worked to find her center of gravity from what I imagined was a spinning room.

"Come on. Let's get you outside before your dad takes me to court."

Mia made her way out of the locker room on uncertain legs with me trailing behind. As we wound through quieter corridors of the club, I kept a careful eye on her wobbly gait and directed her toward the kitchen. As luck would have it, we were able to make our way through the service door relatively unnoticed.

She covered her eyes as we stepped out into the glaring Florida sun, and I looked for any sign of her dad. Beyond the asphalt of the parking lot was a pro shop and the tennis courts, which made it hard to see the traffic on Via Tuscany or beyond, so I pointed to a shaded tree and said, "Let's get out of the sun."

We had taken only a few steps, though, when an exotic sports car pulled in front of us, and a man who looked peeled from the pages of a *GQ* spread stepped out. His eyes were fixed on his daughter, but she just stared down at her Keds.

"Mia. What the hell?" He lifted his arms in exasperation. "Do you know how dangerous it is to drink until you're sick? Where's Katie?"

"She split." Mia trudged to the passenger door of the sports car without another word.

"What kind of friend leaves you sick in the bathroom?" he called after her, but she just flopped into the car and closed the door, pulling her knees back up to her chest.

He turned back to look at me, and our eyes met for the first time. A spark of attraction registered in my core as I realized he was handsome. Mia's mean lawyer dad was all chiseled features, broad shouldered, and *hot*. His presence should have been intimidating, but he was somehow accessible.

"I'm sorry about this." He shook his head. "Her mom and I got divorced last year. Between that and the impending teenage years, it's like she's trying to give me a heart attack."

"It's okay," I said. "She'll be all right. My parents split up when I was about her age. It knocked me sideways for a minute, but I turned out just fine." This was a pretty audacious lie, considering I was standing barefoot in a bathing suit in front of the location of my second job, but if he noticed, he didn't seem to care.

"I'm Will." He extended a hand, and I shook it. Weird how some handshakes pass like perfunctory nothings, but this one didn't. His hand was warm, and I would have sworn goosebumps traveled up my arm when we touched.

"Nora." I took my hand back and folded my arms, rubbing them to make sure there were no actual goosebumps.

"Thanks for being discreet about this, Nora. She's supposed to be with her mom this week, but that won't stop Constance from making this my fault somehow."

"No problem." I gestured in Mia's direction. "I gave her a little bit of water and some crackers. You should probably get her home before it all comes back up on the console of your spaceship."

A light chuckle escaped his lips, and the sound was decadent. "Nice to meet you, Nora." He nodded before turning to leave.

Will, the Hot Mean Lawyer, is delicious. Good for him.

The next week, I was returning Spencer and his wandering claw hands to his mom when Mia stepped out on the pool deck. She was bright eyed and fresh faced, a welcome contrast to the last time I saw her. Her dark hair was neatly gathered in a ponytail, and she was wearing a green sundress with her Keds this time. She spotted me walking toward the locker room and waved as she headed toward me.

"Hey, Mia." I smiled. "How are you feeling?"

Her cheeks flushed red. "I'm grounded."

"Oof." I sighed. *Good for Hot Mean Lawyer dad.* "For how long?"

She squinted as if doing the math. "Until my dad can trust me to make more responsible choices? So probably, like, until next week, when I go back to my mom's house."

"Mia," Will cautioned, appearing beside her in a custom designer suit.

Hot Mean Lawyer looks good in everything. Swell.

She offered me a small cream-colored envelope. "Thanks for looking out for me last week."

I took it with a smile. "Glad to see you're doing better."

"Can I get a soda?" She looked to Will.

"Sure." He added, "*Just* soda."

She gave me an annoyed look, as if to say "Dads, am I right?" and headed off to the snack stand.

I gestured toward her. "She looks like she's doing better already."

"Don't let her fool you. Her status is a minute-by-minute thing at this age."

"Well, it was nice of her to say thank you." I held up the card.

"We both agreed it was a good idea to show proof of life and try to win back some dignity after last week."

"It wasn't that bad. Really. But hey—" I raised a hand in warning. "Be careful about her friends. She said they all think you'll sue them if something bad happens to her."

He frowned as if in disbelief before saying, "That's crazy. I'd never sue her friends. They're all minors." And then after a beat, "I'd sue their parents."

If not for the hint of mirth in his eyes, I might have thought he was serious. He played the straight man perfectly, and so help me, I let out a giggle. He grinned a cover-model, megawatt smile back at me, and my knees went a little wobbly. I blushed for being so ridiculous.

Christ, Nora. Act cool. Don't get drool on his designer loafers.

I looked away, trying to fight what felt like a gravitational pull toward him. But when I looked back up at him, his face bloomed with a half smile and he said, "Can I take you to dinner?" And then, "To thank you for scraping Mia off the bathroom floor?"

"Is that the going rate for babysitting these days?"

"I got divorced last year."

"I remember you saying."

"So . . . I don't know how this is supposed to go."

"Thanking someone?"

"Asking a beautiful woman on a date."

My stomach fluttered.

Is this seriously happening?

"I will skip the part where I ask if you hit on all the swim coaches here," I said.

"You've got me. I do. But no hard feelings if you're not interested. Patrick turned me down last week and I was okay with it. He's a little hairy for my taste anyway."

"I'm not sure if that makes you funny or indiscriminate in your dating life." I smiled.

There was a charming hint of vulnerability in his blue eyes. "What do you think?"

"I thought lawyers weren't supposed to ask questions they didn't know the answer to?"

"It's a rookie move," he said. From the way he was smiling, I could tell he was pretty confident in my answer. "But I am banking on my dazzling wit to win you over."

I couldn't think of a time I'd been asked on a date. In college, we hung out in groups, pairing off here and there, growing into couples, then breaking apart. It was so much more organic and disorganized. I had been on a few dating apps, but that hadn't led to anything civilized either.

Will was urbane and accomplished. And there was something about him that was different from all the other arrogant, manicured men who came through the oak doors at the front of the club. He seemed humble and kind. I considered the age gap between us—was it fifteen, twenty years? What in the world could we possibly have in common?

I hesitated longer than I meant to as I weighed the worst that could happen. Then, I heard myself say, "I'd love to go. Thanks."

I knew full well there was no way this could be the reboot I'd been pining for during all those lunch breaks in the park. But after so many long days at the museum or the pool, maybe dinner with Mia's Hot Mean Lawyer dad would be a nice change of pace. I gave him my number.

A boring night out can't be worse than all the boring nights I've spent at home.

CHAPTER **10**

TWO DAYS AFTER

check my phone, wanting desperately for there to be the call or the text to end this madness. I hear Alma let herself in the kitchen door, and I start a little. This is a new habit of mine. I'm on edge. My senses heightened to catch every sound and shift.

I was never meant to live in this house alone.

I realize I've been sitting on the end of the bed for what must be an hour. Time has become a flat circle in the last forty-eight hours.

As I step into the shower, I catch myself smiling about how Will usually comes to find me here. The pipes from our bathroom run along the far side of his office downstairs. In the beginning of our relationship, the hum of the water running was the siren call that beckoned him to casually walk upstairs like he'd forgotten something in the bathroom, but I was smart enough to know that he was there to see me naked. Because he could. Something about that memory rocks me, and the tears come as darker and more forbidding fears bear down on my mind. None of this is making any sense. Where is Will? What was that weird car I saw creeping past the house? Ardell is treating me vaguely like I had something to do with all of this. And what was with Fritz's comment about the firm?

Overwhelming panic-attack tingles vibrate through my body. I'm in control of nothing, and I don't know where my husband is. I need this nightmare to end. I shake my hands rapidly, hoping to get out of the cycle my brain is in before I pass out in the shower. By the time I shut the water off, I realize I can't just sit here and wait for someone to call me. Wait for something to happen. So, I throw on some clothes and head downstairs.

Alma is in the kitchen making an egg-filled something for me. Her gentle maternal energy soothes me for a second.

"Morning, Ms. Nora. How are you? Did you hear from Will?"

I shake my head.

"I'll make lamb ragu so it's here when he gets back later."

If *he comes back later. What if he doesn't?*

"Thanks." I force a smile. I can't let my foreboding thoughts send me back to tears. I grab my keys and purse and head out the door.

Twenty minutes and a Barnie's Coffee stop later, I walk into the reception area of Will's office. Even though Fritz, and his father, are dyed-in-the-wool good ole boys, the office has none of the trappings of plaid or SEC championship memorabilia you usually find around their species. Instead, it's a masterpiece of Gianna's design. Fine art adorns every wall, plants accomplish a perfect feng shui, and the delicate mix of solids and patterns all in neutral colors makes this feel more like a showroom and less like the place you land when you need to sue the pants off someone. It's too frilly for my taste, but I can appreciate why someone would call it beautiful.

Lenore appears from behind a formidable mahogany door that separates the lobby from a maze of offices and associates, a fresh cup of coffee in her hand. She's been with the firm since it belonged to Fritz's father. Fritz, for all of his bombastic frat-boy tendencies, is smart enough not to be a ran-away-with-the-hot-secretary cliché. Or maybe—for once in his life—he's just as scared of Lenore as everyone else.

Either way, Lenore in her sensible shoes and pussy bows has been the mainstay of the firm. Associates are known to give her a wide berth out of fear. She's smart, funny, doesn't suffer a single fool, and if she'd been born to a different family, she would've crushed law school. She's the constant minder of the files, the watchful guardian of the calendars. On weekends, she hosts a high-brow, invite-only book club to discuss serious philosophers and famous tomes. Will has angled for an invite only to be rebuffed more than once.

"Oh, Nora, I'm happy to see you," Lenore says. "You must be worried sick about Will."

"Hey, Lenore. Yeah, this is all very strange. But I'm glad to see you. Can you unlock Will's office for me? I couldn't find his keys at the house and I, uh, just—"

"Of course, dear. I wouldn't want to wait on the Winter Park Police to have to sort it all out either."

I want to ask her what she means, but you don't really question Lenore. You wait for her to offer up whatever information she chooses to dole out.

"Yeah, I really don't know what to do," I say instead.

"Keep the faith, dear. I know I am."

Lenore lets me into Will's office. Despite the beautiful oak walls and expensive furniture, the well-appointed space mostly looks like the file cabinets exploded all over. The surface of his desk is covered with files and Post-it notes. I can't even see his keyboard.

"He assures me he has a system, though I've never been able to crack it." Lenore chuckles to herself. "Let me know if you need anything."

I walk in half-horrified, half-curious about how Will gets anything done in this clutter. But, like Lenore said, it works for him. He doesn't keep much at home, hence his office looking knocked over.

I freeze and listen for a moment, wary of any associate passing by while I start digging through Will's things. When all I hear is the faint echo of desk phones ringing, I start to sift through some of the folders on his desk, but it all looks like lawyerly stuff. I don't see any dated files or urgent notices for a court appearance— nothing stands out as the reason he might have fallen off the grid. His bottom-left desk drawer has toothpicks, deodorant, and a host of half-chewed and broken pens.

What a brilliant weirdo.

Will always chews on his pen when he's thinking hard about something, leading to at least two ink-stained lips events and one ruined custom shirt in the past year.

The bottom drawers on both sides have notebooks and other random files. They're so disorganized they could induce hives. The top-left drawer has a bunch of random golf tees and ball markers, a small glass plaque he was awarded at a conference, and that's about it. I shift the tees around and see a folded-up Post-it note taped to the bottom of the drawer. I pull it up and open it.

The only thing on it is a phone number I don't recognize: (863) 555-0142.

I flip it over, hoping there's a name or something else, but there's nothing. I open my phone to google the digits, but before I can, Fritz is clearing his throat in the doorway.

"Lenore told me you were here."

I tuck the piece of paper into the palm of my hand so it's out of sight and step closer to the desk, instinctively hiding the open drawer from Fritz's view. I don't know why I feel guilty. With Will gone two days, I am fully within my spouse-snooping rights.

"Yeah, I didn't know what else to do. I just want to find Will."

"We all do, Nora," he placates. I can't get a read on the emotion behind his knitted brow, whether he's annoyed or concerned. "Travis is working on it. But you shouldn't dig too much in here. There's a lot of confidential evidence and information that's protected under attorney-client privilege. The firm could get in a lot of trouble." He's not scolding me exactly, but his tone is reminiscent of a disappointed sitcom dad. "I'll call Travis again and see what he's found out, okay?"

Fritz comes toward the desk to escort me out. Something about it doesn't sit right. I slide the Post-it into my pocket and push the drawer closed before he notices, letting him lead me out.

Five minutes later, I'm sitting in the parking lot outside Will's office, studying the curl of the numbers in his handwriting. It feels like a weighty secret, and I consider giving the number directly to Detective Ardell. But it was tucked away in Will's desk, almost as if he was hiding it. Wherever the number leads feels like my secret to keep, too. At least for now. So here I am in my car, playing Harriet the Spy. I punch in 863, then 555.

Nope.

I hit delete, clearing the screen nervously. I should think this through. On one hand, the owner of the number might know where Will is. But then again, they might be the reason he disappeared.

A quick Google search informs me that the 863 area code serves a staggeringly large chunk of the center of Florida that starts just south of Orlando and stretches all the way down to the top of the Everglades—almost one hundred and eighty miles. Where the number's owner might hail from is anyone's guess.

Did you get into something you shouldn't have and skip town, Will?

That sounds nothing like my husband. He's all rules and polish.

(863) 555 . . .

In my mind, the balance between risk and reward tips toward reward, and I decide I have to know.

. . . 0142

I hit the call button and feel my blood pressure instantly spike.

It rings four times before there's a click. I gasp, thinking someone's about to say something on the other end. A feminine robotic voice rattles off a familiar script.

"You have reached the voice mailbox of." Then a gruff male prerecorded voice chimes with a name: "Dean Morrison."

Who the hell is Dean Morrison?

I hold my breath, trying to decide if I should leave a message, but the line goes dead. Emboldened, I try the number a second time, but this time the lady robot voice tells me the mailbox is full. Driving out of the parking lot, I try a third time while pulling up an address on Google Maps, thinking I might know where to go next.

I try the number over and over as I drive. But I don't get the voicemail again. Just the same rhythm of ring, click, message, disconnect.

CHAPTER 11

BEFORE

On the night of our first date, Will's contact information was in my phone as: Hot Mean Lawyer. That's how temporary I expected his presence to be.

Keep it light, Nora. Have some fun.

I dressed for the date like I was playing a part, leaning into the role of the twentysomething going on a date with a divorced dad. I drew on a slight cat eye eyeliner and fire-engine red lipstick. Not too edgy, but a little more fun than I imagined Will and his circle of friends were used to. I pulled on a sleeveless black Anthropologie dress with a trendy cutout in the back—one of the pricier pieces in my wardrobe—and thought: *Hot, mean lawyers probably like the color black, right?*

It wasn't that I didn't take the date seriously. Quite the opposite. He seemed like a good guy, a dedicated dad, and an accomplished professional. A real-life, in-the-flesh adult. He defied my affinity for men that no one in their right mind would describe as "husband material." The more distant or in need of reform they were, the more I loved them.

Will might have been the first suitable man I'd ever dated. But I didn't want to get my hopes up too high about anything coming from our dinner. I could imagine plenty of pitfalls that might accompany dating a busy divorced father. And I wasn't sure how seriously he took me either. So, I put on a suit of armor in the form of a great outfit to feel just a little insulated from getting hurt.

I didn't tell anyone about the date. Not my co-workers and certainly not my mother. Not because it was a secret, but since moving back to my mom's, I had slipped into my old habit of keeping to myself. All of my friends from college were trying their luck in bigger cities like D.C., Boston, and Atlanta. My social circle was nonexistent—a casualty of my failure to launch.

Will picked some swanky Michelin star place near Park Avenue, and we agreed to meet at the restaurant. I took a rideshare to avoid having to hand my battered Honda key fob to the valet. As I arrived, I noted the row of expensive and rare sports cars lined up like a little boy's prized collection of Matchbox cars. Only there must have been a couple million dollars in vehicles on display. I clocked Will's car, the one he'd used to pick Mia up, in a standout position at the end.

Hot Mean Lawyer is punctual. An interesting development.

And then I saw him under the overhang outside the restaurant, in dark jeans and an untucked white button-down. But in an unwelcome turn of events, he wasn't alone.

He was engaged in what looked like an upbeat and animated conversation with a man and a woman. Unable to picture anything more awkward than trying to make small talk with your date's acquaintances on a first date, I slowed my pace to avoid interrupting whatever the discussion might be and pulled out my phone, preparing myself to look busy.

"Nora." Will looked up from his conversation and waved.

I breathed a small sigh of relief—grateful I wouldn't have to pretend to be on my phone composing a work email about . . . what exactly? A shortage of name tags at the museum's front desk? Too much chlorine in the club's pool?

God. I'm going to get through this date and then I'm going straight home to research grad schools.

He tapped the man on the back in a warm but wordless goodbye and headed my way.

"You look great," he said, grinning like a goddamn homecoming king. There was that fluttering in my stomach again. "Have you tried this place before?" He gestured toward the building behind us.

"You'll be shocked to hear I don't get out a ton." I shook my head as we made our way toward the entrance. "But if Zagat ever needs a comprehensive review of everything from the snack shop at the club, I'm their girl."

"I will keep that in mind the next time I'm on the fence between a chicken salad sandwich and the BLT."

"Chicken salad. No contest."

He reached ahead to open the door for me.

"Welcome, Mr. Somerset." The hostess beamed at the sight of him.

"Hey, Lily." He nodded.

He's on a first-name basis with the hostess. Bet he doesn't even have to order his drink.

Lily grabbed menus and led us through the crowded dining room. As we made our way, I became acutely aware of how many people took notice of our arrival. A few waitstaff smiled in recognition at Will as he walked by. One of them even gave a little wave. We arrived at a small table near the window in the back and sat down while I pretended to be unaffected by the attention.

Lily batted her eyelashes just a little bit in Will's direction. "Would you like to see the wine list tonight, or will you be having the usual?"

I can only imagine what Hot Mean Lawyer's usual is. A James Bond martini served on a hardbound copy of the Declaration of Independence?

"Do you like red?" he asked me.

I nodded.

"Does Chef have any of that Barolo left? The 2016?"

"I believe he does."

She smiled at him while I watched surreptitiously to see if he noticed her fawning over him.

Tack on another point for Hot Mean Lawyer: He didn't.

Lily flitted off to the front of the restaurant as a pair of bussers arrived right behind her to fill our water glasses.

"Evening, Mr. Somerset. Good to see you again." They both nodded before returning to their stations.

"So you *never* come here, huh?" I said once we were alone.

"Turns out being a divorced dad means I'm on first-name terms with about half of the hostesses in the city and most of the takeout delivery drivers. It's pretty embarrassing actually."

"Mr. Somerset." A man in a blazer with open arms was walking our way. "How are you this evening? Such a pleasure to see you again."

Will pretended to wipe his mouth with the back of his hand, hiding a guilty smile.

"I'm Michael. I'll be taking care of you all this evening," the man said.

"Hi, Michael. I'm Nora," I replied. "Can I ask—just between us—how many times do you see this man in a calendar month? Be honest."

Will chuckled. "Thank you, Michael. Give us a few minutes."

After Michael walked away, I looked at Will. "Seriously, do you live here? Because that is so sad."

"You know, it takes months to get a table here." His eyes were alight with humor. "Some people would consider it a flex that I'm able to get a table here so often."

"Is it a flex? Or are you sleeping on a little cot in the back?"

"You got me. Michael happens to be my emergency contact."

"It's nice, though. I'm flattered. Most guys let a few dates go by before introducing a girl to their closest friends."

Now, we were both grinning.

"Do you want to go somewhere else?" he asked.

"So badly."

We made our exit—leaving a bewildered Michael in the dining room—and started walking a quarter of a mile to another spot.

Ten minutes later, we were tucked into a tufted leather booth at Fiddler's Green, the noisy Irish pub filled with a live band covering everything from the Cranberries to Dropkick Murphys. And in a welcome change, we weren't being greeted every thirty seconds by someone Will knew. The floor was sticky with beer, and the laminated menu featured bar food, like shepherd's pie and fish and chips. We ordered potato wedges and chicken tenders to split along with pints of Guinness.

"Don't tell Michael about this," Will said as the food arrived. "He would be utterly crushed."

Because of the volume in the bar, he had to lean in a little so I could hear him when he spoke, putting just the faintest hint of clean laundry and cologne in the air between us. Despite his designer jeans and French-cuffed shirt, he didn't look out of place in the rowdy bar's dim lighting. He looked mouthwatering.

The silliness from the previous restaurant had subsided. Maybe it was something to do with the tight quarters of the booth. The way, when a room is rowdy, you have to look at someone — *really* look at them — to follow along with the conversation. Whatever it was, the air between us was charged.

"Your secret is safe with me." I crossed my heart with one finger. "But for the record, 'dive bar' looks good on you."

He raised an eyebrow at the compliment. "I'll remember that."

"So, what kind of law do you practice?" I asked, deciding it might be better if I broached the career conversation before he asked me about my thrilling adventures answering phones.

"I'm a plaintiff's attorney."

"As in, you sue people?"

"Only if they really deserve it." There was that winning smile again.

Juries must swoon for this guy.

"How'd you get into that line of work?"

"I met my partner, Fritz, when we were roommates in law school. His dad had a practice that he wanted to keep in the family. We decided to take it over from him when we graduated. The firm was struggling by the time we took the reins, but we've built it into something I'm proud of. It's nice to know that our work really helps people who, in all likelihood, have been through something terrible."

I wish I could say Will's speech sounded rehearsed, but his humility was almost more attractive than he was. I wasn't above googling a guy before meeting him for a date, and from what I had been able to find about Will and his law firm, Hall & Somerset, had amassed a fortune in damages for clients, recovering billions of dollars, meaning the firm had earned at least hundreds of millions in revenue. To hear Will talk about it, though, his work was just like any other salt-of-the-earth endeavor.

"What about you?" he asked. "Have you found a career you're passionate about yet?"

"That is, perhaps, the politest way anyone has ever asked me if teaching swimming lessons is my life's calling. Sadly, it is not." I took a sip of my drink. "But you'll be riveted to hear that I have a second job I'm also not passionate about, working the front desk of the children's museum in Loch Haven."

"Wow," he said, playfully matching my sarcastic tone. After a chuckle, he added sincerely, "I used to take Mia there when she was a kid. She loved the alligator exhibit."

"I get to see the alligators every day. One of the many perks."

"Very impressive."

"I know. It's a lot of humble bragging for a first date." I took another sip, the Guinness giving me a warm buzz. "But the swimming stuff and the museum are just stopovers. I'm thinking of going back to school." I didn't elaborate to say that the thought had only just crossed my mind for the first time about an hour ago, and I prayed he wouldn't ask me what I would study. I had no fucking clue.

You might be conquering your field, but I'm busy treading water, Will Somerset.

Mercifully, he just nodded and said, "You've got plenty of time to figure it out."

It felt like a comment on my age, which opened the door for something that had been bugging me since he first proposed this dinner. "Are we going to talk about the age thing?"

He feigned confusion. "Age thing?"

"We haven't traded birth certificates or anything, but I'm thinking there might be a slight, small, almost imperceptible age difference between us."

"Are you calling me old?"

I clutched at imaginary pearls. "Never. That would be rude. I just feel like it would be wise to understand . . ."

He leaned in a little, and I got another hit of the bergamot from his cologne.

Jesus, he smells good.

I couldn't lose my nerve now. "Is this . . ." I pointed at him and then back at myself. "You've mentioned your ex a few times. And the divorce."

"I have."

"Seems like it would be good to clear the air about . . ."

Spit it out, Nora.

Then it all came out at once like some kind of awkward word salad. "Are you just out with a younger woman because you're hoping to impress your friends, or win back some bruised ego, or piss off your ex-wife?"

His eyes widened.

"God, it sounds so stupid now that I've said it out loud. I'm sorry. Ignore me. I just—" I was using my hands to talk now, feeling defensive. "You must think my ego is, like . . ." I stretched my hands apart. "But you're, like, this great guy. And I'm . . ."

Just stop, Nora. Don't make yourself sound even more insecure.

I held back the rest of the thought about me being an aimless swim instructor slash receptionist and let the incomplete sentence die between us.

"The divorce wasn't easy," he said. "Constance and I were together for almost twenty years. When she ended things, I was pretty lost. I didn't want to admit that we had grown apart." He took a breath and smiled. "But if I wanted to piss her off, I could do a lot worse than take someone out on a date. Like cut off her credit cards. It's been a year now, and I just want her to be happy. We've got Mia. We ended things friendly enough."

I took it all in. I had spent the last hour or so looking for a weakness, a flaw, the hamartia to put this fantasy to rest. And in that moment, I knew—down to my bones—that Will was just a nice guy. A nice, successful, handsome, honorable guy.

For fuck's sake.

"And you?" he added. "At the risk of ruining everything with sincerity, you are a breath of fresh air."

My cheeks were hot. "So, you're one of those elusive, drama-free, red-flag-repellent nice guys I've been hearing about?"

"I'm not so sure about that."

"I thought guys like you were a myth, like Bigfoot or a perfect credit score."

He smiled, but I feigned concern.

"I'm so sorry, Will. But I don't think it's going to work out between you and me." I leaned in so he could hear me, inching a little closer than before.

"Oh?" His eyes held mine in a warm gaze and he leaned in, too. That fluttery feeling in my stomach was back.

"Yeah, I'm into dirtbags."

"Shit." His lips curved into a half smile, and I couldn't stop thinking about how kissable they looked. "I guess I can forget about a second date."

"Mmm," I said with a nod. The air between us felt a little thicker now. "I'm afraid the only way to redeem yourself at this point would be to steal my identity to finance a dogfighting ring."

"That would get me disbarred."

"See, that would be hot. We would be instantly more compatible if your career was suddenly in shambles."

"Are you saying you don't think we're compatible?" And we were so close that if he leaned in just one more inch, his lips would be on mine.

A very large part of me knew better than to fall for the perfect guy. This guy. He was a mirage. Just a fantasy.

"Would it help if I could dig up some unpaid parking tickets?" he whispered.

I sighed. "You're going to have to do a lot better than that."

I knew it was a terrible idea. But I still wanted to kiss him. Just once. Just to know what it felt like.

So I leaned in, closing the last inch between us. His lips were soft and warm, and the fluttering in my stomach turned into a heat that spread through my entire body.

Hot Mean Lawyer is fucking edible. Shit.

It wasn't until the next morning that I realized he lived in a massive house not too far from the bar. He hadn't bothered to give me a grand tour. Instead, we fell through his front door. A tangled ball of lusty energy and fists in hair. Somewhere in his foyer, I had feverishly unbuttoned his shirt and pulled it off to reveal a well-toned upper body.

But he slowed things down as he led me up to his palatial master suite, where he kissed every inch of my body, peeling off the Anthropologie number. It was a foreign experience to be with someone like Will—someone older—who was in no rush. He *liked* the foreplay.

You go to bed with the Hot Mean Lawyer on the first date. Trust me on this. You just do.

My skin heated under his touch—every nerve ending keenly,

maddeningly alert. I felt worshipped, possessed even. I was so aware of the heat building in the center of me—and he was, too. When he knew I wasn't going to last much longer, even then, it was purposeful.

I'm ruined.

The orgasm rippled through my body in a way that I wouldn't have thought was possible, and I was pretty sure I'd never experience it again.

As we both fell back in his bed, I held my breath a little. I knew from previous trysts, this was where things could get weird. I prepared myself for Will to start awkwardly distancing himself from me or worse, professing his love or bursting into tears or something. But he just looked over at me in bed, sated and a little starry-eyed, and said, "You are really beautiful. You know that?"

Sometime soon, I will walk-of-shame my way out of his place and I might never see him again. But there isn't a doubt in my mind that I will fantasize about this night for the rest of my life.

I blushed a little as I looked around the room. "What *is* this place? Do you live in a luxury hotel?"

"Sorry it's not a cot in the back of a restaurant." He propped himself up on his bent arm, watching me carefully, like he was studying me.

"I'm sure the cot has its advantages. Like fast access to snacks." I sat up, sheet wrapped around my chest, and took in the room. There was a row of windows that looked out over the lake, and I could see lights from surrounding docks. "It must be a dream to watch the sunrise from here." I didn't bother to hide the awe in my voice.

"Come here." He pulled me back down into the warmth of his arms.

And the feeling of his chest on my bare skin was all it took. We were back to that feeling from the booth at the bar, from the car ride to his place. I was breathless and lust-drunk. He was tugging at my hips. Around the time the edges of dawn started to eclipse the night, we finally fell asleep, intertwined limbs and sheets all wrapped up in the center of the bed. And all I could think was that I would give anything to do it all over again.

I was treated to my first taste of the Winter Park gossip mill a week later when I noticed a pack of moms at the club watching me much more closely than usual. Quinn was practicing her freestyle, and their appraising eyes followed me up and down the length of the pool as she and I worked through her lesson.

"Do I have something on my face?" I finally asked her as we reached the shallow end for a break.

Quinn looked me over. "I don't think so."

"Feels like people are staring."

She just shrugged and said, "Maybe it's because my mom says you went on a date with Mr. Somerset."

My cheeks flushed as I looked back at the moms. Thanks to my sunglasses, I was able to take a longer look without them noticing me staring. I could see it now. The judgmental "Her?" glare in their eyes. And as I scanned their faces, I recognized one of them. The woman from the couple Will had been talking to when I walked up for our date. She was in the middle of some kind of monologue with her audience, sneaking discreet glances my way here and there.

"Do you like-like him?" Quinn asked, drawing my attention back to her.

"If I tell you, are you going to go tell all of them?"

She flashed a cheeky grin. "Are you going on another date with him?"

"A lady doesn't kiss and tell."

"Bo-ring."

"Come on," I said. "Let's get a Diet Coke. My treat this time."

We climbed out of the pool and headed toward the outside bar. I did my best not to notice the disapproving looks of the mothers who had gathered to speculate about Will and me. In truth, their harsh glares felt like knives in my back.

CHAPTER 12

TWO DAYS AFTER

For the better part of thirty minutes, I've been at the Verizon store trying to get Austin, the store's twenty-year-old ace employee, to help me track down Will's phone records, only to be sidelined at every turn by company policies.

"Can you just tell me if any calls came from an account under the name Dean Morrison?" I ask. "I have the phone number right here. If you could just check?"

Austin gives a useless shrug.

The thing about second wives is that by the time I came along, Will had a system for everything. He even had a money manager who handled his bills, so I never had to worry about details like how or when the mortgage or taxes got paid. When we'd gotten married, he'd handed me a black card.

"Is this decorative? Feels like a paperweight," I had joked, feeling the heft of the card in my open palm, heavier than any other I'd ever held.

"This will take care of whatever you need," Will promised. And the card worked like a magic wand anywhere I went. It seemed so practical at the time. After years of living paycheck to paycheck, I could swipe all of my problems away. If I wanted to sign up for a yoga class . . . *swipe.* If I wanted highlights in my hair . . . *swipe.* A new outfit to go to dinner with Will? *Swipe. Swipe. Swipe.*

It was all so easy. Too easy. The vise grip money worries had had around my chest kept loosening until I almost stopped thinking about money at all.

But at the moment, I'm struck by how little I know about the logistics of his money—our money—which is really too fucking bad because being able to retrace his steps on, say, a debit card would go a long way right now.

So, that's how I ended up here, laying my troubles at Austin's underpaid feet.

Unfortunately, as with so many things in the life Will and I share, I'm not the account holder, so Austin is fending me off with all the authority of a mall cop.

My phone rings, and I step away from Austin to answer it.

"I'm at your house," Este announces. "Where are you?"

"At the Verizon store."

"Ew. Why?"

Will's not the only one who outsources his bills and errands. I suspect Este hasn't seen the inside of a cellphone store since grad school. I hold the phone away from my ear a little and make sure Austin can hear me as I respond to her. "I found something in Will's desk and I'm trying to get more information that could help us find him."

"Oh, yeah? How's that going?"

"Terrible," I concede with a sigh.

"Hey. Where did this frittata on your stove come from? It's amazing."

"Alma made it. She likes to cook for me when I'm sick."

"Are you sick?" I hear a rattling clang that can only be Este dropping her fork, and I picture her holding her phone away from her ear as if germs could be transmitted via telecom. For as fierce as she acts, she's a bit of a germaphobe.

"No."

She exhales in relief. "Okay, well. Come home. We're going to Kyle J's HIIT class at noon."

High-intensity interval training. The ritual sweat sacrifice of Winter Park wives. I'd rather run a marathon, barefoot over broken glass.

I have to find out who Dean Morrison is and what business he had with Will.

"I don't—" I begin, but she's not finished.

"And then we're going for Botox. You've been frowning too much, and it shows."

"Thank you. That's a very nice thing to say." I contemplate hanging up, but she has been by my side almost every second since Will left. "I'm not entirely sure that going to get Botox right now is the thing to do. Something about it feels . . . wrong."

"You've been told that there is nothing for you to do while the police do their thing and run down all the leads and look for all the things. You can't just sit with the stress and the worry. It's good to stay busy, keep moving. Practice a little self-care. Put your phone in your pocket in case Ardell calls. I won't rat you out to Kyle J."

"Fine." I relent and head for my car, giving Austin one more glare. There's got to be another way to find Dean Morrison.

Will, I hope you aren't up to something bad.

CHAPTER 13

I am running faster than I ever have in a workout class. But even maintaining a ten-mile-per-hour clip on a treadmill, I can't outrun the unanswered questions that haunt me.

Kyle J is proud. He rewards me with a high five and stands next to my treadmill, yelling about how I'm a "bad bitch" as I pump my arms and knees as fast as they will go. My body aches and my lungs burn.

Este is walking next to me on her treadmill. She looks over and scowls. "What the fuck is your deal?"

"You said we had to move," I huff. "I'm moving."

When Kyle J winds the class down by telling us to "shake off the negativity" and thank our bodies for "the gift of movement," I can't tell if I feel better or even more unhinged. My entire body buzzes with adrenaline. Este hands me a gym towel from the back of the room and I attempt to mop the sweat off the floor around me.

Tippy Schaeffer heads toward us, a mawkish look of concern on her face. "Nora, we're all so worried about Will," she says, dabbing her forehead with a towel. I hadn't realized she was in the class until now. I must have been too hyperfocused on trying to burn off every ounce of frantic energy. Since the night I saw her and Ardell—secretly getting hot and heavy at the Christmas party— I always feel a pinch of secondhand embarrassment for her. As a high-ranking member of Gianna's tennis clique, she'd surely be exiled if they knew about her extracurricular activities.

She cocks her head at me now and adds, "How are you holding up?"

I open my mouth to respond, but my mind is blank. There's something about the tone of her voice—niceties masking skepticism—that makes Will's disappearance feel more real. Too real. It lands like a punch to the gut, and I struggle to take steady breaths. I look between Tippy and Este. I hadn't counted on having to manage other people's reactions to Will's unknown whereabouts.

How stupid of me. Of course everyone's talking about Will.

"Sorry, Tippy." Este makes quick work of grabbing both of our towels and guides us toward the door. "We're late for an appointment."

As we move toward the exit, I can hear Tippy stage-whisper, "I can't believe she's here given the circumstances." In a low voice, someone responds, "I'd be sitting by the phone at home. Especially considering the fact that he's her meal ticket."

The words sap the adrenaline right out of my body.

Don't look back. Don't look back.

I keep my gaze fixed on the door, but once we're out of the studio and headed for Este's car, I say, "I'm not sure I'm up for Botox."

She just looks at me and points at my forehead. "That's the frown I'm talking about. Keep it up and you'll age like a raisin."

"Este," I protest.

"Nora. Tippy is a moron. She just wants everyone to hate themselves so her own shitty life choices don't seem so bad. Don't let her keep you from looking after yourself."

Este climbs into her car, and I consider storming off in the opposite direction, but the thought of being alone overwhelms me. I decide that needles and botulism are preferable, no matter what people may think.

I was wrong. The medspa visit is brutal. Tippy's judgment plays on a loop in my head as they ask me to frown and pucker my lips. The sting of every injection feels personally wounding, like a punishment for leaving the house. Cosmetic self-flagellation.

I shouldn't be here. I need to find Dean Morrison. I have to find Will.

While excruciating, the visit is mercifully brief, and within twenty minutes, I'm holding an ice pack to my forehead as they send us on our way.

"Was that so bad?" Este's chipper as we make our way to the lobby. She gets a special rush from turning back the clock one injection at a time.

"It was torture." I try to frown, but my face is still a little numb. "Can I go home now?"

"Fuck." She looks down at her purse. "I left my phone."

"Este," I snap. "Goddamnit. Take me home."

But she's off without another word, winding back through the halls of the building toward the treatment rooms where we just were. I watch her go and then pull out my phone to dial Dean Morrison's mystery number again.

"I heard you were out today, but I honestly didn't believe it," an unwelcome but familiar voice tsks.

I spin around and find myself face-to-face with—

"Constance." I drop the baby ice pack I've been holding to my forehead, mortification creeping up my neck.

"Tippy said she saw you at the gym, and now Botox?" There was an air of superiority to her posture as she folded her arms across her chest. "Fritz had said you didn't seem too concerned with Will's disappearance, but this is beyond the pale. Even for you."

For me. Who had the audacity to marry her ex-husband while also being nearly twenty years his junior. For me. Who probably eats people like some mythical monster.

Constance and I had gotten off to a rocky start, and suffice it to say, things did not improve from there.

I consider asking how she heard from Tippy so quickly, but that line of questioning feels like a dead end. There must be some Winter Park Wives group text chain I am too plebeian to be invited to join—reserved for Hill House's Nap Dress drop alerts, Herend china cleaning tips, and now, Nora sightings.

"Of course I'm worried about Will—"

"Are you? Because it really doesn't seem that way." Constance takes a step closer so that I can hear the vitriol hidden just beneath the surface. "This is my daughter's father we are talking about, and you're out exercising and maintaining your beauty regimen."

A tense silence settles between us, and I can almost see the battle lines being drawn at our feet.

She continues after a beat. "This side of two years ago, Will and I were figuring things out. We were co-parenting quite well and finding our new normal after the divorce."

It takes effort not to roll my eyes at the phrase "new normal."

"And then you came along and now he's . . ." She makes a gesture with one hand as if to say "poof."

Like some kind of fucked-up magic trick. Now you see him. Now you don't.

The insinuation is bullshit. There is so much more to the story. For starters, Constance divorced Will. Not the other way around.

"Who knows how long you would have kept his disappearance a secret from the rest of us," she continues. "Fritz said you fed him some preposterous story about Will working hours so long he disappears for days at a time—"

"Some story?" I finally clap back, fed up with her tirade. "Will disappears for work all the time. You know that better than anyone else. Isn't that why you left him?"

Her eyes narrow at me. This is the first time I've ever come close to standing up to her, but if she's surprised, she masks it with rage. "As hard as Will ever worked, he never disappeared for days," she snaps. "And now you've *wasted* days when the police could have been helping us . . ." She stops herself as if too overwhelmed to continue.

Someone bring in the fainting couch.

"It's almost as if you waited on purpose. To give yourself time to clean up whatever evidence—"

"Mrs. Somerset," a voice calls from down the hallway, and we both turn to look.

"Yes," we both say at the same time.

Of course she kept his name.

A young nurse comes around the corner and looks at the two of us.

"Hi, Dylan. I'm here," Constance says. She looks back at me, taking a parting shot. "I've barely been able to get out of bed since

Fritz called me with the news. The Botox is for migraines. I suffer from terrible headaches in times of stress."

And there you have it. The picture of what a good wife would be doing under the circumstances. She would be bedridden. She'd be swearing to avenge her daughter's father. She gives me a flaying glare, and then she's gone in a huff.

This is hell. I'm in hell. Fritz has Ardell in his pocket. Constance has Tippy, her self-righteousness, and the weight of Winter Park social capital. And I can't even get Austin at the Verizon store to be on my side.

Este finds me a few minutes later still standing where Constance left me. Stunned.

"Sorry," she sighs. "It must have gotten balled up in the paper they use for the exam tables. We had to go through the trash, but they found it." She holds up her phone as proof of the victory. Then she looks me over. "You're pale. Let's get you something to eat."

By the time we're about five minutes from home, I still haven't spoken more than three words. All I managed in the parking lot was "I saw Constance."

But with a little distance and some ice on my forehead, I see it so much more clearly. Constance doesn't think I'm some mythical monster. She thinks I'm the kind of monster who disappeared Will. And she's positioning herself to be the hero who does everything right until Will comes home.

Will needs to come home. Now.

As we pull into Este's driveway and I get out of the car, I think I see that gray sedan rolling by.

"Hey, I've seen that car before." I'm trying to sound calm and collected, but it's freaking me out.

Este is slow to turn, and by the time she does, the car is gone. "What car?"

I don't want to come off as paranoid, so I just try to brush it off. "Never mind."

"Let's go order sushi."

Este walks in her house, but I'm slower to catch up as I try to squash the anxiety rising inside of me.

CHAPTER 14

BEFORE

The gossip about Will and me dating was the subtle, whispering kind at first. When I would walk by the moms at the club, I could hear them say "that one" under their breaths. Or as soon as I approached, voices fell silent as if they had just been talking about me. But what started as soft sidebar talk only grew as Will and I started seeing each other regularly. When we met for coffee at the Farmers' Market one Saturday morning, curious eyes followed us. When he took me to a play at the Annie Russell Theatre, I could see people craning their necks to get a better view—not of the stage, but of us.

The stares weren't necessarily unkind, but they were loaded with questions. Or maybe just one question: What was someone like Will doing with someone like me? He was one of the city's most successful names, and definitely their most eligible bachelor. They all glowered at me like I had stolen their prom king.

"You're making a scene," I said to Will in a hushed voice one night while we were grabbing a late-night glass of wine on Park Avenue. We were facing each other, sitting on two barstools, and I had my knees tucked in between his. Despite my teasing, we weren't doing anything to draw attention. About half the bar was watching us anyway.

"Me?" He put his hands on the outsides of my legs. I was wearing jeans, and the feeling of his hands running over the fabric gave me goosebumps. He leaned in and nipped at my ear while one hand slid subtly up my thigh as he whispered, "Have you seen you?"

His warm breath sent a shiver down my spine. And his hand sent heat pulsing elsewhere.

We had been dating for about a month, and we had fallen into a little rhythm. Dinners Friday or Saturday night, Sunday coffees or a walk around Park Avenue. On weekdays, he was tied up with work, but he would text or send flowers just to say he was thinking of me. Every time he called, I got this dreamy feeling.

It was all so heady and new. But I kept his contact name as Hot Mean Lawyer in my phone as a reminder not to get too far ahead of myself. We were just having a good time.

Still, it was weird having our good time scrutinized under the unforgiving microscope of small-town gossip. Especially when, everywhere we went, people seemed to know Will. Mia's old teachers, his old clients, the judge that swore him in when he was admitted to the Florida Bar—we couldn't go anywhere without someone stopping by to say hello, reminiscing about some story from a hundred years ago, or asking about Mia and Constance. And with Will being Will—polite, kind, decent Will—every stop-and-chat conversation would inevitably trigger him to introduce me.

"This is my friend Nora," he had said to Mia's piano teacher one morning in Winter Park's mini–Central Park.

"She's awfully young to be a friend," the little old lady had mumbled as she walked away.

Will just laughed, but I knew that every introduction could become fodder for more gossip. And on this particular night at the wine bar, we had already been approached by Will's dentist for a "quick hello," which included a twenty-minute story about the dentist's new Grady-White.

"I don't think I'm the problem here," I teased, taking a sip of my wine. "Before I started going out with you, I was essentially invisible."

"I'm sure that's not true."

"I'm just saying if the legal work dries up, you could run for mayor."

"I'll keep that in mind," he said with a chuckle. But he didn't seem fazed.

"Don't you ever worry what all of these people say to your ex-wife about this?"

"Constance knows about you."

I raised my eyebrows.

"After I bumped into the Lawtons on our first date, I thought it would be best to give her a heads-up that I was seeing someone. I wanted her to hear it from me."

Noble. Obviously . . . But he's "seeing someone"? That sounds like more than just having fun.

He tucked a strand of hair behind my ear. "People are going to talk. Let them."

People weren't just talking. They were shooting daggers at me with their eyes. Whether I was teaching their kids to swim or checking them in for an afternoon at the museum, the country club moms glared at me like I was a predator—a threat to the natural order of their world.

"You told her that you were seeing me or that you were seeing 'someone'?" I asked. He frowned, failing to see the difference. "Will, I know women. My mom's been married four times, and there's never been an ex-wife in history who didn't have an axe to grind with the new girl."

"Constance isn't like that."

I remembered Mia's warning from the pool the day we met. "You don't understand, my mom is crazy."

But doesn't every teenager think their mother is certifiable?

"Maybe she's not, but her friends could be. Everyone has at least one crazy friend," I said. "I just want to know if there's a Chanel-wearing, Birkin-swinging mafia out there calling for my head."

"You're not really afraid of my ex-wife, are you?"

"Just tell me you didn't give her my name specifically. Tell me you said, 'I'm seeing someone from the club.' Or something equally untraceable."

"All I gave her were your fingerprints and social security number."

"Perfect."

"You said it yourself, the moms at the club are already giving you dirty looks. It was all going to get back to her either way."

"It's different if someone else tells her who I am. It's less . . ." *Serious.*

He reached for my barstool and tugged it toward him. We were inches apart now, inches away from truly making a scene. "Maybe we should get out of town for a little while."

"Like witness protection?"

"Like, let's go to Miami or New York."

"Or Helsinki."

"Seriously." He lowered his gaze to mine. "Let's take a trip. You and me."

I considered that for a minute. A trip would be raising the stakes. It would be a next-level, capital T Thing. Traveling together exposes all the inefficiencies in a relationship—which, arguably, would be a problem only if this was actually a relationship. But since it wasn't . . .

"What is that face you're making?" Will searched my face with downturned lips.

"Oh, it's not a face. Sorry, I was just—"

"Worrying if we can endure a trip together?" The twinkle in his eye when he was gently teasing was enough to melt me. "I think we'll manage just fine."

A trip. Hot Mean Lawyer wants to take me on a trip . . .

"Okay. Let's go to New York."

CHAPTER 15

After a weekend in New York with Will, I was prepared to forget about Winter Park forever and start a new life in the city that never sleeps. We stayed in a hotel suite that would have made Marie Antoinette proud, forty-seven floors above Fifth Avenue with a view of the real Central Park.

"Let's only do this forever," I said, curled against Will in the four-poster bed.

He breathed a gentle laugh, and I savored the feeling of his chest rising and falling underneath me.

I had been to New York City only once before, on a school field trip. It was an excursion that was heavy on educational mainstays, like the Museum of Natural History and the Central Park Zoo, and then we went to Times Square to have our middle school minds blown by the sky-high billboards and fluorescent lights. The three-day trip was a highlight from childhood, but when Will asked me to go to New York with him, I understood that it wouldn't take much for him to overshadow the glamour of being thirteen and staying in a Westin with a pack of eighth graders and a handful of harried chaperones.

I also knew that—unlike Winter Park, a city frozen in a shiny, glittery snow globe—New York is one of those places that changes like a kaleidoscope. Turn the lens this way or that, and your view transforms completely. Everyone has a different vantage point.

But once the trip was under way, I came to understand something that I couldn't have fully prepared myself for ahead of time: Will Somerset's take on New York was a sexy, opulent glimpse of the lap of luxury.

We had brunch at the Pierre, walked along Central Park to the Museum of Modern Art, then took a car to the Battery for drinks and dancing at some exclusive rooftop bar Will somehow had access to through a legal colleague.

Now that we were unencumbered by the watchful eyes of basically everyone Will knew, PDA seemed to be a requisite activity at every stop. We held hands at restaurants. Will draped his arm around my shoulder as we strolled through the museum. Then we made out feverishly in the car on the way back to our hotel before staying up half the night, tangled up together in the puffy, cloud-like bedding of our room.

"Let's never leave here."

"What would we do in New York?" he said. My hand was on his chest, and he was tracing the outline of my fingers with his own pointer finger.

"Oh, I'm not talking about New York. I'm talking about this bed." I nuzzled closer. "Come on. Talk dirty to me. Tell me more about the legal protections afforded through squatters' rights in New York."

"I think the firm would come looking for me sooner rather than later."

"Boo." I gave him a sarcastic thumbs-down. "I demand better dirty talk."

"I'm not even sure Fritz could take a deposition if I wasn't there."

"Don't you have an army of associates on the payroll? Let's talk passive income. Let's talk colonizing this mattress."

He shifted his weight to prop up on one elbow, curling his arm around my waist and pulling me against him. He kissed me deeply before sliding me underneath him, sending molten heat down my body as he trailed kisses from the back of my ear to my collarbone.

"I'm suddenly feeling completely unmotivated to get dressed for dinner," I said breathily.

"A pity." Will looked up at me, one eyebrow rising, and made a *tsking* sound.

"We have to go back to the real world tomorrow." I tried hard not to think about reporting to work at the museum on Monday. "Let's order room service."

When he started nipping at my inner thigh, I dug my nails into his back, and I thought I heard him moan a little. But it didn't stop him from pushing me so far over the edge that I was pretty sure the entire hotel could have heard me.

The dreamy rush I got from just the scent of him felt like a drug. And after weeks of holding the fantasy of Will at arm's length, New York had weakened all my defenses. Being with him—being a real couple and not just some fun distraction—suddenly seemed so logical, so attainable. And I fell headfirst into the daydream of being his as we explored the city.

The only downside to the trip was how quickly it ended.

"I miss New York already," I said the next day, unable to help myself as I stared out the window of the limo at the palm trees and low-level buildings of Winter Park. "I wonder what it's like when it snows in the city."

Will reached across the backseat bench and took my hand. "We'll go back at Christmastime."

That's months away. A few weeks ago, I might have shrunk under the pressure of him saying something that serious, but now, everything just felt . . . right. So I allowed myself the indulgence of another little fantasy—this time, one where we returned to New York to catch a show or maybe visit some fancy art opening.

I squeezed his hand like a lovesick dope and said, "I would really like that."

He held my gaze for a minute, and it felt like we were committing to something more than another trip. Maybe guys like Will—guys with their lives in order—don't have the "boyfriend" talk. Maybe they just decide.

I was writing his name with little hearts above it in my mind by the time the car pulled into his driveway. The driver made quick work of unloading our suitcases before Will thanked him with assurances that we could get the luggage inside.

"I'm going to put our bags in my room and order takeout," he announced as he unlocked the front door. "Why don't you grab a bottle of wine from the wine room and meet me in the kitchen? Thai food sound okay?"

"You're trusting me with the wine selection?"

This must be serious.

Will didn't have a wine "room" so much as a wine mausoleum. The temperature-controlled glass enclosure in an alcove off his living room must have housed a couple thousand bottles of wine. There was custom lighting and magnums on display and racks and racks of vintage labels.

"What if I accidentally open something from Monticello or the Last Supper?"

"Go nuts." He smiled.

I kicked off my shoes by the door and headed toward the alcove. As I made my way through the living room, though, I picked up a splinter on my bare foot.

"Ow." I let out a little yelp and lifted the pained foot to check it.

"You okay?" Will called from somewhere in the house.

"Yeah, I think I just . . ." My foot looked clean, so I kept walking. "Never mind."

But as my view of the alcove came into focus, I stopped in my tracks.

"Hey, Will!" I called back, staring at the wine cellar, stunned.

The wine cellar had been pilfered. Not stripped clean but picked off in batches of two or three, leaving Swiss cheese gaps on shelves that—before we left—I would have sworn were full. The magnums had been swiped, too. And there was a broken bottle of red on the floor. I checked my foot again to see a sliver of blood on my heel.

"Yeah," he called back, and I could tell by the sound of his voice that he was getting closer.

"I cut my foot," I began. "And something's going on with the wine."

"Jesus." He was standing beside me now, confused at the cherry-picked burglary. "What the fuck?"

He took a few steps forward, and I grabbed his arm. "Do you have shoes on?"

Looking at his feet, I realized he did. But he looked down at my foot and the trickle of blood that was pooling at my heel.

In an instant, Will scooped me up in his arms and cradled me.

"Come on," he said. "Let's get you a Band-Aid, and then I'll clean this up."

I turned my head sideways to read an Opus One label amid the pieces of broken glass and an evaporating puddle of red wine, and a chill slid down my spine.

Twenty minutes later, Will had bandaged my foot, and we had cleaned up the broken glass. But we were still staring, bewildered, at the wine cellar. Someone had made off with Will's priciest wines, leaving the lesser labels behind.

"You don't think Mia would do this?" I said, not believing for a second she could.

"Mia wouldn't know which bottles were the most valuable." He shook his head. "She can barely tell the difference between Merlot and Welch's."

"Of course. But who else could even get in? Don't you have a security system?"

He exhaled a sigh and twisted his neck to one side. "Damnit."

"What?"

But he was on his feet, headed for his home office. I followed a few steps behind him.

He pulled out an iPad from his desk drawer. "There's a camera on the doorbell."

"*That's* your only camera? For the whole house?" This seemed almost as shocking as the theft. "This is a big place, Will."

"Yeah." He was barely listening.

He opened an app on the iPad and a video queued up. A live feed of the front door. He slid his pointer finger to rewind the timeline, scrolling past snippets of him and me walking in the front door a little while ago. The video feed would go blank if there was no activity, so he scrolled past some stretches of time easily. When there was activity, though, like the mail delivery or a drop-off from UPS, he slowed down the playback to watch a little more carefully.

Then, there she was. Saturday morning around ten. A pretty, petite brunette carrying boxes of wine out of Will's front door.

"Godfuckingdamnit." He dropped the iPad in disgust and reached for the phone in his pocket.

I watched as the brunette in the video looked directly at the camera and flipped up her middle finger. Perfect blowout. Fresh manicure. Chanel sunglasses. "Is that—" I knew before he even said her name.

"Constance—" he said into the phone. A roar of anger came from the other end of the line.

Will held the phone away from his ear, and I was able to make out the words "twenty-year-old twat" before he muffled the phone with his hand and stepped out of the room.

So much for "Constance and I parted as friends."

"That's Mia's key, Constance," I could hear him shouting from another room. "It's not meant to be an all-access pass to my fucking wine room."

And then silence, followed by "Maybe you should have brought it up in the divorce settlement." Then, "She's not. She's a good—Goddamnit, so what if she is! It's none of your business."

There was another tense stretch of silence and then, "The only reason I'm not calling the police right now is because neither one of us wants Mia to have to hear about it."

I felt like I should leave. Like I was intruding on a family matter. That love cocoon I had wanted to keep whole was now in pieces. But I just paced his office. Frozen by indecision over whether to stay or go. And then, about ten minutes later, Will came to find me.

"Dinner will be here in twenty minutes," he announced, as if that was the thing on our minds.

"Are you okay?"

"Yeah." He shook his head.

And by the time our Thai food was delivered, he was back to his light, cheerful mood.

Somehow, that was that. Will never pressed Constance to return the wine, and he never filed a report about the theft. The locks were changed the next morning. And shipments of wine arrived steadily until the wine cooler was completely replenished as if the whole thing never happened.

I gathered he had too much respect for Constance—she was Mia's mom after all—to drag her through the mud. I was too wrapped up in the bliss of being with him to care. I should have given more thought to Will covering for her bad behavior.

CHAPTER **16**

THREE DAYS AFTER

'm sitting on the floor of my bathroom, googling "Dean Morrison." I had started to wash my face when I got distracted by the near-compulsive idea that I have to find Dean. To find Will. Unfortunately, there are millions of hits, even when I search "Dean Morrison Florida."

That doesn't stop me from scrolling so long my feet go numb. When I finally give up, my legs are jelly as I stand to brush my teeth and then head downstairs.

The house was always too big for just Will and me—even during the weeks we had Mia. But without him home, it's cavernous. The air is so still it feels brittle. The spacious rooms and echoing hallways only magnify his absence. As I walk downstairs to the kitchen, I feel a sharp, heavy silence that permeates every square foot.

When I clear the landing, I hear something—someone talking maybe?

It's muffled. An unfamiliar sense of fear grips me, but then, a flicker of hope.

Will?

I follow the sound through the house with one hand at my neck. "Hello?"

"Babe, Will's on the news," a voice calls out from the living room.

Este.

I move quickly to reach her—my blood feels like ice in my veins.

"In a developing story, local authorities are searching for a well-known attorney today after family members reported him missing," Kristy, the female anchor says, her voice infused with a synthetic somberness. A photo of Will that I've never seen before flashes on the screen—him in a white button-down and shorts at the beach. "William Somerset of the Hall & Somerset law firm was last seen at his Isle of Sicily home early Sunday. Authorities are currently looking for any information that might lead to him being found."

Just below the photo, there's a caption so tiny you would miss it if you weren't looking: PHOTO PROVIDED BY SOMERSET FAMILY.

"What is that?" I point to the caption. Este pauses the playback, and we both walk toward the TV screen with narrowed eyes.

"Somerset family?" I look between Este and the TV. "I didn't give anyone that picture. I've never even seen it."

"Oh. Well, I mean . . ." Este looks back at the TV. "You're not his *only* family."

It dawns on me. "If Constance gave them this photo, so help me . . ."

The photo disappears, and Kristy turns to her male counterpart, who says, "Now, for the sad update on a story we covered the other day. The driver of the vehicle that crashed on Via Tuscany has died from injuries he suffered during the crash."

"Authorities have identified the man as Dean Morrison," Kristy says. "Mr. Morrison had been in the hospital since the accident and earlier today succumbed to his injuries. While the crash is still under investigation, our thoughts are with the family at this time."

"Wait, Dean's the one who crashed into Carol's fence?" I gasp, thunderstruck.

"Who is Dean?" Este frowns.

Dean Morrison.

I instinctually pull out my phone and open my call log.

(863) 555-0142

I've been calling the number periodically over the last twenty-four hours, hoping like hell someone would magically pick up. My stomach sinks. Now I know no one is going to.

I look at Este, completely at a loss for words.

"Nora, honey, are you okay?"

The only clue I might have about where Will went is now linked to a dead man. I want to tell her everything. The words almost fly out of my mouth, but I bite my lip to keep them in.

How would I even begin to explain? What is even happening? Will's missing and Dean's dead. What does that mean?

A frantic knock at the door smacks me back into reality, and I start at the sound.

"I'll get it." Este touches a gentle hand on my shoulder.

"I came as soon as I could," the person on the other side of the door says eagerly. Her face is almost obscured by the giant gift basket she's gripping, but I'd know that chipper voice anywhere. Autumn. She enters with a frenzied burst of energy and chatter. "I was in Jacksonville for work—a baby shower, of all things. My God, you poor thing. And Will! Oh, it's all so awful." Rushing past me, she makes her way toward the kitchen.

Este rolls her eyes at Autumn from the couch. "Oh. It's you."

Autumn ignores Este, hoisting the basket onto the island. "I brought some fresh flowers to brighten up the space, some snacks—it's so hard to remember to eat but you have to keep your strength—chamomile tea to soothe anxiety, Carole Radziwill's book about the summer everyone she loved died. Sad, but somehow inspiring . . . and . . ." She digs toward the bottom of the basket to produce a floral notebook. "A journal from Rifle Paper."

Autumn visits the flagship Rifle Paper store on New England Avenue the way some people go to church—often and with solemn reverence. For her, it's a perfect sanctuary of jewel-toned flower graphics, peacock throw pillows, and quirky greeting cards.

Este's off the couch and picking over provisions in the basket with a dismissive scowl. "Who died?" Her tone is glib.

Well, Dean for starters.

The thought makes my heart beat faster, the sound of my own blood pressure spiking dulls the conversation around me.

"*Este,*" Autumn hisses, shooting a pointed glare in her direction. "Nora needs our support right now."

Este rolls her eyes. "We're not sitting shivah, Autumn."

This is when I realize Autumn is dressed in all black.

"Can you please both stop talking?" I say, trying not to sound wounded.

Autumn opens her mouth as if she's going to say something, but then closes it. When she speaks again, it's in a calming, sweet voice, "I'm going to make some fresh iced tea." She pulls a Harney & Sons tea box and Meyer lemons out of the basket. "Have I told you about my lemon tree? I know everyone is obsessed with their chicken coops, but lemon trees are so much more useful. You can use lemons to clean, for skin care . . ." She busies herself with the teakettle on the stove.

Este puts a finger gun to her temple and says to me in a hushed voice, "I could not possibly care less. Can we send young Martha Stewart on her way now?"

Before I can tell her to be nice, my phone rings from the corner of the kitchen. The sudden sound startles me, causing me to give an involuntary jump in response.

Maybe it's Will.

Propelled by anxiety, I nearly lunge across the room to reach the phone, ignoring the concerned expressions on Este's and Autumn's faces. But it isn't Will.

It's Marcus.

Autumn and Este exchange questioning glances, and Este mouths, "Who is it?"

I raise a finger to signal "just a second" and slip out the back door onto the pool deck.

"Hello?" I whisper. Aware that Este and Autumn can probably see and hear me, I keep my back to the windows from the kitchen and walk toward the side hedge. I don't want to explain to either one of them why Marcus is calling me. Este knows we're friends. At least, I assume she knows. But the kinds of friends who call each other? She might think she's the connective tissue between us. I can't handle her questions about him. It's not a can of worms I want to open.

"Hey. People are talking about Will up at the restaurant." His worry is palpable — earnest and a little frantic. "What's going on? Are you okay?"

And I think, begrudgingly, that Fritz might have had it right the first time when he questioned the benefit of filing a report. Autumn and Marcus are just the beginning of a string of people who'll be worried about Will now. At least more people will be looking for him, too, I suppose.

How am I rationalizing the pros and cons of this nightmare?

"Saturday night after the party . . . I don't know. He said he was going down to the dock for Mia's sweatshirt," I begin, struggling to explain a situation I don't even understand. "It's been two days. He's not answering his phone. He missed a meeting with Fritz. Everyone's freaking out."

"Jesus."

"I know," I admit.

My helplessness comes into focus and neither of us says anything for what feels like a long time. I'm about to tell Marcus goodbye when I glimpse a flash of gray from the corner of my eye. Looking toward the street, I see the gray sedan roll by. It's the same one that's been driving through the neighborhood since Will disappeared. I freeze.

"Are you still there?"

"What? Yeah. Sorry. I just . . . Yeah."

Marcus finally offers a hollow "Is there anything I can do?" And I think we both know there's nothing he can do.

"Nora!" Este calls from an open living room door. "Mia's here."

Even from the other side of the lawn, I can see a stricken look on her face.

"Marcus, I've gotta go." I hang up and quickly close the distance between Este and me. "What's wrong?"

I look past her to the living room, where the TV's still on and Autumn is fluffing pillows. As if a cleaner home will be the baited trap to finally lure Will back.

"Where's Mia?" I look back at Este.

"Her bedroom." Her voice is tight. "She said she left her Air-Pods here."

"Okay. What's with the face?"

"I thought you said she called Will that night?"

"I did."

"I thought you said it was because she left her Taylor Swift hoodie on the boat."

"I *did*. Este, why do I feel like I'm on the defensive? That's what happened."

As if on cue, Mia appears in the living room, AirPods in hand, wearing the exact hoodie Will said he had gone to retrieve.

"What the fuck?" I spit out.

"Exactly," Este agrees.

I walk past Este to try to catch Mia, who's headed for the door. "Mia, hey, I didn't know you were coming. How are you?"

She stops in the foyer and shrugs. "I don't know."

"Yeah. Fair."

It's a weird thing being the second wife who is only fourteen years older than the kid. I never know what role I am trying to fill. Big sister? Stepmom? Fairy godmother? Mostly, I really like Mia and think she's caught in a tricky situation between parents of a busted marriage. I try to send a lifeline where I can.

"You know you can come over anytime you want, right? Your dad doesn't have to be home for you to come hang out. I put the snacks you like in the fridge by the pool."

"Thanks. That's—"

A car horn blows from the driveway.

"Sorry, my mom's outside, so . . ." She thumbs in the direction of the door.

"Can I just ask . . . how did you get your sweatshirt back? Did your dad drop it off?"

She frowns. "What are you talking about?"

"The other night, he said . . ." I take a breath, not wanting to sound like I'm accusing her of anything. "Did you call about leaving that sweatshirt on the boat the night of his birthday?"

"No. I would never leave this sweatshirt anywhere." She gives herself and the sweatshirt a little hug. "I stayed up making Tik-Toks with Katie that night."

Mia never called Will. Dean Morrison is dead. And Will is still MIA. I look around the house, and it's suddenly unrecognizable. Like I might be in an alternate universe.

The car horn honks again. This time, it sounds for so long I get a mental image of Constance putting her entire body weight against the steering wheel. My nerves are so frayed I jump about a mile. Mia just rolls her eyes in her mother's direction.

"See you later," she says and reaches for the door.

She leaves me standing in the foyer like she hasn't just dropped a bombshell on me.

If she never called Will that night, then who the hell did?

CHAPTER 17

As Constance and Mia pull away, I get a call from a number that reads WINTER PARK POLICE on the caller ID. I'm buoyed by the vague hope that they've found Will, and this bullshit bad dream can be over now.

"What is it?" Este asks.

I show her the phone screen and then answer.

"This is Nora." My voice is shaky, and it catches as I say my name.

"Hey, Nora. Detective Ardell here. Was hoping you have a minute to swing by the station to look at something?"

"Of course. I'll be right there." I hang up the phone.

"What the hell was that?"

"Detective Ardell wants me to come look at something at the station. Can you take me?"

"Obviously. Also, don't call him detective. He's a man-child playing dress-up. Plus, he's plowed half the women in this town. It's just Ardell."

"He is a community servant."

"Well, he certainly services some people." Este lets out one of her low cackles, but I can't find the energy to laugh.

Minutes later, Este's foot is heavy on the accelerator, ripping through Winter Park. My heart rate speeds up as she zips down the two-lane road that leads to the station. I'm not sure she even realizes how intensely she's driving.

She pulls into the station parking lot and finds an empty spot among a bunch of blue-and-white police SUVs. I am awash with nervous energy. My stomach gurgles, and I'm sweaty and cold all at the same time. I quickly do my best to hold it together. I don't want Este to think I'm going to lose my shit, but she notices and reaches across the console to grab my hand.

"Whatever happens in there, I've got you. So does Beau. And it's not like they found Will—they would've told you that much."

"Is that supposed to make me feel better?" I must be looking at Este like a wounded puppy, because she pulls me into a hug I didn't know I needed. My body relaxes and I can feel the tears coming, so I squeeze her back and pull away. I can't cry now. Not here.

"I was hoping so, but honestly, I'm so bad at this shit. I'm much better at telling people they're dumb and demanding they get out of my way. You're really broadening my horizons as a human with this intense missing Will shit."

Her gallows humor eases my mind, even if it's just a bit. Este hands me a pot of expensive foundation. "Here's some cover-up for your injection sites—you bruise easily. You might have been onto something with what getting Botox at a time like this might look like."

"Ohmygod, Este, I'm going to kill you. And of course yesterday is the day he did eight spots, not four." I flip the sun visor down and get to work trying to cover up the vanity holes in my forehead from our doomed medspa trip.

Bye-bye, vanity holes.

Este sweeps gloss across her lips and instantly looks refreshed. She really might be a sorceress. "Okay. Let's do this." Este gets out of the car. I take a deep breath, steeling myself, then follow her.

The air feels thicker and hotter than it did when we left my house. Maybe it's all the cars and asphalt in the parking lot. Maybe the air on the Isle of Sicily is just ten degrees cooler than the police precinct.

I am a step behind Este as we walk toward the front door when I see him. He's trying to look like a passerby, but the iPhone at chest height pointed directly at me tells me he's not just a guy in front of the station.

"Este, don't look anywhere but at the door, that guy on the sidewalk is filming us." Este starts to turn her head and hiss at him. "Don't look."

She snaps her head forward and we start walking a little faster for the door. I obscure my face with my hair as I climb the steps quickly.

Este and I sit in the waiting area for what feels like hours. There's a man across the way chained to a bench looking like he has had the worst day of his life, but my gut tells me it might only register in the top ten worst days for him. I shift a little, acutely aware of the six-carat Asscher-cut diamond engagement ring stacked above my wedding band. There is nothing I can do to pretend that people don't notice it. Haves and have-nots alike come here to be humbled, apparently. My discomfort is rising when Detective Ardell comes out from behind a door.

Ardell. Don't be scared. He's just Ardell.

"Nora, sorry to keep you waiting. Been a helluva day today. Come on back with me."

"Can Este come, too?" It comes out sounding weaker than I mean it to, but I'm scared about what's on the other side of this door.

"Sure enough."

We follow Ardell down a cinder-block hallway with a bunch of solid doors to a room that, I'm grateful to see, has a window in the door and a large conference table in the middle of it. I stop short at the door when I see, in the middle of the cheap mahogany table, a shirt.

"That's Will's shirt," I say.

Este looks over her shoulder at the run-of-the-mill French cuff shirt on the table. I can tell it used to be white, but it's tattered and torn and stained with dirt.

Or is that blood?

"That could be anyone's shirt," she tries to reassure me.

"I can see his initials on the cuff from here." My voice is distant.

"He's not the only person in all of Florida with those initials," Este pleads.

I walk toward the table and stare down at the shirt. On the tag, scrawled in Sharpie across the white Peter Millar tag: *Somerset.*

I want to touch it, but I don't dare. Ardell sits down across the table from me by the collar of the shirt.

"The shirt was found on the shoreline of Dog Island. It was in rough shape. We're not sure why yet. The Rollins crew team was out rowing, and they spotted something during practice. The coach fished it out and called the police when they recognized the name on the collar from the news."

Este looks at me, finally letting the horror of what might be possible sink in.

"When I met Will, I didn't own a single thing that needed to be dry-cleaned," I say, numb. "I wanted Will to know that I could be a good wife, so I took his shirts to a dry cleaner I had seen downtown. I didn't know what I was doing. There were a bunch of shirts, and the dry cleaner wrote his last name on all the tags with a Sharpie. I panicked. I figured he would kill me because the marker looked pretty ghastly. It bled through some of the fabrics. Even though, in theory, no one should see the inside of his shirt but me, the dry cleaner, or Alma." I stop and stare at the shirt. "He had to throw out some of the Sharpied clothes. But he loves this shirt, so he wears it anyway."

Shit, Will. What does this mean?

Ardell clears his throat. "Do you remember what he was wearing the night of the party?"

"This shirt."

The air hangs in the room, and he doesn't look surprised.

"What does this prove?" I demand, feeling denial creep in. I don't want to be here. Don't want Will to be gone. I have to find something that will explain it away. "He easily could have taken it off and left it on the boat. It's windy down by the dock. The wind could have blown it into the water." I remember how I had helped him unbutton it by the pool. Ardell studies me, and I'm suddenly aware I'm being evaluated. The look on his face keeps me from sharing that I'm not even sure he went down to the dock that night. Mia has her sweatshirt, and I don't know what that means. I retreat further into disbelief. "He leaves things on the boat all the time."

But my protests are flimsy, and I am sure we are both chewing on the same questions.

Did he drop the shirt? Did he fall in? Is he . . . dead?

I don't know the answers, and I'm feeling claustrophobic and a little dizzy.

Ardell pushes his chair back and stands up. "We just needed you to confirm that the shirt was Will's."

"And now what? Is there any evidence on it? Anything that tells us where my husband is?" I am standing and don't remember getting up, and the heat coming out in my words is unintentional. Ardell registers all of it.

"Nora, we're not quite sure what it means, but thank you for confirming that the shirt was Will's. We're digging. We won't stop until we find him. No matter what that means."

Something about that last sentence sets me off. I feel light-headed, and I'm starting to see stars in my vision. I need to get out of the room. Quickly.

I grab my phone and head for the door, but Ardell stops me. "Nora, I need you to think really hard if you can remember any-thing else from that night, even if you didn't tell us the first time around. We won't be mad; we just really want to find Will."

I decide to pull out the Post-it I've been carrying around in my purse. "I want to talk about Dean Morrison." The corners of the small note have rounded a little from being handled over the last few days.

Ardell sits back in his chair. "That guy that ran into Carol's fence?"

"Yes. Will had his phone number." I point to the note. "Do you think it means anything?"

"That's what you found?" Este sounds shocked.

I shoot her a look as something like hope or dread starts climbing up my back.

"I don't think you need to worry about that, Nora. The theory on that guy is he had a coronary and ran off the road. They're still waiting on the autopsy, but there's nothing else there. Maybe Will talked to him, but lawyers talk to everybody. I'm sure you know that." Ardell moves to stand. "Try to keep thinking and see if any-thing else comes up. I'll check in when I know more."

I cut through the door, feeling like the walls are narrowing around me. Ardell shutting down my belief that Dean could be a lead stymies me from sharing that Mia wasn't the one who called Will the night of the party. All of this means something. It has to. But I don't trust Ardell to figure it out.

I dart through the lobby, Este on my heels, and push out the industrial doors to the parking lot. Este is talking to me, but I can't hear anything past the blood rushing in my ears. When the heat hits me, I instantly stop and put my hands on my knees, trying to steady the hyperventilation, but I'm not sure it's working. I feel woozy, like I'm somewhere between floating and falling. Este gets me into her car.

"Este, do you think there's a chance I'm in danger?" I ask.

"You've had a long day, Nora. Let's just get you home."

My stomach aches, and I curl into a ball in the car seat.

The only person who would know what to do right now is Will.

As we pull out of the station, I swear that I see the weird gray sedan again.

CHAPTER **18**

BEFORE

9:20 A.M.

I need a favor. Are you free?

My phone lit up with a text from Will.

He was being polite. He knew I was free because I was off from work today, and he had left me in his bed less than an hour ago to head up to the office. We had been dating for three months, and I barely went home anymore. So the fact that I had no intention of leaving his house, let alone his bed, wouldn't have caught him by surprise.

9:22 A.M.

Sorry. I have a packed schedule of catnapping.

9:27 A.M.

I left my briefcase on my desk. Can you bring it up to the office?

Will's office. The two-story brick building was off Park Avenue, and in a place deeply in love with its own history, it was no accident that Fritz and Will's office held a prime spot on Winter

Park's historical registry. I had seen it a zillion times, but I had never actually set foot in the place.

Maybe that was why the idea of strolling into his office with a briefcase felt like more than a harmless errand. Maybe that was also why the hairs on the back of my neck stood up just a little when I responded:

9:29 A.M.
Sure. Give me 10 minutes.

Even as I hit send, I knew ten minutes was not enough time to make myself sufficiently presentable to walk into Will's office.

While I slept at his place most nights, there had been no romantic overtures about cohabitation—it had been only three months after all. So every few days, I quietly rounded up any clothes that had accumulated at Will's place and took them home.

This was me hedging my bets. This was me playing "the cool girl." The one who doesn't push a guy into a serious commitment too early. This was me . . . setting myself up to wear last night's sequin top and jeans to his office.

Fuck.

I looked down at the white T-shirt I had slept in. It was his, but if I knotted it at the waist, it didn't look terribly oversize. I pulled my jeans on, deciding it was better to look casual than sparkly, and silently willed his office to be vacant as I hopped in my car with his errant briefcase.

After parking, I walked timidly toward the building and peered through the window from the sidewalk. One look at the hum of activity inside told me I was not going to get my wish of slipping in unseen, so I pulled out my phone and texted Will.

9:44 A.M.
I'm outside, but I'm wearing your clothes. Probably better you
come out to grab your briefcase.

I was waiting for a response when a male voice broke my concentration.

"Can I help you with something?" the voice boomed, infused with authority and somehow a touch of charm.

I recognized the character approaching me from photos in Will's home office and the advertisements for the firm. It was his partner, Fritz—a Winter Park institution. One look at him telegraphed a radioactive variant of privilege and an air of invincibility—gilded Teflon—like he could dodge DUIs as easily as sexual assault accusations with a bought-and-paid-for impunity.

"I'm waiting for someone." I tried to make my tone as neutral as possible.

He thumbed toward the building. "Someone in there? I can help. I own the place."

Bully for you.

I bit my tongue to avoid being rude. "It's nice."

"You want a tour?" He took a step in my direction with a glint in his eye. I shifted uneasily.

The front door of the office pushed open, and Will exited as if on cue. "Babe." His face broke wide into a smile.

"Babe?" Fritz frowned and looked between the two of us.

Will stepped past him to draw me in and plant a full kiss on my lips. It was a kiss that was more territorial than romantic. A staking of claim. And under Fritz's leering gaze, I was more than happy to be claimed.

"I see you've met my partner, Fritz." He turned to Fritz, draping a possessive arm across my shoulders. "Fritz, this is my girlfriend, Nora."

"Girlfriend?" Fritz asked, unable to disguise a sort of mild horror. "You're dating someone new, and you haven't even mentioned it?"

It was a title we hadn't discussed, but I wasn't going to contradict him in front of Fritz.

"We've been keeping things discreet for Mia's sake," Will explained.

"And Constance's, too, no doubt," Fritz said in a pointed tone. "How's she taking it?"

Will bristled a little. "She's happy for me, of course."

This was more than a stretch considering Constance's recent wine caper, but I bit my tongue as Will painted a pretty picture. For Fritz's benefit? Or his own?

"I've gotta get back to work." Will kissed me on the forehead. "Thank you for coming."

"Nice to meet you, Nora." Fritz nodded.

As they headed inside, Will took a casual look behind him and winked at me.

Will and I had cleared our fair share of milestones after three months of dating, including our first date, a first trip, and his ex-wife's first breaking and entering. But I must have passed some new kind of test after meeting Fritz, because that night when Will got home, he scooped me up and kissed me.

"I want you to meet Mia," he announced.

"But I've met her," I countered. "That's how I met you. Remember? There was, like, a *lot* of puke involved. Maybe you've blocked it out."

He laughed as he continued to kiss my neck, my shoulder.

"Hey. I've been meaning to ask: Why does she call you Pal?"

"Mia struggled with 'Bs' and 'Ds' when she was learning to read and write. She figured out that 'pal' was easier to spell than 'dad' and it stuck."

Sweet. God, everything about this man is insufferably perfect.

"So, about that date . . . ," he said.

"The date wherein you sacrifice me to a teenager?"

"I want her to get to know you." His lips curled into a half smile. "As my girlfriend."

"*Girlfriend.* There's that word again."

"Has a nice ring, right?"

And it was the twinkle in his eyes that made it so easy to say yes to both the title and the Mia introduction.

And once I agreed to meet Mia "as Will's girlfriend," the wheels started turning—like a train on a track or a meat grinder in a factory. The plan for my debut was a low-key pizza dinner at Will's place. Something that gave Mia plenty of space in a familiar environment. Will's housekeeper, Alma, was famous for her pizza dough, and Will had pulled a favor with her to get a full-spread, make-your-own pizza bar for the night.

Everything was set to go off without a hitch until his work calendar usurped our best-laid plans.

"I've got to take this." He held his phone up as Mia and I were spreading pizza sauce on individual pies.

Mia rolled her eyes like she had heard this a zillion times before as Will picked up the call en route to his home office. An awkward silence settled over the kitchen. Mia had been standoffish since her arrival. Now, she busied herself with topping her pizza, not even bothering to look up.

She liked me so much better when she was drunk.

I thought about all of the men my mother had dated when I was a kid. Countless boyfriends and even two more husbands after she and my dad divorced. Most of them left as quickly as they had arrived. And each one seemed to inspire a new personality in my mom—she quickly rearranged her preferences to match theirs. Still, I found spending any time getting emotionally invested in them pointless. All I wanted from them was to be left the hell alone. Maybe Mia felt the same kind of guarded indifference toward me.

I weighed the pros and cons of speaking versus silence and tried to remember what I cared about when I was her age. But Mia broke the silence first.

"You don't have to be afraid of me. I'm not going to try to Parent Trap you," Mia said without looking up from her pizza toppings.

"What?" I couldn't help the short laugh that escaped.

"I'm not one of those kids that's, like, secretly hoping her parents get back together. I'm not going to put a lizard in your bed or anything."

"Thanks . . . I think?"

"They fought all the time. Like, *all* the time. About everything. I was so happy when they finally got divorced. They're a lot easier to get along with one-on-one. Now, they only fight about the fact that my mom thinks her new house is too small. Which it's not. She's just pissed she's not waterfront anymore."

"My mom dated a lot of cringey guys when I was your age," I offered. "I see your offer not to put a lizard in my bed, and I raise you a promise not to attempt to bond over some weird shopping makeover montage."

"Sounds fair," she said. "Just go easy on my dad."

I gave her an inquisitive look.

"You're the first person he's dated since the divorce. Just . . . don't break his heart too bad."

She thought she was being coy, but I knew a declare-your-intentions inquiry when I heard one. For once, I didn't want to trot out the we're-just-having-fun sound bite. I didn't want to insult her intelligence or make her worry I was being reckless with her dad's heart.

"I like your dad. Like, a lot," I said. "I don't have any plans to break his heart."

In the grand scheme of things, it wasn't much, but coming from a teenager, I understood that Mia had generously extended herself.

"Thanks, Mia."

"What are we thanking Mia for?" Will came back into the room with a burst of energy, wrapping his arms around me and kissing my shoulder.

I didn't have any time to respond, though, as a wild rapping on the front door interrupted the moment. The three of us exchanged questioning looks. And then the doorbell started ringing relentlessly.

"Mia!" a woman shrieked. "Will!"

Terror ripped through the center of me, but Will and Mia seemed calmer as they swapped a knowing look of dread.

"I'll get it," he bit out, already exiting the kitchen and heading for the door with purpose.

What came next was loud and frenetic commotion and then stomping footsteps heading our way.

"Get your things, Mia, we're leaving." Constance, the brunette I recognized from Will's nest camera, was glaring at me as she shouted at Mia. "Now!"

"Mom." Mia huffed a sigh. "Go home."

Constance practically cackled. "This used to be my home before your dad tried to erase me from his life and rewrite history by replacing me with a younger model."

Mia dropped her pizza toppings and walked out of the kitchen. "Just let me know when it's over, Pal."

The lack of response from Mia only fueled Constance, who turned back to Will. "You let her ignore all of the rules here, don't you?"

"Constance," Will said. His voice was measured, carefully considering each word. "You should go."

"Why?" she fired back. "So you can have your midlife crisis in peace?" She gestured to me—the apparent personification of a midlife crisis. "You spent your life buried in your work, ignoring me and Mia, and you choose *now* to pull your head out of the sand? And you introduce Mia to your *girlfriend* without even telling me?" She turned her vitriol on me next. "I sacrificed everything for this family. Gave up my career ambition so that he could have the career *he* wanted."

Was she looking to me for pity?

"I never asked you to do those things," Will interjected.

"No! You never asked. Don't you see how that's so much worse? You just left me holding the bag on everything to do with Mia and building *this* house and managing our social calendars. It's so much worse than if you had asked, Will. You just took and took—my help, my time. You took everything!"

Will threw his arms up in the air. "I can't have this fight anymore. You need to leave before I call the police."

"The police!" Constance was incensed. She leveled a glare at me. "You're just a placeholder, dear. A warm body for when he gets plus-one invites to business events. He only cares about himself and his work. And I hate to be the bearer of bad news, but time moves faster than you think for women like us."

My cheeks were hot.

"Get out now!" Will huffed.

She turned on her heel, and he followed her to the door. But she didn't miss the chance to get in one more swipe. "You're young. You have your whole life ahead of you. You'll blink and ten years will disappear, and he'll still be working."

I recognized the ire in her expression. It was the look my mother had in her eyes every time a man walked out of our house for the last time. Before I could collect myself enough to either run or seriously contemplate therapy to unpack my innate desire not to run, a selfish sort of comfort coiled around my waist.

Will wanted me. He was choosing me.

Once Constance was out the door, Will returned to me in the kitchen.

"I'm sorry." He buried his head deep in my neck.

Mia came around the corner with a pizza on a stone, completely unfazed by her mother's performance, and somehow the evening resumed. It felt like a trial by fire. I was proud to have made the cut, but after Constance's outburst, I was left wondering what exactly I had earned my way into.

CHAPTER 19

FOUR DAYS AFTER

I've *given up sleeping. Who needs it?*

Lately, I just lie here, my mind running until the sun rises and someone comes to pull me out of bed.

Today is different, though. I don't lie awake, waiting for something to happen, and rather than fight the insomnia for some rest, I make myself go for a run. My adrenaline is somewhere between maxed out and numb, and the endorphins might help me recalibrate.

I hardly make it past the driveway, though, before my legs feel heavy. I turn up my AirPods, blasting the most cheerful pop music I can find, but I can still hear my own breathing, my feet pounding the pavement, my throat swallowing sticky saliva. Every step is brutal, but once I'm going, I don't let myself stop.

An hour and a half later, I'm nearly home when I see Carol Parker climbing into her car in her all-Lululemon ensemble with a Stanley cup full of some green-dirt concoction of superfood. I hide behind a hedge so I won't have to talk to her. I like Carol fine, but I don't have the energy for some stilted small talk about Will this morning. Or worse, the beloved fucking fence. I hear her car door close, and I scoot across her driveway, hoping she doesn't see me.

As I check behind me to be certain I've escaped Carol, I barely manage to skirt the gray sedan coming toward me, headlights on. The driver must not see me either, because in the instant I clock the car, it swerves to avoid hitting me and then speeds up to go around me.

What the hell? Are they trying to kill me?

I look around wondering if anyone else saw what just happened but only hear Carol's car coming down the road. Not wanting to wait around to give the gray car a second swipe at me, I take off running to clear the hedge line and make it back to my property alive. Turning up the driveway, I can see through the front door window that the big TV in my living room is on. My heart skips a beat.

Is Will finally home?

I charge through the front door, my heart pounding, my thoughts racing. I rush through the foyer, only to find Este on my couch, watching the morning news.

"Where have you been?" She looks up.

"Running, why?"

Este rewinds the news, and my stomach drops when I see a reporter standing outside of the precinct talking to the news crew back in the station. I hear Will's name and then the TV screen is filled with an image of Will's shirt. *The* shirt. The one Ardell showed me behind a closed door. The one they found. The photo looks like it was ripped from an evidence file.

I feel the air leave my body. Este must've heard my gasp because she yells at me to sit down before I pass out.

But I'm too busy pacing. "How the hell does the news have the shirt? Isn't that supposed to be, like, privileged information?"

"I have no idea. I would've thought the same thing."

Did Constance do this?

On the TV, I see Ardell come out of the precinct and walk toward the reporter. The look on his face tells me that he's surprised they have the shirt, too. In fact, he looks like he's ready to pounce. The reporter quickly wraps up his on-the-ground coverage and throws it back to the studio. The news desk picks up right before they accidentally air a confrontation between Ardell and the reporter.

Back in the studio, the anchors haven't given up on the story. And what happens next actually causes me to faint.

When I come to, I'm still on the floor, and Este is running a cold rag on my forehead, saying my name soothingly. She's a walking contradiction. Equal parts gentle and brash. I have a flash of thinking how grateful I am that she's here.

"Jesus, you went down fast. I barely caught you before you hit your head."

"Este, why did they have my picture on the news?"

"Because you're the wife of a pretty prominent local figure who seems to be in the wind."

"Oh god. What did they say?" I try to sit up, but my equilibrium is not back yet. I settle with propping myself against the arm of the couch. The room is still sloshing back and forth a little.

"It wasn't a big deal. They said like two things and moved on."

"Este, your nose twitches when you're lying. Give me the remote."

"Just leave it, Nora. It doesn't matter."

I push myself up, fighting off the dizziness, and grab the remote from the table. I rewind the news and watch as a picture of Este and me walking down Park Avenue pops up while the TV-pretty news anchor talks.

"Will's wife, Nora Somerset, was seen in and around Winter Park the past few days. Frequenting a gym with a friend—"

"I wasn't frequenting anything, and why are you in the picture?"

"—a coffee shop, and the police station."

"They're making it sound like I'm on some kind of press tour around town. They made me come down to see the shirt." They're not directly accusing me of taking Will's disappearance lightly. But with the picture they're painting, they don't have to. I look completely self-absorbed, unconcerned with Will's disappearance. And they save the best one for last: me walking out of Dr. Demi Novaro's medspa with an ice pack on my forehead.

"And even a spa that's well known for Botox treatments and fillers."

"Botox and fillers aren't exactly newsy in Winter Park." Este rolls her eyes. "They're just trying to stay on top of the story. They've already reported the search, so what else is there besides his hot, younger wife? It's just a slow news day."

"But why would they want to follow me around? It's creepy and not getting anyone any closer to Will."

The voice-over from the television continues, "While we're told she isn't currently a person of interest, the police *have* been in contact with her multiple times over the past few days."

"Multiple times? It's been twice. Two times. Just two. God-damnit." I stand up, steadier from the adrenaline coursing through my veins. "Who the fuck is their source? Constance?" I get up to grab my phone off the kitchen island.

"What are you doing?" Este says, trailing behind me.

"I'm calling Fritz."

"Why?"

"Do you have a better idea of who could find out why these reporters know about confidential evidence? And why they're splashing my pictures all over the news? And don't say Ardell. I'm not calling him."

This is Constance's doing.

The certainty is bone deep. I pull up Fritz's contact in my phone and anxiously pace, waiting for him to answer. But he sends me to voicemail.

What the fuck is with everyone today?

I hang up the phone and stifle the urge to throw it across the room.

Possessed by an out-of-body kind of anger, I head for the door. Maybe it's instinct or blind rage. Or maybe I'm fueled by the ava-lanche of fury gathering momentum inside of me. I only know I need answers, and no one has them. I can't sit here any longer. I can't wait and see if Fritz and his buddy Travis can figure this out for me.

"Hey," Este calls.

"I'll be back," I offer as I leave.

I can't say I even remember getting into the car and pulling out onto the street, but a few minutes later, I'm sitting in front of Constance's house. She doesn't live far. Although to hear her de-scribe the way she left the Isle of Sicily property after she and Will divorced, you might think she was exiled to a third-world country.

Will bought her the white Spanish Revival on Genius Drive as part of their divorce settlement. He even agreed to fund an extensive renovation to suit Constance's tastes. But she never lets him live down the property's shortcomings. First, while it is still among the largest and most coveted properties in Winter Park, Constance's plot on the exclusive road is not lakefront—a massive blow. The house is also smaller than Will's by about three thousand square feet—a Greek tragedy. Finally, the original Genius Drive was not a road at all. Instead, it was a walking path through a sprawling citrus grove, and the wild peacocks that laid claim to the property back then still consider it theirs. Constance complains relentlessly about the way the peacocks wake her up with wild cries at the crack of dawn. Picturing Constance being awakened by howling peacocks tempers my anger by a fraction.

I ring the doorbell and stand back, arms folded.

I hear the dog first. Constance's hell-born Pomeranian, Duchess, is on the other side of the door, yapping as if her life depends on it. Will always says Duchess has much more in common with Lucifer than she does with any royal.

"Duchess! Hush!"

The door swings open, and Constance's face immediately falls when she sees me.

"Enough is enough, Constance," I growl. "Stop fucking giving pictures to the press."

"Well, I would invite you in, but clearly, we're all going to forget our manners today." She doesn't even try to hide her disdain.

I want to laugh. Or slap her. Instead, I try to match her detached, mean-girl tone. "It's the strangest thing. I was watching the news the other day, and not only did they have the story about Will's disappearance but they had a photo. Courtesy of the family."

"Kristy is a friend. She needed some pictures of Will, so she asked me."

"I'm his wife. I'm the one the press should be talking to. And, I don't want them to have a goddamn thing."

"You can't be serious. You've been his wife for five seconds. I was his wife for twenty years. Do you really think you're the one people are going to reach out to?"

"You know what, fine. I don't care as much about the damn photos. But evidence? Will's shirt? It's low. Even for you."

She touches a hand to her head as if another migraine may be threatening. "What are you even talking about?"

It's maddening to watch her pretend to be the sensible one between us when she and I both know she came unglued when Will and I started dating.

Does she think I've forgotten?

I don't know whether to roll my eyes or bare my teeth. "So, what? You called in a favor with your 'friend' Kristy and leaked Will's shirt. You turned police evidence into—"

"I'm going to stop you right there. You don't get to come over here and accuse me of leaking evidence that I've never even seen." She's condescending to be sure. But it's hard to tell if she's lying.

My sense of self-righteousness falters. "Will's shirt is on the news," I sputter. "And you just said Kristy was a friend and—"

"I'm not an idiot. I wouldn't share evidence with Kristy, and I don't know what shirt you're talking about." She clears her throat. "It baffles me that you think you get to ask all of the questions here, Nora. Fritz and Travis Ardell may be caught in your spell, but I'm wide awake."

"Oh, you are? Perfect. Is Travis Ardell up to speed on the time you broke into Will's house and stole his wine? If you're so sure I'm to blame for whatever is going on here, you won't mind if I fill him in on how contentious things can get between you two."

Her expression settles into a frigid glare. "You really think Ardell is going to believe you? Over me? My ex-husband has vanished, and you're the last one that saw him alive."

The word "alive" evokes its antonym: "dead." A chill races from the top of my spine down to my core, and I want to throw up.

"All we know is that Will is missing," I fire back, refusing to accept any other possibility.

"You don't really believe that, do you?"

Nausea morphs into rage, but I don't think clawing her eyes out is going to get me off anyone's list of suspects. I turn on my heels to go.

"You can pretend all you want. But I know the truth. I know he wasn't happy before he disappeared, Nora," Constance calls

after me. Her tone is a little singsongy, with a heavy dose of men-
ace. "He told me your marriage was falling apart."

The words make my feet fumble. My ankle wobbles precariously. But I recover, and I don't give Constance the satisfaction of
looking back at her as I climb into my car and peel out of her
driveway.

CHAPTER **20**

My face is hot as I drive away from Constance's house. Her corrosive taunts about Will's happiness and our marriage eat at me like acid.

Constance doesn't know the first thing about my marriage. Will never would have talked to her about us. But . . . God, what if he did? Would he have seriously said he was unhappy?

I'm rage-spiraling, calling her every name in the book as I monologue out loud about all the ways I should have put her in her place, all the things I would have said if I was thinking more clearly. The anger is so all-consuming that I almost miss the flicker of gray in my rearview mirror.

Mother. Fucker.

The gray sedan that I keep seeing pulls in behind me.

Am I seriously being followed?

To test the theory, I turn off the busy road onto a smaller side street that curls around a half-century-old park. Lakefront and secluded, it might not be the best place to confront a total stranger, but I'm not thinking too clearly.

The gray sedan takes the turn behind me. The posted speed limit on this road is twenty miles per hour—not exactly a high-speed chase. But when I hit my brakes, the gray sedan comes within inches of my back bumper.

I'm out of my car in an instant, rounding on the sedan and

slamming my hands on the hood with a hollow *thump*, palms burning from the hot steel.

"Get out of the car!" My scream is guttural. Primal. The weight of the day, of Will and Constance and her shitty comments and my seemingly irreparably fucked-up life, has broken me.

And now I'm this car's problem.

"Get out!" I repeat. "Who are you? Why are you following me?" I hit the hood of the car again.

The door opens and an older man emerges, clad in an ill-fitting short-sleeve button-down and front-pleated khakis. He must be in his sixties—his pepper-gray hair losing ground to a sea of white, and the hands he's raised above his head are trembling a little. His timorousness might be endearing if I wasn't blinded by rage.

"M-miss, I'm sorry if I startled you," he stammers.

"Like hell! You keep driving past my house, at the police station, and now here you are. Who are you?"

He lowers his hands with an air of caution. "Well, my name is Perry Conroy." His words come slow and a little winding, like a Sunday drive down a country road. "The thing is, my friend Dean was in a car accident—"

"Dean?" I say, shock nearly bowling me over. "You know Dean Morrison?" I take a step toward Perry, feeling like I've spotted water in a desert.

He knows things.

"Yes. He told me he was helping Will with a problem he was having. Then there was that terrible accident. Dean's wife, her name is Ann, and her health isn't the best. So I told her I'd come on up here and find out what happened. I did stop in over at Mrs. Parker's house, where Dean crashed, just to see if she had any information, but she wasn't particularly helpful. Mostly carried on about her broken fence, and the police seem to be operating under the assumption that he was either drunk or had a medical event. But, you see, even though Dean was my age, he was in far better shape. He walked two miles a day with his dog. Kept up with his doctors. He's been on the wagon for a while." He pauses as if he's trying to do math on all of this. "Something feels off.

"They should have a toxicology screen and all the things that come with accidents like that. At least, that's what happens on

Law & Order: SVU." I recall what Ardell said about the autopsy still being in progress.

Is Ardell giving Dean's family the same patronizing runaround he gave me?

"I see your point." I pause, biting my lip. Not wanting to be rude, but eager to pull the conversation back to Will, I say, "Perry, I'm still not following how Dean is connected to Will."

"Dean was a private investigator for Will," Perry explains. "Will called, saying he needed Dean's help. Dean was confused. Why not use the folks that live up this way to do the digging? Will was pretty cagey about it. Dean figured it must have been something Will didn't want folks around here knowing much about. Dean said there was something about Will's voice that made him agree to come up here and do whatever Will needed."

"A . . . private investigator?"

"Yes. By way of retired police officer."

Knowing that Will had someone up here looking for something that he couldn't trust any of his usual PIs with made my stomach turn over.

My inner freak-out must be loud enough that Perry can hear the thoughts as they fly by. He reaches out to gently squeeze my arm. "Are you okay?"

"Sorry. I'm Nora Somerset," I say, realizing I haven't even introduced myself.

"I know."

"Is that why you've been stalking me?"

"I'm sorry. I wasn't trying to. But, you see, Will told Dean he didn't want to use any of his usual private investigators. What I can't make sense of is what Dean was investigating. And I've got a bad feeling that whatever it was, it might have gotten him killed."

I knew Will used PIs from time to time for work, but I've never heard of a Dean. I feel a pang of anxiety—or maybe even guilt. Constance's comments about our marriage falling apart taint my thoughts. Hiring someone from outside his usual network would be a great way to keep the details of what Will was looking for out of the gossip mill.

"You said Dean had a soft spot for Will?" I shake my head, still confused. "How did they know each other?"

"We've always been really proud of Will back home."

Back home?

Will seldom mentioned his hometown. A one-stop cattle town southwest of Central Florida that he left to attend college and never looked back. It had never occurred to me that he would keep in contact with people there. Both of his parents were dead.

"You know Will from Arcadia?"

"We go way back. Dean and I were good friends with Will's dad. His father . . . struggled. With a lot of things. Mostly alcohol. And, well, every few months, Dean and I would try to drag him into a meeting or two and try to dry him out before he would fall off the wagon again. We both felt bad for Will. It was no way to grow up. Dean did all he could. When Roger passed, Will was in college. Dean stepped up and helped Will with his law school applications and such."

"Will hadn't told me much about his family. I guess now I know why." My cheeks heat with embarrassment.

Maybe I am the interloper everyone keeps saying I am. How can I not know these things about the man I am married to?

"I don't mean to pry, but do you have any idea what Dean could've been working on? Is there any chance he was . . ." He trails off.

"Was what?"

"Marriage is a complicated business. I should know. I've been married close to forty years."

I understand the implication. "You think Dean was here looking at me?"

Did Constance put you up to this?

"It would explain why Will wanted to keep things confidential. I'm sorry to imply anything untoward. I just feel like nothing is adding up here."

I wonder if this is why he's been following me. Was he trying to make sure I wasn't having an affair? To gauge whether I'm trustworthy?

"I love Will," I say with all conviction. "He's my person."

"Right." Perry nods. "Again, I don't mean to suggest anything untoward."

Silence settles between us, and I realize we've been standing out here for a while. Beads of sweat from the midday sun have gathered on Perry's forehead.

"I wish I knew more about what Dean was up to. I really do." I'm not ready for Perry to leave without getting his help, too. I think back to useless Austin at the Verizon store. "Do you know how Dean did any of the investigative things he did?"

"I'm not a PI, but I have some favors I can call in with Dean's friends back home. There're a lot of people who are torn up over his loss. What did you have in mind?"

I look at Perry, not sure that I should trust him. But at this point, I don't have anyone else to turn to. And if Will was bringing people in from Arcadia because he trusted them, maybe I can follow his lead.

"Will got a phone call the night of the party," I say. "I thought it was his daughter calling—that's who he told me it was—but it turned out not to be. Maybe if we knew who called him, it could help us figure out why he left?"

Perry nods at me. "I can try to do a little digging around. But it might take a day or two."

"Thanks. I just need to see if I can figure out who called him." *And why.*

Perry offers me a business card for refrigerator sales. "I'm not a salesperson anymore. Just an old retired guy, but that's my number."

As I finish texting him my number, another text comes in from Este.

2:17 P.M.
Where are you? Ardell is in your kitchen.

"I have to go." I turn for my car, but then stop and turn back. "I'm sorry I slapped your car. It's been—"

"Don't give it another thought. I'll call you if I find something."

"I hope you do." And then I remember that Perry is grieving the loss of his friend. "I'm sorry about Dean."

Perry tips his head in appreciation.

"Please call me if you find anything."

"I certainly will," he says.

I watch Perry get back in his car and wind along the narrow road, then climb into my own car, shaking my head. I'm putting my faith in the hands of some random guy who has been following me. Will hired a private investigator in secret, and now the private investigator is dead, and Will is still missing.

What were you into, Will Somerset?

I thought I'd feel better once I tracked down more information on Dean Morrison. Somehow, I feel so much worse.

CHAPTER **21**

BEFORE

Somewhere south of the British Virgin Islands lies Nevis, a small, tropical island that—with its nearly thirty-six-square-mile footprint—is three times the size of Winter Park, Florida. And until Will suggested we take a trip there, I had never even heard of it. One Friday night, he called from the car to announce we were leaving in the morning.

"Pack a bag," he said. "Or don't. We'll buy you whatever you want when you get there. I called in a favor with a party planner here in town—Autumn Kensington. She's booked everything."

I laughed a little. His energy was becoming contagious. "When will we be back? I have work on Monday."

"Tell them you're going to need the week."

"That's not really how that works." I chuckled.

"Then, I'll call the head of the museum. She's a friend."

It's all just so easy when you're Will Somerset.

I hadn't seen him in weeks, even though I was standing in his kitchen when he phoned. He had been staying in a hotel a mile from the Orange County Courthouse for some big trial. Every morning, he reported to the courthouse for a grueling full day of trial, and then he went back to his hotel room to prep witnesses, text me good night, and go to bed. All just to wake up and do it all over again.

But after two weeks of that cycle on repeat, all his hard work paid off, and he had won a king's ransom for a client with a traumatic brain injury.

Will didn't like to think of the end of any trial as a time for some big revelry. He didn't win the Super Bowl. Someone had been hurt. But his advocacy meant that his client would be able to afford round-the-clock care, and that was good news. Knowing someone would live a better life because of his help was the part of his job that he loved.

"Also, get dressed," he added. "We're going out to celebrate."

I don't know why I thought "we" meant Will and me. But as I met him in the driveway, he scooped me up, kissed my cheek, and said, "Come on. Fritz is hosting a little celebratory cocktail party at his house."

Right.

I had never been to Fritz's house before, but I had passed by it countless times without knowing it until now. The Spanish Colonial mansion was hard to miss, situated across the street from the Winter Park Golf Course, a public course just a stone's throw from Park Avenue. This was one of the oldest and most storied parts of Winter Park. If you headed south down the street, you could find the city's oldest church, established in 1884, or the location of the condominium Kenneth Lay rented when he was still working for Florida Gas Transmission—long before his infamous Enron days.

Fritz's property was huge—a monument to the Hall family's generational wealth. On just over three acres of some of the most coveted land in the city, the main house was tucked back against Lake Osceola, behind a gated entrance and meticulously maintained hedgerows.

I was struck by how much of a party this was—the valets and white lanterns hanging from the trees signaled that this was more than a casual get-together. If I didn't know better, I would have thought we were at a wedding venue.

Christ, Will. Don't you know any normal people?

A smattering of applause and cheers erupted as we entered the courtyard, and Will rested a humble hand on his chest, waving them away with the other hand. The adoration in the eyes of his colleagues was a mix of respect and awe, and before I knew it, I had lost Will to the crowd, leaving me standing on the sidelines.

"Nora?" a bubbly redhead trilled. "Are you Will's Nora?"

Will's Nora.

"I'm Nora," I offered, my apprehension lacing my tone.

She clasped her hands together under her chin and let out a little squeal. "Oh, I'm so happy to finally meet you. I'm Autumn. Will has told me all about you. Gosh, does he think the world of you. Are you so excited about Nevis?"

Of the people I had met in Will's world so far, she was the only one who seemed wholeheartedly pleased to meet me. Not suspicious or resentful, or harboring some thinly veiled disappointment. Just happy. It was like the first hint of sunshine after months of rain.

"Autumn." She thrust an ardent hand out. "It's really nice to meet you."

I shook her hand with a smile, and she beamed back at me.

We stepped a little closer to the bar, and I reached for one of the signature cocktails that had been premade and left waiting for guests.

"Don't drink those." She shook her head and gently pushed my hand away from the offending beverage. "I wanted to serve palomas, but Fritz insisted on sazeracs—absinthe and whiskey. Someone's going to black out tonight, but it doesn't have to be you." She looked at the bartender. "Two palomas, please."

"Thank you," I said. "You must plan a lot of these. I can't believe how quickly you pulled all this together."

Her expression went gravely serious. "Oh, I plan all of them. For the last decade. Vacations, parties, weddings. These people don't socialize without me." She handed me my drink. "The timing was easy enough to predict. Juries never want to go past Friday, and Will winning was inevitable. That man's a mastermind." She clinked her glass to mine. "He's not bad on the eyes either. Here's to you, girl."

The Will Somerset hero worship is strong.

I quickly learned that standing next to Autumn at a party was like mainlining the town's gossip. She quietly pointed out which associates were most likely to black out tonight, which ones were on the chopping block for performance issues—there was a decent amount of overlap between those two categories—and which ones were secretly carrying on torrid affairs. She had the dirt on the spouses, too, dishing freely on tummy tucks, shaky finances, and prep school admissions scandals.

The sheer volume of gossip she had on tap should have terrified me, but my mind was preoccupied with visions of sandy beaches.

Three days later, we were lounging by a private plunge pool, with me sprawled out on my stomach in a bikini, soaking up the West Indies sun and Will in his bathing suit, reading a book he'd picked up at the Museum of Nevis History.

"Did you know zoning codes here mandate buildings can't be taller than a coconut tree?"

I lifted my head from the chaise lounge and squinted at Will. "Oh really, Professor?"

"There's so much history here. Alexander Hamilton was born just down the road."

"*Really?*" I tried my best to sound bowled over by this information when I was mostly just charmed by his nerdy enthusiasm. I climbed out of my chair and into his lap, putting one leg on either side of him.

"Did you know Nevis and the neighboring island, Saint Kitts, collectively used to produce twenty percent of the British Empire's sugar yield?"

"That's a lot of sugar." I kissed his shoulder.

He set the book down on the side table and wrapped his arms around me. "I needed this."

"The Four Seasons? Or the West Indies trivia?"

"You." He pulled me close for an unhurried kiss. "We should stay a few more days."

I frowned. "I have to work."

"Quit." The word came out of his mouth like it was the easiest idea in the world.

"To do what? Be your harem girl?"

"I like the sound of that," he growled, nipping at my bare shoulder.

I pulled back. "Seriously, I can't lose my job."

"Why not?"

"It's . . . my job? The thing I do for money? It's the reason I can afford food and coffee and these bikinis that seem to amuse you."

"So quit, and I'll bankroll your lattes and your bikinis."

How does his blasé tone still ooze charm?

"You're not doing that." I tried not to sound offended because I could tell by his tone that he was offering something he would be happy to do. Something that to him seemed like a foregone conclusion.

"Why not?" He opened his arms as if to showcase the exotic view around us. "Why do I have all of this if I can't share it?"

He was being sincere, but I bristled. I had been through this with my mother. Ramona used me as something of a litmus test for whether a suitor was playing for keeps. And the men she chose provided for both of us financially. Not out of kindness, but out of indulgence of her. I was well versed in being a kept object, and I really didn't want Will to think of me that way.

"Why not? Because I'm not your . . . problem."

He pulled me into a bear hug and kissed my neck as he breathed, "What if I want you to be my problem?"

When I didn't laugh, he leaned back and looked at me more seriously. "Take a few months off then. And then I'll help you find a job you're passionate about."

"The museum job isn't perfect, but it's a start to something."

"A start to what?"

"Are you trying to Pretty Woman me? Like dress me up and turn me into someone you can take to cocktail parties? Are you Richard Gere now?"

He laughed and took my hands, kissing each one. "I'm trying to take care of you."

It could be that simple. He could take care of me. And then all of the shit that seemed insurmountable, like my dead-end career and my second job and the question of how I'd ever move out of my mother's condo . . . it would all just disappear. I could stop fighting so hard and share his life with him.

It was easy to get swept up in the fantasy, but I told myself not to get carried away. I had to keep my feet on solid ground. I couldn't give in so easily. I was still clinging tight to my pride and my deep desire to avoid following in my mother's footsteps. I would not and could not believe that a man was going to fix me or be the magic solution to my problems.

"Give me your phone." Seeing the hesitation in my eyes, Will reached for my phone on the side table as if he could sense that, despite my protest, I was seriously considering his offer. Ever the negotiator, he didn't miss the chance to land a deal once a window of opportunity had cracked open. "We'll write the email to the museum together. You won't burn any bridges. Just tell them you're taking a sabbatical."

"A sex sabbatical." I rolled my eyes as I moved to take the phone back, but he already had the home screen open.

He paused as he opened my contacts. "Hot Mean Lawyer?" He looked up at me, arching an amused brow.

I laughed.

Had he never seen it before?

"Why am I in your phone as Hot Mean Lawyer?"

"When we first met, I just . . ." I waved a hand, pushing away the insecurities that still flared every so often in Will's presence. "It was just a little joke. After Mia almost hurled on my shoes and told me her friends were all scared you would sue them. I just . . . It was a little reminder to myself to have fun. Not to take things too seriously."

"You think I'm hot?"

I laughed harder. "You know I do."

"I don't think I'm particularly mean, but it's good to know you're not taking things too seriously." He was teasing now, still looking at the screen as I held out my open palm for him to return the device. "So it's been like this the whole time we've known each other? Every time I call it says Hot Mean Lawyer?"

"That's how a contact card works." My palm was still open and out. "Now give it back."

But he was typing.

"What are you doing?" I raised up on my knees to try to see the screen. "Don't you dare quit my job."

"I promise I won't." His voice was a little less playful than it had been a second before. "But I think it's time I got a new title."

"Hey, I kind of like Hot Mean Lawyer."

"You might not be taking this seriously. But I happen to be

very serious." And as he handed me the phone, I could feel him watching my reaction. "Tell me what you think about this."

His new contact card said: Husband.

"What are you—" My breath caught at the top of my throat.

I looked up, and he was tying his drink straw into a ring.

"Nora Davies."

Is this real? If the ring is a straw, does that still make the proposal real?

"Mm-hmm," I whimpered, wondering if it was possible to faint from happiness.

"I didn't think I could ever be happy like this. I didn't think I'd ever feel this light and hopeful about the future. Knowing you has brought me to life. And you have become everything that's good about my life. And I want to spend the rest of it feeling that way."

His eyes were soft and pleading, and I could see the hand that offered up the makeshift ring trembling just a little. We had been dating less than a year, and we had never discussed marriage.

"Marry me, Nora."

It reminded me of the first time he asked me on a date—he was out on a limb again, asking a question he didn't quite know the answer to.

"Yes," I whispered. And then with a quiet giggle, "Yes, please."

He pulled me against him and kissed me in a rush. Then he carefully slid the plastic ring on my finger. "I'll get you a real one when we get home."

I was still half weeping, half giggling when he kissed me on the forehead and said, "This next part is going to sound crazy. But hear me out. Marry me tonight."

"Really? Seriously?" I felt giddy, like we were scheming some kind of secret mischief.

"Totally. Seriously."

Cynics would have told you that this was the moment it all went to hell. I was too young. We didn't know each other well enough. He was a workaholic. And we couldn't have rushed into things much faster. We shouldn't have rushed into things at all.

But we loved each other.

And so on the white, sandy beaches of Nevis, we got married. I wore a gauzy white dress I found in the hotel gift shop, and the concierge, who had agreed to be our witness, brought me a bouquet made of fresh flowers from around the property.

Then, we stayed in bed for days, living off room service and champagne.

And all the while, there was a tiny voice in the back of my head that couldn't join in the celebration. A whisper of hesitation I couldn't shake no matter how hard I tried. When the corner of my eye caught on the drink straw on my left hand, the whisper got louder.

It's too soon. Too good to be true.

But he seemed so certain, so I let myself believe him.

CHAPTER **22**

"Jesus. Fuck!" the voice boomed from down the hall. "What in Christ's name were you thinking, Will? You fucking eloped on a goddamn beach? You didn't think about what that would expose us to?"

Will answered calmly, "I really didn't think my personal life had anything to do with you, Fritz."

"Like hell!" Fritz roared.

Autumn found me in the kitchen, pretending not to listen to Fritz and Will fight in Will's home office. Or, to be more accurate: pretending not to listen to Fritz yell while Will responded in a voice now too low to hear. I did my best to look composed even though I felt like a kid about to be sent to the principal's office. I looked down at the outsize diamond now sitting on my finger. True to his word, Will had replaced the plastic straw with a massive stone and diamond pavé wedding band within a few days of our return from Nevis, but I kept the plastic ring in my jewelry drawer. The sentimental feeling I got when I spotted it was in sharp contrast to the shame I felt listening to Fritz yell.

Am I in trouble for getting married?

"Nora, I'm thinking we should do the champagne toast in about twenty-five minutes," she said. "Just before sunset."

"You could have called!" Fritz went on. The sound of his voice reverberated up the hallway. "I could have sent you something basic. Something to protect the firm."

What the hell does that mean?

Since we returned from Nevis, everything felt shiny and new. Maybe it was naïve, but the wedding ring on my finger made me feel like a bona fide member of Will's circle. My mom had been so excited she shrieked, and I swear I could hear her all the way from Bali. Even Mia had been by to deliver flowers and a hug. She was genuinely excited for us.

Constance tacked in the other direction and completely ignored the fact that anything had happened. Where she had been brazen in her outbursts before, she suddenly fell silent, offering zero acknowledgment of any kind. I would have taken a half-hearted congratulations as a sign that we could start to coexist, even in the most tepid sense. But blatantly ignoring the whole thing was as cutting a choice as she could make.

Well played, Constance.

Will had roped Autumn into planning a wedding celebration at the house. And, over the course of a day, she had transformed his place—*our place*—into one of her picture-perfect parties. She arrived bright and early that morning with a burst of energy and a take-charge attitude. Furniture was rearranged, service stations created, and floral arrangements tastefully distributed. She moved quickly through her tasks, talking layouts and itineraries. And when she finally had put order to chaos, she came to help me choose an outfit.

"So you just got married? Just like that?" she had said as she stood in the closet wide-eyed, holding the dress she'd chosen. There was a combination of wonder and horror as I told her about the wedding. For an event planner as meticulous as she was, such a spontaneous affair was one of Dante's innermost circles of hell.

I'd ignored her judgment and nodded blissfully. "It was perfect."

Maybe she didn't care for elopements, but Autumn knew how to throw a party. And once the event was in full swing, it felt like something out of a movie. Like Jay Gatsby himself had come back to life for one last hurrah. The air buzzed with excitement and laughter and the faint sound of clinking champagne glasses. She had insisted the servers pour only Dom Pérignon for the first hour, and I didn't even want to imagine the bill for that. There was a dance floor and a fourteen-piece band, working their way through the wedding reception hits.

But as the night went on, it turned out Autumn was in the majority with her shock over Will's decision to elope. When I passed pockets of people chatting, I kept catching weird snippets of conversation. Phrases like "gold digger" and "shotgun wedding" bubbled up from the crowd. It felt like one of those dreams where you're naked on the first day of school. With every errant whisper or comment, I took another sip of champagne—as some deranged, self-punishing drinking game.

So by the time Fritz and Will were having a fight in Will's home office about why I hadn't signed a prenuptial agreement and I listened in from the kitchen, I was well and truly hammered. Enough so that it took a minute to even occur to me that Autumn was hearing Fritz's shouting, too.

I looked desperately at her for help. "Do you think people can hear them?"

Am I slurring my words?

"Everyone's outside," she said confidently. "I'll bring Fritz another drink. That should break things up."

I quickly drained the champagne flute she handed me. "Thanks. I smight need another one of these."

Shit. I am slurring my words.

She shook her head and handed me a glass of water.

"Go outside and get some fresh air," she soothed. "Be back in twenty minutes. I'll tell the band to take their break around that time, and when you hear the music stop, that will be your cue to meet me by the dance floor. Try to be a little bit less . . . drunk by then, okay?"

She was managing me. I had just been managed. But I could see it was coming from a good place, and when the room swam a little, I knew she was right. I needed some water and a little fresh air. Autumn headed for the bar without another word.

I stood in the kitchen for a few seconds, drinking water and wondering if Will would come looking for me. Then, deciding I didn't want him to see me in this state, I meandered out the side door and along the side of the house, where a hedge served as a barrier between our house and the next. By my champagne logic, that seemed like as good a place as any to sit down for a second. But as I leaned against the hedge, I fell straight through the shrub branches, bonking my head on the ground hard enough to ring my ears.

"Ow." I rubbed the back of my head.

"You okay?"

A celestial-looking woman appeared above me. Everything about her was breezy and flowing, from her long, golden brown beach waves to her silk caftan. If I didn't know better, I would have thought she was some kind of fairy or an angel. The thought almost made me laugh, but I bit my lip to quell my giggles. I had just fallen into her yard. No need to further alarm her.

"I'm Este." She cocked her head at me.

"Nora." I blushed as I walked my hands back until I could sit up on her side of the property line.

"Okay, Nora. What are you doing in the hedge?"

"Sorry to be . . . I was just—" I shook my head, trying to lose the champagne spins, and pointed back toward the party. I took a breath to compose myself. "I live next door. I was sent outside to sober up," I confessed.

Something close to recognition settled on her face. "You're the young, new wife I heard the country club moms prattling on about at yoga." She shook her head. "Boy, do they *hate* you."

It should have hurt. Her repeating this gossip back to me should have registered as something in the vicinity of pain. But she wasn't saying anything I didn't already know. And at least she was saying it to my face.

"Don't worry." She smiled gently. "I'm the new-money bitch from California. They hate me, too."

"We should start a club." My words sounded a little more solid than they had in the kitchen. Maybe the change of scenery, or a whack to the head, was helping to sober me up.

"Or a coven." She shrugged. "Who gives a fuck what they think anyway?"

It wasn't exactly a groundbreaking point of view, but after spending the day with Autumn—the executive director of giving a fuck—it was nice to exhale a little of the tension I had been holding on to as I tried (and failed) to keep perfect composure.

"Come up to the house." Este motioned with one hand.

"You've got a little . . ." She waved her other hand around my face.
". . . shrubbery. In your hair."

As we walked up the side of her house toward her pool deck,
I noticed a man about Este's age sitting in a lounge chair outside.

"Nora, this is my husband, Beau."

A wave of nausea rolled over me, and I had to stop and bend
over a little. I should have been embarrassed, but liquid courage
was propping me up.

"Hey, I'm Nora."

"Nice to meet you. You look a little . . . green. I've got an edible
that might help?"

Beau looked to Este, who made a face at him to play along.
She didn't think I saw, but I did. Bless her. And him.

"You look great. But by Beau's math, there's nothing an edible
can't cure." She looked back at him. "Nora belongs to the party
next door. She's the bride."

"Nice," he said. "Congrats." Then he frowned and looked at
Este. "Wait. Are you supposed to congratulate the bride or the
groom? I can't ever remember."

"Those rules are stupid." Este waved the question on. "Beau is
an engineer. If it's not ones and zeros, he needs a road map."

"Este likes to think she's the brains of this operation," he said
and winked at her, then gestured around the property. "But it's all
a part of my long con to get her to take care of me."

"Shut up." She laughed. "I'm going to take her inside and let
her borrow a little makeup."

"Welcome to the neighborhood. Don't be a stranger," Beau
called behind us.

As we walked into her modern mansion and out of earshot of
Beau, Este said, "Beau sold his tech company back in California,
and we made a killing. Now, he spends most of his time mentoring
start-up founders. He's thinking of teaching a class at Rollins. But
mostly, he's impossibly rich and does whatever he wants. That
qualifies as genius these days."

She explained this the same way most people explained their
professions.

*He's an attorney. She's an architect. Este and Beau are essentially
retired gazillionaires with zero fucks.*

In a place that seemed to be built on double-talk, it was

refreshing to be in the company of someone who called things as they were. Este didn't talk to be crass or boisterous. She couriered the truth with an ease and sense of perpetual relief. I was immediately jealous.

We wound our way down a hall that led to a well-appointed master bedroom, sparsely decorated and furnished with pieces that were simultaneously sleek and serene. There was a vanity in the dressing area between Este's bathroom and closet that I was pretty sure I'd seen on a decorator's Instagram touted as "one of a kind."

"Sit there," she said, pointing at a velvet bench. And I flopped compliantly into the seat as she handed me a Diet Coke from a minifridge in the corner.

"Sip. Slowly," she instructed as she reached for a brush.

"You have a minifridge in your closet? God, rich people think of everything."

Sniffing a little laugh, she said, "I'm just going to zhuzh a little."

She brushed and spritzed my hair with product before applying a few touches of makeup. "Just a little extra," she narrated as she tapped eye shadow into the inside corners of my eyes. "To brighten you up."

I felt like she was throwing me a lifeline in the middle of the ocean.

"Thank you. And I'm sorry, by the way. I didn't mean to crashland in your yard." I realized I hadn't given any thought to what she might have been in the middle of. "I thought this party would be fun, but it is . . . *not.*"

"With that crowd, I can't say I'm surprised. You know that expression 'Never let them see you sweat'? It doesn't really work here. They're out for blood." She reached for a bottle of Evian face spray and misted my cheeks. "Not a hint of sweat *or* blood in sight. Only a youthful, dewy glow for you, my dear." She handed me the bottle. "Take this with you. It will keep you looking hydrated."

I checked the mirror and was relieved to find that I looked almost sober again.

Thank you, Boho Fairy Godmother.

Once she had cleaned me up, Este walked me outside and

practically patted me on the butt, as if I was an athlete returning to the field.

"Go have fun," she encouraged. "And don't take any shit."

I wanted to hug her. Instead, I said, "You should come with me!"

"Not a chance. I don't socialize for sport." She didn't hesitate. "But I'll come over tomorrow—we'll get a coffee and some Advil."

"You're a really good neighbor."

"Yes, I am."

Autumn was vibrating with stress when I made my way toward the dance floor. "Where have you been? You were supposed to be here five minutes ago. The sun is almost down."

Don't take any shit.

"Almost isn't completely," I countered confidently. "There's still time. Let's do it."

Autumn opened her mouth to speak, and then, as if realizing there wasn't a moment to waste, dashed away, likely in search of Will.

Instead of Will, though, Fritz appeared. He flashed a wide grin when he saw me, but I could see the hint of weariness in his expression. He was smiling by rote. Still, he extended his hand to me, and I took it with my own polite smile.

"So happy for you two," he said.

"That's such a nice thing to say." I dropped my hand. "I'm glad to hear you finally came around."

He cocked his head to the side. "Came around?"

"It's a big house, Fritz. But sound still travels. Hard to miss the screaming match in Will's office."

He cleared his throat and punched his hands in his pockets.

Stonewalling. Fine.

Autumn was approaching with Will. I was going to have to be brief but firm.

"I'll sign whatever Will tells me to sign," I said in a tone I was sure Fritz could hear but Will couldn't. "Just have the paperwork drawn up and stop beating your chest, okay?"

"I'm going to hold you to that," Fritz promised.

I straightened my spine a little.

Champagne-fueled bravado is powerful.

"There's my wife." Will pulled me against him and planted a kiss on my lips.

The fake smile I had turned on for Fritz gave way to genuine joy for Will. "Hi," I cooed as I wrapped my arms around him. And then I turned to Fritz. "Thanks so much for the well-wishes. I'm looking forward to hearing your toast."

There was a dark flash in Fritz's eyes. But it passed in an instant.

Will didn't notice, and after a beat, I didn't care anymore. We were too busy drinking each other in as the sun set over Lake Maitland.

CHAPTER **23**

FOUR DAYS AFTER

I call Este as soon as I'm back in my car, still thinking about Perry, the stranger I met on the side of the road. "What do you mean Ardell is in my kitchen?"

"I came over looking for you, and he was at the front door," she whispers. "Says he needs to talk to you."

"Did he say anything about Will? Why are you whispering?"

"I'm hiding in your half bath."

"What? Why are you—"

My phone signals an incoming call and I let out an audible groan when I see Fritz's name on the screen.

"Hang on," I sigh to Este and then kill the call with her as I click over to Fritz. "Hey."

"Nora, what the *fuck* are you doing?" The accusation is harsh even if the volume of his voice is relatively normal.

What the fuck am I doing? What the fuck are he and Ardell doing?

Maybe it's because Constance has just castigated me, or the revelations from Perry, or maybe I am tired of Fritz yelling at me, but I unleash the most sarcastic tone I can conjure. "Hello, Fritz. Thanks for returning my call—" I check the clock on my car. "Three hours later. And yes, I'm doing the best I can under the circumstances. Thanks for asking. How are you?"

"Cut the shit, Nora. I told you to do one thing: Stay home and don't speak to anyone."

"That's two things."

"Don't be cute. First of all, stop getting mani-pedis with your friends, all right? This is a missing person investigation."

He's seen the coverage of Este and me out. Fucking perfect.

I don't fold. "Is that what you called to say?"

He changes his tone, and I can tell he resents having to placate me. "We're on the same team here, Nora. We all want Will home as soon as possible. But going out with your friends during all of this is irresponsible. It's only going to distract the public from the real story."

"Well, then maybe you should be calling Constance. Because she's feeding information to her good friend Kristy at Channel 2. Seems to me that falls well outside of the realm of responsible behavior. And who put you in charge of the narrative anyway?"

"Let's not blow things out of proportion, Nora. Just calm down."

There's something so patronizing about being told to relax when your husband is literally missing.

Yes, Fritz, I'll try to smile more.

"And about Constance?" he says. "Look, Nora, you have to leave her alone."

"Excuse me?"

"She just phoned me, very upset. You can't just show up at her house."

How the shit did Constance turn herself into the victim in all of this?

While I try to swallow my shock and indignation, Fritz goes on, "Things are looking bad enough as it is. The news has the story now and that's going to make things worse. You have to keep your head down."

"It would be a lot easier to keep my head down if anyone could explain to me how the news got the information about Will's shirt."

"Travis and I talked about an hour ago. We both agree that's a problem."

Travis Ardell and Fritz are a "we" now. Will hired a PI to look into me, and Constance thinks Will was unhappy in our marriage before he went missing. Do they know Will and Dean knew each other? Are they trying to keep that from me?

I can feel myself being set up to take a fall. But, for what? I start to tell Fritz that Ardell is in my kitchen presently, but decide against it. Fritz is on Constance's side now.

As I turn onto my street, I hear the clang of metal equipment being banged around. And my stomach drops at the sight of cameras on tripods being set up just before the PRIVATE DRIVE sign. A camp of reporters. There must be one for every local station, and every last one of them is pointing their camera at my house. And then I recognize the guy with the iPhone I saw outside the precinct the other day.

Are you the jerk I should thank for leaking Will's shirt?

The press corps setting up camp at the top of my street is the last thing I'm prepared for. I shake my head in disbelief and pull on my sunglasses. I slink a little lower in my seat as I drive down the road, being careful not to hit anyone. I may not understand everything that is going on, but even I know that would be bad.

They notice me. I'm sure of it because I hear voices rising as I pass them. The shouting doesn't quiet until the garage door is completely shut. There's a feeding frenzy outside, and Ardell is in my kitchen. I sit in my car wondering if I can just stay here forever instead of going inside. Probably not. I check the mirror and make sure I look somewhat presentable, mentally organizing what I will and won't share from what I've learned. Between his brush-off of Dean and the leaking of the shirt and how he made me feel like a suspect, I'm not sure I can trust him.

A minute later, I walk in to see Ardell sitting on one of the tall stools at the island in the kitchen and Este standing at the sink, uncomfortably making small talk, which might be funny under different circumstances. At the sight of me, she folds her arms, snapping back to protective mode.

"Hey," she says.

"Thanks for coming home, Nora," Ardell says. "Listen, I've warned the reporters outside not to trespass. The whole drive is private property—owned by the residents of the street—so they shouldn't go past the entrance sign. I can't do anything about them where they are now, but if anyone crosses the line you let us know, and I'll have them removed."

I nod, wondering how the hell things have gotten this out of control.

"And I'm sorry that the press got the shirt and the photos. Fritz has already called about it. We had no intention of divulging any of this information to anyone."

God, Fritz and Ardell should get a buddy comedy.

"You've heard about the road to hell, right?" Este needles. "The one that was paved with . . . What was it again?"

"Este," I admonish.

"I'm just saying." She swivels her gaze back around to Ardell. "Someone should have to explain themselves."

"It was an overzealous rookie. He's been disciplined," he says, definitively shutting Este down. "Nora, I need to ask you some more questions, would that be all right?"

"I—I guess?"

"Why don't you have a seat?"

Why don't I have a seat in my own house, Ardell? Really?

I don't want to sit, but I comply because there's something in his tone that feels different, and I'm a little worried. "Have you all found anything new?"

"Not yet. But we're trying to understand Will's state of mind the night of the party as we continue to investigate possibilities. How was he last Saturday? What was his demeanor?"

"He was Will. We were hosting a party and he was happy to be doing it."

"And how were things between you two?"

"Us? Totally normal. Good. Everything was fine."

"Had you all had any fights lately? Anything you were disagreeing on?"

"None at all." Out of the corner of my eye, I catch Este shifting. *What was that?*

She moves toward the kitchen island, away from me.

What did I just say? I said that Will and I were fine. Why is she being weird?

"This is really helpful, Nora. What about your finances? Have you all had any issues lately?"

Este lets out a little bit of a snort. I cut a look in her direction.

"What?" She puts up her hands. "He regularly drops three grand on dinner out with friends just because it's Friday."

"Nora, can you answer the question?"

"Our finances are fine," I say. But the truth is, Will and I never talk about money. I just know he has plenty of it.

That magic paperweight of a credit card always seems to be limit-less.

"I am going to need a list of all the people who were at the party, and their contact information. I also need to know who all Will was representing, what cases he was on, but I can figure that out with Fritz."

"I'll ask Autumn for the guest list."

"I want the name of the cleaners who cleaned the house the next day, too."

"Fine." I stand up as if to indicate this inquisition is over, but Ardell doesn't budge.

"Had Will been drinking that night?"

"It was a party," I say dryly. "With a bunch of lawyers. We were all drinking."

"Sure. But was he unsteady on his feet at all?"

"No."

"How would you characterize your relationship with Con-stance? And what about Will's?"

The way his questions jump around feels intentional, like he's trying to keep me off balance. I almost slip and tell him that I've just seen dearest Constance. But Fritz has already chastised me about that, so I let it lie.

"She's his ex and I'm the new wife. We're not exactly trading friendship bracelets." I give Este a what-the-fuck look and Ardell catches it.

"What about life insurance? Is there a policy in Will's name?"

"Wait, why does that matter?"

It's a stupid question. I know it is. But I can't believe it's come to this. And I have to ask the question I don't want to ask.

"Do you think he's dead?"

Ardell leans toward me. "Do you?"

Ardell's tone of voice is pointed. Warning signals blare in my head, and I hear Fritz saying not to talk to anyone, especially without him. "Do I need a lawyer here? I think I should call Fritz over."

"No need, Nora. I am going to go track him down to answer the work-related questions anyway. Thanks for your time." Ardell heads for the front door. I'm so mad that I don't even bother to show him out. Este follows him, closing and locking the door behind him.

"What the actual fuck was that?" I'm rattled and angry that Ardell just came over here to grill me with questions when it was his precinct that leaked evidence in a missing person case. "Is anyone looking for Will? Or are they all just gawking at me?"

"The mob of reporters at the top of your street would suggest it might just be you."

It wasn't that long ago that Este told me not to care what people think, but now even she's changing her tune. I don't wait for her to pour me a glass of wine. This time, I go to the refrigerator, pull out the opened bottle, and swig directly from it. Este's eyes go wide with surprise.

"Nora, are you okay? Where were you when I texted?"

I don't want to tell Este where I was, but it's only a matter of time before she pries it out of me. I spare her the trouble.

"I went to Constance's."

"You went to Constance's? Nora . . ." She shakes her head. "That was a mistake."

"Why? Why does everyone say I shouldn't talk to her? I saw the shirt on the news and I figured she should have to explain—"

"Fritz said—"

"Fuck Fritz. Constance appointed herself the family press officer, and she owed me an explanation for all of this Kristy bullshit."

"Are you sure it's Constance you're pissed at? Is it possible Constance is a surrogate for your anger over Will being missing?"

I glare at her. "Do you ever tire of being right?"

"Oh, no. I love it."

"Anyway, I ran into the guy in the gray sedan."

"You ran into him?"

"Not quite literally, but almost. Over on Alabama. He was behind me. Turns out his name is Perry Conroy, and he knew Will when he was growing up."

"Wait, what?"

"I know, it sounds crazy—"

"It sounds fucking insane. Are you sure you can trust what he says?"

"He knew the guy—Dean—who plowed through Carol Parker's fence. The one who died. He came up to check on him. Dean knew Will, too."

I leave out the PI part for now.

"Nora, he could be anyone. Will's face is all over the place. This guy could be a journalist, or someone trying to exploit you."

Even Este is second-guessing me now.

"He wasn't trying to exploit me," I argue. "He was a legitimate person. And he's the only person who has given me any sort of answers." I'm so keyed up I feel my entire body starting to shake. "Okay? So, here's what's going to happen. Perry is going to help me do some research. And then we'll figure out where Will is, and he will come home. Will can do anything. Ask anyone. Whatever bind he's in, he can get himself out of it. He can get himself out of anything. So we're just going to keep doing what we're doing until he comes back."

"Nora, honey," Este says again as she walks over to me and puts her hand on my shoulder. "I know you don't want to hear this, but I think it's time you start to consider the possibility that Will might not be coming back."

Something from deep inside of me starts to boil over and I can't control it. "Goddamnit, Este! Stop it. Stop talking about it. I don't have to consider anything."

"Nora—"

"You can either have a glass of wine with me and let it go, or go home."

Este stands there. I think it's the first time in our friendship that I've fired back at her.

I throw my hands up. "Fine, go home." I storm past her into the living room, bottle of wine in hand.

A few minutes later, I hear the front door open and close, and then I can see Este making her way through the hedge to her house. I flip on the TV to find something mindless. I'm done playing amateur detective. I'm going to watch Bravo until Will comes home.

But watching middle-aged women squabble over who gets the best room on a girls' trip doesn't do much to block out the look on Este's face. It was the same pitiful look she gave me when I claimed my marriage was fine.

She knew I was lying.

CHAPTER 24

BEFORE

"Babe!" Este called. "You ready?" She must have let herself in through the side door by the kitchen. The way her voice traveled through the house told me she wasn't waiting for me to welcome her in.

After the first night we met and she cleaned me up, Este letting herself into my house quickly became the norm. I made her swear to always announce herself—I didn't need her to have some weird I-have-seen-your-husband's-junk story in her back pocket to trot out at dinner parties. So, she often entered by shouting, "It's Este. I am in your house. Please cover your wang, Will."

The morning after the party, she had made good on her offer of coffee and Advil when she knocked on the kitchen side door around eleven with both in hand. I had introduced her to Will, who was already on his way to his home office for a call. He had waved politely, and she and I had gone out to the patio to dissect the gossip from the night before.

We started hanging out together almost daily after that. We had a lot in common. We both felt like fish out of water in Winter Park—although Este couldn't have cared less about this fact. And we were both in search of ways to fill our days. Este had left her job sometime after Beau had sold his company and before they

moved to Florida, and I quit my job at the museum shortly after
Will and I eloped. Between the two of us, we had hours—if not
days—of free time each week. I think we mutually found solace in
the morning runs, shopping on Park Ave, yoga classes, spa trips,
and evening cocktail meetups. We made up our own little world
with a full schedule of diversions.

And I needed all of the diversions I could find. Will had been
so tied up with work since we got back from Nevis that I spent all
my time with Este and Beau. We would stay up late drinking wine
on their back porch while Will texted apologies. Sometimes after
midnight, I would wander home barefoot just to find him in his
office working on some brief or pretrial motion.

I could shake him out of his work fixation by then. A buzzed,
middle-of-the-night me stopping by his home office was enough
to qualify as foreplay, so he'd welcome me in and then whatever
else might follow. But by the time the morning came around, Will
would be gone—already at work for hours around the time I was
rolling out of bed, trying to figure out how to nurse the hangover
from the night before.

This morning, Este was at my house to go to the fish market
on Fairbanks. Lombardi's was a family-owned Winter Park staple
where you could find fresh seafood driven in almost daily from
the coast. The plan was to pick up some fish so that Beau could
grill for dinner to christen the outdoor kitchen they had just in-
stalled.

"Ready," I called down from the bedroom.

As I headed down the stairs, I sent a text to Will.

3:47 P.M.
Grilling at Este and Beau's. Want to come?

"What are we cooking?" Este wondered aloud as we looked
over the glass cases at the fish market.

"Shrimp?" I suggested.

She winced and held up her recently manicured hand. "Do
these fingers look like they're ready to devein shrimp?"

I looked over the rainbow-colored rows of fish. "Wahoo?
Snapper?"

Este snickered. "I'm scared for Beau. I'm not sure he knows

the first thing about wahoo. We better get plenty of sides, or we're going to starve."

She grabbed a bag of crackers and opened them, popping one into her mouth.

"You have to pay for those," I scolded.

She shrugged and threw another one into her mouth. "Minor crimes bring me joy."

I checked my phone to see if Will had responded to my text. Not yet.

Anytime now, Somerset.

I impatiently considered texting him again, but I was so acutely aware of how Constance's criticism of his workaholic ways had ended their marriage. I didn't want to go barking up the wrong tree. At least I could be sure Este and Beau wouldn't judge me for being solo. They never did.

"Okay. We'll get the snapper," Este said by way of surrender to the attendant behind the counter. "Can you give me a *detailed* instruction sheet on how to grill it? Like, imagine the recipe you'd give a child, and then dumb it down even further."

As we left the market with fresh fish and a step-by-step instruction guide, my phone buzzed with a call from Will.

That first-date rush lit up in my bloodstream.

Hey la, hey la. My boyfriend's back.

"Hi," I squealed into the phone.

"Hey, babe," he said softly. "I just got home. Where are you?"

"Este and I are at Lombardi's. Is everything okay?"

He sounded tired or upset about something. I checked the clock in Este's car. It wasn't even four o'clock.

"What are you doing home?"

"Opening a bottle of bourbon," Will said. "I've spent the last twenty-four hours trying to save Fritz from a malpractice claim."

"What happened?"

Este frowned, but I waved her off. She started the car, and we headed down Fairbanks, back toward her house.

"He took on a case without telling anyone. Some favor to a friend. And then he missed a hearing. The judge was about to dismiss the whole thing. A big case. And I've been making phone calls since yesterday to the defense attorney and the judge, pulling favors and even lying to save his ass."

I felt protective of Will, especially when he sounded bone weary. "Why is that your job?"

"It reflects badly on the firm. And Fritz's equity with the courts isn't exactly stellar these days."

It wasn't unusual for Will to take a swipe at Fritz's lack of professionalism. But this was the first I was hearing that Fritz's reputation was on the decline.

"So where is Fritz in all of this? Did they reschedule the hearing?"

Will breathed a heavy sigh. "He's probably halfway to Italy by now. He dumped this mess on my desk and told me he and Gianna were headed out of the country for some trip."

"Jesus."

"Yeah," Will said, and I could hear the sound of a drink being poured. "Come home. We'll take the boat out and blow off some steam."

"Oh." I looked over at Este. "Este, Beau, and I are cooking dinner tonight to break in their new outdoor kitchen. Do you want to come?"

"I'm not in the mood for people."

"I'm people."

"You know what I mean. Just come home."

It was my turn to sigh. I didn't want to tell Will I had plans. He hardly ever asked for anything. And it had been weeks — at least — since we had spent any time together. But I felt guilty bailing on Este after we had just bought a mountain of food for three.

"Okay," I said quietly. "See you soon."

Este would be disappointed, but she would understand. And I would see her again tomorrow. And the day after that.

"I've gotta go check on Will," I announced.

"Is he sick?" Este looked confused.

"No. Bad day at work, I guess."

"Okay." She shrugged. It wasn't like Este to let her disappointment show. But I could see she was irked. Still, when she dropped me off in the driveway, she gave me a hug and a kiss on the cheek.

"Love you," she said. "Let me know if you want us to bring over dinner plates."

CHAPTER 25

Tailoring my plans to Will's work and moods started to become a more regular occurrence after that. One night, when Este and I were in line to see a new independent movie at the Enzian Theater, he called to say that he had just settled a major case, and he wanted to go out to celebrate.

"I'm with Este," I had said.

"Bring her along," he offered. "Drinks are on me."

Other nights—after tougher days in the office—he would come to find me on Este's back porch and walk me home so that he could take me to bed.

He was developing a habit of seeking me out when his mood was right, but the rest of the time, he was too busy to have a cup of coffee with me in the morning. I could tell he was under pressure at work—more than usual, anyway. He and Fritz seemed to be disagreeing more and more, and I felt like a distraction, a way for him to avoid dealing with his problems. I wanted to be flattered that he could count on me and my company for relief from the chaos of his day, but with as often as he was calling all the shots, it felt more transactional than being someone's source of comfort.

I spent more and more time with Este and Beau. Several nights a week, I would stay at their house talking or drinking— occasionally getting high—usually until well after midnight, and then I would walk barefoot across the yard and climb into bed, my heels still sticky from the early morning dew on the grass.

I kept telling myself it was just a season. A tough time. Not a reason for concern.

The stress will pass, and then we'll get back to what made us good.

Will was so wound up that even wandering into his office to flirt with him was a nonstarter. If I went into the office uninvited, he would give me a pained smile and send me away with a few tired lines about how much more work he had to do. It had to be on his terms. I had become a satellite orbiting him, circling him. Waiting on him.

I'm right here.

Every night, I would walk by his home office door, hoping he'd notice me. But most nights, he didn't look up from his computer. Every now and then he'd raise his head and silently wink at me. I'd smile and wave, trying not to look as pathetic as I felt.

"Red rover, red rover," Este shouted with her hands cupped in front of her face. She barely got the words out before she started snickering at the childish rhyme. "Send Beau right over."

Este was on one end of their pool with Beau on the other, and on her signal, Beau charged toward her, scooping his arms through the water to gain momentum and trying to tackle her. They seemed to be taking turns mauling each other, but the rules of their game weren't clear. I was too preoccupied with sulking on a lounge chair near the outdoor kitchen to pay closer attention.

It was a Tuesday afternoon, and Will had been heads down on a medical malpractice case for the better part of a week. I was work-widowed. And while I might have been grateful for their company, watching Este and Beau play like lovesick kids just made the challenges between Will and me feel amplified. Insult to injury.

What a relief it must be to build a life with someone.

Este and Beau had been together for so long that they had each other's histories down pat, and now they got to enjoy the fruits of their labor by palling around all day, messing around in the pool. Whatever they wanted. On nights it was cool enough, Beau would build a fire in the firepit down by their guesthouse, and Este would snuggle into the same crook of his arm every time. Like she had claimed the spot a lifetime ago. Like it was meant for her. Like they had memorized each other. I was happy for my friends, but some nights, I would pour myself an extra glass of wine just to nurse my own jealousy as I sat with them by the fire.

Our time will come. Will can get past this work stress, and then it will be our turn to memorize each other.

"I'm going to get some more rosé." I stood up from my pool chair. I had to shout to be heard over their shrieks of laughter. "Anyone want anything?"

They waved me off and went back to dunking each other underwater. Este was growing more outraged with every plunge.

I was padding toward their kitchen when I heard the front doorbell. I looked back toward the pool to see if Este and Beau had noticed. Este was about to put Beau in a headlock, so I guessed not.

I headed for the door and pulled it open, expecting I'd be signing for a package or meeting the mail delivery person. But there was a man carrying groceries instead. He was tall and tan with a boyish grin and a dark brown, tousled surfer haircut.

Oh.

"Hey," he said. "I'm Marcus, a friend of Este and Beau's?"

"I'm their neighbor. Nora."

Will's Nora.

He raised the groceries up to my sight line. "I come bearing tacos. Can I come in?"

"Sorry." I shook my head. "Yeah. They're out by the pool."

I led him through the house, half expecting to find one or both of them with a bloody nose from all of the roughhousing.

"Marcus," Beau called from the pool as he fended Este off with a stiff arm. "What's up?"

"It's Taco Tuesday," Marcus said as if he was reminding Beau.

That Beau might have forgotten didn't surprise me. He had settled nicely into his patrician lifestyle and taken on an absent-minded professor's way of moving through the world. He made plans and then forgot them, counting on Este to keep his calendar and his life in order. With both of them effectively retired, this system seemed to work just fine.

"Let me help you put those groceries down." Este climbed out of the pool, wrapping a towel around her waist and waving for Marcus to follow her. "Did you meet Nora?" She motioned between the two of us. "Marcus is the owner and head chef at Lemon and Fig on Park Ave. Beau and Marcus met when they were kids at some Lord of the Flies–style summer camp in North Carolina where they had to fend for themselves with just the hiking packs on their backs. Totally normal for nine-year-olds, right?"

"It wasn't really that bad," Marcus countered.

"Beau still talks about the food rationing like he was on a season of *Survivor*," Este said to me. "Anyway, it was a visit with Marcus that inspired us to move to Winter Park after Beau sold the company. Besides you, he's my favorite person in the city. And he's taken a night off from his restaurant to teach us to cook fish tacos because he's an angel." Este kissed him on the cheek.

"Tuesdays are typically pretty slow anyway," Marcus said to me.

"Shut up. You love us," Este said and waved his words away.

In spite of her suggestion that this was a cooking lesson, it quickly became apparent that Este was more interested in Marcus cooking for us than she was in a tutorial on cooking anything. When he handed her a head of lettuce to chop, she acted confused before abandoning the task to turn on some music. And as he tried to explain how to bread and fry the fish for the tacos, she claimed she was too busy searching for Tajín for the margaritas.

But Marcus was a font of information. And there was a light in his kind brown eyes as he described the seasonings he had grown in the garden in his backyard to season the pico de gallo.

"Did you grow up here?" I asked.

He nodded. "Not this side of town, but my folks had a place over near Cady Way."

"Sure."

I knew Cady Way was near Winter Park High School—a quaint middle-class neighborhood with rows and rows of ranch-style houses that were built in the 1960s.

He looked up to ask, "What about you?"

I shook my head. "We moved here for my mom's third husband. I'm from all over, I guess." I laughed as I looked down at my failed attempt to mince garlic. "Maybe that's why I never developed any talent in the kitchen—too much moving around and microwave meals."

"You should come by the restaurant. Tacos are good, but our menu is better." He smiled.

I smiled back, innocently, but my engagement ring and wedding band felt a little heavy on my hand. When I noticed myself looking for ways to go back to the kitchen to help Marcus cook, I switched from rosé to water.

It's fine to think a guy is cute, Nora, but you're not getting sloppy and flirting. You're just lonely.

After dinner, I walked myself home. The light in Will's office was on, but instead of walking by like I usually did, I went straight to bed. It was petty. I know. But I wanted to see if he'd even notice.

After I stared at the ceiling for what felt like an hour waiting for him to come to check on me, I closed my eyes.

He isn't going to come for me.

CHAPTER 26

SIX DAYS AFTER

"You cannot believe the size of this tent we're pulling off for Sweeney Anderson's daughter's wedding. They're spending a million dollars on flowers alone."

Autumn has been flitting around my house for the last few hours, rearranging bookshelves and throw pillows. She had shown up with coffee and a few breakfast pastries, wanting to check in on me.

"I am pretty sure that we've drained the ocean of caviar." She stops and looks at me sitting on the couch, the untouched almond croissant in front of me. "Nora, you have to eat. Want me to warm it up?"

I shake my head. "I'm not hungry yet. I'll eat it. I swear."

"Should I not be talking about this wedding? Am I being insensitive? We should be talking about you and Will."

I don't know what to say to this. Will is all I want to talk about, but I've been painted into a corner. Fritz doesn't want me to go out. Constance thinks I'm some kind of criminal. I haven't heard from Ardell since he was in my kitchen, and every time I think about the lack of information coming from the police and the investigation into Will's whereabouts, my entire body starts shaking. Autumn's mindless prattling about party decorations has been a

HAPPY WIFE · 155

nice reprieve from the anxiety coma my body keeps threatening to throw itself into.

"It's okay, Autumn. Thank you for checking on me."

"Where's Este? She's always here by now."

I don't want to tell Autumn about my fight with Este.

"I'm not sure—she maybe had an appointment this morning, or something," I lie. "Everyone thought it was better for me to just . . . lay low."

You know, since at least half the town thinks I am responsible for Will's disappearance.

"I'm sorry, Nora." Autumn comes and joins me on the couch. "I heard you had a run-in with Constance."

Shit, did Constance launch a newsletter? Maybe it's just a press kit titled "Nora Is an Evil Wench."

"It was nothing."

She just accused me of disappearing Will. No big deal.

"This all must be so much to navigate. So many . . . personalities."

"That's one way of putting it."

"Constance has had a tough go these last few months. I mean, I get it. You fully dethroned her with Will's birthday party. And now Will is missing. She's got to be spiraling like the rest of us."

"Wait, wait, wait. Dethroned? I *dethroned* her?"

"Your party for Will was the party of the year. Everyone was talking about it in the weeks leading up. Tippy flew to West Palm just to get her dress. Constance could feel all of her friends pulling away. Moving on. She's not part of this group without Will. He's the golden boy, and her identity has always been as his wife."

I hadn't considered that until now, but it made sense. The social circle Will moved in was as elite as it was intertwined. Pull one thread and you can start to see how they're all connected. I always worried about bumping into Constance at the events Will and I were invited to. After her antics with the wine and the haranguing at pizza night, I feared our paths crossing would create a scene. But the run-in I dreaded never happened. I should have known other people saw how sticky inviting her was, too, so they just left her off their lists.

My thoughts catch on one detail, though, and I frown. "I heard that Constance had her own party that night?"

"No. I mean, maybe that's what she said she was going to do, but there would have been no way. Ever since you and Will got married—maybe even since the divorce—Constance has known the tide would turn, and she would be collateral damage. She had to have known. That's just how things work around here, and she's been as big a player in the social game as anyone. But that birthday party for Will sealed the deal. Everyone she might have cared about inviting would've turned her down to come here."

"Probably out of morbid curiosity to see how I would fuck it up."

"Even if that was the reason, which it wasn't, everyone was here. Constance got super drunk and yelled at the delivery boy who brought her food."

So Constance was dethroned the night Will disappeared. And now she's working on some kind of fucked-up comeback?

I turned this information over in my head.

"I've said too much." Autumn covers her mouth. "I'm sorry I keep bringing Will things up."

She stands and gathers the dishes. I follow her to the kitchen with my neglected croissant.

"It's okay," I assure her.

Autumn's phone dings with a text. Then another one. Then it starts pinging in rapid succession. She picks it up, and her face falls.

"Shit. They didn't bring the right dimensions for the stage and dance floor." She catches herself. "Which can wait . . ."

"It's okay, Autumn, you should go. Thank you for coming by."

Her phone is still dinging angrily as she comes over and gives me a hug. Then she goes, and I'm left leaning against the counter, biting my lip. I can't stop thinking about Constance suffering a social death the night Will went missing.

How did I miss that?

My mind starts sifting through all the possible things this new information could mean. And while I think, I realize I'm ravenous.

I stand at the sink wolfing down the fig jam, cheese, and crackers from the basket Autumn brought over a few days ago. I can't tell what brings me more relief, the food hitting my empty belly or the new puzzle piece that Autumn has handed me.

Constance was home alone the night of Will's party.

Maybe this is finally a lead. Maybe her vitriol is masking whatever she's hiding. But what would that be? And where does that leave Will?

I hear phone chimes from between two couch cushions and head back toward the living room. It's a text from Perry:

10:23 A.M.

A friend of Dean's is helping with the phone logs.

That's more than I've ever gotten from Ardell.

Walking back toward the kitchen and my haphazard snacks, I look toward Este's house, wishing I could tell her about this development.

I haven't poked my head out since our fight. I'm embarrassed that I was so shitty toward her. She's the only real friend I've had in Winter Park. And I know deep down, even if I refuse to entertain the idea, that she's right. I have to at least leave the door ajar for the idea that Will really is just . . .

Gone.

I shudder at the thought and cram another cracker in my mouth to distract myself from the threat of panic squeezing my lungs. But this is a dread no artisanal charcuterie can deactivate. I dump the cheese back in the refrigerator and pull on my shoes, feeling my heart race. My breaths are short and strangled. All of a sudden, I feel like if I don't get out of the house, I'm going to die.

I'm partway across the hedge when I realize I don't even have a bra on and my pajama pants are pretty see-through, but that doesn't stop me. I'm trying to outrun a panic attack. I cut up the yard toward the pool, where Beau is swimming laps. He spots me, and I'm suddenly self-conscious about my lack of underthings. I instinctively cross my arms. "Is Este here?"

"Hey." He stops swimming and squints up at me. "How are you holding up?"

"Este and I got into a fight. I'm a fucking idiot. This whole thing has been a nightmare. It's like I'm shedding brain cells with every hour that passes."

"She said you needed some space yesterday," he says gently. "Pretty sure she's still up in bed. You can go on in."

I start for the sliding doors.

"Don't worry too much about the fight. Este has a tough exterior, but once you're in, that's it. She'd kill for you, Nora. Whatever happened, I'm sure she doesn't care about what was said. We're all worried. You most of all. She loves you."

My shoulders drop about six inches. "Thanks, Beau."

I wind through the house, and when I call out Este's name, it sounds pathetic. I try again. "Este, you in there?" She doesn't answer back. I push through her bedroom door and marvel at how perfectly decorated her room is.

"Este, seriously. You in here?" I realize she isn't. When I turn to leave, I'm stopped by the amazing black-and-white picture of her and Beau's wedding day. It's like fairies and woodland creatures came and dressed her—a look only she can pull off. She and Beau are perfect. Like they've been sculpted out of some other realm and dropped here with us mere mortals. And she's barefoot. Because of course she is.

I feel a pang of sadness that I don't have this wedding portrait. Just a photo on my phone that the concierge had taken for us. Don't get me wrong, it's beautiful. But eloping means you skip the elaborate photo shoots.

I'm heading down the stairs when I see Este in the yard pulling mangoes from her tree. She looks up when she hears the front door open but doesn't give me much. Just goes back to her tree. I walk over to her, picking up the basket, trying to be helpful. She doesn't rebuff me, but she doesn't offer the opening either. I'm going to have to make one.

"Este, I'm sorry. About all of it."

Este moves around the tree, pulling mangoes and dropping them into the basket.

"I completely freaked out, and I think . . . ," I trail off, searching for what I am really feeling. "I think that I already know deep down that I have to believe that it could all be . . ."

Bad.

Este looks up at me and I watch as the color drains out of her face.

"What's wrong?"

"Oh, god. Nora . . ."

The next two minutes happen in slow motion. As I turn through what feels like molasses, I see Ardell walking up the driveway in full police uniform, flanked by Fritz. When Ardell sees me, he slowly pulls his police hat off. I look at Este. I can see her moving toward me, but I can't hear anything she is saying. Beyond Ardell and Fritz, the press are all firing their cameras toward me.

I feel like I'm underwater.

"No." I shake my head. "No, Fritz." I raise a hand to keep them at arm's length.

I'm insisting, but they don't seem to notice.

Can't they hear me?

"Leave!" I scream. I feel like dropping to my knees and covering my ears like a child.

But they're still talking. Everything comes in weird waves.

"Nora, I'm so sorry to tell you . . ."

". . . we found a body . . ."

". . . identified as Will . . ."

I can feel the world starting to spin. I must have a dire look in my eyes, because suddenly both Ardell and Fritz have either side of me and they're pulling me into Este's house. I can hear Este screaming.

"Beau! Beau, get in here!"

I have no idea how much time passes after that. I'm just sitting on the edge of the couch where Ardell and Fritz set me down, trying to see if my heartbeat will slow down, or if it will race to find the end of my time on Earth.

I have lost Will every hour since that first morning I realized he was gone, but until now, I could find him again. I could picture some cosmic loophole, a silver lining, some impossible comeback where I was wrong and he was alive, and we could fix . . . everything. But now he is gone for good, and I'm free-falling through space. I close my eyes, trying to conjure his face, but I can't. My brain won't let me even go into a liminal space to see him again. One more time.

"I can't—" I start to stand up, but I'm so wobbly I sit back down. Beau comes over and just scoops me up into a bear hug.

"We've got you, Nora. We've got you." Pressed up against his chest, I hear the quiver in his voice and feel his stuttered breath. He's crying. I sink into him, but I'm numb. There's nothing there. No feelings. Just—air and silence.

Ardell comes over and sits on the coffee table across from me.

"Nora, I'm so sorry. About all of this."

"How do you—What—Where did you find him?"

"A pair of kayakers found him snagged in a lily pad near one of the canals. Our best guess is that his body took some time to surface."

I nod like I am taking this information in, but I know that I am going to have to hear it all again. Someone is going to have to tell me multiple times. Maybe for years. I might never believe it.

Because this can't be happening. This can't be real.

"Fritz came down to identify him."

Fritz steps over. "I didn't want you to have to be the one."

I nod at him. He's right. I didn't want to be the one to see whatever that was.

That . . . Will . . . Oh god.

"He looks to have suffered blunt force trauma to the head. We've got our homicide unit involved, trying to get to the bottom of things."

"Homicide?" Este looks like she's been slapped.

"We'll clearly have to wait for our medical examiner's opinion on it, but given the wounds he sustained, this doesn't appear to have been an accident."

I stare at him. So unable to process his words that my entire body goes numb.

Will Somerset doesn't die. He drifts off in his sleep surrounded by his family at the enviable age of a hundred and four. He passes gently into the eternal, shrouded in dignity like some fucked-up American Gothic bullshit.

And he *really* doesn't get murdered.

I stand. "I think I'd like to go home, please. I need to go home."

"The press is en masse. Let's take her through the back." Fritz looks out the window to the front.

Her.

They're talking about me like I'm not here. Like I'm a thing to be shuttled around. That feels about right. Take me through the back. Put me in a padded room. Strap me to a spaceship and send me to the moon. It doesn't matter. Will's gone.

But he can't be gone.

He can't be murdered.

That doesn't make any sense.

I study Fritz's expression like it's a weather pattern, searching for proof, for signs of the grief and horror of being the one to identify your best friend's body. Like maybe seeing his grief will crack open my own. It's barely there, underneath the surface of his eyes. He looks tired, even a shade of broken. But he's in damage control mode—like any attorney. Solve the big problem first. Have feelings later.

Fritz isn't the only one playing a role. Ardell's demeanor has shifted from the last time I saw him. His eyes are on me like he is waiting for my next move.

Will is dead. The game has changed.

He takes a step toward me, but Este puts herself between us.

"I'm going to get Nora home. If you need to talk to her, you can do it later." Este grabs Beau and puts an arm around me. As she cracks the back door to their pool, the shouts from reporters trigger Fritz and Ardell to step up, doing their best to shield me as we cut through the hedges. A few of the press who can't help themselves have started to inch up the street. I'm sure they know it's a private drive, but they're magnets to tragedy. Ardell sees it.

"Get her inside. I'll deal with them."

As we cross the threshold into the house, it all looks different now that I know Will's never going to come home again. I excuse myself and go up to my room, where I stand, stunned, numb. Lost.

Will Somerset dies in a lake? Will—the man who can do anything, the smartest man I know—gets murdered?

That's the most absurd thing I've ever heard.

An unhinged laugh escapes my lips.

This isn't happening.

The laughter gets bigger and louder until it folds me in half. I'm doubled over and howling when Este puts a gentle hand on my back.

"Nora," she says softly.

"This isn't happening," I say, wiping at the tears stinging my eyes as the laughter persists in a painful sort of mania. My stomach aches with every breath. "Will isn't dead. There's no way."

And then the gurgles in my stomach turn and I'm rushing for the bathroom. Fig jam spread, cheese, and crackers come back up in a violent rush, and I reach the toilet just in time.

She hands me a glass of water. "Sip it slowly. It's okay."

I take a gulp and feel my chest tighten as I swallow.

"Here." Her open palm offers half a pill. "Xanax. It's just half. Lay down for a little bit."

I wash my mouth and tromp to bed, downing the pill and water without a word. Crawling under the covers and pulling them over my head.

My phone starts to ping from across the room.

Este hands it to me. "Marcus is texting. The news must be out."

I pull the covers tighter, ignoring Marcus and the news. I don't want to know anything. I never want to hear about anything ever again. I squeeze my eyes shut and wait for the drug to work. I can feel the pill hit my bloodstream as the questions hanging over my head get quieter. But even as I drift off to sleep, they're still haunting me.

How did this happen? What are any of us going to do without Will? And how in the hell did he end up murdered?

CHAPTER **27**

BEFORE

Work-widowed was starting to feel like my permanent state of being. Over a stretch of weeks that turned into months, Will had bounced from one big trial or case to another, breaking only once, to attend a legal conference in Malibu.

"You can come?" he sort-of-kind-of offered.

"That might be nice. We could finally spend some time together." I smiled, swallowing the complaint that I wanted him to insist that I *had* to come.

"I'll be tied up most of the day, but the spas at the hotel are supposed to be amazing."

I'm supposed to spend three days in the spa? I can do that here, where I get to bring Este along.

"It's okay." I shrugged.

It wasn't, but I didn't know how to tell him that. He was so tense that the smallest things had started turning into fights. I forgot to pick up the dry cleaning one day, and you would have thought he came home to find me burning the house down.

"If you couldn't do it, you should have just said so. I would have asked Alma," he had snipped.

"I'm sorry. I meant to. But Este and I got tied up at the club and—"

"Tied up at the club? Was there some kind of emergency meeting you two had to attend? Did the pool bar run out of paper umbrellas?"

"Hey!" I fired back, testy from weeks of neglect. "Don't be shitty to me just because you're stressed."

I must have surprised him, because his eyes widened for a second. It's not like me to push back. Not with him anyway. But I had been accepting the bare-minimum effort from him with our relationship for long enough. Why should I accept meanness on top of it?

It was just a damn suit.

"I'm sorry." He sighed. It was a false victory, though. I knew he simply didn't have the time to fight with me, so the apology lacked sincerity. "It's just that I needed that suit."

"You have a zillion suits."

"I like that one," he huffed as he headed back to his home office.

I started to avoid being home during the times he was working at the house. It was too lonely to be under the same roof but on separate ends of the house, me in the living room or our bedroom while he holed up in his office for hours at a time. I would take myself for aimless walks around Winter Park. I walked to the library and around Hannibal Square and spent hours wandering the acres of Kraft Azalea Garden. I was a sad, aimless work widow.

One Thursday, I was driving up Morse Boulevard when my phone rang. I saw the incoming call from my mother and thought about letting her go to voicemail—she called sporadically and only ever on her terms. But when she was in the mood to chat she was persistent as hell. I knew that if I sent her to voicemail she'd just call right back, and keep calling. Plus, it had been a few weeks since we'd spoken.

"Hi, Mom." I sighed into the phone.

"Nora, you'll never believe the day I'm having." As always, she spoke in a breathy lilt that made men fall over themselves to help her.

I refused to take the bait. Complaining was her primary form of communication. Last month, she called from the middle of a five-star resort in Italy, beleaguered by the low supply of ice in Europe. "How's Sardinia?" I asked.

"Hot. You can't believe how hot. I thought we were coming here to escape the Florida heat. I told Paolo we should have gone to Switzerland, but he has friends he's visiting here. All ill-tempered smokers, of course."

Considering Paolo was an ill-tempered smoker himself, I couldn't muster even an ounce of shock. Paolo, a tall, silver-haired Italian man, wore shirts that were unbuttoned too far down, and though my mother's given name was Ramona, he called her Bella after drinking too much wine. She was Bella most days.

While she had been thrilled by my union with Will, she had ultimately been too busy with her own travels to stop back home for more than a year. When she called to "check on me," that usually just meant downloading her latest calamity to me. Tragedies could include but were not limited to an errant Net-a-Porter delivery in Paris; driving a too-small rental car on the Amalfi Coast; or not getting a pedicure in time to board a yacht where shoes were strictly prohibited.

"Anyway," she said. "I've been trying to get in touch with the plumber all day."

"In the States? Or was there an issue with your hotel room?"

"Well, both."

When I officially moved out of her place and into Will's, Ramona decided to have her Winter Park condo completely renovated. And as it turned out, there was a Four Seasons in Greece with the most divine faucet handles she had ever seen—as if divinity and plumbing fixtures were one and the same—and now, she was on a mission to source the heavenly bathroom hardware. For the majority of the day, she had endured the harrowing task of tracking down the manufacturer by way of a serial number. The vendor—out of Milan—had a patchy work schedule and a limited supply.

I pulled into a parking spot on Park Avenue, still aimless, but tired of driving. Ramona's ramblings on faucets and fixtures had taken almost an hour. Linear stories were not among her strengths. I had zoned out a couple of times as she described the metal filigree and how confusing international area codes could be.

As the call wound down, I considered confiding in her. Telling her I was lonely and sad and that my husband had become a ghost of himself. This was what people with functional connections to their parents might have done. Or at least I suspected as much. I couldn't know for sure.

But asking Ramona for advice was a dead end at best. At worst, I would have to relive the story of some failed boyfriend or engagement as she projected her own relationship issues back to me.

"Can I send you anything from the Mediterranean?" she asked.

As if the Mediterranean is some local grocery store, a quick stop on the way home.

"I don't think so," I started, but I could hear her talking to Paolo now. Something about a nightcap. I looked at the clock on my phone and added six hours. It was almost eleven-thirty at night in Sardinia. "I'm good, Mom. Love you."

She was distracted in a second conversation with Paolo now, but her attention drifted back to me long enough for her to say, "You, too, dear." And then she hung up.

I tossed the phone into the passenger seat and stared at it, thinking about my mom and then Will. I wished I could channel Este in these moments of my life. She'd have the perfect blow-it-off-who-cares attitude about the fact that two of the most important people in my life were pathologically unavailable. If she were here, though, she'd tell me to stop looking for people to be something they're not.

Even though it was nearing dusk, I couldn't bring myself to return to that cavernous, empty house just yet. So, I opted for a walk down Park Avenue and quickly spotted the sign for Lemon & Fig, Marcus's restaurant. I had bumped into Marcus at Este and Beau's a handful of times since the day we first met. I shouldn't have liked running into him as much as I did. He was always so laid-back and easy to be around. And he was nice to me—something I never got from Will's circle of friends. Something even Will didn't have the energy for lately.

What's the harm of going in? We're friends. At least, I think we are.

I pushed open the trendy glass-paneled door leading into a dining room that was just like Marcus—cool and accessible. The warm-wood shiplap and a bright green living wall framed the wide-open restaurant. The atmosphere was a carefully curated encounter with all things earthy and fresh. Wood floors painted white kept the space from being too dark or heavy. There were large black-and-white pictures of beach scenes on the walls—waves at sunset, surfboards gathered in a row on a low fence, and sandpipers chasing low-tide finds.

By all appearances, business was good. The dining room was crowded and lively. I spotted a bar in the back with an empty seat and decided to post up there after confirming with the hostess that seating myself at the bar was allowed.

I couldn't say why, but I felt awkward being there. We had only ever hung out at Este and Beau's. Maybe Marcus was just being nice when he suggested I stop by.

Relax. You don't even know if he's here.

"Hey, Nora," a familiar voice called from the back of the house.

Marcus was coming out of the kitchen in a white chef's coat, holding two artfully plated dishes. "You came," he said, and that boyish smile was on full display. "Let me run this food, and I'll be right back."

So, he's here. Okay. You're not doing anything wrong. It's a restaurant.

He reappeared a few minutes later, this time from behind the bar. "Welcome to Lemon and Fig."

"This is a great space," I said. "How long have you been here?"

"Four years, maybe? We started doing pop-ups and some elevated food truck gimmicks to build word of mouth. But then Paul McCartney's stepson posted something about us on his social media when he was at Rollins. We were off to the races after that."

"Wow," I said. "After the Beatles broke up at that hotel down at Disney World, I thought they were done with Florida for good."

"But for the grace of Sergeant Pepper go I."

I held back a laugh—fearful it could be perceived as flirting. *We're just friends.*

"So, what brings you in?" he asked. "Are you eating or just looking for a cocktail?"

"What do you recommend?"

"Everything." He opened his arms, proudly showing off the space.

"I'm not sure I'm hungry enough for everything. What are you known for?"

"Fresh fish and local produce are the backbone of our menu. We're a little bit of a farm-to-table, coastal fusion concept, leaning into the Florida coastline and the Central Florida farmers that helped to make this part of the state what it is. You know what . . ." He grinned. "Let me make you a little bit of everything."

"What does that look like?"

"Just trust me." He winked.

Friends wink at each other. Probably.

A little bit of everything, it turned out, looked like four tapas plates that Marcus brought out all at once. Butter lettuce, avocado, and mango salad. Fresh snapper. Braised short ribs. Roasted potatoes.

"And to drink." He presented a flight of four wines and started to explain which wine paired with what dish.

"What do you call all of this?" I let out a nervous laugh as he put the plates in front of me, intimidated by the bounty.

"I don't know," he said with a shrug. "It's a new offering. How about the Dear Prudence special?"

I knew the Beatles song, a dreamy melody about Prudence being as beautiful as the sky. And when was she going to come out to play? The song was so full of longing. Was there something else to the joke?

No, Nora. You're just starved for attention.

I tried to change the subject. "Tell me about the photographer." I pointed to the art on the walls. "Where'd you find these photos?"

"Those are mine."

Goddamnit.

"I'm a beach bum at heart," he said. "Maybe that's why I never left Winter Park. It's hard to walk away from everything that keeps this place close to nature. The beach is an hour away. We have nearly a thousand acres of lake here. I'm not sure I could live in a landlocked state and keep my head on straight."

Este would be throwing up in her shoe right now. Or maybe she wouldn't. There was something about Marcus's love of where he grew up that was hard to mock. It was completely unpretentious. He was kind, and straightforward.

"A beach bum?" I asked, sinking my fork into the most tender short rib I'd ever seen.

"They let just about anyone on the semipro surfing circuit."

"Is that right?"

"That's what I hear."

"I'll try out tomorrow then. I could use a hobby. Should I just head straight to the Cocoa Beach Pier?"

"Tell them I sent you."

"I'll do that." I took a bite of the rib and flavor burst on my tongue. "How dare you."

"It's good, right?"

"I'm upset. Nothing should taste that good. We're all doing what it takes to increase our longevity, and you're just out here slinging delicious heart attacks."

"That cow was grass-fed. Does that help?"

"Does that help . . ." I shook my head and went back for another bite. "Absolutely not."

"You're good at this," he said, and his expression was hard to read.

"What am I good at, exactly?"

"I've told you everything about me—where I grew up, my restaurant, surfing—and you've somehow managed to stay completely silent about yourself."

"That was really everything about you?" I raised a skeptical eyebrow. "That would be a very short biography."

"See what I mean? You're like a spy. If the semipro surfing circuit doesn't take you, try the CIA next." He laughed, wiping his hands with a bar towel. "Keep deflecting."

I laughed a little, too, feeling uncomfortable. "I'm not—Am I deflecting?"

Was I?

"I think so."

I put my fork down as a show of really paying attention even though the last few morsels of food on my plate were beckoning to me. "Okay. What do you want to know?"

"What do you get up to all day?"

He was trying to be nice. Make small talk. But it concerned me that I didn't have a good answer other than . . . pal around with Este.

Did I really come all this way—land the guy, move into the big house—just to wind up lost again?

Instead of answering, I said, "I've been thinking of going back to school."

"Oh yeah? What do you want to study?"

I turned to look at him, doing my best to mask my surprise. Marcus was the only person who had ever asked me a follow-up question on the subject.

I took a sip of wine. "Art is the only thing that's ever held my interest for long. But I don't know if it's worth going back to school for that. It's not a real career, you know?"

I expected Marcus to laugh. But instead, he studied me. There was a sense of disappointment in his expression, like he was sorry someone had lied to me. His features softened in that way of his. "Not a real career? Said the artist to the chef."

I took another bite of rib, feeling vulnerable. I had never talked about my artistic goals like this before. Something about saying them aloud to Marcus walloped me with a harsh reality. I'd been longing to make art for so long that I forgot about *actually* making it. When had I given up on the idea of being an artist? Maybe around the time I realized I'd have to fend for myself, and that most artists don't earn a living wage. But now, there was nothing stopping me, and yet I spent my days working out and getting Botox rather than picking up a paintbrush.

"If you want to be an artist, Nora, you should do that." Marcus fixed his eyes on me, his expression so serious it caused a lump to form in my throat. He was right, and I knew it. But something told me truly copping to it would turn this conversation into a long, emotional upheaval, and I didn't want to get into all of that right now.

Marcus must have sensed my hesitation, because he dropped the subject. "You said you're from all over?"

"Yeah."

"That's not a place, Nora."

I laughed. "It's about five different places if you want to get precise about it."

He leaned back on the counter behind him, waiting for more.

"My parents lived in Charlotte, North Carolina, when I was born. After my dad split when I was thirteen, we followed my mom's love interests around like some kind of a fucked-up road show. There was Jim from Connecticut, Don in Providence. Right before my junior year of high school, we spent a summer in Camden, Maine, and she married a shipping heir from Boston, but that quickly ended in disaster. Sometime in my senior year of college, she ditched New England for current husband Paolo in Winter Park."

"Paolo?"

"He's Italian and only sort of nice," I said, remembering the cigarette smell that followed Paolo through every room. "She has a place near Park Avenue that she treats like a pied-à-terre while she and Paolo hotel-surf their way around Europe."

Marcus gave me a look that was somewhere between amused and skeptical. "Who pays for all of that?"

"Husband number three financed the pied-à-terre as part of their divorce settlement. But Paolo pays for the travel. He's like a viscount or something."

"She really knows how to pick them."

"Just their bank accounts, I'm afraid. They weren't all brimming with personality."

"That's a lot for a kid."

I waved a hand to breeze past the more tender wounds. I had gotten an education out of it. I understood early on in life that I was on my own. Lust fades. People change their minds. Relationships fall apart. Even mothers can be flighty. Very flighty.

Marcus didn't need to hear how hard friends had been to come by, since I changed schools with every one of my mother's new romances, or how I spent my teenage years hiding in my bedroom, drawing or painting—a master escapist. No matter how good things seemed, there would always come a time when we would have to give back the zip codes and the cars we'd borrowed—the lives we were trying on. Ramona always left with more than she had started with—alimony or just some kind of cash payment. But it was chaos. By a certain point—maybe after the third fiancé kicked us out of his palatial estate—I just put my head down, and vowed to keep my needs to myself, never wanting to be the straw that broke the camel's back in Ramona's relationships.

Of course, there was always a final straw. Her charm wore thin, or their money ran out. And then it was time to restart our lives elsewhere.

No wonder I took one look at grown-up, stable Will and swooned.

Instead of saying any of this, I shrugged. "White picket fences are overrated."

"Is that right?" There was humor in his eyes. "You're just slumming it in the mansions on the Isle of Sicily then?"

He was trying to be funny, but the joke cut too close to the quick.

Had I run to the closest thing resembling a picket fence that I could find? Worse yet, was I destined to live my life in other people's mansions?

I took a breath and tried to fake a laugh. "Oh, I didn't realize we were the kind of friends that can make jokes about each other's life choices. You want to talk about the tattoo on your arm? Is that Sanskrit?"

"All right." He waved me off with a playful hand. "You win this round."

"Good, because I want to hear more about this amateur surfing career of yours."

I took another sip of my Pinot. It was jarring how easily Marcus saw me.

We stayed late at the restaurant talking. I hadn't realized how late it was until a server approached him to hand Marcus the keys for the night.

I looked around the dining room and saw it was empty.

"What time is it?" I asked.

"Must be after ten."

Hours had passed. I looked behind me, to the front door. It was dark outside and the lights from the lampposts that dotted the sidewalks were glowing.

"I should go," I said, a little dazed. Marcus was just so easy to talk to.

"Want me to walk you to your car?" he offered, and I nodded. The crime rates in Winter Park weren't exactly threatening statistics, but it was better to be safe than sorry. "Give me just a second to let the manager know I'll be right back."

Hopping off my barstool, I headed to the entrance. As I waited for Marcus, his team started to close down the space for the night—turning the lights up and the ambient music off. Without the crowds and low lighting that made the restaurant feel warm and inviting, there was a quieter energy to the space. It was a peek behind the curtain that somehow felt intimate in a way the public wasn't supposed to see.

"Ready?" Marcus met me by the door and we stepped onto the sidewalk.

Even at ten o'clock at night, the Florida heat was lingering in the air, and the temperature change from an air-conditioned restaurant to a humid evening sent goosebumps up my arms.

"I'm over there." I pointed to my BMW X5 on the other side of the brick-paved avenue. I'd sold my Honda about a month after Will and I got married. He joked that parking the beat-up Accord in his driveway was bringing down the value of the real estate in the neighborhood as he handed me the keys to a brand-new car.

I'd loved that Honda. It'd given me my freedom since I was seventeen years old. But Will didn't know that, and I know he didn't mean it as an insult.

Marcus looked left and right and then reached his arm wide to gently touch my shoulder to guide me across. He wasn't putting his arm around me, not really. But the contact still made me jump a little.

We walked to my car with an awkward silence hanging between us. I kept spinning my engagement ring—hooking the large stone with my thumb and turning it around my ring finger.

"Ohmygod." I hit my hand to my head when we reached the car. "I just realized I didn't pay for my meal." I reached for my wallet.

"No," Marcus said and put up a hand. "The Dear Prudence special is on the house."

"Then how do you afford the royalties?"

My stomach did a little twist when I looked into his eyes. He casually pushed his hands into his pockets and laughed. Being with Marcus was like being under a spell. It was hard to reason or even describe, but I didn't want the spell to break.

So, it was under the spell that I took a tentative step toward him, searching his eyes.

Can't we just stay here? Can't we pretend nothing—not the trouble back at my house or all the loneliness—nothing else is real?

He put his hands on my arms, rubbing at the goosebumps that wouldn't fade. But he looked so sad.

"You should go home, Nora," he said softly.

I knew he felt it, too. The pull between us. The almost-chemistry that almost gave way to a kiss. In another world, it might have been the end of a date or the start of something. And maybe one of us would have leaned in.

But this wasn't that world.

I climbed into my car and headed home to my husband, leaving Marcus alone in the glow of a lone streetlamp, watching me go.

CHAPTER **28**

SEVEN DAYS AFTER

I made myself take a shower today. Though, I didn't totally understand why I felt the pressure to do so.

Why exactly is it objectionable, when mourning, to look the part?

For some reason, my grief seems to be making everyone a little queasy.

There have been droves of people in and out of my house in the last twenty-four hours. From the size and volume of flower arrangements, it's hard to tell if we're in mourning or celebrating the winner of the Kentucky Derby. People who, for the past year, have taken unique pleasure in skewering me as the interloping gold digger are now giving me consoling hugs. I guess death trumps social politics. Or maybe social politics still reign supreme and they're just in it for the spectacle. Publicly grieving is merely another way these people socialize. The way they tell me their Will stories—as if they've all just lost their dearest friend—makes it feel like everyone wants a piece of the grief. A piece of the attention.

I do my best to stomach it all with a demure smile, propped up by the wine Este keeps passing me. But every now and then a more sinister thought creeps in about the cast of characters surrounding me.

Which one of you fuckers killed Will?

An incalculable number of casseroles and to-go containers from every restaurant in Winter Park is piling up in my kitchen. No one here would bake a thing themselves, but they'll at least give a show of being polite, civilized, and thoughtful enough to pretend to dote on me.

While all of this pomp and circumstance is happening around me, I still feel like I'm walking on the bottom of a pool. I hear people's voices, but it all just sounds like murmurs. I see Autumn in my kitchen trying to repackage the food into sad single-serving freezer bags complete with little ribbons holding them together. As if attractive packaging will somehow make me feel better about being a twenty-eight-year-old widow.

Oh, look! My spinach lasagna has a green curlicue bow! Who even cares what happened to my husband!

I don't mean to be terrible. I know she is trying to do something nice—she *is* doing something nice. But I'm trapped in a kind of permanent fog. A fog that will never lift, that I will carry with me for the rest of my life no matter where I go, or what I do. My husband will always be gone.

Somewhere under the clutter gathering on my bathroom counter, my phone rings. My mom is calling. It's the fourth time she's called since I left a message that they'd found Will.

"Hey, Mom."

"Nora—"

The sound of her voice catches me off guard, a lump of grief swells in my throat. But no tears come. Just a searing pain in my chest.

"Nora, honey, I just can't believe this news. It can't be happening. Paolo has been talking to the captain since you called, trying to figure out if we can get to any port, or how I can get to you. But he's holding his ground that he can't turn the ship just for me. And now I'm just beside myself. I'm distraught. You need me and I can't be there."

She starts to cry. A familiar whimper that inexplicably makes me angry. I can't console her. I haven't even been able to access my own tears.

"Mom, it's okay. Really."

"Bu—No—I want—flights—can't—"

Her phone starts cutting out.

"Just call me when you get to dry land, okay, Mom?"

I don't get an answer and hang up. I stand there for a second, considering calling her back, but I don't have the energy for it. I head downstairs instead.

When I come into the kitchen, Mia is standing in front of the refrigerator, looking over all the random meals. There's a pile of her clothes on the counter behind her. It's the first time I've noticed how much she stands like Will. She's the spitting image of Constance, but she has Will's easy posture, and his slightly crooked grin. My heart hurts for a minute, but this time it isn't for me. This is happening to Mia, too. Will wasn't just her father. He was her person—her Pal—long before he was mine.

Shit, I'm an asshole. Where has Mia been in all of this?

I think about the first time we met, and Will saying Mia was struggling with the divorce.

How could any of us have known then that things were going to get so much worse?

Mia gives up and closes the door. Her hair has barely been brushed, and she's too young for the circles under her eyes. She sees me and jumps a little.

"Sorry, I didn't mean to sneak up on you," I say. "I didn't hear you come in."

"I probably should've texted." She moves around the island toward her phone on the counter.

"You don't have to. You never did before."

Before. When this was her dad's house. And he lived here. And she just came and went.

I realize that I need to say something, but I don't know what.

"This part is weird. I don't know what to do about it either." Mia unlocks her phone and scrolls through some text messages, answering them rapid-fire the way only a teenager can.

Mia is often more of an adult in any given situation than most adults I know.

"I just . . . needed a break. My mom's house is so crowded. She keeps begging her friends to come over so they can drink wine and watch her cry about Dad. Like she hasn't spent the last millennium badmouthing my dad to anyone who will listen. Everything's always so dramatic with her."

Something about Constance getting to own any piece of Will's loss makes the ache of losing him feel heavier and chafe in all the wrong places. I curse his death for the thousandth time.

How am I supposed to carry all this?

I am about to tell Mia that she can come here whenever she wants, and that I really do want her to still consider me family, but Este comes through the sliding glass door, a bottle of Prosecco in her hand, shifting the mood.

"Hey, Mia. How're you holding up?" Este sets the Prosecco down on the counter and goes to the butler's pantry for glasses.

"I'm okay. But I better go. If my mom finds me here, she'll kill me. I'll, uh, see you guys later, I guess?"

"Of course."

I pull Mia into a hug. It's the kind of hug my mother has never been able to give to me. And for a brief moment, it's exactly what I need. She lingers for a second, her body slumping into mine, but when she starts to shake a little, she pulls away. And so do I. We're not ready to settle into the pain yet. She scoops up the clothes off the counter and shows herself out the front.

I look at Este, the glisten of a tear in the corner of her eye. I can see her fighting it off, being strong for me. Very on brand for Este and her "never let them see you bleed" motto. She hands me a glass of Prosecco and more of whatever stash of Xanax she seems to have an endless supply of. For a flash, I see my future as the subject of a cautionary tale, but I slam them both back. We walk to the living room and I climb into the corner of my couch, pulling a pillow across my lap and hugging it close.

"Has Ardell called?"

Este brings the bottle of Prosecco and her glass over and plops on the couch next to me. "I checked with him, and he said they still haven't heard from the medical examiner. Fritz was going to go down to the office to talk to the guy himself as of about twenty minutes ago."

"I want to talk to him. I want to know what evidence he's been able to gather." I'm wringing my hands with the anxiety of it all.

Este reaches out and stills my hands. "You're about twenty minutes away from being a little drunk. And high. Maybe another day?"

"I have things to say."

"Like what?"

I sink back into my seat. All I can fixate on is that Constance was drunk and angry about her social demise the night Will died. It's the one card I have, so I need to be careful about how I play it. I've even withheld it from Este, because she runs so hot she'd be on Ardell's doorstep in an hour with the information. I need more to back up my theories before I can say anything.

"Never mind," I mumble.

Will is dead—murdered—and everything is upside down. I have so many questions running through my mind. How did we fast-forward from trying to find Will to this? It feels like as soon as his body was found, a switch flipped, and now everyone is in a hurry to bury him. I keep waiting for one of the mourners who've come to pay their respects to pull me aside with their conspiracy theory of how this is all a farce. If they're talking about how this could have happened, they're not talking to me. Everyone gives me a wide berth as I move through the house.

They're all so somber and certain of their grief. Meanwhile, if I open my mouth, I might just scream.

Isn't someone going to do something? Aren't we looking for answers? What could've happened? Was he scared? Did he . . . suffer?

The last thought almost makes me want to puke. And I must look like I am going to because Este reaches over and rubs my knee. I can tell that she doesn't really know what to do or say, and "at a loss for words" is a very weird look for Este. I don't like it.

Este must sense my feelings because she picks up the remote and turns the TV on. She's flipping through the guide, trying to find something mindless to watch when the current channel up in the little box is Lindy Bedford—the nationally syndicated newsmagazine host who makes Nancy Grace look like a kitten—talking about Winter Park. Este clicks on the box and I hear myself gasp when I see Will's face front and center on the screen.

"The body of Will Somerset, a perfectly healthy forty-six-year-old man, was found in a lake in Winter Park, Florida. Officials still haven't released the details, but their homicide unit is looking into the case. That sounds like murder to me. And get this, he's one half of one of the most prolific personal injury firms in the state. For those of you who don't know about Winter Park—this is an area that doesn't try to attract attention the way West Palm

Beach or Miami does, but there's still plenty of money to go around in this zip code. For an area with a population of less than thirty thousand people, the median household income, according to our research, is over a hundred and fifty thousand dollars per year. That's a lot of money for a relatively small city."

"Este, why is this on my TV?" I croak out.

"I have no idea."

"Remind me to send a thank-you card to Kristy with Channel 2 News," I mumble.

Lindy finds the next camera angle and leans forward. "Let's be real honest here. In domestic homicide, they always look at the partner. And in this case, the wife is a beautiful twenty-eight-year-old who likely wouldn't have married someone almost twenty years her senior if he hadn't been standing on his wallet. If I'm the police, I'm thinking the cause of death is 'suspicious,' and she's my number one suspect. Period."

I don't remember standing up, but I'm now in front of the TV with my own face staring back at me. "Este—"

"I'm already on it."

A series of pictures from my Instagram account start flipping through on the screen. I hear my heart beating in my ears.

Me, blowing a kiss to the camera in a bikini in Nevis.

Will, sitting in front of a birthday cake, blazing with candles as I kissed him.

"I guess it's time to make your social media accounts private," Este says softly.

The next picture is an older photo of me and Este at a bar one night. That one lingers on the screen. Este and I are sweaty and beaming. We had just survived a half marathon and were celebrating. The camera pushes in on me and my smile looks . . . garish. They pull up the picture of Will next to mine. The prominent attorney and the window dressing. The shame cuts deep, and I want to shout back all the reasons she's wrong. But Este and I are silent, waiting for the next punch to be thrown my way.

"Here's what I want to know," Lindy goes on. "Why did she wait so long to call the police? Our reports are that he went missing sometime late Saturday night, early Sunday morning. She didn't make the call until Monday? So, you can't find your husband and you just . . . go about your day? Do some yoga with a friend? Some say she was even seen getting Botox the day her husband was reported missing. Are you kidding me?"

"It was Kyle J's HIIT class," I hear Este say.

"How did they know that?" I murmur in a voice that's too small to be my own.

"If someone wants to exploit your pictures for ad revenue, fuck them." Este changes the channel to local news, but they're covering Will's story as well.

A talking head is in the middle of saying, ". . . according to our sources, there are questions about the wife and why she waited so long to call the police about her then-missing husband."

"Turn it off, Este." I didn't mean to say it so loud. Este turns off the TV and puts the remote high on a bookshelf. "What the fuck is happening?"

Este looks at me. "Nora, come sit down. I'm trying to find Fritz."

But I don't move. I can feel the tingles of panic in my hands again. My arms go numb. I try to shake it off, but I can't get out in front of it. I walk out of the room and out the front door without even thinking. I almost walk smack into Marcus, who is carrying a bunch of grocery bags.

Marcus.

"Hey, Nora, I didn't want to just walk in—"

I hear the shouts from the press stationed at the entrance of the neighborhood, like lawn ornaments from hell. It looks like the number of news trucks has doubled since this morning. It's more than I can handle.

"LEAVE ME ALONE!"

"Hey, hey, Nora, are you okay? We should go inside." Marcus tries to shield me, but I can hear their cameras going off rapid-fire as Este descends on us.

I put my hands over my ears. "Why is this happening?"

"Nora, get inside. Now. You, too, Marcus." Este pulls us both in. She slams the door and looks at Marcus. "You shouldn't have come without calling."

Marcus furrows his brow at her. "I didn't realize there was this much press here."

"It's national news, for fuck's sake."

"I don't own a TV."

"How incredibly fucking millennial of you."

I hear someone screaming the most visceral, unearthly scream. And it takes me a minute until I realize that it's me. "STOP IT! STOP TALKING."

Marcus puts the grocery bags on the counter and pulls me into a hug. He tries to whisper so that I can't hear, but I know he's telling Este that he's got this, and she can take a break.

Take a break. I'd like a fucking break from this.

Este protests. She's been here, it's fine. But Marcus is insistent, and I know in the back of my head that Este must be exhausted from sitting in this cesspool with me for days.

I'm too tired to fight with either one of them. After a moment, Este lets herself out through the side door, and Marcus releases me to start pulling things out of drawers in the kitchen.

All I want to do is put this misery back in its box. Sleep. Sleep will do that. A tiny taste of oblivion. I trudge upstairs, get into my bed, and drift away.

CHAPTER 29

I wake up confused, my head still swirling with thoughts of who could've killed Will. Or, more important, *why*. I can't let go of the fact that Constance has no alibi. But is she the type to do something so drastic? I know she wants Mia to have her father, which contradicts the narrative I am concocting about why she would have shown up drunk and shoved Will off our dock. But if she was drunk, maybe . . . Maybe it was an accident? But how would she even get on the dock?

I need to start one of those boards with suspects. I'll need pushpins, red yarn, and Will's printer—which never works.

I pad downstairs, where I find Marcus reading on the couch. He springs into action when he sees me.

"Nora—"

"What time is it?" I rub at my eyes, adjusting to the lights of the house and the darkness outside.

"Nearly ten P.M."

"On what day?"

"Still Saturday. You must be hungry."

I'm not, but I am a reasonable enough person to know that I need to eat. I walk over to the island and sit down as Marcus starts pulling plates out of the warming drawer. Never one to do anything in half measures, he pulls together a meal worthy of a Michelin star, setting a plate in front of me that looks like a still life.

The baby carrots' greens wrap around a pork medallion adorned with mushrooms and mustard sauce. Pearl onions are perfectly placed in a brown sauce that is drizzled delicately on one edge of the plate. And there's a pile of arugula, golden raisins, and walnuts that looks like birds in a bush. He's an impossibly talented artist.

People here think he's just a chef. How silly.

He hands me a silver fork with a little peacock engraved at the bottom.

"Nice fork. Did you bring it?" I say, hoping small talk might keep the swells of grief at bay.

Marcus looks at me confused. "Uh, no. You have a whole set in the butler's pantry. You don't know what cutlery you own?"

"Marcus, the chef, meet Nora, the queen of DoorDash."

He chuckles as I push a pearl onion a little with my fork, then force myself to take the first bite. It's the most perfect soft-but-firm sweet onion in the history of the world. As soon as it hits my taste buds, I realize that I am famished. I can't remember the last time I ate.

It turns out you burn through the calories of Prosecco pretty fast.

He pulls out a plate for himself and stands kitty-corner from me. It's the spot where I always stood when Will got home late to a foil-covered dinner and wanted to talk.

"You shouldn't have waited," I say.

"It's okay. I ate a late lunch. Plus, I eat alone almost every meal. Figured you'd be up at some point."

I nod toward the seat next to me. Something about this tableau is too painful to stay in. Marcus obliges and sits down.

We chew in silence for a while. I don't know if it's his years of working around the people of Winter Park, or in high-end restaurants, or both, but Marcus has an incredible ability to just wait. To be patient. To give space to something. I'm grateful.

After we've eaten, I help Marcus do the dishes—much to his protest. But *doing* something is making me feel better. People have been catering to me for most of the week. Este basically dresses me every morning.

It's a strange thing, the way people react to grief that isn't their own. It's the monster no one wants to get too close to. It's too scary to think about it being their own horror-filled story. So people cook, and clean, and bring casseroles, and do laundry for you. The work, the movement, the physical toil become sandbags in a hurricane. If they stay in motion, maybe they can keep the grief just far enough at bay that they won't absorb it and have to face any of their own. Everyone around me is keeping their foundations dry while I sink farther to the bottom of an ocean of sorrow.

It's nearly midnight when I sit back down on the couch. I'm exhausted, but there's no way I can go back to sleep now. Marcus comes over with a glass of red and hands it to me.

"I opened one of the good ones. I hope that's okay."

"Why have it if you don't drink it?" I swirl the glass a little. "That's what Will says." *Said.* I can't go past tense yet. "Holding on to expensive wine is a waste. Buy it and drink it."

"Smart man."

I swirl the wine again, watching it rise and fall against the glass globe. The gentle swirl of maroon is . . .

Mesmerizing. Like Will.

I stop and down two-thirds of the glass.

"At least make me feel a little better and enjoy it? It's a 2003."

I stifle a giggle so I don't spit wine all over the white cloud Restoration Hardware couch Will and I picked out after we got married. He said he wanted me to feel like this house belonged to both of us. Now it's only mine.

I'm a widow, Marcus. This isn't funny.

It's like the flip of a light switch. Something about laughing or feeling anything other than soul-crushing dread or fear feels like I'm cheating. On Will? No. Maybe more like I'm gaming grief.

Will is dead and I'm cracking jokes with Marcus?

The guilt seeps into my bones until I start to shiver and ache. I sit up and put my wine down, and instantly I feel a wild squall of anger move in.

"Why are you here, Marcus?" I ask quietly.

"What do you mean?"

"Why are you here with me, at my house?"

Marcus shifts a little and sits up, confused. "Because it's what you do for your friends. Especially given the circumstances."

"But we're not friends. We were never friends."

I don't know why I am saying any of this, but I can't stop myself. My brain and my heart are no longer in sync—they no longer have any connection to each other.

"Nora, what are you talking about?"

"You and I—We're . . . something else. Something terrible and wrong."

"What?"

"Will is barely dead and you're here cooking me dinner and plying me with wine—"

"I'm not . . . *plying* you with anything. I'm not—"

"I'm not some pity case for you to take on. I'm not some poor little interloper widow who can't handle her own shit. Okay?"

Marcus stands up, shakes his head. "Nora, I'm sorry. I didn't mean anything other than trying to help out a little. I can't imagine what you're feeling right now."

"You're right. You can't."

"Okay, that's my cue." Marcus takes his wineglass to the sink and washes it.

Even with me shitting on him, he can't help but be a chef. Never leave the kitchen undone. It's always ready for the next meal, the next masterpiece.

Marcus heads for the front door. He stops and turns back to me. "I never meant anything other than a show of kindness, Nora. I'm sorry for what's happened. For everything that's hurt you." And with that so-sincere-it-rips-my-heart-out sentiment, he leaves.

The door closes, and I'm left in total silence. I have no idea what just happened. No idea why I said what I said. I can feel a wave of emotional destruction building in my throat, but I'm not ready for it. I can't lean into this pain. If I do, I'm not sure I'll ever be able to pull myself out of it. I down the rest of my wine, scoop up the bottle, and head upstairs to my room.

In the back of my mind, though, I know there's no amount of shouting I can do at Marcus to undo everything that's wrong. And there's not enough Malbec in the world to wash away the fact that someone killed my husband.

CHAPTER **30**

BEFORE

After my Dear Prudence dinner, Marcus started stopping by Este's house with fresh produce every few weeks. He'd bring strawberries or cucumbers or spring potatoes and make a dish for all of us to share. I chalked it up to coincidence that he stopped by on the nights I was there for dinner, because when wasn't I there for dinner?

It became a relaxed little routine for the four of us. Marcus would teach us a recipe or Beau would fire up the grill. We'd eat in the outdoor living room of Este's backyard with the ceiling fans spinning and watch the wakeboarders and the crew shells glide by. It was nice to have people to share the days with while Will was buried in work, but sometimes, when we were sitting out on the deck, I would catch myself staring at our house, looking for the light in Will's office and silently begging him to come out and join us.

Maybe that's why, when Will proposed we go out to dinner one night, I leaped across the kitchen to hug him.

"I would love that." I smiled.

His face screwed up a little at the sight of my enthusiasm. Like he hated to be the one to break the news to me. "There's a catch,

I'm afraid." He sighed. "It's a work thing. I'm sorry. Fritz thinks it would be a good idea for the four of us to get dinner."

My shoulders fell. "Like you and me? With him and Gianna?"

"I know she's not your favorite person. And I told him I barely have time to have dinner with you thanks to his latest fuckup, but he insisted."

"I don't hate her. But I am certain she . . . disapproves of me."

"What? Why?"

Does he really not know what people say about me?

"I don't know. She's just Gianna. And I'm . . . not."

"Yeah, you're you. My wife. Right?"

Right.

He needed this. I could see it in his eyes.

"Of course. We'll go. It'll be . . . fun." I nodded, walked toward him and wrapped my arms around his waist. Determined not to let this turn into a fight. "But you'll still play footsie with me under the table, though?"

He smiled weakly. "Sure."

God, he looks so tired.

"Is everything okay? You've been working like a madman, and it seems like you're always stressed and cleaning up Fritz's messes."

He pulled me close, and I rested my head on his chest. I heard his heart beating, and I tried to listen for signs of distress. He kissed the top of my head. "Everything's going to be fine. I promise."

"Wow, Nora." Will took in a breath and pulled one hand to his chest when I walked into his office the night of the dinner. He was already dressed for dinner but had gone back to his office to knock out a few emails when I told him that I needed ten more minutes to finish my makeup.

I had spent hours on TikTok, searching for the perfect smoky eye makeup tutorial. If I was going to have to sit across from Gianna all night, I was going to look perfect. Because she was perfect.

"You like it?" I turned in place to show off the form-fitting designer dress I had borrowed from Este's closet. "I went shopping at Este's."

She might be a boho fairy by day, but Este's evening wear could make a *Vogue* editor weep.

"Tell her I'll buy the dress from her." He came toward me.

"I'll see what I can do." I giggled.

It was nice to see an emotion that wasn't exhaustion or frustration from Will. Maybe this double date could be fun.

"Let's go." He touched the small of my back and guided me toward the garage.

Once we were loaded into his car, though, he looked over at me. "I just realized I forgot where we're going."

Will had left the reservations to me, and I called in a favor with Marcus for Lemon & Fig. Apparently weekend reservations were booked weeks—if not months—out. Even though it was the first time my name, not Will's, was the fix for snagging a restaurant reservation, I didn't offer up the fact that Marcus was a friend of mine.

"Lemon and Fig. Este and Beau are friends with the chef."

Will nodded and reached a hand across the center console to hold mine as we headed down the driveway.

"We must be early." Will looked at his watch as we were seated near a window.

I couldn't help the look I gave him. "It's six forty-five. The reservation was for six-thirty."

I knew a snub when I saw one, and Gianna never missed the opportunity for a power play. Will, on the other hand, never missed the chance to give people the benefit of the doubt.

"Let's get a drink," he soothed, landing a small kiss on my shoulder and rubbing my back.

It was after seven when Gianna and Fritz finally rolled in. I expected some flare of drama over their late arrival or a show of remorse and maybe even an elaborate—if flimsy—story as to why they were delayed, but they simply strolled in as if they were right on time.

I guess when you're Fritz and Gianna Hall, you're always exactly where you're supposed to be.

Will stood to greet them, but I kept my seat, a quiet protest.

After the requisite air-kisses and backslaps had been ex-changed, Fritz took the seat across from me while Gianna opted to sit in the corner, opposite Will. The server was quick to attend to our table and take down their drink orders, hurrying off with a similar urgency to retrieve their requests. It was like watching someone wait on royalty or a celebrity—pathetically obsequious.

"Nora," Fritz said and slapped a hand on the table. "How the hell are you? I feel like I haven't seen you in ages."

"Surely not ages, Fritz," Gianna purred. "Nora and Will haven't even been married a year."

Subtext: You're brand-new and do not belong.

"I've been well." I smiled politely. "Thank you for asking."

"What do you get up to in that big house all by yourself?" Gi-anna asked as she sipped her tequila and soda.

Translation: You do not run in our circles. And like any other strag-gler in a pack of animals, we should leave you for dead.

"This and that." I shrugged, very aware that anything I said to Gianna would make its way back to Constance in short order.

Will put an arm around my shoulder. "She practically lives in the yoga studio with our neighbor, Este."

This made Gianna's sharp eyes go wide. "I didn't know you were so athletic. You should come by the club sometime. The girls and I have a little tennis group. We'd love to add one more to the clan."

In other words: I'd love to isolate and bully you for sport while my friends watch. We can bring tennis rackets.

"Oh gosh." I tried to sound innocent. "You're so kind to offer. I'm afraid I've never been very good at tennis. The scoring makes me dizzy. What is it with country club sports and made-up scoring systems? Golf, tennis, cricket—it's all Greek to me."

Considering you already think I'm an unsophisticated idiot, I might as well play dumb to get out of whatever kind of hellscape socializing with you and your friends would be.

"It's very nice of you to extend the invitation, Gianna," Will chimed in. "I'll help Nora brush up on scoring."

"I'll bet you will." Fritz wagged his eyebrows.

Gianna just rolled her eyes. Will took a sip of his drink.

"Don't mind Fritz," Will said to me, but loud enough for the table to hear. "He's never been able to move on from sophomoric

humor." Then, directly to Fritz, he said, "Even when it's completely inappropriate."

Fritz didn't exactly look contrite, and Will didn't quite look
angry. But an awkward silence settled over the table. I'd never
seen them like this.

Gianna kept the smile frozen on her face, then tried to break
the silence. "How are things with the firm, Will? Fritz tells me
you're working on the case of a lifetime. Martinez something or
other?"

*Is this the thing that keeps him up all night? Why does Gianna know
about it but not me?*

My chest stings.

Will looked at Fritz for a second, and there was something
strange and unspoken in the way he eyed his partner.

"Among other things," Will said, noncommittally. "I've been
swamped. And I've had to pull a few favors with the courts to keep
up with all of the deadlines." There was another look in Fritz's
direction.

For his part, Fritz was completely unaffected by Will's veiled
swipes. But everyone else at the table seemed to be aware of the
tension. Will was mad at Fritz for something, and it was bigger
than just a crass joke.

While Gianna had thrown out superficial topics—the weather,
Mia's schooling, rising property taxes—to keep the conversation
going, I had listened for clues about what was really going on. But
Will was polite, engaged on each topic and kept a sort of distance
from anything that might draw Fritz into the conversation. That
didn't keep Fritz from chiming in in his usual big way, taking up
any available space and calling the attention back to himself.

Fritz trying to take control of the conversation only for Will
to wrench it back was an unusual tug-of-war. Usually, Will gave
Fritz all the rope he wanted, shrugging off the wild stories and
lewd language as "just Fritz being Fritz." That night, though, he
wasn't laughing Fritz off, and when Fritz had piped up to add a
comment, Will had diplomatically and firmly changed the subject.

When the tension got to be too much to bear, I had excused
myself for the bathroom, and took my time walking through the
restaurant. In no hurry to return to the conversational standoff at

the table, I checked the news on my phone as I'd stood by the sinks in the ladies' room.

After I had wasted the maximum time allowable—enough time that it was plausible I had used the bathroom, but not so much time that Gianna could start a rumor I had some kind of digestive disorder—I emerged and bumped squarely into Marcus.

"Sorry," I sputtered as we collided.

He put both hands on my arms to steady me. "Hey, Nora! I read the note that this was a work thing. That's too bad. I would have pulled together a Yellow Submarine tasting menu."

I smiled. "Yeah. It's for my husband."

We were in a narrow hallway, set back from the dining room. He looked behind himself to see if he could spot our table.

"By the window." I pointed surreptitiously.

"Ah," he said. "So that's the elusive Mr. Nora."

"Will. And Fritz and Gianna, the witch."

"Witch, like she's got powers?"

"Witch, like if she had powers she'd use them to make me disappear." I shrugged. "I'd love to see her turned into a newt or something."

"Got it." He turned back to me. "So, if you two can't stand each other, why are you at dinner together again?"

As if it's that simple.

"I don't know. I haven't seen Will in, like, a hundred years, so I said yes to spend some time with him." I bit the inside of my cheek. Complaining about Will to Marcus felt like a betrayal. I looked back at the table and saw Will watching us.

His face was inscrutable, but as I caught his sight line, he winked, his face softening into a smile.

I turned to Marcus. "I should get back."

"What was that?" I asked as we were driving home at the end of the night.

The tension at the table had not gotten any better. In their own, conflict-averse ways, Will and Fritz covertly sparred with each other for the entire meal.

Will just shrugged and said, "It's complicated. And what was with the conversation between you and the chef?"

"Don't turn it around, Will. Marcus is a friend. What's going on with you and Fritz?"

"Fritz and I aren't seeing eye to eye at work."

"About what?"

"Almost everything."

Another nonanswer.

"You know you can talk to me about work stuff, right? I am happy to be a sounding board. I'm your wife—"

"Leave it alone, Nora. The work stuff doesn't concern you."

It was a real shutdown, and it hurt. It was the first time he had made me feel like the ditzy young wife everyone gossiped about.

I couldn't help but fire back, "Then don't concern me with stuffy dinners with Fritz and Gianna."

I crossed my arms and shifted toward my window. Will let out an almost inaudible sigh, but I heard it and tried to fight back the tears that were stinging at the corners of my eyes.

He reached over and pulled at my left arm. I let him. He took my hand and kissed it. "This will all pass. I'm going to take care of it. I love you."

I didn't say another word the rest of the way home.

CHAPTER 31

EIGHT DAYS AFTER

At dawn, I wake to the sound of egrets and sit at the edge of the dock, watching them take flight, willing myself to feel *anything*. A couple of paddleboarders skate by on the early morning calm of the lake. They wave, and I wave back.

Over here! I'm the widow that everyone is talking about! Did you hear? Do you know it's me?

They're gone as the sun breaks over the tops of the houses. A glare bounces off the metal trim of the boat. I shield my eyes for a second.

I used to love the view down here, watching the water change with the weather patterns. Big, puffy cumulus clouds often build in the morning and early afternoon as the ground heats up. Some days the clouds are so close it feels like you can reach up and touch them if you stretch a little. This morning, the water's so calm it reflects the sky above.

Will loved these days.

"Look at that water. It's like glass," he'd say before insisting we take the boat out.

I consider lowering the boat now, but something stops me. The same question that's been hanging over my head since they told me he was murdered.

How could this have happened?

I find myself looking around, examining the grains of wood on the dock for clues or blood. I scrutinize the smooth fiberglass and the swirling script of the boat name: *Don't Settle.* Then, I'm climbing in and out of the boat to try to see if there are any signs that a struggle occurred here. I raise the boat in its lift, then lower it.

Nothing makes sense. I look out over the open water and consider how easy it is for anyone to get here from the lake, passing through the canals, in the dark of night. I shake off the shivers that this thought triggers.

Was someone else here?

I walk up the dock, back toward the house, and take a few steps into the lake where the dock levels off with the shoreline. The water's cold and my steps are weighed down by the soft sand sinking under my toes. From where I'm standing, I can see that the water level at the end of the dock is well below six feet. If he had been conscious going into the water, he would've been able to swim or even stand up and stumble his way to shore.

Desperate for more information, I head back down the dock and climb back into the boat.

Five minutes later, I'm powering across the water almost full throttle. The wind rushing by my head is the white noise I've been desperate for. The static in which I can find the oxygen to breathe. I take in a few deep breaths, feeling almost like myself again for a second. And then my phone dings. I suppress the impulse to pitch it into the lake. I see that it's a text from Autumn, and I have three missed calls from Este.

Shit.

I throttle back and turn the boat for home as I read Autumn's text.

8:49 A.M.
Nora, I'm at your house. We need to talk.

What now? What could possibly be happening now?

I pull the boat back into the slip, and as I'm knotting the line, Autumn and Este come out of my house, heading down the lawn.

"Did you take the boat out?" Este asks, almost confused.

"Yes." I don't offer anything else up. I'm not in the mood for her judgment. Although it is nice that she's not treating me with kid gloves anymore.

"Just . . . for, like, a ride?"

"Yes, Este. I took my boat out for a ride. It was pretty out this morning, and I can do those kinds of things, right? It's allowed? I'm allowed to be a human person who does things?"

"Ooohkay. Of course it's allowed." Este folds her arms. "Listen, Nora, we have a bigger thing to talk about."

Autumn seems awfully skittish, but I assume it's because of me and my . . . "state."

"Can it wait? I need coffee."

Autumn nervously checks her watch and glances at Este.

"For fuck's sake, Autumn, you can't be a chickenshit about this now," Este snaps. "She'll be here in like ten minutes."

"Her who? And here, where?" I ask.

"Constance. She's coming here. Fritz called Autumn and said that Constance feels it's important that you plan Will's service together."

I guffaw at the idea of that. "What the fuck?"

Will is dead, and Constance wants us to put on a united front. Nothing is real.

"I know." Este wrinkles her nose at me.

"She was thinking because of Mia that you should work together," Autumn says, and even though I'm ready to start a fight with almost anyone these days, I soften when I think about the spot she's stuck in. She has the worst position in this whole thing. Her livelihood is so embedded in this community. She can't alienate her clients—not me or Constance. She adds, "I am super happy to help."

"Constance said the word 'together'?" I ask.

Autumn frowns. "Well, not as such—"

And just like that, the slightest sign of goodwill vanishes. "What a joke. Constance is incapable of even making eye contact with me. But I have to just slap on a smile and let *her* plan *my* husband's service?"

Este raises a hand. "I don't think you should, personally—"

"Este, I think we have to try to be inclusive here. For Mia." Autumn shrugs a little.

"Fine. Sure. Whatever. For Mia." I push past Este and Autumn and don't stop walking. I need to get to the house to make coffee.

Fifteen minutes later, I open my front door to find not only Constance but Gianna Hall on the other side.

Oh, this is perfection. My living nightmare gets worse by the hour.

Any hope I had of contributing to the planning of this service has evaporated. I'm glad there's Baileys in my coffee.

"Constance. Gianna. Thank you for coming by." My voice is wooden even to my own ears.

Constance feigns a weak smile but doesn't say anything.

"That's quite the collection of reporters you have out front," Gianna says as she crosses the threshold first. Even next to Constance, Gianna's a royal wrung higher. Maybe when Constance and Will were still married—before I dethroned her—maybe then they had equal footing. But I doubt it. Gianna always wins.

"All within their reporter rights, I'm afraid," I say.

"We're so very sad about Will. All of us." Gianna places a bony hand on my shoulder and leans in for what I think she thinks is a hug, but to anyone watching could also look like she is about to push me into the glass window by the front door.

"Thanks, Gianna."

Constance comes in, and I look her over, unable to quell my suspicions. I tense up. The last time I saw her, she was accusing me of disappearing Will, and now he's dead. I brace myself for a fight, but to my surprise, she gives me a hug. And I'm momentarily stunned that the embrace feels authentic for half a second.

What is this charade? She knows what she accused me of. I know she has no alibi for the night Will died. We could have it out right here. But instead, we're planning Will's funeral with a level of decorum that would make the Social Register proud. This is next level, even for you, Winter Park.

Constance pulls away, righting herself, and the air between us settles into thick unpleasantness. I look to Gianna, realizing that she knows everything that has transpired between Constance and me in the past few days.

Does she know what I said? Probably. Constance must have asked Gianna to come as backup. Like a bodyguard or an enforcer.

"Shall we talk in the kitchen? I hope Autumn got my call to meet us here." Gianna starts for the kitchen with an entitled air, like my house is just another property in her portfolio of real estate holdings.

And what if Autumn hadn't? Were they just going to come here and surprise me? Funeral by ambush?

I know the answer is yes, which makes this all that much more exasperating.

Constance trails Gianna on their way to the kitchen, and I see it as my window of opportunity. Even though the last time that I saw her things were ugly, it occurs to me that there's a chance she knows something about Dean Morrison. If he's from Will's hometown, maybe she met Dean in her past life with Will. Despite everything between us, it's possible she has useful information.

"Did you know Dean Morrison?" I ask, and we both stop in the living room.

There's a flicker of recognition in her eyes that she quickly covers.

"Only from on the news the other day."

But she's avoiding direct eye contact, which makes me want to pry more. "Will never talked about him?"

"Will knew him? How?" She frowns.

This is bad theater. If she had a day job, I'd tell her to keep it. Does she know Dean was a private investigator? Does she know Will trusted him?

Whatever she knows, she's not sharing. I'm no better. I'm holding on to every scrap of information—hoarding it. But I'm considering what details I'd be willing to trade on to find the connection between Dean and Will dying so close together—it's all just too coincidental—when Autumn calls from the kitchen. Gianna must be growing impatient.

As we come into the kitchen, Gianna is seated at the head of my breakfast table, priggishly waiting for us to gather.

Seated beside her, Este shoots me a look filled with disbelief that Gianna is making herself at home. I return a clandestine nod. Este smiles back at me as if to say "game on." I try to signal my gratitude by way of best-friend telepathy.

As Constance and I take our seats, Este pops up to give Constance a hug that is mostly unreturned. "I'm so sorry for you and Mia. This is just awful."

Constance looks at me, and I see the cracks in her polish today. "Yes, it is." Her eyes are liquid, but she holds the tears at bay. I'm surprised by her grief—but maybe I shouldn't be. For so long, she played the part of Will's concerned first wife. Poised, if a little stiff. Now, her emotions appear closer to the surface. More real. I can't figure out what to make of it. But I wonder if the house looks different to her, too, now that Will is gone.

"Good morning, ladies." Autumn gives Constance a hug and Gianna an air-kiss. "Can I get you all something to drink?"

"No, nothing for us. Thank you. We should really dive in," Gianna responds.

So, Autumn pulls an iPad out of her purse and sets it on the table. "I had some preliminary ideas for the florals at the church and the centerpieces at the club for the reception. Fritz and Gianna are going to host that for you, Nora."

She powers up the iPad, and a funeral vision board is displayed.

A funeral vision board. I'll never get over these people. Behold: Queer Eye for the Dead Guy.

I feel my blood pressure kick up a notch. "Oh, I'm perfectly happy to host—"

"Fritz and I insist," Gianna says. "I've called Daisy at the club to make sure we can have the ballroom Tuesday. Constance called the church, and they can accommodate Tuesday as well. We thought that would be the appropriate amount of time to get things settled."

We. The royal, Constance-and-Gianna "we." I am so annoyed, and a little indignant. I want to ask what the rush is. Will is barely gone—my denial is still following me around like a thick fog. But I do my best to just play along when Autumn opens a file titled "Suggested Seating Chart" for the church.

"You did all of this already?"

Where have I been? Oh, only scraping myself off the floor.

Autumn's cheeks flush, but I'm not sure if she's embarrassed by my naïveté or by how much planning they've done without me. "Uh, well, I—"

"We knew how hard this would be for you to plan on your own," Gianna says. "And since Constance and I have been in Winter Park for so long, we thought it'd be easier if we just took the reins."

"The reins. Of *my* husband's funeral."

I am too blinded by my anger to do anything with even a glimmer of rationality to it. Este must see the hues of red filling my complexion, because she steps in.

"Nora, did you have any ideas of things that you wanted at the service? Or anything Will might have wanted?"

I turn and look at Este. She has given me a place to put all my seething rage.

"Thanks for asking, Este, but no. I hadn't realized that I was going to be planning a funeral that other people decided had to happen on their schedules and by their rules. So, I hadn't put a lot of thought into any of it. But since you asked, I'd like to speak at the service."

Constance and Gianna exchange scandalized glances, not at all subtly.

"What? What is the problem?" I say with all the confrontational venom I can muster.

"Constance and I felt that, since it might be hard for Mia to hear from you and not her mom, Fritz should deliver the eulogy," Gianna advises primly.

"*Fritz?*" I stare at her.

"Yes. He's known Will for so long—"

"And I haven't."

"That's not at all what I meant to imply—"

"You didn't imply. You said—"

Autumn steps in. "It might be nice if Nora, Constance, *and* Mia lay a wreath at the table with the urn at the start of the service and then sit together with Gianna, and the other Hall family members. As a show of solidarity. And I thought that Nora might like to use a wreath made of poinciana—the national flower of Nevis." Autumn smiles at me, hopeful.

Este starts to say something, but Autumn shoots her a look that makes Este go silent.

Whoa. Autumn shutting up Este is the Major Leagues.

I wait for Este to unload, but she doesn't. She just shrugs at me.

God, even Este knows I can't win this.

I take a sip of my boozy coffee. All I can do is watch the rest of it unfold before me. Gianna and Constance put me in *my* place in *my* house about *my* dead husband.

About a hundred rounds later, including the one where I got to pick the memorial photo we were going to use—a *small* victory—Gianna, Constance, and Autumn show themselves out with the service planned from tip to tails. Autumn in her magical way has gotten us all to agree to everything, including the idea that Constance, Mia, and I won't wear black—it's too drab—but that we'll all wear different shades of blue—like the lakes and the island waters Will loved.

"The Stepford Sisters thing was too much for me," Este mutters as we regroup in the living room. "I'm not even completely sure that I understand what just happened. Should we scoop them and have a pop-up service tomorrow?"

"A what?" I lift my head from the couch, where I'm currently horizontal.

"Like an impromptu service." She doesn't expound. She's already launching into another thought. "And why isn't anyone talking about the fact that literally everyone is a suspect? Like, how the fuck did Autumn get a funeral planned so quickly? Did she know she was going to be burying Will?"

Those last few words make me shudder a little. "Lay off Autumn, Este. She's the nicest one of that group of vipers, and she was in Jacksonville the night Will . . ."

I can't finish the thought.

"Okay then, what about Gianna? Isn't she Satan's mistress?"

"Gianna doesn't even collect her own mail."

For a brief second, I wonder if she'll mention Constance next. But before she can list the entire roster of Racquet Club members, I wave her off. "Can we make another drink? I have a headache."

"Fine. But keep your eyes peeled at that funeral. I'm going to bring a notepad." She heads toward the butler's pantry. "Do you have any olives anywhere?"

"Check the bar." It's all I can say. Este's heightened suspicions send me back to my questions about Constance. I'm consumed with the fact that she had no alibi, and she knows more than she's letting on.

CHAPTER 32

TEN DAYS AFTER

'm sitting at the vanity in my bathroom in a director's chair and a hairstylist and a makeup artist are moving around me. Two navy dresses hang from the shower, yet to be decided on. I always thought moments of glam like this were reserved for happy occasions. Like weddings, or movie premieres. But instead it's for my husband's funeral.

I watch them transform me from the epic disaster of a human that I have been for the past week — something vaguely akin to a bridge troll that barely sleeps, gobbles wine, and lashes out at the townspeople — into something resembling a tasteful painting that would be titled *Mourning Wife*. Subtle jewelry, subtle makeup, subtle nude heels.

Everything about me is subtle. I've been reshaped into something more palatable for polite company. In this getup, you can't even see the axe-wound-size grief in the middle of my chest or my raging paranoia.

I come down to the kitchen to find Beau and Este waiting for me. I beg them to ride in the limo with me. I can't bear to show up alone. My mom is trapped at sea. Este laughed when I told her. It wasn't mean. She was delighted to learn someone else's family is as fucked up as hers. I make a mental note to ask her about that someday, realizing we've never talked much about the past. I wonder if we will now. Would there be a "before Will" or "after Will" time stamp on all of our shared memories?

The limo ride is awkward. What do you talk about on the way to a funeral? Beau notices and squeezes my shoulder twice as we pull in front of the church.

Autumn has coordinated the funeral so well that our limo arrives directly in front of the limo carrying Constance, Mia, Fritz, and Gianna. She walks purposefully down the church stairs toward us, making her best attempt to look both somber and stately.

"Great. You're all here. Fritz, Gianna, Este, and Beau, go ahead and go in. Most of our attendees are seated. I'm going to hold the family just another minute."

I recognize a congresswoman and her detail standing by. Autumn politely ushers them inside and signals to us to ascend the stairs.

I feel like my feet are stuck on the sidewalk as a wave of dread washes over me. The thought of making this walk with Constance, of all people, is too much for me to bear.

Maybe she'll burst into flames as she crosses the threshold of the church.

Mia must sense it because she slips her hand into mine and her other hand into Constance's. It's such a generous gesture. And if I had been able to shed a single tear since Ardell told me Will was dead, I might cry now, too. Fortunately for the spectators who have come out to bear witness to this affair, my tear ducts are fused shut. It's for the best—no one likes a messy widow.

The three of us walk in as the organ gently pipes some epic drudgery of somber music. It's so bleak it's almost funny. I feel like I am going to have to fight off a fit of laughter, the kind that comes only when you know for absolute certainty that you cannot laugh. I can't look at Mia, or Constance, even though I think they, too, are realizing this is utterly ridiculous.

We walk up the aisle, generally trying to avoid eye contact with anyone. I'm almost completely undone when I get to the front of the church and Mia squeezes my hand. I pull myself together as we lay the wreath by Will's urn.

His urn.

The picture I chose of him is a carefree one. That's why Constance and Gianna hate it. He's sitting in the captain's chair on the boat, his hair is in need of a trim, sunglasses are slung around his neck on a neoprene lanyard. His crooked smile is so quintessentially him. I love that picture. And here it is staring back at me in front of what must be twelve hundred people.

My Will. How did it come to this?

Autumn ducks in and shuffles us to our seats before I can really let the emotions sink in. I barely listen to the funeral as people talk, and eventually Fritz bellows from the pulpit like a preacher. As the eulogy concludes, Fritz gets a little choked up talking about how he and Will were brothers. They met at the University of Florida after Will's dad died. And Fritz's family took Will in. I feel like there might be one story in all of this about Will, but Fritz goes on to say how the Hall family was responsible for them both getting through law school and then Fritz's father handed over his firm to them. Fritz's ego paints him as the hero of Will's story, helping to set Will up for a better life all built on Fritz's back.

I stare at the tile floor, wishing desperately that I could give Constance and Gianna the I-told-you-so glare they so deserve.

Pompous ass. You were right, ladies. That was far better than me talking about my husband.

The organ blast of the recessional almost launches me out of my seat. I follow Constance and Mia out of the church and into the blast of Florida sunshine, where I see Marcus. He makes his way over to me, and I freeze. I'm not sure if I should talk to him here or not.

"Nora, it was a beautiful service." He leans in to hug me. I only half hug him back. And as I pull away, his hand lingers on the small of my back.

That's where Will used to put his hand.

"Thank you for coming, Marcus. I should . . ." I gesture to the limo, feeling guilty for blowing him off so quickly. I take a breath. "Seriously, though. Thank you. And I'm sorry I screamed at you the other night. I'm still polishing my grieving widow manners."

He shakes his head. "Don't worry about it. You get a pass for as long as you need it."

"You're a good friend. I'm not sure I deserve it."

"Ah, you'd do the same for me if the shoe was on the other foot."

"Let's hope we never have to find out." I scan the crowd and stop when I see Detective Ardell staring up at Marcus and me. I feel "caught." I step back from Marcus, and Ardell notices it.

"Nora," Autumn calls from the waiting car.

"Go ahead." Marcus shrugs in Autumn's direction, and I take my exit, bounding down the stairs, hating that I feel like I might be a little flushed. Mostly from embarrassment for yelling at him the other night. I was horrible to him, and still he came today.

But did Ardell see Marcus put his hand on my back?

As the limo pulls away, Marcus stays on the steps, talking to a few of our neighbors. The windows are tinted, so he can't see me. But I watch him glance ever so slightly in my direction as we bank left around the church.

thought the surreality of the funeral couldn't be beaten, but then I got to Interlachen for the reception.

If aliens descend from space, the level of confusion over what this party is might send them packing to explain to their leaders that Earth is too complicated for their own kind.

Consider a different galaxy.

I am watching Constance work the room better than I could even imagine doing. We keep catching looks at each other and trading icy glares. Gone is the illusion of playing nice in God's house.

I spot Mia and debate whether to approach her. She's stock-still as the party moves around her. Her wide, tired eyes watch the scene playing out like she's stuck in a horror movie. I want to pull her into a hug. As if it could shield her from any of this.

When I move toward her, Ardell steps in front of me.

"Nora. How are you holding up?" He tips his head to one side. He's going through the correct motions to convey sympathy, saying all the right words. But there's a current of something else in his body language. Something that feels like condemnation.

"Thanks for coming," I say, trying to dodge the possibility of him questioning me more. Here of all places.

"It's the least I can do to pay my respects."

When he doesn't offer anything else, I make up an excuse

about needing to say hello to a few more people—trying to ignore the feeling of his eyes on me. Este finds me with what looks like a club soda but mercifully is a very, very large glass of tequila with a hint of lime.

"What the fuck is going on here?" She slams back whatever's in her glass and looks to see which of the five—*five*—bars in the room has the shortest line.

"I have no idea. But this tequila was a clutch choice."

"I just heard Constance tell some sappy story about Will and then go on to say how hard it is to be a widow. She's not a fucking widow. She's the ex-wife. The—"

"She broke into Will's house and stole his wine."

"Wait, what?"

"When we first started dating. She stole his wine. Just the expensive labels."

Este laughs so hard she snorts. Which cracks me up. But I can't crack up. Autumn is about ten feet away and will tackle me if I do. I bite my lip to keep it together. For a second, I think Este is going to hurt herself laughing so hard. But then a flash of recognition changes her expression, and she snaps into place. I follow her gaze and see Mia, standing in a corner on the opposite side of the room. She looks lost and so little. I smile and wave a little wave. She waves back, but I can tell she's dying to be anywhere but here.

"Este, no matter how weird this is, we get through it. For Mia."

"For Mia."

Este and I clink glasses as Carol Parker walks up to me, and I realize that behind her, there's a line of people waiting to talk to me.

There's a receiving line now? Like it's my fucked-up widow corona-tion, and they've come to kiss my sad-girl-widow ring.

Twenty minutes and four hugs from Alma later, I'm longing for hand sanitizer and a new way to say "I'm holding up as well as can be expected" when I spot Lenore bringing up the end of the line. I'm so happy to see her I throw my arms around her.

Finally. I'm in the company of someone who doesn't submit to the pretenses of these people.

When she says, "Nora, honey, I'm so sorry. What a nightmare

this must be for you," I know she means it, unlike half of the people I just spoke to.

I've lost any filters I had at the start of today. "It's utter bullshit, Lenore."

She pulls me into another hug. "I thought Fritz had a lot of nice things to say about Will today. I'm glad. They've had so many fights recently at work."

"About what?"

"Oh, this and that. Being business partners is hard."

The wheels turn in my brain. "Lenore, do you know if Will was meant to meet with someone named Dean?"

"Yes. But I'm not sure it actually happened, since . . ." Lenore looks at me knowingly.

They're both dead . . . but why?

Lenore's expression tightens a little. "We shouldn't talk about work today."

Then I remember something from the night we went to dinner with Gianna and Fritz. "What about that Martinez case of Will's?"

Lenore's face registers surprise—as if I am not supposed to know about it.

"Gianna mentioned it one night over dinner," I continue.

Why is it fine for Gianna to know about this case and not me?

"Oh, I see. There was a difference of opinion on whether they should have taken the case at all, but you know what, we don't need to talk about this today. Today is for Mia, and . . ."

Constance, Autumn, and Gianna? Me? It sure as shit isn't for Will.

I don't want her to stop talking. Something was clearly up with Fritz and Will. I want to tell her to pull up a chair. I want to grab a notebook and hear everything.

What did Lenore hear? What does she know?

"Would it be okay if I stopped by sometime to talk?" I ask.

She bobs her head noncommittally. "We're all here for you. I just loved Will."

"Thanks, Lenore. I might come by for a few things from his office this week."

"Of course, whatever you need."

Without another word, Lenore turns to go, and I feel the

tingling in my hands. I set my glass down and quietly slip out a side door.

I'm not sure if it's the tequila or the fact that I'm at my husband's funeral, but I want to escape. Through the door and down a hallway, I find a small nook with a bench, hiding where I hope no one can find me. Except that Marcus does.

"I saw you sneak out," he says. "I just wanted to make sure you were okay."

"I am definitely not okay."

"It would be weird if you were." Marcus closes in on me a little. I know he means to offer kindness and consolation, but I find myself almost recoiling. I don't feel deserving of any comfort.

"I should've gone to check on him." My voice cracks as I say it. "I should've gotten up and gone down to the dock—"

"You can't go there, Nora. Whatever happened, it's not your fault. You did nothing wrong here."

"Tell the press that."

Marcus brushes a piece of hair out of my eyes, and I let him. But there's an unintended intimacy about it that I can't handle, sending my dissociative stare back toward that ballroom we're hiding from.

That's when I see Ardell is watching us from the door I slipped through. His judgment of me is plain now. I can see the disapproval etched into the frown on his face as he holds my gaze.

To an outsider, Marcus and I might appear to be standing too close. But to the man investigating my husband's murder, I might as well be wearing a scarlet letter with blood on my hands.

Fucking perfect.

"I have to go. Thanks for coming today, Marcus."

When I look back at the door, Ardell is gone. I slip out of the nook, brushing past Marcus, and I disappear back into the ballroom.

Este and Beau stay with me for an hour after we get home. We are all exhausted beyond words, and we sit in my living room—staring at nothing, barely speaking, and sipping whatever cocktail Este mixed up. As they get up to let themselves out the side door—the press is still en masse out front—I see Perry is outside, and he's about to ring my doorbell.

"Who the fuck . . . ," Este says as she walks toward the door.

I'm on my feet in an instant, feeling fully alert for the first time in maybe days. "I'll get it."

Perry, what did you find?

I rush past Este and pull the door open, hurrying Perry inside before the reporters can snap any more photos.

"Come in," I insist. "Perry. I'm so glad you're here. What's up? What did you find?"

"We're talking to weird old townies now?" Este whispers, but she's not quiet enough.

Perry looks sheepish. "Oh, Nora, well, hi. So sorry to bother you, I know the funeral was today, and—"

"It's okay," I insist.

The only thing that can salvage my day of playing Pretty Princess Funeral Barbie is news about what Perry's been able to find on Will.

Desperation pinches my voice as I say, "Did you find anything?"

"Find anything?" Este looks at me sideways. "Who is this guy?"

"Este, this is Perry." I try to speed through the introduction. "He's a friend of Will's who—"

"Perry, the weird gray car stalker?" Este looks unimpressed.

I don't let her rattle me as I continue, "Perry was doing some digging into Will's phone records to see if he could figure out who Will was talking to the night he . . ."

"Shouldn't we leave that to the police, Nora?" Este's tone is on the edge of scolding.

"You can't be serious. You're choosing right now to put your trust in Travis fucking Ardell?"

"At least we know a little bit about Ardell, unlike Pierre here."

"Perry," I correct, but I think she's gotten it wrong on purpose.

"Nora," she says and pulls on my arm. "Can we talk?"

I shake her off. "No, because I want to talk to Perry."

Perry looks down at his tattered boat shoes. "I'm afraid I don't have much of an update today. Some folks back home are still trying to see what they can do." He's crestfallen to be letting me down. His eyes go a little watery as he says, "I came to pay my respects. I'm just so sorry about Will's passing. I wanted a different outcome for this whole thing."

"Oh." My gaze falls to the floor.

"Listen." Este looks to Perry and in her kindest hostess voice says, "Maybe you should come back some other time. It's been a difficult day."

Difficult. As if the day was just a tricky puzzle we were trying to solve. Difficulty level: soul-crushing.

There's no update. Perry doesn't have anything that will help me. And Dean is still dead. And now there is no more Will. And I am trapped here in this life. A life without Will and without answers. And I'm starting to wonder if Ardell thinks I killed my husband.

I can practically hear it, like the click of a door closing. Or the last tick on a time bomb. Something inside of me detonates. "Fuck."

"What?" Este turns her head toward me.

"What the *fuck* is happening? Damnit. I didn't choose this— I didn't want—" I stop myself. I can't say that. I did choose this. In every way. The Hot Mean Lawyer picked me, and I leaned in so hard, even when things got bad and then worse. And now look at me. The press is hounding me, there are no answers to how Will ended up dead in the lake, and I'm . . . all alone. Worse than alone, I'm a murder suspect.

Did you get what you were after, Nora?

I look at Perry and then to Este and Beau, and their sympathetic faces are more than I can handle. The dam breaks. But it's not what I thought it was going to be. It's not the puddles of tears I've refused to cry over the recent days. Instead, I'm marching down the back lawn, Este calling after me, and I can hear my voice, but I don't even know what I am saying.

And when I get to the dock, I pick up my pace, and run right off the end of it. Hair, makeup, and a two-thousand-dollar designer dress be damned.

Grief is ugly.

The water hits me, and I just stay under the surface. It's silent here. Maybe I'll never come back up. But my lungs start to burn. I hadn't exactly taken a good breath before jumping.

I kick my way to the surface. Este's on the end of the dock, pulling a towel out of the storage bin beside the boat. She doesn't say anything—just offers me a hand out of the water. Perry and Beau are on the pool deck. I watch Perry clap Beau on the back gently and mutter something I can't hear. Beau nods as Perry heads up the side yard, presumably to avoid this epic shit show. Este wraps me up in a towel and pulls me into a big hug.

Something snaps me back to reality, and then the truths I haven't wanted to believe are suffocatingly real. And that's when I finally let it all go. Thick, choking sobs fight their way to the top of my throat as I gasp and wail. Este doubles down on her squeeze as the tears come in crushing waves.

Will is dead. Will is dead. Will is dead.

And then a sickening thought comes to me.

What if his killer was at the funeral?

CHAPTER 34

BEFORE

Will and I barely ate together most days, but after another long week of work for him, I thought changing the scenery and setting the table for a nice meal would finally give us the dinner I had wanted to have the night that we went out with Gianna and Fritz.

As I walked along the aisles of Whole Foods, I couldn't help but think that when I was Nora Davies, grocery shopping had been a fight for survival. I made so little money between the museum and the swimming lessons that I was relegated to palm-sweating fear of whether my card would be declined every time I swiped it at checkout.

But now, as Nora Somerset, I could lazily walk up and down each aisle—each aisle!—and read labels, and place however many nine-dollar bricks of cheese I wanted to put in the cart. I didn't. I usually tried to find the cheapest one in the bin—old habits die hard.

Somehow hours of shopping had passed before I came home with the ingredients to make Will's favorite slow-cooked short ribs over polenta. I had gotten a little more confident in the kitchen thanks to cooking with Marcus. And I was extra grateful that Will's favorite food mostly involved throwing a bunch of ingredients into a Dutch oven and walking away to watch someone else going through a painstaking two-hour prep of a meal on *Iron Chef.*

Things were starting to come together by late afternoon. But I felt like a little girl playing house as I pulled out Will's bone china and silver flatware and started to set the table.

When everything was perfectly placed, I checked my phone. I had added location sharing for Will and me after one too many nights when I thought he was on his way home, only to find out he was pulling another all-nighter somewhere. The Find My app booted up and showed him at the address of his office.

I sent a quick text.

7:21 P.M.
Still on for dinner?

I ran upstairs to put on the dress. *The dress.* I had returned Este's after borrowing it for dinner with Fritz and Gianna, but after seeing how much Will loved it, I spent days scouring consignment shops online for the same vintage Dolce & Gabbana dress in my size. I was busy stuffing myself into the bodycon silhouette when my phone pinged with an incoming text.

7:46 P.M.
Leaving in 10. I have to make one more call.

I spoke fluent Will. Ten minutes was more like thirty. I took a breath.

That's fine. It gives me more time to primp.

But when thirty minutes turned into an hour, my composure started to fray a little. I had moved the short ribs to the warming drawer, but the polenta was beginning to rubberize into a sad, sticky little Frisbee. I should have known better than to cook it so soon.

I was searching the pantry to see if I had the ingredients to start over when I heard the garage door opening. I planted my feet where I was standing, determined not to run to the door to greet him.

I won't look desperate. And I'm not going to pick a fight.

He came in through the mudroom and let out a sigh as he put down his briefcase and shrugged off his sports coat.

"Will," I called from the pantry, trying to sound casual.

"Yeah," he said, and I could hear the stress of his day in his voice.

I stepped out of the pantry to find him leaning in the doorframe connecting the mudroom to the kitchen.

"Hey." I smiled.

"I'm sorry. I know I'm late." He rubbed at his face with an open palm.

"It's fine. I made dinner?"

He dropped his hand and took in my dress. "Damn. Now I'm really sorry I'm late."

The first traces of a smile started to curl his lips.

"You like the dress?" I did a playful little shimmy.

"I love the dress." He stepped toward me, kissing my collarbone. "I love you," he said into my neck.

"Not so fast." I laughed. This was classic Will Somerset foreplay. If he got his way, we'd be upstairs in a matter of minutes. "I made dinner."

He looked up, a little confused. "You actually cooked?"

I walked over to the warming drawer and pulled out the blue Dutch oven. "Short ribs," I said, a little embarrassed of how proud I felt.

"Shit." He slapped a hand to his forehead.

The smile on my face quickly fell. "What?"

"I had a late lunch," he said with a wince. "I'm not really that hungry."

I will not lose my shit. I will not lose my shit.

"I thought we said we would have dinner together." I tried to sound calm.

"I didn't know you were cooking." His voice was tight with something that sounded like either guilt or frustration. He crossed the room, heading for the bar in the butler's pantry.

"But I told you I was cooking." I sounded like a whiny child. I could hear it. I took a deep breath and considered ways that I might be able to salvage the night.

"I must have forgotten." He made a gesture as if waving the misunderstanding away, but it felt like he was waving me off.

I followed him into the pantry, which was lined with cabinets on one side. Along with the bar setup, there was another dishwasher, a sink, and a coffeemaker built into the wall. The auxiliary prep and serving space was bigger than the kitchen in my mom's condo. He poured himself a bourbon into one of the lead crystal rocks glasses that stayed lined up neatly next to the bar. I remember thinking he seemed like such a sophisticated adult when I first saw the crystal decanters arranged in this part of the house. Now, I just glared at him.

He could fix this so fast.

Say you fucked up. Just lie to me and say you're hungry. Say that you can see I went to a lot of trouble. Say something.

"I can't take it when you look at me like that." He was clearly annoyed by my disappointment.

"How am I looking at you?" I asked, but there were so many other questions filling up my head.

When did I become an inconvenience? Just another needy little thing to manage? Where's the man who swept me off my feet? We've been married less than a year and I'm already an afterthought? How did we get here so fast?

"We'll go out when all of this blows over," he offered, but he was still staring at the ice in his drink.

"When what blows over?"

"Nothing. Just work stuff. We'll go out. Wherever you want."

"When?"

"Soon." He shook his head.

"Soon is not a time, Will." I couldn't hold my impatience back, and I was sure he heard it. "We used to spend every weekend together. Now I'm begging for just a few hours."

He breathed out a rough sigh. "You don't understand, Nora. I'm fighting for my life."

"I don't understand? I don't understand because you don't *tell* me anything. You won't tell me what you and Fritz are fighting about. You won't tell me about this big case. You just expect me to be here waiting for you when you want to go to dinner or to go to bed. But you don't talk to me. You're 'fighting for your life'?" I threw up air quotes, which earned me a death stare. "Seems like I should know why!"

He drained the glass and slammed it on the counter. "You

enjoy the house, right? And hanging out with Este and Beau all day and shopping whenever you want? Don't you have everything you want? Do you understand that it all takes hard work?"

The words stung, but the tone of his voice hurt more. He was right. He had lifted me up and out of all the complications and bad days of my old life. Every money problem had been erased. Maybe feeling lonely was better than being alone. It was possible, I guess, but not probable. When I had been alone, I was fine with it. I didn't know otherwise. Now, I knew what I was missing out on. I resented the way he spoke to me like I was stupid. He looked at me like I was too naïve to understand the real world.

Your friends think I'm a joke . . . Do you?

Tears welled in my eyes. "I'm not an idiot," I shouted back. "I know you have to work. But it's never been like this. And if it wasn't for Este and Beau, I'd be completely alone."

He poured another drink, shaking his head.

I lowered my voice, trying to pull us off the rails. "Maybe we should see a counselor."

He shot me an incredulous look. "Marriage counseling? Don't be dramatic, Nora. I'm not some shitty husband. I'm just busy."

"And I'm not some gold-digging moron. I didn't marry your house or your money. I married *you*, Will."

When he didn't respond, I attempted to smooth my tone over a little. "Maybe we could get a dog then. Someone to keep me company when you work late." I was begging for scraps. It was humiliating. And then I said the worst thing I could have said, "Maybe we could try for a baby."

He glared at me like I was a stranger. Like I had broken into his house and asked him to father a child with me. My heart sank. Something about that look made me question if a child was ever going to be a thing we did.

"I can't talk about this with you right now." He moved to leave, but I caught his arm.

"Wait," I pleaded.

He turned around on me, eyes blazing. "My career. The firm. Everything I've worked hard for disappears if I don't do this work. Do you understand?"

"Stop asking me if I understand." I straightened up and glared right back at him. "And I'm not asking for anything unreasonable. I just want to spend time with you."

"Fritz is going to *bury* me if I don't clean up the mess he's made."

"What does that mean? Is he threatening you?"

"Nora. I can't! For fuck's sake!" he erupted, throwing the glass of bourbon against the wall. It breezed past my ear and shattered on the wall behind me with a startling crash. He charged toward me like he might push me up against the wall. Suddenly aware of how small the room could feel, I stepped back and he kept walking out, turning right before he got to me—leaving me in his wake. He went into his office and slammed the door.

When I got lightheaded and almost passed out, I realized I was holding my breath. All I could do was stare at the broken glass swimming in a pool of dark amber liquor at my feet.

CHAPTER **35**

could have gone to Este's. I probably should have. But I was too
ashamed of how Will had acted. Too disappointed by how bad
the fight had gotten to let Este know. If I told Este, she might
never forgive Will. Even in my shock and anger, I was protecting
him. I didn't know what to make of that. Was I weak? Was I pathetic? I was starting to feel like both were true, so, yeah . . . I
didn't go to Este's.

There was also a part of me that knew if I told Este, I might
actually have to do something about Will's outburst. Este would
never let Beau get away with something like that. She'd key his car
and then leave the divorce papers on his windshield.

All I wanted to do was forget the whole thing ever happened.
I wanted to erase it. I wanted to rewind time and take the whole
fight back.

A few minutes after Will locked himself in his office, I walked
out of the house, leaving the bourbon and shards of glass scattered on the floor. I felt like I was fleeing the scene of a crime, but
I didn't go far. I got in my car and started driving. And no matter
how many times I thought about driving straight home, I found
myself making a few turns and basically just circling the city,
crying.

By eleven, I had expected or maybe just hoped that Will would
call. But he hadn't, and I still didn't want to go home. To make

matters worse, a storm had moved in and decided to sit right on top of the city with fat, splashing drops of rain that fell so fast I could barely see between swipes of my windshield wipers. It got so bad that I didn't spot the knocked-over cone alerting drivers to the pothole in the road, and as my tire hit it, I knew I'd blown it. I pulled over and put my head on the steering wheel, letting the tears fall.

Suddenly, the storm picked up enough that I started feeling like I needed to get off the road. I wiped my eyes, trying to focus on my phone screen, giving up a few times as I tilted my head up and let the tears stream down the sides of my face. Finally, I managed to type:

> 11:13 P.M.
> I blew a tire. Can you come get me?

Ten minutes later, Marcus rolled up and got out of his car with a large golf umbrella.

"There's no way we'll be able to get this changed right now," he said. "The storm is supposed to pass in a while. We'll come back. We can go to my house, I'm just down the way."

I probably should've argued that. But I was spent and so soaked to the bone that his house sounded like the perfect place to wait for the rain to let up.

He lived in a dark blue bungalow behind Trismen Park. The earthy smell of the rain and a sticky humidity washed over me when Marcus helped me out of his car and under the umbrella. We hurried through his front door as a few pops of lightning lit up the sky.

"Thanks for coming," I said, acutely aware of the scene that I was causing. It was after eleven o'clock at night and I was in Marcus's living room with puffy eyes and a rain-soaked designer dress. And I couldn't go home because my husband threw a glass at me. Near me? What even was that?

Welcome to rock bottom, Nora.

His place had an open-concept layout, so I could see through to the kitchen, outfitted with everything a chef could want, including an island large enough to fit six stools for entertaining.

The space was like his restaurant—warm, cozy, with touches of a bohemian influence that reminded me of the beach. From the slouchy linen sectional couch where we sat, I could see white lights strung over a swimming pool in his backyard, and beyond the pool, there was a little greenhouse with surfboards racked against one wall.

Marcus looked me over carefully like he wasn't sure what to make of my late-night appearance, but he didn't ask about it. He just handed me a napkin and I did my best to clean up my eye makeup without a mirror.

"Can I make you some tea? You want a glass of wine?" he offered.

"Tea would be nice," I said in a voice that sounded as small and defeated as I felt. The truth was I was starving. I had been so wrapped up in cooking that I had forgotten to eat lunch, and of course I never made it to dinner. Maybe the hot water would take the edge off my hunger pangs.

He headed for the kitchen, and I stood up to follow him. My eye caught a gallery wall of photos in the corner of the living room. Candid snapshots from different chapters of his life. I took in the pictures as he held the gas stove control knob and it let out that familiar click, click, click to ignite under a teakettle.

It's weird, trying to piece together someone's history through a series of photos, but as I looked over the wall, I told myself stories from the framed scenes. Marcus had backpacked through Europe, scuba-dived around coral reefs, and surfed in Australia. He had jumped off the back of a sailboat somewhere that looked a lot like Greece. He had loved a black Lab and his parents. There were friends or siblings—I couldn't tell which—who had accompanied him on all of these adventures. He lived life with open arms and a friendly smile, and I felt a selfish twinge of jealousy for how light and cheerful it all seemed to be.

This is how life turns out for people with stable suburban parents. They get a zillion options and even a few do-overs, because they always know they will have a safe place to land if things go sideways.

"You okay, Nora?" Marcus asked as he looked over from the stove.

Considering I was so clearly not okay, I understood there was no point in downplaying the situation.

"Will and I got into a fight," I admitted. "I just need some space."

Concern shaded Marcus's face. "What happened?"

I shook my head. "Nothing. Everything. Death by a thousand cuts."

As I said it, I pictured a slowly assembled unlit pile of kindling. Every few days, Will would be late or inconsiderate. Or he'd give another nonanswer or allude to some stress I couldn't possibly understand. And I'd gather my hurt feelings into a little pile, like stacking up twigs for a fire. Tonight, we'd tossed a lit match into my careful collection of sticks—my pile of swallowed feelings and repressed loneliness—and they'd ignited like a bonfire.

"It was bad," I said. "We were both shouting, and Will threw a glass. And I feel so stupid for how out of hand it got. I feel so stupid for coming over here and bothering you. But I didn't want Este to know."

There was so much more I wanted to say, but I didn't because it wasn't Marcus's problem to solve. And I think deep down I knew that Will would be mad that I was airing our dirty laundry. And the more I turned it all over in my mind, the more I spiraled.

Am I stupid for getting married so fast? For thinking I could just live in a world like this—Will's world? "Just add a rich husband" for a fantasy life.

"Nora, did I lose you?"

I snapped out of it to see Marcus looking at me quizzically.

"Sorry."

"No need to be. Hungry?"

"Starving."

He pulled things out of the refrigerator like a magician pulling rabbits out of a hat. I sat down on a nearby stool. Even as I watched him get to work, my mind was reeling.

I didn't think I regretted the marriage, and I didn't think I wanted to leave Will. There was so much about our life that was good. I liked the protection living in his world offered, even if it came with the stigma of being his young wife. I loved him. But I hated feeling like a burden to him, and the way he looked at me—like I was just a naïve kid—made me wonder if he was having regrets.

The teakettle whistled, and we both looked at it. Marcus

turned the burner down and started to assemble a mug with raw honey and a chamomile tea bag.

"Here." He offered me the mug, and my hands were warmed just by holding it. Then, he pulled something out from the broiler and put a plate of food in front of me. It looked like cold cuts on toast, but after my first bite, I realized it was heaven on a plate. Some perfect, toasty grilled cheese comfort food thing that I devoured.

"I like your place. It's just like you."

"Oh yeah?"

"Warm, down to earth, a little arty."

"Your deflections come with a side of compliments tonight, I see." I could tell he meant it as a joke, but his eyes were pulled down a little in concern. "We can talk about the fight."

"I'd rather not."

He walked back to the living room and took a seat on the couch. I sat down on the other side. I'm not sure why, but I put an oversize pillow between us.

"What are you going to do about it?" he asked.

"The fight?" I shook my head. "I don't know. I just want to undo it. I want it to have never happened. But it did. I walked out of the house hours ago. I thought he would call, you know? I keep thinking he's going to fight for me. To do something to try to keep me . . . But he won't."

As I said the words, the lightbulb went off in my head—the realization was as clear as day.

Will isn't going to fight for me. He doesn't like to fight anyone. He doesn't like to fight.

When Constance stole all his wine or burst into his house to yell at me, he didn't want to confront her about it. And when Fritz made a scene, Will just shook his head. The biggest reaction I'd ever seen from him was tonight, when I goaded him into a fight he didn't want to have.

"Everyone deserves someone who will fight for them," Marcus said softly, and there was a hint of regret in his voice.

"Well, I might be out of luck."

"Have you tried telling him that's what you need?"

"I asked about counseling. I told him I was lonely. He shut it all down."

Marcus nodded, taking it in. "The only marriage advice I have is don't take marriage advice from a single guy like me." He chuckled gently. "It sounds complicated, and I really hope there's a solution where you get what you need."

I could tell he was choosing his words carefully and trying hard not to criticize Will.

"You're being kind."

"You want me to be mean?"

"I want to know what you'd tell your sister to do if you had one."

"I have a sister." He straightened up slightly. "And I'd want her to be happy. But you have to decide what that means. What do you want your life to look like in five years?"

Five years felt like a lifetime from now. Before I met Will, I was living paycheck to paycheck. And then when we started dating, I got so swept up in the moment. I lived life looking forward to the next date or weekend together. It was so all-consuming that we never talked about the long term. Now, thinking about the way Will looked at me when I asked about a baby made my stomach hurt.

I put my head in my hands. "I've made so many mistakes."

Marcus put a gentle hand on my shoulder. "You don't have to have it all figured out tonight," he reassured me softly. "It's late. Maybe you just need to get some sleep. If you don't want to go home, I have a guest room." He looked at my designer dress. "And a T-shirt you can borrow."

I might kill Will if he stayed the night at another woman's house. But it was just in the guest room. Just so that we could both cool off, I justified. Then I checked my phone, hoping there would be a text from Will begging me to come home. But it was after midnight, and he hadn't tried to call me since I left.

"Okay." I nodded, taking the last sip of my tea and resting the mug on the coffee table in front of me.

I woke up to the sound of a knife sliding across a cutting board. It wasn't staccato, it sang. I rolled over and looked at the clock on the wall: 5:47 A.M. I picked up my phone, wondering if Will had called, but there was nothing but an alert for some headline in the local paper. I was immediately split between blind rage and worry.

He didn't call.

But what if he hadn't called because he was unconscious or something? I checked Find My. He was at the office. Not in a hospital bed or lying mortally wounded on the living room floor.

Fine.

I sat up in bed and felt the last ounce of optimism drain from my body.

My dour attitude was in sharp contrast to Marcus's warm décor. In the morning light, his house was even cozier than I noticed last night. There was an herb garden, and multiple tomato plants that were flourishing, with tiny red tomatoes. I flinched a little when I saw Marcus walk out to pick some herbs. Like I'd caught him in his own intimate, perfect life. I couldn't help but wonder what my life would have looked like if I had a place all to myself. A house of my own.

Will's taste had become mine. His life was my life now.

I watched Marcus walk back inside, breaking me from my weird reverie. I got out of bed and slid back into my couture, realizing that this was threatening to become a strange not-walk-of-shame.

I came into the kitchen as Marcus put the finishing touches on a crepe-style omelet that looked so good I didn't even pretend I was going to pass up eating it. He slid a cup of espresso my way as I sat down and dug in.

"I called to have your car towed to Leroy Tire. Hope that's okay. You sleep all right?"

"Yes, thanks. It's quiet and away from the lake. Listening to all the frogs' nightly calls is something I didn't realize that I now take for granted."

"Yes, we simple people live without the frogs."

I blushed. "I didn't mean it that way."

"I'm teasing." Marcus plated his own breakfast and sat down next to me. "For those of us who didn't grow up with fuck-you money, it's like we're in the bubble but not *in* the bubble. Right? I'm just the chef they all want to say they know, but not the guy they're going to bring completely into the fold."

"Right. Interloping."

"It's not interloping when they give you a key and the combination to the safe, Nora."

I turned and looked at Marcus. He was right. I wasn't an interloper. I was invited in, given the access. And that realization made me even more mad at Will, who brought me in and now, in his own way, was treating me like the interloper that the rest of them acted as if I was.

No, no deal. I've got the combination to the safe.

"I should get home." I was calm, but there was a fire under the surface.

Marcus nodded and cleaned up the breakfast plates so he could take me home.

And a quick ten minutes later, he was depositing me at the top of my driveway.

"Thanks for everything."

"I hope you work it all out, Nora. But I'm around if you need . . . anything."

I smiled and watched as he drove away, but my smile faded when I realized I didn't know what I was going to say when I finally talked to Will. Still, I stalked up the driveway with unyielding purpose. I was so ready for whatever would come that I didn't see Este standing at the end of her driveway, taking in the whole scene.

CHAPTER 36

ELEVEN DAYS AFTER

Time is passing. I know that it is. Because I'm watching the sun move across my living room trying to think of something to do other than sleep or wander aimlessly from room to room. The funeral ended, people went back to their lives, and I am here. Sitting in this house, wondering what the hell is next. Wondering what the hell I am going to do. I haven't heard from Ardell. Fritz says we have to give Ardell space to do his job. Fritz also says I'm not supposed to leave my house.

What the fuck does Fritz know anyway?

"Wow, you're vertical." Este chases a mosquito out of the house and slides the door shut again. It's been so hot here the past few days, and I can feel the AC trying to keep up. The house has the edge of humidity to it.

"My back hurt from being in bed too long." I can feel Este eyeing me as I pull some last little wedge of a casserole out of my refrigerator. The kitchen counter is littered with dishes and half-full glasses of almost every different kind of beverage.

"Where's Alma?"

"There's a clause in her contract that she gets bereavement if someone dies. Ironic, isn't it?" I put the casserole in the microwave and dump out a few glasses, but putting them in the dishwasher feels too hard. At least they're in the sink.

I absentmindedly walk to the front window as Este goes over to finish the dishes for me.

That's when I see the police car pull into my driveway. And then another one. Then three more.

I should have seen this part coming.

"Uh . . . Nora . . . ," Este says.

Ardell gets out and a dozen officers exit the cars behind him. *They're coming for me.*

Ardell makes eye contact with me and holds my gaze. *I've got you now.*

I open the front door, and Ardell closes the distance, saying something that I think sounds like "official capacity," and then I'm sure I hear the words "search warrant."

The reporters are shouting questions from the street, and I'm horrified as Ardell hands me a piece of paper.

"Nora, we have a search warrant for the house and cars. Are both cars here?"

"What?"

"I'm sorry, but I'm going to have to ask you to step aside and not touch anything."

I look down at the piece of paper he's handed me, but I can't make out what it says. Este pulls it from my hand.

"Is this really necessary? What the hell are you looking for?"

"I'm afraid I can't discuss that with either of you."

Ardell nods back at his team and they all start filing in the house, none of them making eye contact with me. Out the window, I see a team of divers heading down toward the dock.

"Mrs. Somerset, you can't be here when they search the premises. Anyway, I'm going to need you to come to the station with me to answer some questions. I can drive you down."

Mrs. Somerset? Is he for real?

Este instinctively steps in front of me. "What for?"

"I need her to come down to the station with me, and I think it's best that she does so willingly."

"Am I under arrest?" I am so confused about what is happening.

The room is spinning a little and I don't really know what to do. I reach out to Este, my hand gently squeezing her arm.

"We just need you to answer some questions at the station."

"Oh. Okay. I, uh, just need to get my shoes," I say as I walk off dazed in search of some sneakers.

"Nora, you need to call Fritz," Este says behind me.

I don't want to.

"It's okay, Este. I'll just go with Ardell and then he will bring me home. Whatever this is will be over then." It's a weird turn for me to be placating Este.

I really hope it will be over by then. It has to be.

She looks like she's ready to lunge at Ardell and snap his neck. I slide into some shoes and grab my purse.

"Really, Este," I say. "It's fine. You stay here and close up when they leave."

It's the first time I have ever seen Este look genuinely scared. She reaches out and squeezes my hand. I squeeze back, wishing it was enough to reassure us both.

Walking to the car is chaos. The crush of reporters camped out at the edge of the neighborhood goes wild. I can hear pictures being taken and questions being hurled my way, but once the car doors slam shut, the air gets tense and quiet and stays that way for the duration of the trip to the station. Ardell doesn't say anything. I am certain he is now following some protocol, and while I am completely scared out of my mind, I am trying not to show it.

Ardell parks his cruiser toward the back of the lot and hurries me by the elbow to a back door, but a few photographers and press from the front of my house have clearly been on our heels, and I can hear them yelling my name.

Inside, we walk past a bunch of offices and down a hallway where Ardell stops and opens a door to a windowless room with a table and a few chairs around it. There's a metal loop in the middle of the table, presumably to hook handcuffs to.

"Is this really necessary?"

"I'm afraid so."

I feel my body go numb and start to tingle as I walk across the threshold into this room. My hands start to shake, and I know that there is nothing I can do to hide it. I sit down in the chair, unsure where to look.

"I'll be right back."

He walks out and closes the door, and I have to do everything in my power not to throw up all over the table. A few minutes pass before Ardell walks back in with a notebook and a bottle of water. He slides the water across the table to me and sits down, then puts a digital recorder in between us on the table.

"I need you to state your full name and date of birth, as well as acknowledge that you know that this conversation is being recorded."

This is bad. I have no alibi, and they know it.

"I'm, uh — " My voice is shaky and meek. I clear my throat and try again. "My name is Nora Davies Somerset. My date of birth is April 6th, 1996, and I'm aware that this is being recorded."

"Thank you." Ardell opens his steno pad and pulls a pen out of his suit jacket. "When was the last time you saw Will?"

"Haven't I already done this?"

"Yes, but I need you to do it again."

A blend of frustration and fear rushes through my bloodstream. "We had a party at the house for his birthday. After everyone had gone home, he and I were upstairs . . ."

Over the next five minutes, I do my best to recount the story of the night of the party exactly the way that I have told it since this all began.

Exactly the way it fucking happened.

Ardell listens with his eyes narrowed like he's focusing hard on me, and every now and then I'll say something that inspires him to scribble down a quick note. I catch myself trying to figure out the rhyme or reason to what gets jotted down.

"You said there's just a security camera on your doorbell, right?"

How do I explain that the richer people are the less security they seem to have? Sure, Este and Beau's place is all smart-housed to the gills, but that's because Beau likes to be able to run everything from his phone. Will could not have cared less about that kind of stuff.

I nod my head.

"That's weird, right?" Ardell says. "A big house like that and no cameras. Do any of your neighbors have cameras?"

"I don't know." I try to sound helpful as I ask, "Are you looking for something in particular?"

"We've got some new questions about that night."

"Like what kind of questions?" Under different circumstances, I would be thrilled. I have questions—God knows I have questions. But I'm in an interrogation room. And my house is being searched.

I feel my palms go clammy. How many cumulative hours has Lindy Bedford spent on cable news implying that Will is dead because of me, the young wife? Winter Park is small, and it is fueled by optics.

Is Ardell getting pressure to arrest me?

"Why don't you tell me what happened at the end of the night?" His pen stays at the ready in his hand, balanced over the notebook, which he angles away from my line of sight. "You were waiting for Will to come to bed, and you believe that you fell asleep around one A.M., but you don't have anyone who can corroborate that for you, right?"

"I was in bed, alone, yes. And because I was in bed, alone in my own house, where I live, it's accurate that I don't have anyone who can verify that. But I was alone. In bed. In my own house." I am not even trying to hide the defensiveness in my voice now.

"You didn't think it was strange that your husband never came back to bed?"

"Maybe I would have if I'd been conscious."

"And then you wake up, and he's still not there. Tell me about the next two days. What did you do then?"

I want to tell him to shut the fuck up, but I also want to avoid the inside of a jail cell. I purse my lips and say nothing.

"Look, Nora, I am going to level with you. We've had some evidence come to light—"

"What evidence?" I ask.

"I'm not at liberty to say."

"Then why am I here?"

"Because something very bad happened to Will."

"No shit, *Travis*. He's DEAD!" I slap my hands on the table between us.

Silence falls over the room, and I'm acutely aware that I'm in the middle of a storm.

"You think the evidence points to me," I say grimly.

Travis doesn't respond, and I look around, feeling the cameras, the two-way mirrors, the weight of suspicion bearing down on me.

I'm not the enemy here. I did not kill my husband. I did not kill Will.

The words finally come rushing out of me. "Why aren't any of you looking at Constance?"

"Constance?" Ardell says her name with an offensive level of incredulity.

"Yes. Constance. She didn't have a party the night of Will's party like everyone said she did. She doesn't have an alibi. No one can account for where she was. And she was angry. She yelled at her food delivery guy. I bet you could get the time from the delivery service, but that night, all her friends came to Will's house instead of being with her. That's a motive."

Ardell looks at me like I'm baby Bambi personified. So cute. So stupid. "Nora, Constance was one of the first people we questioned."

I wind my hands up as if to say "Spit it out."

"She does have an alibi. She was on a Zoom with her . . . well, her psychic for over four hours that night.

There's a ringing in my ears as my thoughts catch up to what Ardell's just said.

"And the psychic confirmed, and we've verified the times with Zoom. Apparently, they talk a lot."

Constance was home. She's going to be alibied by Madame Cleo.

And Marcus was right; I wasn't an interloper. I was the person who knocked Constance off her pedestal, sent her running to consult with the stars.

Constance is saved by some cosmic medium. What does that say about karma?

I shake off the disbelief and try to regroup. "What about Will's phone records?" I almost can't believe I'm mentioning it after how quickly Ardell shut down my questions about Dean, but it's the only card I have left to play. "What about that Mia call?"

"Oh, we know that you weren't honest about that call. It was never Mia."

He's going to turn that call around on me?

"I wasn't *dishonest* about the call," I say. "And I told you there were things to look into and you basically patted me on the head. So, about the call, Will told me it was Mia. If it wasn't her, who the hell was it?"

My heart is racing. I've been waiting a long time to hear the answer to this question, and Ardell looks over the folder in front of him like the answer is right there. I sit forward in my chair—waiting for him to say something.

He clears his throat. "Well—"

There's a knock on the door, and he gets up.

Fritz comes barging in. "Come on, Nora."

Behind him, I can see Este standing in the hallway, looking ready for a rumble if the situation calls for it.

I put up a hand to stop Fritz. "Just a second."

"Nora, stop talking. You're going home." Fritz has me on my feet and heading for the door, pulling hard on my elbow.

"Fucking *ow*! I want to hear this," I protest. "Ardell, who called?" I have to get this answer before Fritz inserts himself.

Ardell tries to get between Fritz and the door. "Fritz, I've got to talk to her—"

Fritz snaps a look in Ardell's direction. "Have you charged her with something?"

Ardell shakes his head, practically cowering.

Bad dog.

"We'll be going now."

Fritz stands next to me and then escorts me down the hallway with Este in tow. "I really hope you didn't say much. You should have asked for a lawyer."

I shake my arm loose from Fritz. "I didn't think I needed one, Fritz. I didn't *do* anything. And Ardell has information that might be helpful—"

"I fucking hope so. He's leading a murder investigation. You are not a detective. You are a housewife. Go to your house." His nostrils are flaring. "Este, take her home. The press is here, so I want to keep your face as hidden as possible, and don't let them get a good shot of you. I will talk to Travis."

I don't budge for a minute. I'm tired of being bossed around by Fritz Hall. He takes a step toward me and lowers his voice, "Nora, go the fuck home and stop talking to people without me."

I fold my arms and give him a mutinous glare.

"What's your plan here, Nora?" His voice is at the edge of taunting. "You want to cause a scene in the middle of the police station? You think that's going to help your case?"

Este steps between us and pulls me away. "Come on," she encourages in a gentle voice.

I go, because deep down, in the part of my rational mind that hates to admit Fritz is right, I know I can't get him to budge, and it would be a mistake to try to argue in such a public place.

Este offers me a sunhat, which I pull on and sling low over my face as I walk out the door without another word to Fritz.

We have to crawl through the crush of reporters, who are now desperate to get a shot of me. I'm curled up in a ball, back to the window, hat obscuring my face. Este expertly parks her car at an angle, so I can slide out directly into the garage, shielded from the press.

Este really does think of everything.

She gets out of the car, flipping off the reporters as she slips into the dark garage, and promptly closes the garage door.

I walk to the kitchen, hating the feeling that lingers in the air. The house looks almost normal—almost. But little things here and there are just out of place, moved or picked up by the officers sent to search the house. It feels like someone has just broken in, like someone is watching me.

I pick up two different prescription bottles.

"What are you doing, Nora?"

"Just going to head back into oblivion, thanks." My nerves are shot and I'm exhausted. I start to unscrew one of the bottles, thinking a three-hour nap might take the edge off, but Este slaps my hand down.

"No. No more Grey Gardens bullshit. This is serious now, and as much as it pains me to say it out loud, Fritz is right. Don't talk to anyone else. Not without him around."

I huff. But I know she's right.

"Did you see how many reporters are out there? They're mul-tiplying like fucking rabbits." I slump down onto the couch, and Este joins me. "I didn't do anything, Este."

"Oh, come on. You and I both know that doesn't matter now. You're the perfect poster child for people like Lindy Bedford to splash all over the news. 'Young, dumb, pretty wife is actually a young, dumb, pretty murderer.' America eats that shit up with a spoon. The whole world does. Give them a few more weeks and they're going to try and convict you on cable news before Ardell can move on to another suspect."

Fuck.

I pull out my phone and google my name to make a point. I stop dead when I see the first thing that pops up in Google search.

"What the—"

On my screen is a picture of me from the funeral, talking to Marcus. His hand is on the small of my back, and the headline blasts out that I'm a prime suspect in my husband's murder, look-ing "cozy" with an unidentified man. Even I think the photo makes me look suspicious, maybe even guilty of murder.

Este takes my phone and scrolls through a few pictures that are up on some rag-mag site. "This is why the press is all over your house and the station." She chucks the phone on a couch cush-ion. "These people live for a murder. And they are waiting with bated breath for you to be the one who did it, looking for all of the so-called evidence that they can get their hands on. They're going to sell a million magazines to a million murder-obsessed house-wives. And then the TikTok murder girlies are going to find you. Lindy's chumming the waters with every new broadcast. Some-one's going to start a fucking podcast."

She stops and takes a breath, and I can tell she's holding back the last thing she was going to say.

"What's wrong?" I demand.

Este shrugs it off. Shakes her head in an unconvincing no.

"Fuck you, Este. What's wrong?"

"I saw you one morning. Coming home. I saw Marcus drop you off at like six A.M." She looks at me and there's genuine sad-ness in her eyes. "I didn't want to tell you, or ask, but . . . those pictures, that morning. What's . . . going on there?"

"Fucking *nothing*." I'm pissed. I stand up and pace around in front of the fireplace. "Why didn't you just ask me? Or tell me that you saw me?"

"I didn't think you wanted to be seen, so I was waiting for you to tell me what was going on."

"The answer is still fucking nothing. Will and I had a shitty fight, a really shitty fight, and I left and was driving around, and I got a flat. I called Marcus for help. And then Will didn't bother to call me or find me, so I stayed at Marcus's. In the *guest* bedroom."

I can feel my blood pressure ticking up and don't want Este to know it, so I sit back down and hang my head in my hands. "That is all that happened," I say, my voice muffled through my fingers.

"I am going to ask you something one time, and whatever the answer is, I'm here. I'm your ride or die. Okay? But I have to know so I can help you."

I drop my hands and hold her gaze. I've never seen her look so serious.

"Are you in this? Did something happen?" she asks. "Are we talking about a murder weapon buried somewhere that we need to go make disappear? Maybe it was all just an accident. Something went too far in a heated moment? Just tell me and I'll get a shovel and a convertible, and we'll ride off into the sunset and no one has to know."

"You're really asking me this?" But I know I can't even be mad. The Marcus pictures, Constance's accusations, my nonexistent alibi. None of it looks good.

"A good friend holds your hand. A best friend gets the shovel."

"Este. Have you buried a body?"

"No. Have you?" she bandies back.

"I didn't kill Will, Este." I look at her and I hear myself panting. "I didn't kill him. I loved him . . . I think."

Is it possible to feel yourself coming unglued?

"Okay." Este must see the wild look in my eyes as a cry for help. She softens and puts a careful hand on my arm. "Sweetie. You're exhausted. And you smell a little bit like a police precinct."

"Hurtful."

"And still shockingly accurate." She gives me a little pat. "Go take a shower. I'll run home and figure out something for dinner."

A shower. Some food. I know Este is right. I have to find Will's killer before I end up taking the fall for his murder.

CHAPTER 37

BEFORE

I took advantage of the fact that Find My still showed Will was at the office when I got home. Walking past the pantry, I checked the floor for the puddle of glass and bourbon from the night before. It was gone, and so was the mess I had made getting his ill-fated short ribs ready. Everything was perfectly tidied. As if nothing had ever happened. He's a lawyer. He can't help himself. Evidence is evidence.

I headed upstairs to peel the day-old, rain-soaked, and then air-dried designer dress off and put it with the dry cleaning so Alma could run it up to the cleaners and help me bring it back to life. I gave it one last I-know-it-to-be-parting look before heading to the shower.

It's too bad. It really was a great dress. Now, I'll probably never wear it again.

I was already dreading seeing it hanging in my closet, thinking all the tears and bad energy from last night might have sunk into every careful stitch in the fabric. But I quickly shook the self-pitying thought off, remembering the pep talk Marcus had given me.

I'm not wallowing. I'm going to be assertive. I belong here as much as any of them. As much as Will.

I planned to confront him about it when he got home. I was

going to fight fair, but firm. It would be different this time because I wasn't going to leave things up to chance.

At least that was the little speech I was giving myself. Then almost without thinking, without hesitation, I opened the web browser on my phone and searched: *Winter Park divorce attorney.*

Stop it, Nora. What are you doing? It's not like the museum has called to beg you back.

Watching the results populate made my stomach hurt.

I'm not leaving. Who the hell would leave this?

No one in their right mind would walk away from this world. This life. But my younger self knew that you have to have contingencies. You have to have a plan B. My mother's only plan B was find another guy. Until that happened, the mornings I had to scoop her off the bathroom floor to make sure that I got to school on time were too many to count. While she could sink herself into another romantic story line, I couldn't be so naïve.

I didn't *want* to leave, but I had to know my options. I had to know that if I needed to go, I could, and that I wouldn't be left with a weird couture wardrobe and not much else. This world had taught me that you have to fight for what's yours. If Will was going to stay distant and cryptic and act out, I needed to be responsible. And I was so hurt by his inaction that I had to make a plan. I needed to know how to right things if they went wrong. And if this marriage was going sour, I was determined not to cower while it all played out.

I scanned reviews and logos, seeking something that looked professional and not sleazy. I scrolled past aggressive attorney taglines and revenge-driven slogans before I landed on one that was straightforward and simple.

With a shaking thumb, I clicked on the number.

"Fisher-Grant Family Law," a pinched female voice answered after a few rings.

"Hi . . ." My voice shook a little. "I would like to schedule a consultation with one of your attorneys?"

"Sure, dear. But this is just an answering service. Can I take down your contact information? I'll have someone return your call when the office reopens on Monday."

"Okay," I said before reciting my name and number.

As I hung up, I let out a big breath.

*There. You're just getting information. Getting information isn't be-
traying your husband. He's a fucking attorney. He doesn't have to call
anyone because he already knows all the information. I should at least
have some.*

I showered and pulled on leggings and a sports bra, thinking
a run before he got home would help me feel clearheaded.

Endorphins are good. Endorphins make you feel powerful.

Turning the corner to go downstairs, I walked straight into
Will.

"Fuck. You're home." I jumped back, startled.

"Hey," he said in a soft voice. "God, I'm so happy to see you."
He pulled me into him, and the hug was warm. But I was frozen,
keeping my arms at my sides. "You were right about everything."

He released me, and I looked up at him, perplexed.

He's contrite. I was not counting on contrite Will.

"What are you . . . ?" I frowned, taking in his face, expecting
him to be bleary-eyed, like someone who'd waited up all night for
me or something. But he wasn't. He was just sorry.

"I acted like an ass last night. I don't mean to shut you out.
I've just been so busy looking out for the future that I haven't
looked out for us. I fucked up."

"Fucked . . . up? Will, fucking up is forgetting an anniversary
or something. You threw a glass. It was scary and not okay."

"You're right. I'm so embarrassed." He nodded. "I've been
thinking about what you said. Maybe we should go away next
weekend. I'll have Autumn plan something for us. Let's go to the
beach. Why don't you go spend an offensive amount of money on
bathing suits?"

"The beach?" Twenty-four hours ago, I would have swooned
over this offer. But now . . . I can't just whisk off to someplace that
makes it all seem like problems can be blown away with fairy dust.
"We can't ignore last night, Will."

"I know. I was inconsiderate and childish, and I'm sorry."

"Why didn't you call? After I left, I mean. Don't you want to
know where I was all night?"

"I assumed you went to Este's to cool off. Didn't you?"

"I drove around most of the night," I lied. "I popped a tire
near Phelps Park. I had the car towed to Leroy Tire to get fixed."

My second lie.

Staying at Marcus's was innocent. I don't know why I was covering it up. I just didn't want to make things any worse than they already were.

He frowned in concern. "Why didn't you call me? I would have come to get you."

"What's going on at work, Will?" I parried.

He took in a long, drawn-out breath. "There's a big case—Martinez. If we handle it the right way, it could be an earth-shattering win. Eight or nine figures. A career milestone. Maybe I could slow down, and we could spend more time together. But Fritz keeps trying to let his ego get in the way of things. All he sees is dollar signs. I'm having to manage him *and* the case. It's twice the work. Sometimes three times."

"That's the case Gianna mentioned at dinner," I said.

"Fritz shouldn't be running his mouth about cases at home."

"Fritz's ego getting in the way isn't exactly new."

"True. But when there's tens of millions of dollars on the line, the stakes *and* his ego are . . . heightened. He keeps trying to insert himself, and if I don't keep him on a short leash, we're going to end up with a fraction of what the case is worth. It takes patience to work a case like this up. Not a strength of his." He put his arms around me. "None of that is an excuse. I'm so sorry, Nora."

I looked at him for a long minute. I was grateful to be let into the conversation, but I couldn't overlook his bad behavior. "Will," I said. It was equal parts a plea and a warning.

"I love you."

"I love you, too. But if you ever pull shit like last night again, I'm leaving, and I will not come back. Not ever."

He kissed the spot on my forehead where my hairline begins. "If I ever pull shit like last night again, I'll handpick your divorce attorney. Just to make sure I get taken to the cleaners. Because I'll deserve it for fucking something this important up."

I laughed a little.

Damnit, Nora.

He was saying all the right things, but something still didn't sit right. I wanted to believe my hesitance was just the regret-hangover from the fight.

He kissed my cheek. "It's a beautiful day."

"Maybe so."

"You want to take the boat out for some fresh air?" He kissed my other cheek. "I don't need to work anymore this weekend."

"No," I huffed in fake annoyance.

His brows knitted.

"I was prepared to have a big conversation and tell you that you were wrong. And I was going to be so respectful and mature and tell you I belong here just as much as you. And you can't shut me out anymore."

"You're right," he said softly.

"I had a lot of really good things I was going to say."

"I want to hear them."

"Well, you're just taking the wind out of my sails completely."

"You want to do this over? I could go out and come back in. We can start from the beginning, and you can say all the things you want to say. I promise to agree with you."

"When you say it like that, it sounds like overkill."

"Do you really think you don't belong here?"

I shrugged. "People say something to you often enough, it gets easier and easier to believe it."

"Fuck them. You belong with me. Don't let anyone tell you otherwise."

"I just wish other people saw it that way."

"Oh, Nora. These people are wretches. Trying to win their affection is Sisyphean. They don't like people. They like shiny things—diamonds, private jets, black cards. But how about this? I will throw you a party. Ply my nearest and dearest friends with alcohol until they fall in love with you. It wouldn't take much. You're easy to love and my friends are all lushes."

I stifled a laugh, warming up to him again. "What about your birthday? You're going to be forty-six soon."

He looked up at the ceiling for a second. "Don't remind me."

"I could throw you a party. *And* ply your friends with alcohol until they fall in love with me. Think of it as strategic altruism."

He snorted as he brushed my hair away from my face. "Would that make you happy?"

"Celebrating you? Or being beloved? Because I'm mostly in it for the second thing."

He laughed as he kissed my neck. "I'll ask Autumn to give you a call this week. She'll have people eating out of your hand by the time they cut the cake."

I stared at him for a beat, letting him wonder if I was in, even though I was sure he knew I was.

"Now, can we go to bed?" he murmured into my ear. "I've got a few other ways to make it right with you as well."

It might have been wrong to fall back into his arms so quickly. But love makes you do crazy things. As he slid a warm hand under my shirt, I began to mentally erase the darkness from the last twenty-four hours.

Fuck it. I'm his.

And my little lies about Marcus faded into the background.

CHAPTER 38

THIRTEEN DAYS AFTER

I turn on the TV in the bedroom while I'm waiting for the shower water to heat up. I tell myself it's opposition research while I'm pacing and rerunning my conversation with Ardell at the police station. It takes effort not to flinch at the photo of me and Marcus as Lindy Bedford flashes it up on the screen for the umpteenth time. As I step under the hot water, Lindy Bedford's voice is jabbering on in the background, echoing off the shower glass. Este's right. I can't shut out what they're saying about me or hide from the fact that I might be one step away from being arrested for murder.

What the hell happened that night? How did Will and I end up like this?

"We're told this man, Marcus Campbell, owns and operates a very popular restaurant in Winter Park. And the way they're standing next to each other in the photo, you have to wonder, just how close are these two? And does the chef know anything about what happened to Will Somerset that night?" Lindy says. "We'll be joined by a body language expert after the break."

A fucking body language expert. Is this a joke? There must be bigger news happening elsewhere. What's the karma of praying for a natural disaster at a time like this?

I kill the shower water and have just started to dry off when I hear the trilling of my phone. It's Fritz.

"Shit." I pause for a second, wanting to duck the call, but I know I can't. "Hello?"

"Nora, Ardell called. They have the murder weapon."

"What?"

The murder weapon?

I feel dizzy. A fog of disbelief settles around me, and I want to curl up in a ball. But I remember what Este said.

Pay attention.

Fritz exhales a heavy sigh. "The divers found it buried in the mud under your dock."

"What was it?" I ask.

He hesitates before saying, "A hammer."

I'm gripping the phone so hard that my fingers go numb. I stand in my bathroom, naked, water pooling all around my feet.

"I want to see it," I finally say, trying to make my voice sound assertive.

"That's not going to happen. Forensics has it now."

A fucking hammer.

I squeeze my eyes shut, trying to block out the mental images that rush forward. No matter what I do, though, I can't stop *imagining* the sound of a hammer making contact with someone's head. Will's head.

Fritz walks me through a few scenarios of what could happen.

"Hopefully, there's nothing that could tie the hammer to you," he says. And it's not at all comforting.

I feel lightheaded at the thought of Will being attacked, of him enduring such a violent death. I put a hand out and hold on to the wall to make sure I stay upright.

"Nora," Fritz calls through the line. "You still there?" He sounds almost annoyed.

I hang up and my hands are shaking. My memory flashes to the last time I had seen someone with a hammer.

Fucking hell. This is not real.

CHAPTER 39

BEFORE

"Hey, Nora," Beau called from what appeared to be a scattered pile of lumber as I crossed the distance from my backyard to his and Este's. "You look great."

Este was on a lounge chair in a bathing suit and sarong, reading a book about Eastern healing. "That's because she's got that dreamy love glow after a long weekend at the Breakers."

I looked down at my sundress. It wasn't anything out of the ordinary, but maybe I was smiling a little bigger than usual. After our epic fight, Will had booked an oceanfront suite at the famed hotel, and we spent four days on the sandy coast of Palm Beach. After months of feeling lonely and cut out of his life, it seemed like that rocky season of our marriage was finally coming to an end. Will was attentive and supportive again. Even after we got back from Palm Beach, he had made time to eat dinner with me a few times a week. I wasn't too surprised that Beau could see the lightness of relief on my face.

The setting sun reflected a glare off the lake that made me squint as I looked back at Beau. "What are you working on?"

He gestured proudly at the pile of tools and supplies surrounding him. "Planter boxes for the garden."

"They'll be ready in three to five years," Este chimed in.

Beau fired back, "What's that healing book say about negative energy, Este?"

She rolled her eyes. "Hey, stranger." Este patted the chaise next to her. "Come sit with me."

"Stranger?" I dropped into the chair. "I saw you three hours ago at yoga."

"Yeah, but we haven't done dinner in forever. You've been too busy making heart eyes at Will."

I had been making heart eyes at Will most nights. But even on the nights that he had a work commitment or some late-night brief to write, I steered clear of dinner at Este and Beau's. I hadn't seen Marcus since the night I stayed at his place. And dinner with Este and Beau meant I might run into him. And then I might have to talk about that awful fight again.

We've moved on. I'm not looking back.

"It's good to have you back. Can I get you a drink?" Beau offered on his way to the house. "Marcus is making margaritas in the kitchen."

"Marcus is here?" My stomach lurched.

"You think I'd let Beau use power tools without adult supervision? I made him show me where his living will is before I even let them go to the hardware store."

I tried to laugh, but it wasn't convincing. "I'll pass on the margarita, but thanks."

Este handed me her glass of rosé with a knowing expression. "Take this. I'll go get another."

What was that? Did Marcus tell Este I stayed at his place? No, I don't think he would do that. And if he did, I'm pretty sure she would have let herself into my house at any hour of the day or night to get to the bottom of the story.

The look was gone by the time she returned with a fresh glass of wine in her hand.

She settled back into her lounger and took a sip of her drink. "How's the planning for Will's birthday party coming?"

"Oh, God." I sighed, touching my forehead with one hand. "Autumn keeps sending me Pinterest boards. I feel like my head's going to explode. She keeps asking me about table linens and color palettes. I mean, fuck. I didn't even know drink menus needed an aesthetic."

"Jesus, this town is the worst sometimes. Drink menus don't need an aesthetic." Este snickered. "What the hell does that even mean? Sounds like she's just padding her hourly rate so she can charge you a fee every time she gets the urge to google 'twinkle lights.'"

"It seemed like the right idea at the time, but I'm starting to dread it."

"It's going to be fine. I'll be there, and Beau will bring weed if you want."

I stifled a laugh. "When doesn't he bring weed?"

"You know . . ." Este shifted in her seat to face me. "You should see if Marcus will cater this fête."

Another look.

Does she know something?

It's not like Este to be coy. Still, I saw her watching my face for a reaction, but I kept my expression neutral.

"I'll let Autumn handle that." I waved the thought off casually. "I'm pretty sure she thinks I'm where logistics go to die for this party. And I don't want to mess up all of her spreadsheets and planning documents."

"What a nut."

"She's *nice.*"

"She and Carol Parker might as well be best friends. I bet they're planning a trip to Magnolia Farm together or something equally clichéd and sad. And the way she worships the old biddies at the Garden Club. It's all a bit fucking much."

"Not everyone can afford to fuck off to a private island if being a member of the civilized world doesn't pan out for them, Este. Some people have to go along to get along."

"Touché." She sipped her drink with an unapologetic smile.

"Hey, Nora," a familiar voice called out. "Did you come to lend a hand?"

I turned around and smiled as nonchalantly as possible. Marcus was wearing a pair of beaten-up jeans and holding a hammer by the head. "Hey, Marcus," I said.

I don't need Este clocking my reticence.

But the way she could read a room was practically preternatural. She stood and grabbed her glass of wine. "I'm going to go check on Beau. He said he was looking for drill bits, and I'm not even sure he knows what that means."

"Do you?" I asked.

She waved me away with a good-natured smile. "Fuck off."

Marcus and I both laughed mildly. But I wanted to beg her not to leave. I couldn't, of course. It would be too dramatic. The impulse was there all the same.

Marcus put the hammer down on Este's chair and then sat facing me with his elbows on his knees. "How've you been? We've missed you at dinners."

"I've been good." I took a sip of my wine and tried to avoid his sight line. "Busy. We went to Palm Beach."

"I've been worried about you."

I frowned. "Why?"

"When I dropped you off, I just wasn't sure how that was going to work out for you."

"We're not going to talk about *that*." I looked back at our house, feeling paranoid, as if somehow Will had superhero hearing and might catch the edges of this conversation. I know it was dumb, but going to Marcus's had been foolish.

He looked confused and maybe even hurt. "What? Why not?"

"Because I don't *want* to," I hissed. "Did you tell Este anything?"

"No!"

"She keeps looking at me like she knows."

"Knows about what?"

I look at him like it should be obvious.

"Deflecting. Again."

Now I'm getting annoyed. "That's not funny anymore."

"I'm not kidding."

"What do you want to know?" My hands started for my hips, but I stopped them. If I took that posture, I would have to explain it to Este later. I'd seen her wandering by the window twice.

Marcus pushed his hands through his hair. "I've been worried is all. Did you stick up for yourself? Did you get what you need?"

"We're perfectly happy now." It came out a little haughtier than I intended, and I felt guilty. Marcus had never been anything but kind to me. "It wasn't that bad. It was just a fight. Married people fight."

"Yeah. They fight, but they tend to avoid property damage."

"Okay. We are *definitely* not talking about that."

I immediately regretted that I'd told him about the smashed glass. That's not something you can untell someone. Especially someone like Marcus.

His expression grew wounded. "So, you just let him off the hook then?"

"I said what I needed to say, and he agreed."

"And then he took you on a trip and you forgot all about how miserable you've been for months?"

"What's your point?"

"Stop letting Will bribe you, Nora. Stop giving him all the power just because he has money."

"He didn't bribe me. I was not bribed."

Was I?

I had been floating on a cloud since the beach trip. Marcus was yanking me back down to earth, and I kind of hated him for it.

"What do you want me to say, Marcus? And why are you so caught up in what happens in my marriage? Don't you think it's a little strange?" I narrowed my eyes at him.

Congratulations, Nora. You've hopped the median and now you're headed the wrong way in the express lane to the low road.

"I'm sorry," I said and took a breath. "I am trying to make it work. I am trying so hard."

"Who told you it should be this hard?"

I took a sip of my drink, regretting how much Marcus knew about that night. Wishing it was just something Will and I could bury.

"Have you thought about how this works out for you if you succeed at making things work?" he asked. "You asked me what you should do. Have you thought about what you really want? I mean, kids? What about art? Or art school? Do you want anything for yourself?"

What I want is to keep my manicured life together. If I walk away, all of this goes away. I have no job and no savings, and I live nowhere. Not to mention the most important thing, no Will. And I love him.

"I'll figure it out. I have the combination to the safe, right?"

"Sure." He shrugged. "So, are you going to use it?"

"What does that mean?"

"It means: You deserve the things you want in your life, and you don't have to bow down to these people to get them."

"I'm not," I snapped back.

He raised his hands in surrender. "All right, Nora."

Shit. This isn't Marcus's fault. I called him that night.

"Marcus, I didn't—I'm—"

Este stepped back out on the deck, looking back and forth at the two of us.

"Hey, Marcus?" she called. "The oven's making a weird beeping sound." She waved her hand around, blissfully unaware of how anything in her kitchen worked. And, I hoped, unaware of the disagreement Marcus and I had just had.

Marcus picked up the hammer and headed back toward the house.

CHAPTER 40

THIRTEEN DAYS AFTER

I killed the call with Fritz and flew into action, making no effort to dry off. The black T-shirt I had yanked on as I was running for the door is wet and sticking to my skin. The next thing I know, I'm banging on the service door of Lemon & Fig—my hair still stringy and knotted from the shower.

About a minute into my nonstop fist rapping, Marcus swings the door open on a wild-eyed, drowned-cat version of me standing in the back alley of his restaurant. The clock in the galley says it's just after 11:00 A.M.

"Nora." His face is stricken by the sight of me. "Come in. Are you okay?" He gently pulls me by the arm into a dry storage area of the kitchen, sending my eyes down to his toned forearms. I picture him holding the hammer. He's strong enough to pull it off. The thought makes me recoil, and I draw my arm back and wrap it around my waist.

"What time did you leave my house?" I shrug off his grip.

He frowns. "When?"

"The night of the party. The night Will died, Marcus. How late were you there?"

"I don't know. Maybe midnight?"

"Maybe?" I don't disguise my incredulity.

"What the fuck are we talking about here, Nora?"

"You were so upset about the fight with me and Will and the glass. Did you try to talk to him about it? Did you two get into a fight and something happened?"

Marcus's face falls. "Are you asking me if I—"

"Everyone thinks I did it, but what about you? You were there and you didn't like Will very much after I told you about that fight."

"Nora . . ." He shakes his head slowly. "You need to go home."

Marcus is the most benevolent person I know. Even now. Even when I've rushed over to his restaurant to accuse him of murder, he's not angry, but I can tell he's wounded.

Of course he is. What am I doing? Am I actually accusing him of murder?

My lower lip starts to tremble, and I rub at my face. "Fuck." I cover my eyes as the tears rush down. "I'm sorry."

"Yeah." He shakes his head. There's a distance in the way he looks at me that makes it clear I've fucked up. Again. "Hey. What's a murder accusation between friends?" The sarcasm in his voice stings.

Keeping my face hidden, I say, "Everyone is talking about me. Everyone thinks I killed him." I already know I've taken this too far. But I can't stop myself. "They think I *killed* him, Marcus. I have to ask you—"

"I didn't kill him, Nora!" The boom in his voice startles me, and I drop my hands to look at him. The stormy expression in his eyes hollows me out. "Are you happy now?"

But even in his anger, there's something about the way he says my name that makes my heart ache. Maybe it's just that there's an underlying tone of . . . he *actually* cares. He cares and I keep hurting him.

"You're right. I should go."

He doesn't move to follow me, but I can feel his glare on my back. As I slip back into the alley, I wonder if he'll ever forgive me.

Getting into Marcus's restaurant unnoticed was easy once I found the alley where shops and restaurants on his strip receive deliveries and let in service teams. But getting to my car is going to be another story. Parking on Park Avenue is always at a premium, so I had to take what I could get when I found a street spot near the park.

I put on my oversize sunglasses in the alley and skulk back toward Park Avenue to retrace my steps. I keep my head down and my eyes on the sidewalk to avoid catching anyone's attention. But when I see the black scalloped Chloé ballerina flats headed straight for me, I know I'm a goner.

"Nora?" a saccharine-sweet voice trills. "Is that you? Goodness. I almost didn't recognize you."

Fuckity fucking fuck.

I look up and see Gianna and her pack of tennis twits. They all fake-smile at me with barely restrained abhorrence. They are gleefully mainlining my demise. I bet they record Lindy's program while they're up at the club drinking spritzes.

Never mind the fact that someone died. They're burning a second wife at the stake! Grab the popcorn!

I take small comfort in the fact that Constance isn't with them today to witness my humiliation. She's been lying low since the funeral. Probably because Fritz told her to, and she's a better listener than I am.

"Hi," I respond, wishing to sink into the sidewalk.

Gianna doesn't miss a trick, looking me all the way up and down before she makes a *tsking* sound. "You're too young to just give up on your appearance, dear."

"Touché, Gianna," I concede, knowing better than to bring a knife to a gunfight. Where the gunfight is trying to defend myself in front of Gianna and her minions, and the knife is the clumps of conditioner that might still be in my hair. "It's good to see you."

She makes a noncommittal "hmm" sound. "I'm surprised to see you. Fritz said you were trying to keep a low profile."

The iciness in her eyes informs me the gloves are off. Now that Will's funeral is behind us, I can either fade into the background or expect to be confronted with what she really thinks of me—thoughts she only vaguely showcased when Will was around to protect me.

"I had to pick something up." I gesture behind myself at nothing in particular and hope she won't notice the fact that I'm empty-handed.

"At Lemon and Fig?" She smirks. "Do you really think that's wise? Did Will know you and Marcus were so . . . close?"

I will not punch Gianna Hall in public. I will not punch Gianna Hall in public.

"This has been . . . *fun*," I mutter. "But I have to go."

"I would want to get home, too, if I were in your current state."

I move past Gianna and her posse and pick up the pace to get to my car, dying on the inside the whole way.

CHAPTER 41

Driving back to my house, I am simultaneously beating myself up over accusing Marcus and trying to figure out what my next play is going to be. Processing the public shaming from Gianna will have to wait.

I have to find a way to prove I didn't do this. I have to find out who did.

There's a missed call from Perry on my phone, and I try him back, but it goes to voicemail. Pulling into my driveway reminds me why I can't just drive around to try to find him. The reporters and press trucks that have flocked to Winter Park to cover Will's murder are everywhere, but the center of their operation seems to be the entrance to the Isle of Sicily. They snap frantic photos of me and yell as I drive past them now. Their energy is voracious, their breath bated. It's clear they understand that I'm the prime suspect and they want B-roll for the six o'clock news.

I would love to give Lindy Bedford the same treatment she gives to others. Splash her name all over the tabloids for being so close to something spectacularly terrible. Though, sadly, she probably enjoys attention of any variety. She chose her line of work for a reason.

God, when she gets the intel about the hammer . . .

I'm not sure anyone can do anything for me now. Except maybe Perry. I need to know if he called because he found something.

When I get inside, Este is in the kitchen.

"Hey," I say.

"You okay? Marcus just called and asked me to come check on you."

I sigh. "Yeah. I'm okay."

"He said you stopped by the restaurant looking pretty upset. I thought you were showering."

"I was, but then I got a call."

"Did the caller tell you to go accuse Marcus of murder?" She folds her arms. I am being scolded, and I probably deserve it.

I definitely deserve it.

"He mentioned that?"

"Marcus is a golden retriever in human form, he wouldn't—"

"I know. It's like every time I think I've hit rock bottom there's a mini-earthquake and a new layer of low opens just for me," I say. "It was wrong. I'll apologize, but listen, I need to find Perry. I'm pretty sure Will hired Dean to look into me."

"About what?" Este's eyes go wide.

"Maybe the Marcus thing? If you saw me getting out of his car early in the morning, maybe Will did, too. I have no idea." My brain catches up to my mouth. "But none of it might matter now. They have the murder weapon."

"What? How? Where?"

"A hammer. Under my dock."

"That sounds bad."

"It's bad."

"Like really bad."

"Yes, the level of badness knows no bounds, Este. That's why I need to find Perry, see if he's found anything."

"Well, then, how much do you love me?"

"The most?"

"Perry is staying at the Citrus Inn on Lee Road. I'll drive."

My jaw drops. "Why do you know that?"

"You sent him away in a bit of a . . . state after Will's funeral, and I got his information as he was leaving."

Everyone should have an Este.

The hotel is only about fifteen minutes away, but it takes us almost as long to get past the reporters.

"Damnit." Este inches her car slowly out of the driveway. "We've got to start sneaking through the hedge to my house. The last thing we need is to run over one of these asshole's feet."

"But it'd feel kind of nice if you did."

She giggles and so do I—nothing has been funny about the press being camped in front of my house. The thought of smashing a few toes sounds delightful.

It should be said that not every square foot of Winter Park is historic sprawling mansions and aspirational McMansions. And the houses get lower and smaller as we drive away from the Vias. The Citrus Inn is just a block from Eatonville, the oldest black-incorporated municipality in the country, and the town where Zora Neale Hurston grew up. It's a tight-knit community beloved for its charm and history.

But none of that charm can be felt at the Citrus Inn. The motel is more of a sad relic of another era in Florida than anything else. One so old that they actually *do* have a pink flamingo in the patch of grass in front of the entrance. Ironic or not, I applaud their moxie.

We bypass a small building that houses a check-in desk and pull into the parking lot. All of the rooms have exterior-facing doors, and Este spots Perry's gray sedan parked beside one. "My guess is he's a first-floor guy. Probably has at least one busted knee."

"Hey. Maybe don't call him weird and old like last time?"

"Don't you think that if I could censor myself I would?"

"I do not think that. No."

"Fine. I'll do my best."

I climb out of the car, see the gray sedan I've come to know so well, and take the chance of knocking on the door it's parked in front of. We wait a minute, and no one answers. Este rolls her eyes and knocks much more loudly. A moment later, an exhausted look-ing Perry cracks open the door.

"Nora. What are you doing here?" Over his shoulder, Lindy Bedford is on a muted TV with another talking head. I see a picture of Will pop across the screen, and then one of me walking into the police station.

Neat.

I can't get sucked into self-pity, though. I launch into my apol-

ogy speech, knowing I need to make things right with Perry before I even consider asking him for a favor.

"Perry, I'm really sorry for the way I lost it the other day. The
funeral and everything just got to me, and I felt really bad."

"Oh, there's no need . . . no need to apologize. I can't imagine
what all you're going through. But I'm glad you're here. I was able
to collect Dean's personal effects from the hospital yesterday. Do
you want to come in?"

Perry moves out of the doorway and motions us inside the
room. He quickly tidies up the bed and turns off the TV. He moves
some clothes off the couch and motions for us to sit. He's been
living here for two weeks now, just trying to help his friend. The
gloom is practically wafting off the old polyester curtains hanging
around his windows.

"Aren't those a fire hazard?" Este whispers.

"Shh," I hiss. "Clearly, you've seen what's going on with me,
Perry." I motion toward the now blank screen on the TV.

He shakes his head. "I'm not sure I've ever seen anything
quite like this town. Seems a lot of these people have more money
than sense."

Este snickers.

"You're not wrong, Perry." I offer a faint smile. "And I'm obviously in a bit of a bind. So, I was hoping that you might still be
willing to talk to me, despite what the news says—"

"She didn't kill Will, obviously—"

"Thanks, Este." I look at her, sternly. "But the police have
taken a shine to Lindy Bedford's young-wife-killed-her-rich-
husband storyline, and we need to know what you know so that
we can find out who did this. So, Perry, I'm really hoping you've
been able to find something that can help."

He sighs the way he talks, long and drawn out. "It took some
doing, and my friend with the phone company might lose their
job for this. It wasn't Mia who called Will that night. The call came
from Fritz Hall's phone."

All the air leaves my lungs.

Finally . . . the one thing I had to know.

"Fritz? Are you sure?" I gasp.

Perry nods, like he really hates to be the bearer of such bad
news.

Este and I trade glances, and my brain is already racing as I try to digest this information. "I don't follow."

But maybe I do?

When Ardell interrogated me at the precinct, he said Mia hadn't called Will. He hadn't said *who* called—before Fritz stormed in.

All the acrimony between Will and Fritz over the last few months runs through my mind. They seemed to be disagreeing about everything.

Was it bad enough that Fritz would kill Will?

I hear Will's voice in my head. *Fritz is going to bury me if I don't clean up the mess he's made.*

"Well, the, uh, thing I had found on my own was that there were some calls between Fritz and Dean in the phone records I got ahold of, but that's not much of anything to go on. From the look of it, Dean was running down all kinds of different angles about Fritz. Affairs, business dealings, all of it. Will wanted Dean to take a hard look at Mr. Hall."

Perry's words land on me like a ton of bricks. Dean was looking into Fritz.

Which means Will was looking into Fritz. Why?

I am up and pacing.

"What are you thinking, Nora?" Este asks.

"The night of the party. Will and Fritz were arguing. It was heated and I didn't catch the context, but they had been fighting for months. Will said they were at odds over some big case and how to handle it. Maybe it came to a head that night at the party. But why would he lie and say Mia called?"

Perry shakes his head, clueless about that as well.

"How long did they talk?" Este perks up and leans in.

Perry shuffles through some papers he has on a nearby table and pulls up a phone record, flipping through the pages until he lands on the night of Will's birthday party.

For a heart-rending second, I hear Will in my head from that night. He was so happy. *I have a good feeling about forty-six.*

"It looks like they talked for about forty seconds."

What did Fritz say? Did he tell Will to meet him on the dock? Or did they go somewhere else?

"What the hell does that mean?" Este throws up her hands.

I look at her. "I have no idea. We have to find out why Will asked Dean to dig into Fritz. There must be more there."

Perry nods. "I agree."

"I'll go to Will's office and see if I can find anything."

"I will keep digging, too."

"Won't Fritz be at the office?" Este asks.

"Not this time of day. This is about the time he posts up at the bar at the club for his 'afternoon meetings.' Drop me by the house, Este?"

Este lobbies hard to come with me, but I hold my ground. I have to do this myself. I'm not sure if it's the blinding rage of knowing that Fritz has a hand in what happened, or my own desperation to do something to find justice for Will. Either way, I hope Will would be proud of me for taking matters into my own hands. It's what he would have done.

Get ready, Fritz. I'm headed straight at you.

CHAPTER 42

I park out front of the Hall & Somerset office, taking note of the fact that Fritz's car isn't here, and head inside. Lenore is at her desk, scanning and filing the mountain of papers in front of her.

"Nora, dear, Fritz isn't here."

"It's okay. I came to see if I could get some of Will's personal things from his office. He has a few photos here that I love and wanted to take home." It sounded good in my head. I hope she buys it.

"Of course. Let me get the key."

Lenore leads me back to his office and unlocks the door. I walk inside for the first time since Will was found. I heave a dramatic sigh, hoping Lenore will observe my grieving widow act and give me some space, but my heart actually aches.

The main office phone rings from Lenore's desk.

"Let me go grab that, and I'll come back with a box for you."

"Thank you so much."

I guess I shouldn't be surprised Lenore leaves me unattended. I had been expecting it to be a little harder to get time alone in the office.

But they all underestimate me. I'm just the young, dumb, pretty wife.

I watch Lenore turn the corner and know that my unsupervised time is limited. I open a few of Will's filing cabinets searching for anything to do with the Martinez case. Most of what he does is digital now anyway, but I'm hoping there might be one of Lenore's perfectly cataloged hard-copy backups in the drawer that I can just grab. Coming up empty, though, I abandon the cabinets and turn back to Will's desk, opening his drawers. I found that Post-it before; maybe there are other treasures here for me?

The top right drawer has a bunch of ties I had bought him for the next time he spilled coffee or chewed through the ink cartridge on a pen. I pull out my favorite one, pale purple with tiny dogs on it. My subtle hint that maybe we could have a dog. Will missed the intimation. The lower drawers are full of random files that I'm sure give Lenore a headache. But when I slide open the bottom right drawer, something catches my eye. There's a folder with the logo from Mia's school on it.

Odd.

Constance is the keeper of Mia's stuff at school. That was decided on in the divorce. And this folder looks "school official." I pull it out, flip it open, and find a bunch of papers about the Martinez case with Will's sloppy handwriting all over them. There's a page of what looks like phone numbers, or maybe account numbers. I am reading so fast and it's all so jumbled and I'm terrified that Lenore is coming back in here—I can hear her squeaky pumps heading down the hallway.

I close the folder and shove it into my bag and start winding up the ties that I've pulled from the other drawer. Lenore walks in with a small box and a big box.

"Sorry about that—nervous client. I wasn't sure what size box you needed?"

"Oh, the small one should work."

I put the ties in the box, walk over to the shelf, and start pulling down some pictures, some awards of Will's. None of these are things I even sort of need to memorialize Will, but that is beside the point.

I need to fill this box to hide what I'm sneaking off with.

I grab a photo of Will and Fritz. They're younger and Fritz's face is thinner—he looks almost fit. Both are smiling wide and full of vim and vigor.

"I always loved that one," Lenore pipes up.

"Really? Why?"

"It was taken right after they won their first big case. They were so proud. It was a good day."

I thumb the picture frame and add it to the box. "Seems like they had easier times back then."

"Everything is easy in the beginning."

Tell me about it.

She lingers in the doorway, and I know this is my chance.

"I have to ask," I say. "I feel like things got worse since this Martinez case happened. Or maybe I was just misreading things?"

"Every case is a living, breathing organism, Nora. They take on lives of their own. It's not always easy to navigate through them."

"Right. Of course. I just wonder if it was something bigger. More than just the case?"

Lenore straightens up a little. "I'm not sure why you're worried about any of these things now, Nora. Fritz will handle all that."

Shit. I've lost her.

"Oh, I know. I was curious because I know they were struggling—"

"Nothing they wouldn't have figured out. I'm sorry for all of this, Nora. I'm sorry that you're stuck in the middle. I saw that the police had brought you in for questioning."

She's showing me who is boss.

"Just some routine things," I say.

"Have you found the pictures you want? I think we should close up this office and let Fritz get all of the *work* files out of here before you come back."

"Yeah. I just wanted these few things."

I pick up the box and add my bag to it. I feel like Lenore is eyeing it, wishing she had X-ray vision to see inside. I shift the box on my hip so that my bag slides deeper inside.

"Thank you so much, Lenore. I'll head out."

I walk out of the building to my car, adrenaline surging as I put the box on the floor of the passenger side. As I walk around to the driver's side, I look up at the window and see Autumn.

What's she doing at the firm now? I'm sure they can't be throwing a party so soon after Will's funeral.

She must be carrying out one of Gianna's insane quarterly design and décor updates to Fritz's office, or changing out the flowers. Will and Fritz had asked Lenore to do that exactly one time before, and she had let the flowers wilt until someone commented about the smell, making it clear that she was the gatekeeper. Not the gardener.

I shake it off and get in the car. I've got a file burning a hole in my bag.

Once I'm home, I use our dining room table to spread out every single piece of paper from the random folder I swiped. Most of it doesn't make sense to me. But one page has what I think is an account number circled and *Dean?* written next to it. Another paper seems to be some email regarding the Martinez case that is so steeped in legalese it's lost on me, but at the bottom of the page, something catches my eye. Scrawled in Will's handwriting it just says: *Talk to Autumn.*

Autumn? Was that just a random side note about something else? His party, maybe?

The French door by the pool opens, and Este comes through it.

"You're back. What did you find? I've been texting you and you didn't answer."

"Sorry, I found a folder. Something about this Martinez case, but of course, thanks to Will's chaotic organization, I don't really get what any of it is. I think this might be an account number. I texted it to Perry. We'll see."

"Look at you, Angela Lansbury. That transition from wife to retired widow detective happened fast."

"Shut up. Something strange is going on, and I have to figure out what."

"I mean. Fritz is an ass, but do you really think he's a killer?" Este surveys my haul.

I shake my head and say, "I don't know. But, more important, why did Will hire a PI from his hometown? Someone who would be loyal to him? Someone with no ties to Winter Park?" She's turning this over when I add, "Fritz is friendly with every cop, every judge, every anyone that matters. If Will was looking into him with someone local, Fritz would have found out."

"But they all liked Will better. The ones with taste anyway."

"This must have been too serious to take the chance."

"You think Will had something on Fritz and Fritz found out?"

"It would have to be big. No chance Fritz could run that firm without Will. And he knows it. He always left his biggest messes for Will to clean up."

I flip another piece of paper over and see a note around some circled numbers: *Autumn.* I don't make a thing of it, don't show it to Este. I can't listen to her long list of grievances against Autumn.

"What's this?" Este pulls at a little piece of something that is stuck to the inside of one of the folder pockets and holds up a grainy photograph of a very cozy-looking Fritz and Autumn. I snatch it from her.

Autumn and Fritz?

I drop the photo back on the table like it might be hot to the touch. "Holy. Shit."

Este huffs out a short guffaw.

They're having an affair? For how long? And why the fuck would Autumn do that to herself? And if Will knew, how does this factor into all of the fights Will and Fritz had been having?

"Wish that was surprising, but I told you I didn't like her," Este says, looking satisfied that we've finally found the perfect evidence to justify her Autumn hating. She flips through some of the other papers on the table.

"Hey, listen, I need to run an errand. I'll be back in a little bit. Okay?" I scoop up the files and start shoving them back into the folder and then into my bag.

"An errand? Really?"

I pause, then say, "I just need to go see about something. I've got a hunch."

"Now you have hunches? We're doing hunches? Should I buy you a trench coat?"

I don't respond. I'm already halfway to the door when she calls, "Just be careful, okay?"

CHAPTER 43

The buzzer on the door says A. KENSINGTON. I press it twice to be sure she answers. Autumn lives in a modest three-story apartment building that probably had its heyday in the late 1980s. Mirrors and black lacquer finishes adorn the lobby.

I buzz one more time and finally I get an answer back.

"Who is it?"

"It's Nora, Autumn. Can I come up?"

There's a pause just awkward enough that I might need to ask about it later, but for now, the door buzzes.

"Grab the elevator to the third floor. I'm down the hall to the left. Three thirteen."

When the elevator doors open on the third floor, I catch a hint of mildew in the stale air. I'm surprised that this is where Autumn lives. With the way she carries herself, I always pictured her in some pristine, new building.

I find Apartment 313, and the door opens before I knock.

"Nora! Hi!" She pulls me into a friendly hug, which I only sort of return. I'm a woman on a mission now and I don't have time to slow down. "Please, come in."

The inside of Autumn's apartment is exactly what I expected. It's exquisite, even if the backdrop of the building is outdated. You can see every single curated choice, down to the potted lemon tree on her balcony.

"Can I get you some iced tea or water?"

"No, I'm fine, thank you."

We walk into the living room, and I pick a beautifully tufted bench to perch on across from the couch, where Autumn sits down. Then, I realize that I don't really have a plan of what to do here.

"What's going on?" Autumn asks, a slight edge of worry in her voice.

Time to ad-lib.

"I was surprised to see you at the office earlier. I didn't remember there being anything on the social calendar coming before . . ." How do I even shorthand the last few weeks? "You know what I mean."

"I was changing out the flowers. Fritz did ask me to look over an invite list for the trial attorney dinner that's coming up."

Right. Life goes on for the living.

"Listen, I don't mean to be too forward, but I know you and Fritz are . . . Well, it's none of my business, but I know that you're . . . close."

Autumn blanches. I have to be careful. I'm a sentence away from being thrown out of her apartment.

"I really don't care, Autumn. I'm sure you heard, but people—mostly Ardell and some cable news demon—think I had something to do with Will's murder. I can't let Will's killer get away in all this noise, and I've got to find out who really did this. And—" I pull the grainy picture from my purse—"I found this when I was cleaning some things out of Will's office."

She stares down at it like I've pulled a weapon out of my bag.

"Nora, that picture was from a while ago. That's over. It was short-lived and a massive error in judgment on my part. Please, *please* don't tell anyone."

There's honest desperation in her voice, and it makes me a little sad.

"Will hired a private investigator to look into Fritz," I say. "I suspect that is who took that picture—"

"Nora, you don't think I had anything to do with Will—"

"No, but I think Fritz did. And I need to know if you know anything."

Autumn's clutching her hands so hard that her knuckles have

gone from red to white. I know she knows something—will she tell me?

"Please—"

Autumn stands up and walks around the back of the couch, putting distance between us. If she could run, I think she might. Not because she's guilty, though. It looks like she's having a panic attack.

"Autumn, I'm sorry. I am not trying to upset you, but if you know anything that might help with this whole thing, I would really appreciate it. I got dragged into the police station the other day, and Ardell searched my house."

"God, Nora. I'm sorry—"

I sit patiently and don't press. If she's going to tell me, she has to get there on her own. Whatever she knows, it's enough to put her in this state. She comes back around the couch and sits in the chair closest to me, then leans in.

"The night of the party . . . ," she says in a low whisper. "The night of the party, I heard Will and Fritz fighting."

"About the Martinez case?"

"What? No. Remember that guy, the night before the party . . . ? The guy that ran into Carol's fence?"

Dean Morrison.

"Apparently, there was some kind of chase going on. Fritz was trying to catch up to the guy in the Buick, but Fritz chased him right into Carol's yard. So at the birthday party, Fritz was on Will, demanding answers about why Will had him followed, and Will just kept asking Fritz 'where all the fucking money went.' It got pretty heated, so I left before they realized I was listening in."

My God.

Autumn knew all of this and told no one. Even as Will was missing and when they found out he'd been killed. Even as she was bringing me grief gift baskets. In a flash, I see red. I feel such a deep sense of betrayal that I want to scream. I want to flip her perfectly arranged coffee table display. I know—I *know*—that getting mad at her won't accomplish anything, but I still want to slap her.

"Why didn't you tell anyone? After what happened to Will? Why didn't you—"

"Because I only overheard a few things—"

"Autumn—"

"No, Nora. Do you know how many secrets I carry about the people in this town? About the Halls? Do you have any idea how many things I hear or *almost* hear happen when people drink too much and it's the end of the night? Half the time, I don't even know if what I hear is true, but I hear it all. The affairs, the fights, the bounced checks. Do you know how much I know because I plan the parties and I'm in their houses and they talk freely because I'm basically invisible to them? I stay out of everything. I do what I have to do."

"So where does Fritz factor in?"

"Getting involved with Fritz was a mistake. A transgression I'd prefer to keep to myself. We both stayed too late at a party one night." She sighs. "I know it's hard to believe, but he can be really charming sometimes." She fidgets with the hem of her shirt. "I understand how messy it sounds. But I try to stay out of all of it. Because these people will never be held accountable for anything they do. They hold all the cards. And I'm the only one who loses if I talk. I'd be out of a job. They all know it. Discretion is part of my livelihood. If I keep their secrets, I get to keep working."

It always comes back to money and power with these people. I think about Andres at the club the day I met Will. The day Mia was stealing drinks, and Andres wouldn't lift a finger to help her, for fear of losing his job. There are different rules at this altitude. The people with the money and power always have the upper hand. I hadn't thought about how that affected Autumn. But I understand now. She couldn't do the right thing without blowing up her own life.

I feel a pinch of empathy for her. Just a little.

And I know she's right about the power her clientele wield, but I also know I am going to have to convince her that this time, she's going to talk.

This time, *we'll* find the ace up the sleeve.

CHAPTER 44

BEFORE

There are plenty of legitimate debates to be had about how much of Florida will be underwater in the next decade or more. But it always strikes me as funny how quickly people forget the ways Florida had to be doctored, polished, and propped up to be habitable in the first place. Still, no matter how much air-conditioning is pumped into this veritable swampland or how many housing developments are built, the wild nature of this place—the weather and the water and the gators and the snakes—can be tamed but never counted out. That's why sinkholes spontaneously open up on the highways. And why, when the Interlachen Country Club was built in the 1980s, one-point-five-million yards of earth were needed to turn two hundred and seventy acres of muck into the golf course and club that stand there today.

This entire town is built on quicksand.

The hyperbole crossed my mind as I handed my keys to the valet and headed into the club.

Will had been golfing with Fritz all day. I'm not sure who initiated the outing, but I suspected it was another attempt to mend fences between the two of them. From what Will had shared lately, things were still tense, but he was doing his best to keep the peace. Which, apparently, included golfing.

"Why don't you come up to the club after? We can meet for dinner." He had kissed my shoulder as we sipped our coffee in the kitchen early that morning.

The club wasn't my favorite place to eat. It was teeming with a little Lilly Pulitzer mafia of women who all disapproved of me. But I was doing my best to remember that I belonged in this world now. Interlachen was at least better than the Racquet Club. I hated ordering drinks from Andres. And it was almost impossible to resist the urge to pick up a dish towel and start wiping down loungers or offer to help whenever the pool staff started clearing drinks and plates.

I'm not an asshole. I swear I didn't become one of them.

I agreed to head up to the club around six and wait for Will at the pool bar. There was zero chance in hell I'd dress up to sit with the vipers in the main dining room. But it was a nice night to eat outside. A calm breeze blew among the alfresco tables and chairs.

I ordered an Arnold Palmer and kept my sunglasses on so that I could people-watch. But before my drink arrived, Fritz sidled up to the table. He looked freshly showered, his hair still wet and combed back. But there was a hint of sweat on his brow. Maybe it was the humidity, though day-drinking on the course for hours seemed a more likely culprit. He dabbed at his forehead with a monogrammed handkerchief and then tucked the fabric square back in his pocket.

"Hey, Nora." His face lit up with that politician's smile.

I stood and gave him a hug with one, tentative arm. Polite but distant. "It's good to see you, Fritz."

Oh, hell. Did Will invite him to join us for dinner?

The server appeared with my drink and offered to take an order for Fritz.

"Thank you kindly." He waved her off. "But I can't stay."

I feigned disappointment.

"Gigi's got dinner reservations for us," he explained. "Will's still getting cleaned up in the locker room, but I told him I'd keep you company while you wait."

Yippee.

"Well, that was very kind of you."

"I'm afraid it was a little selfish on my part. There's something I've been wanting to talk to you about."

What on God's green earth could Fritz Hall want to talk to me about? Maybe it's about Will's birthday party. Maybe he wants to give a thirty-minute oration once everyone's gathered.

"You wouldn't believe how small the legal community is, Nora. Especially for someone like myself."

"I'm sure." I slapped on a placid expression.

Where is he going with this?

"And we all like to help each other as much as we can. Even outside of the plaintiff's field. We all stay pretty tight."

Fun story.

I wanted to roll my eyes and tell him to get to the fucking point. "What is it that you need from me, Fritz?"

"A friend of mine over at Fisher-Grant Family Law said you were calling to get some advice." The expression on his face darkened a shade. "Now, why would that be?"

Oh, for fuck's sake.

I'd kept meaning to follow up with the family law firm after our fight. But Will had been so sweet since then that the phone call kept slipping farther and farther down on my to-do list. Had Fritz told Will? I doubted it. Will would have said something. Honestly, I wouldn't have cared if he did. After the way Will had behaved, could anyone really blame me?

Still, my skin prickled—grossed out by the idea of Fritz and some attorney speculating about the state of my marriage and why I'd called. But I straightened up in my seat. I wasn't about to let him see me flustered. "Marriage is complicated, Fritz."

"That's fair enough, Nora. Thankfully, Mark Fisher is a close friend of mine. He's assured me he'll keep this information confidential. But I need assurances from you, too."

"You seriously think you've got one over on me because your colleagues would rather gossip than keep their clients' confidence?" I didn't even bother hiding my contempt. "What do you want, Fritz? What are you talking about?"

"I'm talking about the postnuptial agreement that you were supposed to sign in case you and Will ever decide to go your separate ways."

I scanned the pool deck, hoping Will would turn up.

"Listen." He gave a jovial chuckle. "You two do whatever you want. Lord knows Gigi keeps a divorce lawyer on speed dial, but if you're leaving Will, we need to get it in writing that you're leaving with no part of the firm."

He was trying to good-cop me.

No, thanks.

"I don't know what to say." I smiled sweetly, playing up my role as the young, dumb wife. "Will never gave me a postnup to sign."

After the wedding party, I'd half expected him to. But then, he stopped talking to me about almost everything for a while because he was so busy.

"*Nora.*" Fritz leaned in and his voice got quiet and tight. "If you leave him and you try to take even one dime from that law firm, I will end you. Do you understand?"

I rolled my eyes. "Take this up with your partner, Fritz. I told you. I'll sign anything he puts in front of me. I don't want your firm."

"I'd love to take this up with Will, but he won't hear of it. So I'm bringing it to you." His eyes were blazing with a quiet fury. "Make this right. Do what you've already said you're happy to do. I can have something drawn up and couriered to your place tonight."

The rage in his eyes was unmistakable, but there was something I almost missed. Fear.

Fritz Hall is afraid of me? Oh, I'm going to savor this.

"No deal."

"What the *fuck*, Nora?" He was speaking low, trying not to cause a scene, but he punctuated the word "fuck" with a firm rap of his fist on the table, causing a few people to look over at us.

If Will didn't want me to sign something—whatever his reasons—I wasn't going to.

Fritz tried again. "You said—"

"I said"—I raised a hand to stop him—"I would sign whatever Will asked me to. So—and evidently I can't stress this enough—take it up with him."

Fritz stood so quickly and impulsively that he almost knocked his chair over behind him. I kept my seat, staring up at him with an unbothered expression on my face.

He tapped at the table with his pointer finger. "Why won't you just do this?"

"I don't know. Because I don't have to? Maybe because I don't bow down to you like everyone else?" I shrugged. "Here comes Will now. You can ask him about the paperwork yourself."

Fritz waved a defeated hand in my direction, taking his exit with a nod in Will's direction and then mine. I watched him stalk out of the pool area with his head low, occasionally looking up to offer a distracted wave to the acquaintances he passed.

"Hey." Will kissed my cheek, and the smell of his body wash was a welcome hit of comfort. "I just missed Fritz, huh?"

"God, am I happy to see you." I reached for his hand. "Hey, listen. Do me a favor? Don't ever fucking leave me alone with him again." It was a voice I didn't use often, but one that conveyed I was serious.

Will recognized the gravity right away. "You're right. I think that's for the best."

The somber way he so quickly agreed made me shiver a little.

CHAPTER 45

FOURTEEN DAYS AFTER

Fritz Hall has been living a life of easy money and no consequences for forty-six years. That ends now.

But I know the same thing Autumn did the night she heard Will and Fritz fighting: No one is going to want to believe me. In fact, at this point, most of them would probably love nothing more than to watch me burn.

Fritz killed Will with a hammer and he's trying to frame me for the murder. Fuck that.

No, if people are going to believe me in this place where Fritz is king, I will have to prove everything irrefutably. And I can't leave anything to Ardell. He's too in love with the lore of this place, too eager to please the higher-ups to be trusted with just a hunch. I have to bring him a heap of evidence tied up with a bow.

Perry texted this morning, and I told him I had something big but didn't want to put it in writing.

I've been sitting on the floor of my closet for the better part of an hour. I started getting dressed but then got pulled down into grief. The sorrow comes out of nowhere. I'll see a cuff link or a book Will left out and fall head over heels into a paralyzed state of sadness. This time, it came when I realized that at some point I am going to have to deal with all of Will's clothes. All of his things. I entertain the idea of donating them for a second, but I can't stand the thought of someone else wearing his suits, his shoes. I'm clutching at his favorite old T-shirt, but I'm all cried out.

My phone rings, snapping me out of my spontaneous grief paralysis. It's Marcus.

I think about answering but don't because I hear Mia calling out from downstairs. I don't need her to find me here.

"Hey, Mia. Coming down." I splash a bunch of water on my face and pull myself together before heading downstairs.

She's rummaging through the refrigerator when I reach the kitchen.

"Sorry, I don't think there's much in there," I say. "I threw out most of the food. I couldn't keep up with the casseroles on my own."

Mia pulls out a LaCroix and sits down at the island. She looks pale, but at least the sparkle in her eyes is coming back.

"Is your mom outside?" I ask. "What's going on? Everything okay?"

"No. My friend Ashleigh dropped me off. My chemistry books are here. Please don't tell my mom I came. She said this is your house now and I'm not allowed to be around you."

Shit. Constance hates me and Will is gone. I might be a murderer for all they know. Why *would* Constance allow Mia to have a room here?

"Oh, Mia, you can come here anytime you want."

She looks at me with a "yeah, right" face. And, I get it. Constance is drawing her line in the sand.

"This is all so awful, I know. But, just because your dad . . ."

Is gone. Dead. No more. I can't say it out loud one more time.

"Just because he's not . . ." I shake my head. "I really am still your family, Mia." I mean that when I say it. I had worked hard to build my relationship with Mia. Clearly, Constance is trying to sever all ties as quickly as possible, but I love Mia. "And I didn't do what they're saying I did."

I can tell Mia's not sure what to say to that.

"This is going to blow over."

I hope.

"And you can leave whatever you want to leave here and all you have to do is call if you want to come over. You can stay anytime."

Mia nods, wiping away the tears. "I'm going to grab a few things from upstairs."

Twenty minutes later, I wave at Mia as her Uber backs out of the driveway.

I'm just like June Cleaver—if June's husband was also murdered and she allowed her stepchild to rideshare to school.

In my defense, I had offered to drive her to school, but we both decided that it was better not to have any of Constance's friends spot me in the carpool line. So, instead, I paid for the Uber and watched her leave.

There are a few dutiful reporters waiting just over the bridge, and I can't help but wave at them. They look bored today, but that's because there hasn't been any news on Will's case since word of the murder weapon leaked. True to form, Lindy had delivered a monologue worthy of Hamlet.

What a fucking absurdity this all is.

I am about to head back inside for a shower when I see Perry's gray sedan pull into the driveway. I wait for him, and we walk into the house together.

I pour him a cup of coffee as I tell him everything that Autumn told me.

"That sonofabitch," Perry says.

It's the first emotion other than totally calm and pleasant that I have seen out of Perry since I met him. And I know how he feels: rage the fire of ten thousand suns.

"It took a lot of convincing, but Autumn is willing to go to the police. I told her to wait. We have to have more. These people will find a way to explain what little hearsay we have into nothingness and Fritz's life of debauchery and dishonesty will go on uninterrupted."

"Well, I think I have it." Perry pulls a laptop out of his computer bag and opens it up. "Through a bunch of digging and a few favors, I found something that I thought you should see." His screen lights up with PDFs of account records from a credit union I've never heard of. "Did you or Will ever open accounts here?"

"It's not saying much, but I've never even heard of the place,"

I tell him. "Will's never done any banking other than with Bank of America. He had a whole soapbox spiel about major national banks. It's one place he really didn't count on the 'little guy,' or so he said." I'm scanning the accounts and stop when I see that there is one in Mia's name. "What the hell? There's one in Mia's name?"

"It looks like there are three large lines of credit also taken out, one in your name and one in Will's. And, well, it looks like all the credit's been spent and the payments against the loans are past due. Someone borrowed about two million dollars in both of your names, using the firm as collateral for the loan."

"What the actual fuck, Perry? These aren't ours. Will doesn't owe this kind of money. We *have* way more than that. Which I realize is not a very humble thing to say out loud. But it's the truth."

"Dean had found one of the accounts and the account number matched the one you sent me yesterday from Will's office. If you and Will didn't open the accounts, we need to find out who did."

Fritz.

Autumn's comments about overhearing Fritz and Will fight over money take on new meaning.

For all the things Fritz has done that might be socially dodgy and a little bit dicey in the world of business and trial law . . . this is so much bigger. This isn't just the threat of malpractice for handling a case poorly. This is wire fraud and financial crimes. This is federal prison. If Will knew about this, he would have turned Fritz in immediately. And Fritz knew it. I think about the rage on his face that evening at the club when he thought I might stand in the way of his complete control of the firm. Fritz *really* didn't want anyone to have any reason to go looking into the firm and its finances. His double-dealings would have surfaced all too quickly.

It's like watching the last piece of a puzzle slide easily into its rightful place. Will sensed something wasn't right—Fritz meddling in the Martinez case probably didn't help—so he hired Dean to dig into Fritz's debts and accounts. Then, once Fritz realized Will was onto him, he killed Will in a Hail Mary attempt to maintain the shiny façade that had shielded him from trouble or consequences for his entire life.

"It has to be Fritz."

"Forgive me for asking such a simple question, but if you all have plenty more than what was borrowed, wouldn't the Halls be sitting high on the hog, too? Weren't they equal partners?"

I imagine two million dollars to be a very different sum in Arcadia. In Winter Park, though, two million dollars—especially to someone like Fritz—would be a Band-Aid, not a windfall. Fritz must have been in pretty deep somehow.

Perry rubs the back of his neck. "I am happy to keep digging on my own, Nora—"

"No. I think we have enough now. I've got Autumn ready to talk and we don't have time to let her think and change her mind. There's just one more thing."

Perry pulls his gray sedan into the credit union parking lot as a clerk unlocks the front door, post-lunch. Perry and I had spent most of the drive devising a plan for me to get the information we needed. He's going to wait in the car, and I'm going to go in with my best "recently widowed" performance.

All of these pins starting to drop are lifting me out of the vortex of hell I've been in. I walk into the building, head held high, and scan the lobby for the best mark. I land on a dour-looking older gentleman, hoping that he'll take pity. I walk over, and he motions for me to sit in the chair opposite him.

"How can I help you today?"

"Hi—" I look at his nameplate. "Dennis. My name is Nora Somerset, and my husband . . ." I pause as if I'm holding back a wall of emotions. Something that's not too hard for me to fake, all things considered. "My husband died a few weeks ago—"

"Oh, I'm so sorry to hear that."

"Thank you. I'm trying to sort through all our affairs, and I came across several accounts here at this branch. I need to figure out what they were for because I didn't know about them."

Dennis hesitates a little. I clock it.

"I know there are probably rules, but it's just me now, and I have to make sure that my finances stay in order." I look at him with the biggest doe eyes I can muster.

C'mon, Dennis. You can do it.

"Of course, ma'am. Let me pull that up."

I slide a piece of paper with the account numbers written

down and watch as his face changes when, I am certain, he sees the past-due notices on them.

"These accounts are owed quite a sizable balance that hasn't been paid. But, considering your circumstances, let me see if I can waive the late fees if you make a payment today."

"Thank you. Can you tell me when the accounts were opened?"

He looks at me for a second. "I will need to see some ID to do that." I slide my license across the table at him and he looks at it, satisfied. He clicks through a few things. "It looks like they were opened about three months ago."

"Is it possible for me to see the signature pages on the contracts?"

Dennis considers me, and I know it's an odd question, but I am hoping he'll just keep helping me out.

I continue. "I need the information for my accountant to help me settle my late husband's affairs."

"All right." Dennis prints out the signature pages for me and slides them across the table. "Now about making a payment today."

"Yes, of course. Can I have my accountant call you? I'm just figuring out all these finances and they're the ones who really handle payments."

"That'll be fine. Take my card and have them call today, please."

I pick up the papers, shake Dennis's hand, then do my best not to skip out of the building.

Back in the car, I sift through the three signature pages. It's clear they've been signed by the same person because of the way the ink pools at the end of each signature. It's subtle, but I recognize it. Fritz forged signatures for every document.

Let's go get Fritz Hall arrested.

It took us about an hour to walk Ardell through everything. After telling her part, Autumn went with another detective to give a sworn statement. It all made sense. Dean had figured out that Fritz was stealing money from the firm and told Will. And, the night of the party, Will had confronted him about all of it. After the party, they must have met up somewhere to finish their argument, and Fritz killed him.

I had brought along a handwritten note from Fritz to Will that

I saw on Will's desk at home. Same pools of ink at the ends of sentences. I told Ardell that if he went to the credit union he would find surveillance showing that Fritz, not Will, opened those accounts.

I could see the internal struggle behind Ardell's eyes. He didn't want to believe any of it. He didn't want to believe me. He held Fritz in such high esteem. But as he started processing all the information, he saw it the way we did.

"I'm really sorry for all of this, Nora. What a shitstorm. We'll look into it, and we'll talk to Fritz."

I nod.

I had hoped that I would feel instantly better once Ardell had the evidence we had gathered, but this was all still so much to process. I don't think I'll really believe it's true until Fritz is in custody.

We thank Ardell and leave.

In the parking lot, I give Autumn a hug and try to transfer my gratitude with a gentle squeeze. I know how hard this must be for her. How scary it is to think that they could all write her off. But she waves that away. It's the right thing to do.

Perry and I pull into my driveway at magic hour, that part of the day when afternoon gives way to sunset and the sky is bright pinks and purples. Perry stops the car short when he sees Fritz standing in the middle of the driveway, leaning against the back of his car.

"Why don't you stay here?" Perry offers.

"No chance. Fritz can talk to me."

I get out of the car and close the distance to Fritz with strong, head-held-high steps.

"We had an agreement!" Fritz booms at me.

"Not this again." I roll my eyes.

"You said you'd stop talking to people. You said you didn't want to hurt the firm. So, imagine my surprise when I find out you're trying to frame me for *murder.*"

"Any cooperation you might have thought I owed you all went out the door the minute you killed my husband."

"I did *not* kill Will. This is all some last-ditch effort for you to save your own ass," he taunts me. "Well, it won't work. This is my town. Or have you forgotten? You're nothing. Nobody."

Fritz is making a commotion, and I see Este and Beau approaching from the hedge between our houses. When they spot Fritz, they both start to jog to come to my defense. But I put up a hand to stop them.

"Maybe that's true, but you're also skimming off the top and stealing from your partner." I watch Fritz's eyes flicker with that accusation. "I know about the accounts at the credit union. I know that you were stealing from Will. And I know that you were grinding him to a nub because his abilities as an attorney were the only way for the firm to make any money."

"I haven't the faintest clue what you are talking about."

"It must be so hard to be a hack. To be the golden boy who doesn't actually ever do the work because you can't. So you found Will and you made him do it all. And you just cashed in and dined out."

I must be starting to hit some buttons because his face is getting red. His eyes scan the scene before him like he's trying to plot his next move.

"You were nothing without Will."

"What the fuck do you know about anything, Nora?"

"Rich coming from you after you built your fortune on Will's back. What *are* you going to do now that you've killed your golden goose, Fritz? You're nothing but a hollow suit who squandered a fortune. How pathetic."

Fritz lunges at me. I'm so surprised that I freeze. He's nearly got his hands on my neck, but Beau steps in with a stiff arm and clotheslines him. Fritz is on the ground almost instantly. Perry and Este stand farther back as I take two steps until I am directly over him. Fear registers in his eyes, and it should. If it weren't for the whole prison part, I'd murder him right here.

"Fucking leave. This is private property, and you're trespassing." I walk toward the house without looking back.

Este, Beau, and Perry follow me inside. I can see the questions on Este's face.

"What the fuck just happened out there?" she says.

"Let me grab a bottle of wine. You're going to need it."

We order a dinner of takeout, and I piece together what Perry, Autumn, and I have been able to find over the last day or so. Este is gobsmacked. She looks toward the driveway where Beau laid

Fritz out. That was hours ago. Fritz had gotten in his car and driven God knows where after we went inside.

"How did he make it to your house when he should be in a jail cell?" she demands.

"Ardell said they have to get in front of a judge. But someone from the courthouse must have tipped him off to something. Who knows what they'll have to do to keep him from running." I take my plate to the sink.

After dinner's been cleared, the exhaustion hits me. I feel like I might finally be able to sleep through the night. As I say good-bye to Este and Beau, thanking Beau for stepping in when he did, they leave through the side door.

I turn to Perry and say, "Perry, I can't thank you enough for all your help. I couldn't have done this without you."

"Or Dean."

"Or Dean. I'm so sorry about your friend. Maybe he and Will can keep a lookout for each other now."

Perry smiles sadly. "Maybe."

He gives me a hug and tells me to stop by if I'm ever in his neck of the woods. I think we both know that's as unlikely as him ever returning to Winter Park. I promise to keep in touch, though.

I'll have to add a friends-made-looking-for-my-husband's-killer category to my holiday mailing list.

I stand in the doorway until his car is all the way out of the driveway, then close the door and walk into the living room.

A new air settles over the house. It's quiet and calm, but also empty. I grab the last of my glass of wine and head over to the couch, where I snap on the TV. Lindy Bedford is on the screen talking about a "new person of interest" in the case. I smile to myself and flip over to HGTV, where some pretty female architect is schooling a contractor.

I know tomorrow I will wake up with the same yawning grief, but at least I did what I could to help Will get justice. At least there's that.

CHAPTER 46

THE DAY OF THE PARTY

The morning felt like a dream. Blue skies and calm water stretched out in every direction around us as the boat powered across the lake. Will was smiling that crooked smile of his. The one that made me swoon. And even over the roar of the boat engine, I could hear Mia's soundtrack.

That morning, as we sat down to a breakfast Alma had made for Will—some divine overnight casserole thing—Mia shared the playlist she had made to celebrate his birthday, titled "Pal Turns Old."

"It's perfect, Buggy." He had kissed her forehead, taking the "old" joke in stride. "I love you."

Mia beamed proudly, satisfied with the reception of her gift.

Will's forty-sixth birthday party would be later that day, and we all agreed a boat ride would be a nice way to spend the hours between breakfast and the time Mia would have to head back to Constance's and Will and I would have to start getting dressed.

Even before we could head down to the dock, though, the house was buzzing with activity. Autumn swept into the kitchen around nine A.M., as we were putting our breakfast dishes away. And Marcus wasn't far behind her, arriving with enough food to feed an army and soliciting the help of Autumn's party crew to unload provisions.

"So, this is the famous Marcus," Will had said as he shook Marcus's hand. "Este and Beau are always raving about you. Nora, too, of course."

Marcus's usually friendly smile had a bit of an edge to it, and I wondered if he was still mad at me. I gave him a short wave, feeling like I owed him a huge apology and knowing I couldn't apologize with Will around. "We're headed out on the boat for a little while. Can you tell Autumn I have my cellphone on me if she needs anything?"

"Yeah," he said as his jaw tightened in the back of his cheek. "Have fun."

I could feel the judgment radiating off him.

Not today, Marcus. Today is for celebrating Will and charming the pants off some rich assholes.

We walked down to the dock, climbing aboard *Don't Settle.* As soon as we were on the water, Mia synced her playlist to the Bluetooth speakers, and we zipped around as some of Will's favorite musicians serenaded us. We bounced from R.E.M. to REO Speedwagon before Nick Drake started playing.

Will cut the engine so that Mia could jump in the lake to wakeboard. As Mia was getting ready, I noticed a small box on the captain's dash next to Will.

"What's that?"

He looked down at it like he hadn't seen it before.

"That," I said, pointing this time.

"I don't know." He shrugged with a little smirk. "Open it and find out."

I frowned at him. "It's *your* birthday, Will. I'm supposed to be the one giving *you* presents."

He reached for my hand and tugged me into his lap. "I've already got what I want." He pulled me in for a hug and kissed my cheek. Leaning back, he picked up the box and handed it to me. "Open it."

"Give it to me tomorrow. I feel guilty taking something from you on your day."

"Nora." There was that liquid look in his eyes that I loved so much. The one he gave me when he proposed and when he asked me out for the first time. Pleading and hopeful. He could have anything he wanted from me when he looked at me like that. "Please, open it."

That's my Will.

"I love you," I said.

"I love you. Now, open it."

Inside the small green rectangular box was an amber pendant encircled in delicate scalloped gold on a thin gold chain. The amber had little flowers that looked yellow etched into the burnt orange gem and on the back I could feel the grooves of the etching.

"Oh my God." I looked at him. "It's so beautiful. I love it."

"It was my mom's," he said.

I looked up at him, shocked. I knew his mom had passed away when he was still a kid. All these years later, I was surprised he had anything left of hers.

The second wife doesn't get many heirlooms.

He took it out of the box and opened the clasp. "It's not very extravagant. Nothing like the jewelry you see around the club. My mom didn't care much for opulence. Not that we could have afforded more. But she loved this necklace. She wore it every day."

I turned on his lap so that he could fasten the chain to my neck.

"My mom would have loved you," he said, and he looked like he might cry. "You've never given a shit about any of this." He waved at the mansions surrounding us on the lake. "You just want me. I can't believe I'm so lucky."

I pulled him in and kissed him, wiping a few small tears away.

"Knock it off, Pal," Mia called from the water. "Stop making kissy faces and drive the boat."

He chuckled and gave me another kiss before obliging her.

I touched the pendant, which fell just above my heart, and swelled with a little bit of pride. We had made it through a really shitty time. We were going to be okay. I didn't know what the future held for me. Maybe we'd have kids, maybe we wouldn't. Maybe I'd try to go back to work, maybe I wouldn't. But we were going to be there for each other. We were going to figure it out together.

CHAPTER 47

TWENTY DAYS LATER

I've had the first good night's rest in almost a month, and I wake up ready to go for a run. I text Este as much. Her response comes through as I'm pulling on my shoes.

7:46 A.M.
Fuuuuuuck. I thought we were done with running.

7:48 A.M.
Fine. Ten minutes.

I laugh as I head down the stairs and out the front door.

The press corps of lawn jockeys have retreated, pulling up stakes and hightailing it to the Halls's when it was leaked that the police were looking into Fritz. I watch Este make her way across the driveway, and I almost miss Ardell's cruiser coming down the road.

"For fuck's sake, what now?"

Este doubles over with her hands on her knees. "Oh, thank-christ, we don't have to run."

Ardell gets out of the car and heads toward us.

"Morning, ladies. Sorry if I interrupted your run."

"I'm not," Este says as she lifts her arms in a stretch.

"Can I speak to you in private, Nora?"

I look at Este, who is already ambling back to her house. "Call me if he's hauling you in; otherwise, let's go to yoga at noon. I'm going back to bed."

Ardell and I walk inside.

I offer him a cup of coffee, which he happily takes from me. "The stuff down at the station is at least a third motor oil."

"What's going on?"

"I wanted to come here myself to tell you that we've done a lot of digging, and you were right about all the financial crimes. Fritz and Gianna's cash assets were down to almost nothing. Their checking account was overdrawn by nearly twenty grand and they're carrying hundreds of thousands in credit card debt. He basically bankrupted the law firm. Not only did he steal millions from the business, but he also was skimming off some clients as well."

"Wait. Are we broke?"

We. That habit was going to be hard to break.

Ardell shook his head. "I don't want you to worry. Other than the fake accounts Fritz set up in your names, it looks like Will had taken some pretty aggressive precautions and moved your money far out of Fritz's reach. We've had to hand the case over to the FBI—they handle the fraud stuff. But everything you said he did, he did."

"I sense a 'but' . . . "

"Yeah. The thing is, Fritz alibied out for the night Will was murdered. He left the party in an Uber and went to the club until it closed. We've got him coming and going on camera, and the bartender and about eight other members backed that up. He then Ubered to a club downtown, and we've got the camera footage there. He ended the night at a hotel with a guest; those details I won't go into, but you can probably imagine some of them. Credit card activity tracks the whole thing. It couldn't have been him who killed Will."

My heart sinks. This should be over. Done.

"Now, I don't want you to think we're back on you for any reason. You've done all you can to be helpful. I really believe that, and I want to run something by you."

What could I possibly know? I threw a party and went to bed.

"When we did a search of your house, we were looking for something pretty specific. Something that Will's autopsy uncovered. I talked to my captain, and he agreed that I could share it with you in the hope that it might mean something."

My heart is racing.

"This is going to be a little graphic, but there was something unusual in Will's stomach." He's looking at me, sizing me up to see if I can handle it. I nod for him to go on.

"I've just got a picture of what we found here on my phone. Don't worry. I'm not going to show you any autopsy photos. I don't want to upset you."

He might never apologize for making me a suspect in Will's murder. The kid gloves are back on, though. To him, my tragic status as a grieving widow—not the murderous wife—has been restored.

At least that's something.

He clears his throat, and adds, "Does this look familiar?"

I almost pass out when he turns his phone for me to look at the image.

I'd know it anywhere.

"Oh, hi, ladies!" I give an exaggerated wave as I walk into the locker room at the Racquet Club. They all turn and look at me. Constance, Tippy, and Gianna leading the charge, not even trying to hide their disgust. If it weren't for the Botox, they'd be positively scowling. I blow past them and make a line straight for Gianna, who is busy primping in front of the mirror in her oversize locker.

"Is there something I can help you with?" she says without even bothering to look in my direction.

"I guess me handing your husband over for financial crimes means the tennis invite is off the table, huh? Rats."

She looks like she's sucking on a lemon. But despite the grimace on her face, she really is exquisite. Flawless even—well, almost. The time it must take to pull that off. Too bad she won't be taking her glam squad with her to prison.

I go on, "You know, if anyone had asked me a few weeks ago, I would've told them that you were the gold standard. That I wished I could be more like you. Because I thought you had everything figured out."

"You couldn't be me if you were born a thousand times to the right family." Gianna's nostrils flare ever so slightly.

And there it is. The interloper's crest burned into my core.

"You're right," I say. "I could never be you. I could never sit in a gilded cage acting as if the clothes, the clubs, the *jewels* were enough. Believe me, I tried. But there were so many moments of wondering: What comes next? And worse: Is this all there is? No one ever lets on to just how boring gilded cages can be, you know?"

I find myself closing in on Gianna, making sure I've got her between the wall and me. She can't get out of this conversation. *This is war.*

I watch her take a step back—she's not sure what I'm going to do. But she regains her snake-like composure and then steps toward me.

"I don't have to listen to anything from trash like you," she hisses at me. "Leave it to you to be too uncouth to know that you're not welcome here anymore."

"It's funny. When you parade around a party showing off your forty-thousand-dollar ring with a sapphire that is *such* a rare shade of teal, people take note. I guess that's sort of the point, right? So, imagine my surprise when the police showed me the picture of that exact rare stone. It turns out it's evidence in a *murder* investigation now. And you'll never believe where they found it."

I'm watching all the information cascade onto her like a wave of anvils. I hope every word I say is imprinted on her brain. I want her to bleed out. I want to do to her what she did to Will. To take from her like I know she took from him. I'll settle for a social death. Which for her will be just as painful.

"I never quite understood why you froze me out. But I get it now. I realize now that I *am* the enemy. I am the person who threatened the glass house you put yourself in. I am the little pebble that shattered the image of who you are." I take another step toward her, until I'm inches from her and hear her catch her breath. "Emily Post never wrote a chapter on the protocol for this, but I've come by to let you know I'm not quite finished."

She doesn't visibly react, but there are signs I'm getting through. I can see it in the vise grip she has on her gym towel.

"Oh, please, don't worry, I don't want to be some Messiah Pariah who outs the ridiculousness of all of you. But I owe it to myself and Will to be more than anyone in my life has ever given me credit for. I don't want to be in the shadows, but I am not looking for the limelight either. Maybe I am failing. Maybe I am succeeding. But I'll do it on my own terms from now on. You can have your gilded cage. Oh, but wait . . ."

Now I am so close I can feel her shaky breath on my face.

"It won't be so gilded now, will it?"

One of the tennis biddies snorts at that. She must be picturing Gianna in prison.

Amazing. Her own courtesans are ready to usurp her power and take the mantle so quickly.

"Easy, Tippy," I snap. "I saw Ardell's hand up your skirt at the Christmas party. The sun doesn't shine out of your ass either." The other biddies gasp and shuffle just a hair away from Tippy.

Poor Tippy. I enjoyed that a little more than I should have.

Gianna pulls on my arm. "You've made your scene, Nora. Now, should we discuss this like adults?"

"You can have that chat with the police. I'm sure they'll be eager to talk to you." I check the locker room wall clock. "Any minute now."

"This is slander. You should be ashamed—"

"Will was always quick to remind me," Constance says, leveling a look at Gianna. "That you can't sue for slander just because you don't like what people have to say about you."

To my complete and total surprise, Constance moves right beside me. Gianna backs away from us a little, looking from Constance to me. A pair of Mrs. Somersets. Even as her best friend turns on her, Gianna tries to regain the upper hand.

"The gemstone proves nothing." She huffs. "I could've—lost it at the party. Before I left."

"You're right. The gemstone doesn't prove you killed Will, but it does point cops in the right direction. And now they've managed to gather enough evidence to put you away. Something about a bloodstain on a bimini. Does that ring a bell, *G*?" I laugh a little. "God, I remember when I first learned 'bimini' meant 'boat awning.' The glossary of terms I have had to download just to keep up in this town. Rich people are crazy. So is DNA evidence, it turns out. Shame you nicked yourself that night."

I fight the curl of the corner of my mouth as the color drains from her face. There will be time for smiling later.

Now I know there is nothing left to say. Nothing left to do. I walk toward the locker room exit, stopping only to grab some country club mints. As I push through the door, a herd of uniforms rushes in, calling out Gianna's name. I lock eyes with Constance, and we exchange a wordless "holy shit" right before the swinging doors shut behind me.

I tuck into the shadows of the pro shop and watch Gianna Hall as they stuff her into the back of a police cruiser with half of Winter Park standing by to witness. And, somehow, even in this moment of total ruin, there is still something elegant about her. She's destined to be a fucking felon now, and she makes it look good. A hint of glee threatens to show itself on my face when I realize that Gianna will have to live the rest of her life knowing I was the person who took her down. And with her own jewels.

Thanks for that, Will.

I watch the taillights disappear down the winding brick road, feeling a flicker of hope that this part of the nightmare can finally be behind me now. I turn on my heel and walk past the group of gawking Winter Park wives.

Let them stare. I would, too.

They've just witnessed the minting of an urban legend: the second wife who took down the queen. The buzz of this story will linger in the air at cocktail parties and Park Avenue brunches for years. The chatter starts as I stride away. It's a familiar hum, the whispered gossip that has followed me around like a shadow since the day I met Will. But I tune it out for good this time.

I'm not listening to what they say anymore.

EPILOGUE

THREE MONTHS LATER

am standing in the middle of my empty master closet. It looks so sad with bare shelves and abandoned hanging rods. I had moved into this place when it was fully furnished. This is my first look at the stripped-down version. It's a little unnerving.

My things are in suitcases ready to be loaded out. The plastic, makeshift ring Will had given me is looped around my left ring finger. Widows, I had learned, wear their wedding rings on their right hands, so I switched my diamond ring in accordance with polite society. But when I was alone in the house, I had taken to putting on the well-worn cocktail straw, reliving the memory of when he slipped it on. I'm wearing it now to make sure it doesn't get lost in the shuffle of moving day.

It was an easy decision to sell this house. Too much water under too many bridges for this to ever be a happy place for me again. Este still hasn't forgiven me, but I've reminded her that I'm leaving the neighborhood, not Winter Park.

Of course, I had toyed with the idea of leaving town altogether. I daydreamed about shedding my second-wife-turned-widow-turned-vigilante reputation. But Este is here, and she's my family now. There is no way around that.

I just can't stay in his house. This is one of the last things that was Will's, but it was never mine. My mother says she'll come visit me in the new place as soon as they get to Istanbul. She's booked a flight and everything. I wonder if Paolo's time in Ramona's orbit is running down. I guess we'll see.

I didn't hear Mia come in until she quietly knocked on the doorframe of the closet. "Oh, hey," I say. "You're here."

"Yeah."

Mia and I both stare at the boxes we've filled with Will's clothes, waiting to be donated. It's awful to think about.

I nod to a shelf behind Mia. I had let her choose anything she wanted before someone came to haul away what used to be his. She's here to pick up a tie and a few soft, worn T-shirts.

Mia can't hold back the tears. Neither can I. The finality of it all is brutal. We stand in a hug for a long time, keeping each other afloat in a sea of grief.

When we're ready, we pull ourselves back together and head downstairs. I am floored to find Constance standing in the kitchen. A lot has changed since the last time I saw her.

For starters, her best friend is in jail now.

"Get what you came for, Buggy?" she asks.

Mia nods at her mother. "But I need to grab something from my room. Can you take this?" Mia hands the pile of Will's things to Constance and heads back upstairs.

Constance looks at the tie on top. "I bought him that tie. In the Bahamas."

We stand there in the silence for a minute. After Gianna was arrested, Constance had copped to lying about what Will said — he never told her he was unhappy. But she believed so fervently that I was to blame for Will's disappearance she had concocted the lie to get a reaction from me and pointed Ardell in my direction from the get-go. She was trying to smoke me out. It turns out she did know Dean Morrison. As an old friend of Will's family, Dean had been at their wedding. His car accident was her first clue that shit was going down. When she sounded the alarm about Dean, Ardell didn't listen to her either. But leave it to the first wife. Constance knew something was wrong before all of us.

After a beat, Constance says, "Maybe we can find a way for Mia to come by to see you from time to time. For her sake."

It's the thinnest olive branch. An olive twig, maybe. But I'll take it. Will's gone. Whatever rivalry we had needs to end. At least for Mia. Maybe for all of us.

"That would be great," I say softly. "I would love to have her anytime."

Constance nods, then heads out the front door.

I can only imagine how hard that was for her. Maybe she'll always resent the parts of Will's life that didn't include her. I don't know if we'll ever find a relationship beyond all of the things we begrudgingly shared. Maybe one day.

Mia comes down with a tote bag full of the last remnants of the drawers in her room. She gives me a huge hug. And as we stand there, smiling at each other, Constance's horn blares from the driveway.

The sound cracks us up.

"I mean. She's trying, but my mom is who she is."

Truer words, kid.

I watch Mia get in the car and give a wave as Constance drives off.

It's been a little over two months since Ardell and his team arrested Gianna and got her to confess to Will's murder. He had called me from the station late one night to recount her story. Hearing him go through the details of Will's last hour was surreal—I still can't believe I lived through this ordeal. That this is my story. My life. I hear it repeated in soft whispers as I walk down the street.

Did you hear what happened to Nora Somerset? It's a crazy story.

The night of Will's party, Fritz—extremely inebriated—left with some lawyer friends, and as he was apparently known to do, abandoned his phone and his blazer on a chair somewhere out on our lawn for Gianna to deal with. Which she dutifully did. She and Fritz had taken to boating to our place when they visited, because Fritz liked to skirt DUI laws. So Gianna took their boat home, but somewhere between our house and theirs she had the idea to try to confront Will. Knowing Fritz was worried about the state of things in his partnership with Will, she decided to do what she does best: Handle it. She went back to our dock and called him from Fritz's phone, claiming she was having boat trouble. Maybe he could come take a look? Will, being Will, of course obliged and went down.

Why he said it was Mia calling is the one piece that will never make sense to me, but after years of thinking on his feet in a courtroom, he handled the misdirect deftly. He probably knew if he told me Gianna was having boat problems, I would've told him to let her sink and drown. Will didn't want the fight. He never wanted the fight, but especially not on his birthday. Things were good between us again. Sometimes it's okay to skip the dumb fights. Happy wife, happy life, and all that.

But not telling me set something far more sinister into motion. Something that sent Winter Park into a spiral.

Gianna had heard Fritz and Will's failed conversation by the dock during the party, she had doubled back when the lights around the house were turned down. When questioned by the police, she said she was trying to reason with Will and smooth over his issues with Fritz. She knew about Dean, and the money troubles. For all of their problems, Gianna and Fritz were thick as thieves in that way. She also knew that Fritz suspected Will was planning to leave the firm. All those late nights Will had been pulling were time he had put into working on his exit strategy. Will had stood his ground with Gianna. He had turned a blind eye to a lot of things, but Fritz was committing fraud. Gianna couldn't negotiate her way around that fact—Fritz had driven the ship into the iceberg and Will wasn't going to go down with him.

After they talked and he checked Gianna's boat—it turned over just fine—Will stepped back onto the dock and bade her good night. That's when she came after him with a hammer Fritz kept in the boat, walloping him until he was unconscious, then rolled him off the dock, watching him disappear beneath the water's surface. His shirt snagged on the propeller of her boat— they'd found some threading on it after the fact—which explained why his shirt had shown up before his body.

The whole thing was messier than Gianna had hoped, but a dead Will couldn't turn Fritz in for fraud. She used a bucket from her boat and the lake water to wash away the blood and ditched the hammer under the dock. She had thought of almost everything. But she hadn't thought about the blood on the bimini. Which did, in fact, match her DNA profile.

The rest of the story is something we may never know for certain. At least that's what the authorities have told me. We were left to surmise because Will isn't here to tell us. Ardell and his team spent their fair share of time wondering how the gemstone got in his stomach, but knowing Will, I have a pretty strong idea. Always the lawyer, he knew a good piece of evidence anywhere. And he knew good evidence was to be protected. He must have sensed his demise or at least an imminent loss of consciousness, and when the stone popped out of Gianna's ring, knocked loose during the struggle, he swallowed it. He knew I'd be able to recognize it. And in that one act he gave me his parting gift—the power to take down Gianna Hall.

Gianna was always cleaning up after Fritz. I can't say I believe the bit about her trying to smooth things over with Will. The size of the wounds in the back of his head would suggest blind rage, not steady rationality. But it was almost the perfect crime, because why would anyone look at Gianna? She'd placed a heavy bet on Fritz's connections keeping her out of the pool of suspects and figured Fritz might be able to do some double-dealing if she was brought in. She'd probably covered up enough for him through the years to be able to call in the favor. But with Fritz in hot water for the financial crimes around the firm, his social capital was gone, which meant so were her protections. She hadn't accounted for Dean and Perry. She hadn't accounted for Fritz being arrested. And she certainly hadn't accounted for *me*.

My theory on her motive is that Will was going to dethrone Fritz and Gianna, the royalty of Winter Park, and she wasn't going to allow that to happen. All she had was the life she had created, and maintained at any cost to anyone else. Will had become another one of Fritz's messes that she was going to clean up.

For all of the ways he kept trying to put himself in the middle of the investigation, there were plenty of questions about whether Fritz had known what Gianna did. But both of them denied Fritz's involvement in Will's murder. Even if things were tenuous between them, Fritz wouldn't be foolish enough to kill off his biggest source of income. Will had been single-handedly floating the company with his work and reputation. Fritz was convinced he could salvage things. As for Gianna, she was Machiavellian enough to know there are some secrets a lady takes with her to the grave.

The four of us were sadly entangled—Will, Fritz, Gianna, and me. We had all worked to keep up appearances and hold our perfect lives together, each in our own way.

Cable newsrooms were thrilled. In the end, there *was* a pretty wife who'd committed murder, but she wasn't dumb. She was calculating. Lindy had dined out on the story for weeks. I had secretly felt vindicated by it.

Now, Este is watching me move a few boxes around the living room. "You know you're rich, right? Paying people to move your shit around for you is one of the greatest luxuries fuck-you money can buy. And where is Autumn? I would think color-coding your boxes and running around this house like a maniac with a label maker would be her version of Disney World."

"She's coming by later to deal with the Realtor. I've made her promise to call only if the house is on fire. I don't think I'll ever want to set foot in this place again."

I follow Este into the kitchen, where she turns around and looks at me. "This is such bullshit. I can't even bribe you to stay next door anymore. You're too expensive."

In the middle of all the shit, it really hadn't occurred to me that Will would leave money behind. That all of this was going to be mine. While there'd been a trust for Mia since the day she was born, the account would get a healthy infusion, but she couldn't touch it for anything other than education until she was thirty. Will was adamant that she needed to figure out who she was without money first. Constance would get the equivalent of her alimony until Mia graduated. But the rest was mine. Like I had won some fucked-up dark-web lottery.

Dead husband? Winner! Here's tens of millions of dollars.

The resolution of the Martinez case Fritz had been keeping an eagle eye on was a nine-figure payout, something the Halls had been counting on to take care of their outstanding debts. Fritz's half of the case fee was seized by the IRS. But for me, it was a cherry on top of an already massive pile of money. I had absolutely no idea what I was going to do with any of it.

I put my hand on the amber pendant around my neck.

We were happy. There was a time when we were each just what the other needed.

The memory of Will giving me the necklace is worth more than any of the money.

As for Fritz's finances, the investigation Will had commissioned with Dean had given authorities a strong start. The feds had gone on to uncover proof that Fritz had bled his estate dry on a series of failed investments, a busted Ponzi scheme that he was too dumb to execute, and an ungodly amount of gambling, drugs, and alcohol. Fritz had squandered a few million dollars on bets alone when he got hammered on a trip to Vegas. Their historic house was finally up for sale after months of legal holdups. The Hall family's legal team had high hopes that the proceeds of the sale could shore up all the money Fritz had leveraged our names to steal. And the proceeds of the sale of Fritz and Will's law practice, the building, and the entirety of the Hall estate would be divided among equity partners and Lenore; the rest would go to Mia and the Halls' kids. I didn't want a single cent of that cesspool.

Este told me that in time I would figure out what to do with the money Will had left me. She'd set me up with her fancy wealth manager. I didn't want to think about it now. First, a new start in a rental a few minutes away, then the spoils of this tragic war.

"You know there is no scenario in which I could stay in this house," I say to Este. "But you're going to see me all the time. Instead of waking up and walking next door, you can just call me. But please stop FaceTiming from the bathtub. It's weird and there aren't enough bubbles."

"You say it like it's a crime to do my administrative tasks from the tub. It's called balance; look it up."

She hugs me too hard, and I tell her I love her. "I really don't know if I would have survived this without you."

"And you've decided to repay this debt by leaving me."

I don't know how else to tell her I'm not *leaving* leaving. But she's right that things are changing. They have to. I give her a look, and she softens.

"I'm proud of you," she says. The words come out shaky, and I think she might cry.

She pulls herself together as we see Marcus's perfectly refurbished vintage Defender come down the road. He parks in Este's driveway and makes his way toward us. As he gives me a quick hug, that same hum of energy that's always been between us lingers, but I do my best to ignore it. Maybe if we had met at a different time . . . But I was Will's, and then I was a widow. I'm too fucked up with grief to know what happens next. These days, I'm working on earning his friendship after everything I put him through.

I grab my tote bag, and a Crealdé School of Art brochure almost falls out. Marcus picks it up, handing it to me with a satisfied grin on his face.

"Art school." I nod. "Look at me not deflecting."

It's not a joke this time. There's a great local program I'm hoping to start. I've been working through my grief with a paintbrush, and it's made me more eager than ever to pursue art. Turns out, I care less about a graduate degree and more about doing the thing I enjoy. For the first time, I'm chasing something that's just for me.

"Good for you, Nora," Marcus says.

Este turns to head down toward their dock. It's bittersweet. I still have so many days of unyielding and painful grief, but that's to be expected. Leaving this house, though the right thing, feels like I am abandoning Will. Would Will and I have gone the distance if Gianna hadn't been a housewife from hell? It's useless to wonder. He's gone, and while I'll never regret our marriage, I needed to leave, too. In my own way.

I lock the front door and put the key in the Realtor box. I stand on the front step, staring at the door, taking it all in, and letting it all go at the same time.

"Come on," Este calls from her yard. "Let's take you home."

Marcus picks up the few bags I held back from the moving crew, and we walk down to Este and Beau's boat. My new place is on the water. Just a boat ride away. But as we step onto the dock, I can't deny myself a longing look back at Will's house.

Breathe, Nora. Take it in. Find what's next. That's the job.

All I can do now is focus on chasing my own happiness. He would have wanted that.

Beau turns the engine over, powering the boat forward toward the setting sun in the distance. When the breeze picks up, I take in a long, hearty breath. And another . . . and another. With each exhale, Will's house shrinks in the distance.

I'll miss you forever, Hot Mean Lawyer.

And for the first time in a long while, looking to the horizon, I feel steady on my own two feet.

ACKNOWLEDGMENTS

The book might not exist without Kendall's grandmother, Mary-Ann Kendall Bouldin. She knew just about everyone in Winter Park and sold many of them their houses. She told some of the juiciest stories about the city, including the one where she snuck into the home of an NBA player while it was still under construction. Her passing six years ago still makes us emotional. She would have loved this story, but since she is gone and immune from trespassing charges, we feel comfortable saying: It was Horace Grant's house.

We owe a huge thank you to Nicki Spencer, who read every single draft of this book. Her suggestions and ideas are throughout these pages, and we truly don't believe the book would be what it is today without her. A wonderfully creative writer and talented producer in her own right, she loaned her time and effort to help us. For that, our gratitude is endless.

There is debate on the table for who is responsible for putting the two of us together. Bayless and Megan are both vying for the title. While we'd bestow the credit to either one of them with great joy, we're pretty sure it was the moment that our kids met on back-to-school night and Liam (Meredith's son) let Marin (Kendall's daughter) "cheat" off his Meet the Teachers scavenger hunt sheet to catch up after a late arrival. Since we love all the players so much, we're going with a three-way tie. Thank you to all of you for taking such a vested interest in our pairing.

Having other authors in your orbit when you write a book is another invaluable resource. Marc Cameron, Rebecca Hanover, and Katherine Wood answered roughly a thousand questions, and they have been cheerleading through the entire process. Having read and loved their books, it's wonderful to be among them as fellow authors now.

To our closest and dearest friends who got tasked with being our early readers: Audrey, Bridget, Cara, Carine, Celia, Cort, Cory, Elayne, Holly, Jessica, Laura, Lauran, Liz, Marcie, Maria, Pamela, and Selena, who gave thoughts and encouraged us to keep going: Thank you so much for taking the time and being so supportive.

When we called Kevin Crotty and told him we'd written a book, he said to send it along. About a week later, he called, excited and enthusiastic to share it with a co-worker of his at CAA. We will always be grateful to Kevin for pushing the manuscript forward and believing in it because it led us to . . .

The unparalleled, unrelenting, and impossibly delightful Alexandra Machinist. We're not sure there is a more fun phone call to be on than one with Alexandra. Her thoughts brought together the original manuscript in a way that we truly believe made the difference for not only where the book landed but also where our *Happy Wife* stories can go. Watching her do her thing in taking this book into the marketplace was amazing, and we will never forget the phone call when we sold it. It was a life-changing moment that we will cherish forever.

Coming to the table with the backgrounds in corporate communications and TV writing and producing, neither of us were strangers to editorial processes, but we cannot imagine having gone through it with anyone other than Natalie Hallak. She has opened up the world for both of us to see what happens when you have a highly collaborative person who believes in the thing you created and helps to comb through the pages to make it better. The dance of further excavating this book was made infinitely easier with Natalie in our corner. We're so happy she brought us into Bantam. Thank you, thank you, thank you.

And to our entire team at Bantam, all the people whose hard work has touched this book, thank you.

FROM MEREDITH

I had wonderful mentors along the way who taught me so much of what I know about writing. Jessica Waldoff, Pete Aronson, Jordan Levin, Jim Parriott, and Dee Johnson were all willing to show me how to be better at my craft.

Marcie Ulin and I wrote a spec pilot script in 2005 that my brother shared with Ann Blanchard, who became our first TV agent. I will always be grateful she bet on Marcie and me. I learned how to be a creative partner with Marcie. I'm grateful not only for that creative work but also for the friendship that came along with it. And thanks to her and Tom Halford, I also got a husband out of the whole deal.

Celia and I met on a tennis court in the summer of 1980-something. Most notably, she was wearing suede Bucks instead of tennis shoes, because form over function was (and is) her mantra. She has been an ardent supporter, and I'm so lucky to have a friend like her. And I so deeply enjoyed getting an endless string of texts from her asking, "BUT WHERE THE HELL IS WILL?"

Our best family friends opened their doors when I moved to Hollywood twenty-five years ago. Jim and Gail (my West Coast parents) and Brian, Carrie, Jessica, Tiffany, and Rob (my West Coast siblings). They housed me, fed me, and encouraged my creative pursuits. Having their support all these years has meant the world to me.

John, Jodi, and Chris might be the coolest in-laws on the planet. Their support has been paramount to my ability to pursue my crazy career. I hit the jackpot with them.

To my actual mom and dad, Harold and Judith, everyone always asks you how you ended up with two creative kids. The answer is simple: You always gave us the space to explore and try. And you were there to pick up the pieces if things didn't go as planned. I love you both.

To my brother, Jay Lavender, my OG best friend. You opened the one door I needed opened to launch my career at the same time that I got to watch you write and produce a #1 movie. To say it was awesome would be an understatement. We work in a complex and complicated industry, and I feel very lucky to be doing it with the best kind of ally there is. Between that and bringing Alexis and Lucy into my world, I'd say I hit it big! Love you.

To my husband, Ian. Thank you for wrangling the kids on Saturday mornings and late at night when Kendall and I were trying to get through a draft or an edit. You married a creative entrepreneur—which isn't easy—but you've taken to it brilliantly. I get to do what I do because I have your support and partnership. And to my sweet boys, Liam and Ryan, being your mom is the coolest story of all. I love you all so much.

And to Kendall—what a wild ride we've started. I couldn't have guessed that meeting at back-to-school night in September of 2022 would lead to this place, but I'm so happy that it did. I cannot begin to tell you how much fun I am having both as your friend and your writing partner . . . and how many more memes I have to send you. Xoxo, Meredith

FROM KENDALL

Fresh out of college, I was highly unqualified for the first job I ever applied to, but the man who read my resume saw something in me and created a role for me at the Orlando Science Center. I will always be grateful to Carroll Thrift for that. Over the years, I have had the privilege of meeting mentors, colleagues, and friends who have shaped, supported, and bet on me. It's a privilege to say there are too many to list, but I owe so much to Megan (the original true blue), Liz, Mindy, and Carine. Each of you propelled me forward and made me better at pivotal times in my career. I am so grateful for that.

I would like to thank my siblings, Cort, Audrey, and Trevor, for being my forever friends. To Cort and Audrey, thank you for reading with such enthusiasm. Trevor, I know you'll get around to reading this book, but until then, thank you for knowing about the alligator population in Lake Maitland. And to my mom and my dad, I love you both.

I'm not sure I would have been able to finish this book without the help of Abby, who got me back on my feet when I was injured. Thank you for believing in me and helping me get better.

A special thanks to Selena, who was the first person I told

about this story and who encouraged me to bring it to life. Thank you for cheering on every update I gave, no matter how big or small. And to Jessica, aunt to my daughter, daily subscriber to my life, thank you for being my chosen family and reading every draft. You're so fun.

Most important, to Drew and the kids we were when we met at a smoothie shop twenty years ago. I'm so proud of us. I choo-choo-choose you. And to Marin, the hardest worker, funniest jokester, and kindest-hearted kid. My entire career has been dedicated to showing you girls can do anything. I hope you always know how special you are. I love you both more than words could ever say.

And last, thank you to Meredith. First, for telling stories that inspired me for years before we met, and second, for agreeing to write this book with me. You are a force of nature. And even better than that, you are a phenomenal friend.

ABOUT THE AUTHORS

MEREDITH LAVENDER has spent the last twenty years working as a television writer/executive producer. Most recently, she served as showrunner/executive producer on HBO Max's *The Flight Attendant*, and she is currently in development on multiple television projects.

KENDALL SHORES'S career spans nearly seventeen years and runs the gamut from grant writing for a nonprofit museum in Orlando to internal communications consulting and strategy for large organizations. She likes writing fiction so much more.

Kendall and Meredith both live in Atlanta with their respective families and possibly too many dogs. If there's such a thing.

meredithandkendall.com
Instagram: @meredithandkendall
TikTok: @meredithandkendallbooks

ABOUT THE TYPE

This book was set in Linotype Didot, a modern adaptation of Firmin Didot's (1764–1836) original 1784 design, then called French Modern Face Didot. Considered to be an elegant, neoclassical typeface, it was redrawn in 1991 by Adrian Frutiger (1928–2015) for the Linotype foundry to address the demands of legibility in digital typesetting.